*For the Chicana writers
who by their example and work showed me
que si es posible:
Gloria Anzaldúa, Sandra Cisneros,
Cherríe Moraga y Helena Maria Viramontes.*

1

WITH HER INDEX FINGER, Veronica Melendez shoved the paperback volume of Latina short stories across the table's weathered surface. Avoiding Professor Camille Zamora's gaze, the twenty-two-year-old Chicana crossed her arms and studied the neighboring jacaranda, its feathery leaves spreading like verdant fans. The tree's lavender flowers had long since vanished, and Veronica wished she had been on campus to admire its springtime blossoms.

Camille Zamora outlined the pre-Columbian motif on the book's black and gold cover. "What did you think of the cuentos?" The July breeze toyed with her shingled black hair, revealing occasional glimmers of silver.

"The stories weren't what I expected." Veronica watched a tiny squirrel scamper across an overhead branch. "I had some trouble reading the ones in Spanish."

"It wouldn't take much to improve your proficiency— or your fluency and writing skills."

Veronica met the older woman's eyes. "Camille, I'm hardly a bilingual reader, much less a two-language writer."

The professor laughed. "Y porqué no? That's what I find so exciting about our literature—it can be in English, Spanish, or a combination of both. It's a wide open field, Veronica, and you have the talent to—"

"Sometimes I wonder why you don't practice what you preach."

"I *teach* Chicana lit. Don't expect *me* to write it." The professor smiled and slipped both of Veronica's manuscripts into a monogrammed leather briefcase. "When can I expect your next stories?"

"By the beginning of fall quarter. That was our agreement."

"Yes." Professor Zamora removed wire-rimmed sunglasses and scanned her student's unsmiling face. "I believe in you, Veronica. You've had a very difficult year, pero, vas a ver—"

"I know." Veronica followed the squirrel's jerky movements. "The—experience—will make me stronger."

The professor shifted in the ivory metal chair and sorted through her briefcase. "Maybe you'll be interested in this."

Veronica turned to glance at the outstretched flyer. Bold letters on chartreuse paper announced an upcoming showing of student films in Melnitz Hall.

"Veronica, do you know René Talamantes?"

"No." Her brown eyes again traced the squirrel's erratic progress from branch to trunk.

"René's a grad student here in Film and Television. It'd be a good idea to meet her."

Making no comment, Veronica took the flyer, folded it into her bag and got up.

The professor's fingers lightly grazed her student's arm. "René's film will be shown next Wednesday. Maybe I'll see you there?"

"I don't know, Camille." Veronica gathered her canvas bag and notebook. She did not turn to wave, limping past Rolfe Hall towards the nearest parking structure.

*

On her way home, she slowly guided her brother's silver 280-Z through a street repair zone on traffic-choked Santa Monica Boulevard. Meeting with Camille Zamora had exhausted her; she wanted to take a nap before venturing out again.

Veronica maneuvered the car around plastic orange cones and wondered if her father were in the area. Joe Melendez was a foreman on one of the city crews, but she did not see him among the other hard-hatted Chicanos. She preferred his taciturn nature to her mother's loquaciousness; he tended to listen, not question much. Yet she knew both her parents viewed their youngest daughter as moody and idiosyncratic, unlike her siblings. Even Camille Zamora, for all her encouragement, considered Veronica different from the other Chicana students.

Her fourteen-year-old nephew slammed the condominium's screen door and tossed a stack of mail on the squat oak table.

"Hey, Roni, someone's moving into the Tonelli place."

"Philly—can't you see I was trying to sleep?" Flat on her back, her brown toes tracing the sofa fabric's geometric pattern, Veronica drowsily reached for her "Heal the Bay" coffee mug, but took the mail off the table instead.

"Sorry." Grabbing his binoculars from an adjacent bookshelf, Phil hurried towards the terrace. In shorts and a Los Angeles Dodgers' T-shirt, he slouched against the wrought iron railing and spied at the courtyard below.

For a moment, Veronica surveyed him, amused at his curiosity; no doubt the new neighbor was female. Going back to the mail, she noticed a purple envelope scrawled with Michi Yamada's calligraphic handwriting.

Phil adjusted his binoculars for a closer inspection and uttered a low whistle. "She's really awesome, Roni."

Veronica ignored him and ripped open the envelope. What did she care about his latest crush? She had not heard from her friend Michi in two months.

Phil seemed unaware of her lack of interest in his discovery. "You think she's an actress or something? What a babe!" When he received no reply, he lowered the binoculars. "Is that from Dad?"

"What?" Veronica stared at the letter in disbelief. When she pulled herself into a sitting position, some of the mail fluttered to the carpet, but she took no notice. Michi had not responded to a previous letter and Veronica had hesitated to phone then, thinking her friend had found other priorities while in graduate school.

"Roni, what's wrong?"

"Michi's leaving Berkeley—for good. She doesn't explain, Phil. Just says she'll be home soon."

"Weird." He went back to his spying. "You just have to look at this totally incredible—"

In exasperation, Veronica pulled herself up. She was worried about Michi, but knew Phil would not leave her alone until she had seen the new neighbor herself. Adjusting her oversized T-shirt with its "I survived Catholic school" slogan, Veronica limped towards him.

"Such a voyeur." Veronica caught only a glimpse of a woman with auburn hair, wearing fuschia shorts and a black halter top and carrying a large carton towards the downstairs condominium.

Veronica nudged Phil. "Too vieja for you, muchachito."

"Older women appeal to me." He slipped a steadying arm around her thin waist. For a moment, they stood side by side, dark heads almost touching. Nephew and aunt were both slim and brown-skinned, often mistaken for brother and sister, although Phil's razor-cut hair contrasted with Veronica's curly perm.

"Listen, teenyboppers are more your speed."

He rolled his eyes at her remark and set the binoculars on a patio chair. "How's your leg, Roni?"

"Stiff—especially after dragging myself up to humor a snoop like you."

"Let's go for a walk, then." His sly grin revealed a mouthful of orthodontic braces. "Or for a swim."

"Or anywhere downstairs so you can finish checking out Ms. Redhead." She smiled, too. "Go ahead. I'd better phone Michi."

"Roni, you really need to exercise." His voice cracked with concern.

"Will you just get out of my hair for a while?"

"Okay, okay." With a good-natured shrug, the boy ambled towards the screen door and closed it quietly behind him.

Unsuccessful at reaching Michi by telephone, Veronica slumped back on the sofa. She could not understand why her friend had decided to leave Berkeley. Deep in thought, she jumped at the telephone's sudden shrillness. "Hello?"

"Roni, did Philly leave yet?" Her mother's querulous tone irked Veronica.

"Not till tomorrow, Mom." She closed her eyes, wishing she had not answered the phone. "How're you?"

"Pues, me siento bien. You never call, hija."

"Jeez, it's only been a couple of days. Didn't have time 'cause I had to meet with Professor Zamora this morning. She keeps me hopping, you know. How's Dad?"

"Working hard as usual. Quieres cenar con nosotros esta noche?"

"No thanks, Mom. I'm pretty tired and I have a therapy appointment in about an hour." Veronica faked a yawn to emphasize the point.

"Mira, flaquita, you need to get out once in while— besides going for physical therapy." Her mother hardly paused. "Sabes qué? I saw Michi's mamá in the flower shop yesterday when I was ordering a special arrangement for la iglesia. She said Michi's in San Francisco with Tami and should be home any day now."

Veronica became alert. "Did she say anything else?"

"Nomás eso, hija. Que bueno que tu amigita's coming back. Maybe she'll get you out." Sara Melendez' voice became persuasive. "Pues, how about dinner with us when Philly's gone, eh? I'll make arroz con pollo Saturday night."

Veronica could not refuse; chicken with rice was her favorite dish. Despite her curiosity, she really did not want to discuss Michi with her mother. "Well, okay, Mom. See you then." She gently put down the receiver and went to freshen up.

The physical therapist's office occupied a corner suite in one of the steel and glass structures defining Santa Monica's developing skyline. Veronica stationed the Z close to the elevators, peered into the car mirror, and fluffed her curly black hair before entering the building.

In the waiting room, she sank into a persimmon loveseat, disdainfully noticing a month's worth of *People* magazines spread before her. She sighed and leaned back for a moment, then pulled out Michi's letter.

When the receptionist called her, Veronica stuffed the

letter into her canvas bag and headed down the carpeted corridor to the treatment room. She set the bag on an empty chair and seated herself on the padded examining table. Sighing, she stared at her left leg, slim, brown, and scarred, before removing her sandals.

"Ah, Veronica. At long last." A lab-coated woman with weathered olive skin came in. Her long greying hair was secured with a cloisonné barrette, and her accent hinted at Eastern Europe.

"Hi, Anna." Veronica smiled. "How's your puppy?"

"Nearly grown." The physical therapist's blue eyes glinted. "And your leg, little one? You missed two appointments this month."

"I suppose it'd be better if I exercised more. Sometimes it's hard to make myself do anything, Anna." Veronica felt like a recalcitrant child. "But I swam this morning."

"Good. You want to be tip-top when school starts. Let's begin. No time to waste."

While Anna manipulated and applied strengthening techniques to her leg, Veronica found it difficult to focus on the therapy exercises. She hoped Anna would not notice her distraction.

"Keep doing the leg lifts. I will be back."

After the therapist left, Veronica looked at her left leg, so brown against white shorts, so thin and fragile in the weighted ankle cuff. Never an athlete, she was unaccustomed to an exercise regimen; she preferred to curl up with a book. Yet, gritting her teeth, she resumed the leg lifts, wincing from the effort.

Returning home, she found no trace of Phil and crossed the condominium complex's flagstone courtyard in search of him. Behind its wrought iron fence, the aqua pool was still except for someone splashing at the far end. Veronica saw him sprawled on a deck chair, his gaze riveted on the auburn-haired figure in the pool. At his aunt's measured approach, Phil looked sheepish.

Veronica shielded her eyes against the afternoon sun. "Been here all the time?"

"Nope. I helped Siena move in."

Veronica leaned against a vinyl-backed chair. "Your latest heartthrob? What happened to that cute Gina Rodríguez?"

"Lay off. Gina uses yucky green stuff on her fingernails." He shrugged off her memory.

"Listen, fickle-face, don't forget you have to pack some stuff. What time are you leaving tomorrow?"

"After class. Hey, Roni—did you talk to Michi?"

"Her phone in Berkeley's been disconnected. Then I tried calling her parents, but no one's home. According to Mom, Michi's staying with her sister and should be home soon."

"Yeah?" Phil kept his eyes on the new neighbor. "Anyways, Siena's using the Tonelli condo for the summer." Lowering his voice, he faced his aunt. "She's terrific. Doesn't even treat me like a kid. Want to meet her?"

"Might as well."

Phil called to her. From the rippling water, her head emerged, wavy red hair clinging to alabaster shoulders. She swam to the edge of the pool.

"I'm Siena Benedetti." Her eyes were clear hazel gems. "Phil told me all about you, Veronica."

Awkwardly, Veronica leaned over to accept her handshake. "I hope he hasn't been bugging you." She made herself let go of those damp, yet silken fingers.

"Oh, no. I never would've had time for a swim if it hadn't been for Phil's organizing skills."

The boy squirmed from a mixture of disgust at his aunt's comment and delight at Siena's compliment.

"We even had lunch together. He's quite a neighbor." Siena stepped out of the shallow end, and her round breasts thrust prominent nipples through the bikini's flimsy fabric. Veronica tried not to notice.

Siena reached for a huge Garfield-the-Cat towel. "I hear you're a writer."

Tensing, Veronica shot her nephew a reproving glance. "I'm a grad student in English at UCLA. I dabble in fiction."

"And you're a survivor, too."

"What?" Her brow furrowed. She wondered how much Phil had told this new neighbor.

Siena pointed to the T-shirt's caption. "I should wear that one myself."

"Oh."

Tiny droplets, like transparent beads, clung to Siena's fair skin. Veronica felt light-headed and remembered she hadn't had lunch. She suddenly imagined herself licking those crystal drops, stroking Siena all over. What had come over her? Again, she tried not to stare.

Siena seemed unaware of her effect on either Melendez. "I'm a design student, but I have a modelling job this summer." She dried herself, arching her lithe body.

Joanna had had a similar figure, Veronica mused. That fleeting memory caused her to avert her gaze. Phil, she noticed, was rapt.

"Well, if you'll excuse me, I'd better grab a bite. Nice meeting you, Siena."

"I have some sandwiches inside. Would you like one?"

"No, thanks. I need something a little more substantial."

She tried concentrating on the first draft of another short story, but all she could think about was Siena's gracefulness, her translucent skin and animated eyes. The new neighbor awakened memories—and yearnings. Putting the pages aside, Veronica eventually dozed. Hours later, she felt a warm hand on her shoulder and awoke with a start. "Joanna?"

"No, it's me. Thought I'd better wake you." Phil squatted beside her. "You'll really be stiff if you stay here all night."

With some effort, Veronica managed to sit up. She had cried herself to sleep and wondered if Phil would notice her eyes' puffiness. "What time is it?"

"Almost nine." He plopped himself on the sofa's edge. "You were dreaming about—"

"I think I always will." Her response was terse, and she made a pretense of gathering the pages. She hoped he had not been curious enough to read any.

Phil's voice was quiet. "Sometimes I dream about Mom. Even if I don't remember her too well, she's still in my dreams."

Regretting her curtness, Veronica touched his knee. "It's really hard to lose someone you've been close to, Phil. It takes so long to get over it."

"I know." He cleared his throat. "You must think of Joanna all the time."

She kept her hand on him, noticing the hard musculature of his brown thigh, so different from Joanna's softness. She did not answer.

"Roni, it wasn't your fault."

She moved away. "I was driving."

"But no one blames you. Not even Joanna's parents."

"I'll always feel responsible."

"Hey, that guy in the van was going too fast. He came right at you. You had nowhere to go. And, anyways, there's nothing you can do about it now."

"Except feel sorry for myself, right?"

"You don't mean that." When he frowned, Phil resembled his father, Veronica's older brother Frank.

She sighed and curled one leg beneath her. "Can't be too much fun to spend the whole summer with Ms. Moodiness. No wonder you're excited about going away for the weekend."

Gulping, he seemed to chose his words carefully. "I wish you'd never been in that accident, Roni."

"So do I. With all my heart."

He went on, lowering his eyes. "You've been different ever since. We can't do things together like we used to—roller-skating, bike-riding. You're sad a lot, too. And sometimes I just don't know how to handle it."

"I'm sorry." She bit her lip to keep it from trembling.

"You can't help it. You lost your best friend, after all."

Her voice shook. "I really wish things could be—like before. Everything's such an effort these days, Phil. I don't know if you understand this, but I'm putting whatever energy I have into writing. It's the only way I know how to cope. Camille sure figured that out. But you probably feel cheated that we're spending most of our time at home. When your summer classes are over, we'll get out more. I promise."

"I have lots of friends to hang out with." He sounded petulant, perhaps regretting his candor. "You don't have to do anything with me if you don't feel like it."

"I *want* to, Phil." She leaned towards him, touching his shoulder. "Look, you're going through rough times yourself. Don't you think I know that? Having a step-mother is a major adjustment, especially since you and Frank have been on your own since you were a baby. If you want the truth, I'm a little wary about all this, too."

He gaped at her. "You are?"

She tried to explain. "I'm sure Frank and Joyce love each other. Frank seems happy, and I'm glad because he's finally made time for himself. His life hasn't been easy since your mom died. I just hope he and Joyce'll make time for you, too."

Phil sat closer to her. "Yeah. Who wants a kid around? Not a couple of honeymooners."

"Well, *I* want you around." Veronica's voice became emphatic. "Philly, I don't know what I'd do without you." She smiled a bit. "Have to get back on my feet so I can help take care of you."

"I'm no baby," he insisted.

"Not if you're falling head over heels for red-haired models." Veronica playfully punched his shoulder. She did not want to think of her own attraction to the new neighbor.

Phil laughed and ducked another punch. "Had dinner with her, too."

"I'm surprised you're home this early."

"Siena started yawning. Thought I'd better split."

"Such a thoughtful guy."

"I think she's lonely," he said after a moment.

"Well, she's new in town."

He shrugged. "Once in while, she seems sad."

"Did she say much about herself?"

He shook his head. "She asked about you, though. Wanted to know how come we're hanging out together."

Idly, he traced the Dodgers' logo on his T-shirt.

Veronica grimaced. "You told her."

"She asked why you limp."

"Can't exactly hide my bum leg." She gave it a cursory pat. "Did you tell her about Frank and Joyce, too?"

He seemed relieved she was not angry. "Yeah. Siena has a stepmother, too. She said it takes time to get used to someone new in the family."

"Everything takes time, Philly."

"Time to grow up. Time to get well. Sounds like we've got our work cut out for us." With a grin, he surveyed her.

"Yeah. For now, bedtime sounds right to me." She made a move to rise. "Muchacho, be a sport and help me. My leg's gone numb again."

In her bedroom, Veronica stacked the manuscript pages on the white lacquer desk. The double-spaced paragraphs bore precise one-inch margins on all sides. She had made neat pencilled notations between the typed lines and inserted strings of words, crossed out others. Yet, despite her editing marks, each page was uniformly structured, confined to its predetermined borders. For a first draft, the manuscript presented a clean and orderly pattern. Like her life had been—before.

2

AFTER PHIL LEFT for his photography class, Veronica decided on an early swim. Her procrastination tended to fluctuate between writing or exercising; that morning the latter won out.

Twice she swam the pool's length, then stopped to perform strenuous kicks. Taking a breather, she sat on the rim and dangled her legs in the glimmering water while the sun poked through the grey screen of clouds. She thought of the half-written story upstairs, and her head buzzed with colliding ideas, snatches of dialog.

"I saw you from the window, early bird."

In a peppermint-striped bikini, the new neighbor tossed her towels on a lounge chair, dived in, and effortlessly swam over.

"I needed that to wake up." Siena's hazel eyes met Veronica's dark ones. "How're you today?"

"Breathless. My physical therapist is right. I'm really out of shape."

"Phil told me about—"

"I tend to stiffen up." Veronica shied away from the topic. "Do you swim a lot?"

"Whenever I'm lucky enough to be near a pool."

"I ought to use this one more." Kicking her legs in the water, Veronica noted the dissimilarity between her brown skin and the other's fairness. Joanna's tawny coloring had not been such a dramatic contrast. She kicked the water again. "I hope Phil didn't overstay his welcome yesterday."

"Not at all. I never meet guys my age as sweet as Phil." Siena tossed damp hair from her face. "Do you?"

Caught off guard, Veronica shook her head. She wondered what to say, but she wasn't about to masquerade as a heterosexual for Siena's benefit.

"You two seem very close, Veronica."

She was relieved the conversation remained on Phil. "My parents raised him after his mother died. He was only two years old then, and I was ten. Frank was too broken up to be much involved with a baby."

"And now Frank's honeymooning with his new wife." Siena leaned back on delicate-looking wrists. "Phil would rather live with you."

"What?"

"He feels secure with you. He's worried about relating to his stepmother."

"Thanks for listening to him, Siena. I think he feels pushed aside."

"I know the feeling." Siena slid into the water. "Come on. Let's get your legs working again."

"In a minute." Veronica enjoyed the novelty of being cajoled.

Siena disappeared and darted up at the far end of the pool. "I won't let you escape."

Needing no further encouragement, Veronica cautiously lowered herself in, breast-stroking towards her. They swam in unison, back and forth, until, breathless once more, Veronica tried to raise herself from the water. She became frightened by her sudden exhaustion and its accompanying powerlessness. Her shoulders ached, and her impaired leg felt numb. When Siena offered assistance, Veronica grabbed onto her, allowing herself to be almost lifted out. With trembling legs, she stumbled to a lounge chair, her chest heaving.

"My God, Veronica. Are you all right? I didn't mean to—" Grabbing a towel, Siena was all apologies.

She gasped out the words. "I'm okay—really."

"Let me dry you." Siena ran the towel over her, dabbing gently.

Veronica flinched at that intimate action. "I'll be fine. You don't have to—"

"I'm so sorry." Squatting by the lounge chair, Siena continued to pat her dry.

Veronica coughed, then leaned back. "I overdid it, that's all. Would you hand me that other towel?"

"Let me just—"

"I'm *not* an invalid." She loathed the unreliability of her physical strength, especially when she preferred to impress Siena.

"You just need to build yourself up again. I didn't mean to push—"

Veronica spoke with some sharpness. "Please—just stop."

Siena seemed unoffended by the brusque tone. She put the towel aside. "I love being fussed over. I thought everyone did."

"I'm not used to it. And, anyway, I hardly know you." Veronica immediately regretted adding that. "Look, I'm sorry. You're trying to be nice, and I'm—"

For a long moment, their eyes locked, neither daring to turn away. Then Siena's misted, and she sneezed, several times in a row. Both women erupted into giggles.

"You're getting chilled," Veronica managed to say. "Use that other towel before you catch cold."

"It's just my hay fever. You know, redheads and allergies," Siena joked with feigned nasalness. She sneezed once more. "In a few minutes, we're going in again."

Veronica shook her head, knowing she could be persuaded.

Book bag slung over one shoulder, Phil pushed open the pool gate. "Roni, I phoned a bunch of times, but you never answered."

"Damn. I forgot I was supposed to pick you up. How'd you get home?" She pulled on her terrycloth robe and limped to him.

"The bus. How else?"

"Hi, Phil." From beneath a beach umbrella, Siena offered that radiant smile.

"Hi." He grinned spontaneously, then glanced at his aunt. "Did you pack my stuff?"

"No. I've been out here."

"Jeez, Roni. Steve's picking me up at 2:00." He nearly stamped his foot in irritation.

"Quit whining, and let's do it." She moved towards the gate, irked by his childish temper and her own absentmindedness.

Siena remained by the pool. "Ready for the weekend, Phil?"

"Yeah. Movies today and tomorrow, Sunday the Dodger game—I'm set."

"Steve's poor parents—stuck with both of you." Veronica paused by the gate. "Coming or not?" Deciding not to wait, she walked towards the condo, and he caught up with her soon.

"Can't believe you forgot. Every morning you stay inside, but today when I'm counting on you, you're goofing off."

"I was *exercising*."

"You were stretched out getting a tan, Roni."

"Philip, I am *not* your slave. If you'd listened to me and done your own packing last night, you wouldn't be griping now. Quit nagging or I won't help you at all." She took her time on the stairs.

Disgruntled, the boy passed her. She found him in his bedroom, removing jeans and T-shirts from the dresser drawers.

"You're only going for a couple of days. What's the big deal, anyway? Just be sure to pack underwear and socks. And your toothbrush, too."

"Yeah, yeah." He stuffed everything into a Gatorade sports bag.

"Phil, what's really the matter?" She leaned in the doorway, terry robe loosely belted.

"Want to be ready when Steve and his mom get here."

"That's all?"

"Yeah. Why?" Pushing aside a lock of his black hair, he looked up innocently.

Veronica shrugged. "Sorry I forgot." She wound one end of the terrycloth belt around her thumb. "Look, this weekend will be good for us. We need a break from each other."

Tossing gym socks into the bag, he did not reply right away. "Will you be okay by yourself?"

"Sure, muchacho." She grinned and tightened the belt. "Thanks for asking, though."

"I worry about you, Roni."

"Like I worry about you." Stepping into the room, she removed his Levi's jacket from the closet. "Don't forget this. It still gets cold at night."

Phil reached for the jacket. In the same movement, he surprised Veronica by hugging her against him; lately, he seemed to have outgrown his cuddliness.

"Roni, maybe you should stay at Grandma's."

"She smothers me." She kept her face against his bony shoulder. "I'll be fine."

"Be sure to lock up tonight. Sometimes you forget things. And—I don't want anything else to happen to you."

"Philly, I'll be all right." Holding him at arms' length, she tried smiling, noticing he was teary, too. "Have a wonderful time, okay? Forget about me for a couple of days."

The chiming doorbell distracted him. He wiped his eyes with the back of his hand. "That's Steve. I'll let him in."

Steve Martínez was Phil's height with a stockier build. Humor-wise, the boys were two of a kind. Joking and teasing, they led the way towards Mrs. Martínez' station wagon.

Veronica tagged along. "Rita, do you really know what you're in for?"

"I'm used to it, Roni." In her late thirties, Rita Martínez kept her brown hair frosted to hide the intrusion of grey. She tossed Veronica an appraising glance. "Que cute te mires."

"She's been baking in the sun all morning. That's why she shines," Phil cut in, grinning at his aunt.

Veronica ignored his gibe. "Behave yourself, okay?"

Rita continued studying her with a practiced eye. "You starting to go out yet?"

"Haven't been in the mood." Veronica recognized the coolness in her own voice.

"Well, get into it, girl. You're young. Enjoy yourself."

Veronica forced a smile. All she needed was Rita's offer to introduce her to some eligible Chicanos. She did not

21

trust herself to comment. Waving to the three, she backed away.

Siena looked up from her fashion magazine. "Did Phil leave in one piece?"

Veronica nodded, gathering her towels and suntan lotion. "I'm going in to work."

With a yawn, Siena watched her. "You're so disciplined." She leaned on one elbow. "Are you working tonight, too?"

"Probably." Veronica did not look up, sensing an invitation she both wanted and dreaded.

Pushing her sunglasses atop her windblown hair, Siena revealed her lucid gaze. "How about dinner?"

"Fine." Veronica's heart hammered. "About 7:00?"

"Great. I'll be over then."

She showered and changed into a baggy T-shirt that almost reached her knees. A cherished souvenir, it bore the orange shoestring logo of the Los Angeles Women's Marathon Celebration. In that comfortable garb, she sat at the typewriter and stared at the blank page. She wanted to empty her mind of distractions, but writing about Joanna recreated haunting images of those smooth hands caressing, sepia eyes beckoning. Veronica had never loved anyone else, and she craved Joanna still. With a twinge of disloyalty, she knew she also longed to touch and kiss Siena.

When Veronica heard the doorbell, she groaned and got up.

"Sorry. I lost track of time again."

"No problem." Siena was decked out in an aquamarine gauze sundress, auburn mane caressing bare shoulders. Dangling abalone shell earrings complemented her eyes. She fanned herself with a woven clutch purse and stepped inside, her gaze sweeping over the condominum's living room.

Engineering textbooks, spy and adventure novels, political and sports biographies crammed the twin oak bookcases. Between them stood an oak and glass entertainment center, and the walls featured LeRoy Nieman prints of sports figures.

"Snazzy place. What does Frank do?"

"Structural engineering." Veronica moved towards the hallway. "Excuse me. I'd better change."

"Where are we going?"

"Don't know." She had forgotten Siena was unfamiliar with the Santa Monica area. Fleetingly, she wished she could skip this dinner. She preferred her own company, free of the arousing distraction of the new neighbor.

Inspecting her wardrobe, Veronica found nothing that compared to Siena's finery. "What do you feel like eating?"

"Anything. Maybe we can go somewhere on the beach?"

Taking that cue, she suggested Moonshadows, a steak and seafood restaurant with an unhindered view of the Malibu coastline. Siena offered to phone for a reservation.

With that problem solved, Veronica sorted through the closet. She finally selected white slacks, a silky magenta shirt, and Bass sandals. It was hopeless to try to compete.

*

Siena raised her brows at seeing the silver Z. "Macho car."

Starting the ignition, Veronica shrugged. "Frank made me promise to drive it while he's gone."

Siena adjusted her dress's neckline, manicured fingers smoothing the gauze fabric over her breasts. Her Opium cologne enhanced the Z's leather interior.

"Do you have a car, Veronica?"

"No." At her taut utterance, the memories flooded her: her impetuous offer to drive Joanna's Rabbit all the way home, her lover's appreciative smile, brown hair billowing in the breeze. At a curve in the mountain road—the speeding van, their screams, the crash, the darkness—then endless silence. Veronica blinked rapidly, her long fingers clenching the steering wheel.

"No," she said again. "I don't have a car."

Siena's voice was a whisper. "Oh, Veronica."

She did not respond, manuevering the Z through residential streets. She stayed in the slower right lane. Lately, most of her driving was confined to her hometown; she avoided freeways and hillside roads. She no longer sped through amber lights nor swerved around crawling traffic. She lacked the confidence to resume her previous driving habits.

Veronica felt the muscles in her neck and upper back tense. Whatever had prompted her to suggest a Malibu restaurant? Weekend traffic would be heavy. Despite dinner reservations, there would be at least a twenty-minute wait. She envisioned her abandoned typewriter and wished again she had stayed home.

With the Palisades to her left, the Pacific sun setting on the horizon, she drove past the stately palms and down the winding California Avenue incline leading to the Coast Highway. The scarlet sun radiated on the serene water, transforming the ocean into an endless violet mirror. That spectacular sunset at last convinced her the outing was worthwhile.

"You're so quiet, Siena. Nervous about my driving?"

"Please don't think that. I was imagining how scared I'd be to drive—afterwards."

Veronica lowered the sun visor. She was grateful Siena had stopped asking questions. "I was terrified at first. But every morning before he went to work, Frank would make me drive, even if it was only around the block. Eventually, I started driving him to and from his office. For him to leave me in charge of Phil *and* his car was really an act of confidence."

"He trusts you. And I do, too." A gust whipped Siena's hair. "I really admire you for pushing yourself into conquering your fear. I tend to be lazy."

"Actually, so do I—about most things. Typical summer behavior."

"I guess." Siena leaned back. "In that case, it's a good thing I have that modelling job lined up. My father knows someone in advertising who pulled a few strings." She glanced at Veronica. "I'd rather design, but modelling will give me a different perspective. I designed this." Siena spread her wide skirt.

Veronica gave her a quick glance. "I like it. It'd hang like a sack on me."

"You look terrific in sleek things—like your blue swimsuit. You're not a frilly person, Veronica."

"Definitely no frills." She smiled, relishing that precise assessment.

"Maybe I'll design something for you."

Veronica glanced at those vibrant eyes and wondered about Siena's motivation. Curbing her imagination, she reminded herself the new neighbor had a friendly nature;

there was nothing more to it than that.

"Could you somehow fashion me a new leg?"

A few minutes later, still laughing, Veronica turned the car into the Moonshadows' parking lot.

Siena set down her wine glass. "What are you writing, Veronica?"

"Short stories. At least, that's what I'm trying to do, so I've spent months on the three R's: recuperating, writing and rewriting." She balanced a flat mushroom on her salad fork and wondered how much to reveal. "I had an undergrad Chicana literature class. The prof really took an interest in the students, especially the Chicanas. She thinks writing is therapeutic and encourages me to stay in touch with my feelings by being creative. I've agreed to write six stories by fall, but sometimes I think she wants too much from me."

"Have you been in therapy?" Siena's voice was gentle.

"Saw a counselor while I was in the hospital, but I didn't want to continue. It was bad enough dealing with my physical problems. Writing is my own way of working through the pain. Maybe if I write it all out, I'll be able to resolve it."

"Sounds lonely."

"Sometimes it is."

Veronica remembered how Joanna had understood her persistence in working out a story, in developing characters. Joanna had been a psychology student, and her insights and critical analysis of the characters had proven invaluable. Veronica missed that stimulating give-and-take, as well as the many nights when Joanna had stood behind the desk chair, effectively closing the discussion about fiction by slipping a teasing hand inside her lover's shirt.

Veronica swiftly swallowed some Chardonnay. "But there's joy in writing, too—fulfillment. That's what I strive for."

"I hope you get it."

"Me, too." Veronica smiled, a trifle sadly. Both women were silent for some moments, watching the rolling waves.

"You know something? Sharing a meal with you is so different from having dinner with a man."

"A sexist comment if I ever heard one." Veronica looked up, amused but flattered.

"A man would've bragged all the way to Malibu, about himself, the car, his career. He would've tried to impress me by telling me about his writing. He would've suggested what to order. And he would've assumed I'm helpless, which I'm not."

"Maybe you've been dating the wrong type."

"Absolutely."

"Siena, there *are* sensitive men out there. Phil's dad, for instance."

"He's already taken. The rest are gay. Maybe I just need some women friends. I don't have many."

"Why not?"

"Probably fear of competition. When I was in high school, I had lots of girl friends. In college, my focus changed." Siena shrugged and gazed at the placid sea. "I guess I'm cynical, but lately I've realized how many evenings I've wasted on men—trying to please them and figure them out. It hasn't been worth it." Her eyes met Veronica's. "Maybe you've had different experiences."

Veronica blinked and spoke quickly. "Listen, L.A. can be an intimidating place. Give it a chance, Siena. Once you settle in, you'll start meeting people."

Siena's fingertips rubbed the abalone-embedded design

of her silver bracelet. "I left San Diego because I wanted a change." Her gaze fixed on the Pacific. "Six weeks ago, I had an abortion."

Reflexively, Veronica lay a hand over hers; Siena's felt frozen. "I'll listen if you want me to."

Siena sniffled and pulled a kleenex from her purse. "You're the only person I've told. I'm not even sure why." She kept the kleenex in her hand. "Maybe because you've been through a personal tragedy and you've survived." She laughed shortly, tears hazing her eyes. "Oh, God. That sounds like soap-opera talk. Maybe I'm cracking up. You must think I'm wacko."

"Not at all." Veronica squeezed her cold hand, sensing her isolation.

Their waiter looked like a temporarily beached surfer, sun-streaked hair slicked back. He lingered while serving them. Veronica continued holding Siena's hand, not caring what the kid thought. Neither spoke until he left.

"Siena, if you've lost your appetite, we can leave. I won't mind."

"You go ahead and eat. I'm sort of gathering my thoughts." She fumbled with the kleenex and blew her nose.

Veronica's instincts prodded her to hold Siena, yet a crowded restaurant was not the place. Consolingly, she patted her hand before moving away to taste the char-broiled shark.

"Delicious. So tender."

"Like my feelings." Siena tried to joke, her voice shaky. "You really want to hear this?"

Veronica nodded.

Siena took a deep breath and another sip of wine. "I was going to be married in December." For seconds, she stared at the violet ocean; the sun was almost below the horizon. "Gary's a grad student in biostatistics at UC San Diego, and we got serious last year. He wasn't the first guy I've slept with, Veronica, but with him, it felt special. I thought we were friends as well as lovers.

"Sometime during the spring, we were careless—and I got pregnant." She used the kleenex again; it had become a soggy ball. "The day I planned to tell him, I saw him in the library with someone else. He was holding her hand, and he kissed her. It was more than a friendly kiss, believe me. I was across the room, and waited till she left. Then I went over and told him about me, and about seeing him with her. Gary didn't deny it.

"We started walking outside. All of a sudden, he said he was scared of marriage, and it probably wouldn't have worked out anyway. He said I should get an abortion. I started crying right there on the library steps. I ran away, Veronica. He didn't even try to stop me."

Siena's hand shook when she reached for the wine glass. "A month later—I did a lot of soul-searching in the meantime—I had the abortion. I feel so guilty—I was raised Catholic—but I couldn't have the baby without Gary. I couldn't raise it on my own—maybe in a few years, but not now. And so I killed it." Siena sobbed, turning her bent head towards the window as if wanting to melt into the rigid glass.

"You did what was right for you. You thought it through, Siena. What other options did you have?"

"I don't know. I'm all mixed up. And now I'm even scared to be around men. Maybe they'll somehow know what I've done. I've never felt this way. I doubt if I'll ever find anyone worthwhile. No one will want me."

"That isn't true. You aren't heartless. You spent hours will Phil yesterday; most people wouldn't bother with a kid. And I never would've worked so hard if I'd been alone in the pool this morning. You're a caring, decent woman, Siena. Believe me."

She inhaled sharply, trying to halt the tears. "I want to, but my feelings get in the way."

"Don't let them. Trust me. Earlier, you said you did."

She nodded and touched Veronica, tracing her long brown fingers. At that contact, Veronica's pulse quickened.

3

THE WAITER BALANCED the tray holding another two glasses of Chardonnay and gestured with his chin. "That gentleman over there sent these."

Veronica and Siena exchanged exasperated glances.

"I can't deal with this," Siena murmured.

Veronica's voice was calm. "Please thank him for us, but we've had enough. And would you bring our check?"

"Fine, ladies." The kid smirked and left.

Siena leaned towards her. "Is the guy looking at us?"

"Yeah. He's about thirty-five, open-necked shirt, gold chains. Get the picture? Maybe he'll take the hint and back off. He's flashing a grin now. Don't look."

"I hardly want to encourage him."

Veronica pulled out her wallet. "Do strangers usually send you wine?"

Siena seemed surprised at the question. "I can't believe it doesn't happen to you."

"Well, twice—and I was with another woman then, too." She remembered how amused Joanna had been. "Suppose it's fun if you're a wino."

Siena arched a brow. "Veronica, don't be modest. One of those glasses was for you."

"He's definitely not my type," Taking the check from the waiter, she quickly tossed some bills on the table, and edged out of the booth. "Let's get out of here. You can pay me later."

*

When they passed his table, the man grinned. "Couldn't interest you dolls in more vino?"

Veronica ignored him. Although her leg had become stiff again, she hastened her pace and heard the man's baritone rumble behind her.

"Curly ain't talkin', I see. Hell, the wine was for Red, anyhow. She's the hot one."

Turning, she saw him push back his chair and trail Siena. Veronica swung open the heavy door and signalled to the car valet, hoping her companion would hurry.

Following Siena, the man chuckled. "Night's still young, baby. Plenty of time to get to know each other." He followed her outside and was about to slip a hairy arm around her, but she slithered away, face taut.

Veronica caught a whiff of his boozy breath and grimaced. "Can't you see she isn't interested?"

"Keep out of this, Curly."

"*You* keep out. Quit bothering her."

"You going to stop me, dyke?" With a sneer, he elbowed her.

Veronica flung his arm aside. "Fuck off, asshole."

The man's eyes bulged. Far from sober, he rocked on his white loafers and made a clumsy lunge towards her. At that moment, the valet pulled up and the women scrambled into the Z. Gunning the motor, Veronica drove off without even leaving the baffled valet a tip.

Siena fell back against the seat and giggled. "You were magnificent—Curly!"

Veronica felt exhilarated. Laughing, she guided the Z southbound along the Coast Highway.

"He was nauseating—so plastic." Siena glanced over her shoulder. "Hope he doesn't keep following us."

"He can eat my dust." Veronica kept her right hand on the wheel, left elbow on the door frame.

Halfway to Santa Monica, Siena grew quiet, her hilarity fading. "Is that the kind of guy I attract—a sleaze who wants a good time and nothing else?"

"Hey—you're bound to attract all kinds."

"But I don't want to." Her voice was tinged with despair.

"You can't hide yourself away, Siena."

"Maybe I should."

"Look, don't let that jerk get to you. A few minutes ago, you laughed at him."

"Because he was so ridiculous."

"Right." Veronica noticed the speedometer and realized she had been traveling too fast. Hands trembling, she slowed down, changed lanes, and went past the California incline towards the McClure Tunnel.

"I heard what he called you," Siena said after another silence.

Veronica's heartbeat quickened, but she aimed for nonchalance, manuevering the Z through the fluorescent-lit tunnel. "Yeah, he pulled out his defense mechanisms and fired away. Men call women 'dykes' to intimidate us. That crap doesn't work on me."

"But weren't you scared when he tried to—"

"He was drunk, Siena. I could've knocked him over."

"You're tougher than you look."

Veronica did not answer, unsure if she detected admiration or suspicion in Siena's voice. She was not even sure if she cared. Her exhilaration had worn off.

Leaving the highway, she took surface streets and soon guided the sports car into its stall. For seconds, neither woman moved. Veronica toyed with the car keys.

Siena unfastened her seat belt and clicked open the

door. "Feel like dessert?"

"No thanks. I'm really tired."

"Are you feeling all right?"

She nodded. "Just need some sleep." She locked the car and walked ahead of Siena into the condomium complex.

She was relieved to be alone. The evening had exhausted Veronica more than she had anticipated. For the first time since the accident, she had gone out with someone other than a friend or family member. She had been on her own, unprotected. Most of the time, her family tried to shield her from any unwarranted memories and unpleasant incidents. She imagined how astonished they would have been by her assertiveness at Moonshadows. She had even surprised herself.

Yawning, she headed towards her bedroom, but the telephone's jangle lured her back.

"Hey, Roni—were you snoozing?"

Veronica recognized Michi Yamada's voice at once. "Where are you, Mich?"

"In the shadow of the Golden Gate. I'm driving home tomorrow. Melendez, I really want to see you."

Veronica curled into a corner of the sofa. "What's the scoop? When you didn't write—"

"I can't talk now, but will you fit me into your busy calendar—like on Monday? Sunday I have to spend with the folks."

"How about lunch after my therapy appointment?"

"You're seeing a shrink?"

"Don't start. We're talking physical therapy here." Veronica gave her the office address and appointment time.

"Great. So how's your leg?"

"Better. I swam this morning—the therapist's orders. You know how lazy I am about that stuff."

"Yeah. Where were you tonight, Roni? I phoned about an hour ago."

"Had dinner with one of the neighbors."

"A guy?"

"A woman our age. She's in L.A. for the summer."

"Potential friend?"

"I think so." Veronica was exasperated. "Mich, how are you—really? I don't hear from you in ages and now you're asking about my neighbor, for God's sake."

"Roni—it'll take hours to tell you everything. Right now I have to pack. See you Monday."

For a few moments, Veronica frowned at the phone, stunned that Michi had hung up. What had made her usually talkative friend so evasive?

She tossed her blouse to the floor and struggled to remove the slacks from her stiff left leg. Sitting on the toilet, she finally yanked them and her panties off. She heaved herself up by grasping the bathroom's doorknob. Turning, Veronica faced the full-length mirror on the opposite wall and narrowed her eyes to inspect herself.

The hazy sun had darkened her legs, arms, back and shoulders, giving her the appearance of wearing a buff-colored swimsuit. She flattened her pubic hair, liking its coarse texture, and admired her small, firm breasts, her trim buttocks and legs. Her gaze did not linger on the lengthy surgical scar. Moving her hand, she fingered her vagina; as she had expected after the evening with Siena, it was moist. She wiped her fingers on one thigh and stared at herself again, noting how she favored her right leg.

"Gimpy. I wonder if that's a turn-off."

Shrugging, she moved to the sink and washed her face. She patted herself dry and flicked the bathtub tap. Adjusting the water temperature, she tested it with a tentative toe. Awkwardly, she climbed in, bracing herself against the tiled wall. She eased herself down with caution, letting the warm water cascade to her thighs. She placed a small towel flat beneath her and lay back, spreading her legs. She slipped both hands beneath her buttocks to boost her vulva towards the jetting stream of water. She closed her eyes and imagined Siena bent over her, auburn hair flowing, her face between Veronica's legs. She fantasized Siena's lips teasing, her warm tongue licking her, and became further aroused by the sensuously pounding water.

With a moan, Veronica moved her legs further apart. Splashing water rained on her face. It thudded on her clitoris, and she came suddenly, strongly, shuddering from the spasms. For a long time, she did not move. Then, clumsily, she reached up to turn off the tap. She lay back, her legs sore from being wide apart, and partly, she realized, from the strenuous morning swim. Resting her neck against the porcelain rim, she sighed with deep satisfaction.

Veronica sat at the kitchen table, her drafted story spread before her. She tried to concentrate on editing, but found herself thinking of Siena and Michi instead. She envied Siena's ability to confide, and wondered what revelations Michi would offer. Drinking a cup of almond tea, she was startled to hear the doorbell. On impulse, she took a steak knife from the utensil drawer and tiptoed into the living room. Through the peephole, she glimpsed a pale-looking Siena wrapped in an emerald velour bathrobe.

"Just me," she said when Veronica let her in. She eyed the steak knife cautiously.

Embarrassed, Veronica put the knife on the coffee table. "I'm overreacting to being alone."

"Do you miss Phil?"

She nodded, though he had not been on her mind all evening. "Guess you can't handle being by yourself either."

Siena sighed. "I keep waking up."

Veronica's heart palpitated. A long night of lovemaking would surely exhaust Siena, she thought wryly. "Maybe some brandy would help." She brushed past Siena and squatted by her brother's built-in bar, grabbing a bottle of Christian Brothers' from the bottom shelf. She figured Frank bought the Catholic friars' brand out of habit. Pouring some into a snifter, she handed it to Siena. "This should do the trick."

"Thanks. I'm kind of a nuisance, huh?"

"Not at all." Veronica leaned against the bar, suddenly self-conscious in her wrinkled T-shirt and bare legs.

"Can I stay here? I just don't want to be lonely tonight."

Under her robe, Siena wore a peach-colored, diaphanous nightgown, and her wavy hair framed her face. When she tossed the robe on Frank's king-sized bed, she allowed her hazel eyes to survey the athletic paraphernalia stacked in a corner. "I feel like I've invaded his locker room. Is he your only brother?"

Veronica nodded. "And the oldest—Frank's thirty-four. My sister Lucy is five years older than me. She's a Carmelite nun."

"Phil said your married sister lives in Arizona." Siena sat on the edge of the bed. "Does Lucy know you wear that T-shirt with the Catholic school slogan?"

"She wouldn't be surprised." Veronica rubbed the edge of the Scandinavian-designed dresser on her way out of the room.

"Where are you going?"

"To lock up and turn off the lights."

"Will you keep me company after that?"

Veronica's voice was soft. "Sure."

Seconds later, she stood in the darkened living room, hesitant about her next move, trembling from a combination of fear and desire.

Siena leaned against the headboard of Frank's bed, holding a brass-framed photograph.

Veronica edged into the room, but remained near the door. "That's Frank's wife—Joyce."

"Pretty. Do you like her?"

"Guess so." Veronica rubbed her neck muscles; they were tense again.

"You don't sound too sure."

Veronica grinned in response and wound up sitting at the foot of the bed. "Joyce really needs to get acquainted with Phil. Part of that's Frank's fault. He's been juggling family stuff, his career, and his relationship with Joyce. Now it's all caught up with him, and Phil's the one who feels it most."

"He seems like a flexible kid." Siena returned the picture to its place. "Will you keep living here when Frank and Joyce come back?"

"Oh, no." Veronica crossed her right leg and absently

stroked her knee. "My apartment's sublet to one of Frank's friends. I'll move back there before fall quarter."

Siena swished the brandy and took another sip. "Where is it?"

"About a mile away." She rubbed her neck again. "I've been here about five months. After leaving the hospital, I spent a month recuperating at my parents' and nearly went insane. When Frank asked if I'd rather stay with him and Phil, I jumped at the chance. Anything to get away from my doting mother. She has an advanced case of empty nest syndrome."

"That's to be expected, isn't it? Phil said you were even in a coma for a couple of days."

She frowned at that memory, but felt oddly satisfied to add, "Besides the multiple fractures." She averted her gaze and tried to suppress a yawn.

"Oh, Veronica. You really are sleepy. Snuggle in with me."

For a moment, she appraised her, questioning her motivation, but Siena's eyes held no trace of guile. Too weary to figure her out, Veronica relented. She did not look at Siena as she rolled back the burgundy comforter and reclined rigidly. She pondered how she would sleep next to that tempting body, but lacked the energy to get up again.

Siena lay near, her long hair brushing Veronica's arm. "Sleep well," she whispered.

"You, too."

Eyes closed, pale lashes curling, Siena began to breathe rhythmically. Veronica reached over and switched off the light. She lay on one edge of the wide bed. Her sleep was sporadic.

*

In the morning, she was stiffer than ever. The strenuous exercising had reawakened flaccid muscles. Aching, she stared at the back of Siena's head, auburn hair glinting in the early light. Veronica tried to sit up, but her whole body trembled. She slumped back, shoulders crackling from the strain.

Siena rolled over, eyes languid. "Why are you awake so early?"

"Have to use the bathroom, but the Tin Woman needs oiling."

"Poor bambina. I'll help you up." Siena crawled closer, gently slipped a supporting arm behind her head, and raised her to a sitting position. Although Veronica relished Siena's closeness, she did not look at her, embarrassed by her recalcitrant body, her numb left leg.

"Now all the way." Keeping one arm around her, Siena guided her up. Shakily, Veronica leaned near, keeping her weight on her right leg, fearful of losing her balance.

"How would you've managed without me?"

"Good question." She reached for the bathroom doorknob. "Don't come in."

"Veronica—"

"Honest. I—" Her eyes filled with tears.

Siena helped her to the toilet and lowered Veronica's panties. Then she shut the door and remained in the hallway.

Veronica wanted to cry from humiliation. In a few moments, she heard Siena's voice. "Are you through?"

She squeezed her eyes shut and wished she could sit there alone for the rest of the day. She hated being helpless.

"Veronica, do you have a shower massage attachment? That would really loosen your muscles." Siena spoke soothingly through the closed door. "If we shower to-gether, you wouldn't have to worry about losing your balance. I'd be there to catch you."

Veronica stared at the door and did not know what to say.

"You don't have to be embarrassed. It'll be like high school gym class—"

With effort, Veronica raised herself and opened the door, holding its knob tightly. "I don't like bothering you with my problems." She kept her eyes focused on the bathrom carpeting.

"How can you say that after what I put you through last night?" Siena briskly entered the bathroom and re-moved towels from the shelves. "Come on. Let's shower."

She watched Siena with a combination of exasperation and trepidation. Siena seemed used to getting her way. Veronica did not like to be passive, but her numb leg would not allow her to stalk out either.

After Siena tested the water, she whisked off her night-gown. Veronica caught her breath at viewing those pink-nippled breasts bounce.

"You're next."

Shivering, she sat motionless while Siena removed the baggy T-shirt and knelt to take off the cotton panties. One pink nipple brushed against Veronica's knee. Her pulse quickened when she saw the nipple respond to that sudden contact.

Siena seemed oblivious. "You ought to model. Your coloring is beautiful and you're so slender. Wish I had a body like yours. I'm too big on top."

Veronica blushed; she did not trust herself to answer. No one but Joanna had ever admired her so. With no hesitation, and not only because she was fearful of slipping, she let Siena lead her into the slower. She held Siena's waist, cherishing the feel of that adorable flesh.

"Whenever I visit my grandma, I bathe her like this. She has arthritis." Siena rubbed soap on a washcloth and proceeded to wash Veronica. "She was very self-conscious at first, but it makes more sense than trying to get her in and out of the tub. Now we make a game of it. And showering together conserves water."

Keeping one hand on Siena, Veronica blinked against the cascading stream. This was so different from her bath the night before. Despite feeling helpless, she liked being naked with Siena; it seemed perfectly natural. She only wished the circumstances were more in her favor.

While Siena soaped her, Veronica tried to focus on the conversation. "Where does your grandmother live?"

"In Sonoma with my mother. Mom went back there after the divorce. Dad's still in San Diego running his restaurant. That's where he met his second wife." While she spoke, she directed the shower massage to Veronica's aching neck and shoulders.

"This really was a great idea." Veronica liked the way their bodies and skin tones contrasted.

"When we're through, I'll give you a real massage. Then you won't have any excuse for being stiff." Hair wetly plastered to her head, Siena laughed and her breasts jiggled. Veronica wanted so much to touch, to lick them. She made herself look away.

Minutes later, she lay flat on her tummy on Frank's bed. Wrapped in a towel, Siena knelt over her and vigorously kneaded those sore muscles.

Her words came in quick spurts. "Didn't you say you're not used to being pampered?"

"Mmmhmm." Face pressed against the sheet, Veronica kept her eyes closed, reveling in the constant attention.

"I don't hear any protests about this."

"Enjoying it too much," She admitted with a shy laugh.

"Good. Don't protest about breakfast either. I'll get it started while you dress." Siena moved off the bed. "Think you can get up on your own?"

"No problem, now." Veronica lay still, watching her leave. "Siena, you don't have to—"

"See you in the kitchen."

She remained immobile, her muscles and skin tingling from the invigorating massage. The sensual feel of those soft hands had revitalized her. She did not know how long she could continue being silent about her attraction to Siena.

Fleetingly, she thought of Michi again, but after she got up, she found Siena's enthusiasm for exploring Santa Monica contagious. There would be time for Michi on Monday.

Siena played chauffeur in her blue Honda and laughed at her companion's bewilderment over the yuppie transformation of Montana Avenue. Veronica knew from her father and brother that the northern section of the city had begun to rival Main Street for its trendy appeal, but seeing it herself still surprised her. Once Montana Avenue had been a residential neighborhood with only markets, laundromats, gas stations and a branch library to break the monotony. Now it boasted a variety of art galleries, exclusive boutiques and gourmet shops.

They found a parking spot on a side street and trekked a block to begin their excursion. Siena pulled her into a boutique which sold hand-painted clothing. After impatiently lolling, Veronica left her trying on dresses and wandered into an adjacent shop which featured South-western jewelry and artifacts. She lingered over the display counter, recalling Joanna's preference for turquoise. She would have liked the heavy squash blossom necklaces on view. Reflexively, she twisted the delicate silver ring Joanna had given her, and moved to the rear of the store to browse among the Navajo baskets and rugs. They had always wanted to visit the Southwest together.

When Siena found her, she persuaded Veronica to take a frozen yogurt break.

"We have to find a fabric store. I have a terrific idea for a caftan—I'll try out the design on you. You'd look elegant, and it'd probably affect your work."

"If it'd improve, wonderful. Otherwise, I'll stick to my T's."

4

Sara Melendez smoothed a cross-stitched tablecloth on the dining room table. "Any word from Frank?"

"Mom, he's on his honeymoon." Veronica began to lay out the silverware. After the shopping trip with Siena, she barely had had time to change and drive to her parents' home.

"Frank should at least phone Philly, but he's too busy con su guerumba. That girl isn't right for him, Roni." Her mother sighed and wiped her steaming forehead with a paper napkin.

"He's crazy about Joyce." Veronica put a tall glass at each place setting. "Phil's the one I'm worried about."

"Pobrecito. Remember when he used to sit on my lap and say 'Grandma, tell me stories about my mommy.' It was enough to break my heart." Sara placed a covered casserole dish in the center of the table and gestured for Veronica to sit.

"The boy's practically a man," Joe Melendez cut in. Leaving his easy chair, the husky man carried a folded newspaper under his arm and winked at his youngest daughter. "Phil doesn't need a bunch of mujeres feeling sorry for him. He'll turn out all right."

"It'd help if his father—and his grandfather—paid more attention to him." Sara glared at her husband, her stout figure quivering with indignation.

"Ay, mujer. Déjame en paz," He grumbled. His large

45

workingman's hands held his greying head in mock consternation.

Veronica handed her father the casserole dish containing chicken with rice. She was amused by his exaggerated ways of coping with Sara's volatile nature.

"How's your leg, hijita?"

"Better since I've been swimming."

His dark eyes spread their warmth. "Que bueno. As long as you keep it moving, it'll be like before." He took her plate and served her a generous helping. "If you need anything, let us know. You never ask, Roni."

"Frank's left me plenty of money for the summer, Dad. But—thanks."

"Your brother's always watched out for you." Her mother fanned herself with a napkin. "Ever since you were a baby."

"We probably get along 'cause I'm so much younger." Veronica poured iced tea for her parents and herself.

"Serve yourself more frijolitos, Roni."

"I'll be farting all night if I eat too many."

Her father chuckled. "Que muchacha! Hay tortillas aquí tambien." He scooped up some beans with the edge of one. "What's happening with Phil gone?"

"I've done some writing. And today I went shopping with one of the neighbors."

"Que bueno. We don't like you to be cooped up todo el tiempo. You'll ruin your eyes with all that reading and writing."

"My eyes are fine and always have been."

Her mother's curiosity was sparked. "Pues, who's this neighbor? One of those gavacho bachelors? Ay, hija, ten cuidado."

"Ma, she's white and female. And what's the big deal, anyway?" Veronica pushed the rice about her plate.

46

Sara Melendez let her daughter's comment pass. "Más arroz?"

"I have enough."

"Pues, you do need new friends. Have you heard from Michi yet?"

"We're having lunch Monday."

Joe went into the kitchen and returned with a Budweiser. "See? Michi didn't mean to ignore you. She was probably just busy with school."

"Verdad, mijita," Sara agreed. "When she was home last Christmas, she was with you all the time, remember? Michi practically lived at the hospital."

Veronica blinked at those memories. On many afternoons, Michi had sat and cried with her over Joanna. When her friend had left for Berkeley, Veronica had become even more bereft.

"Have you seen Isabel?" Her mother served herself and Joe another hefty portion.

Veronica suspected Sara was envious of her closeness to Isabel Nuñez, Joanna's mother.

"Sometimes at the cemetery, but not lately." She sipped her iced tea. "Wonder how she is."

"I see her y la familia en Misa casi todos los domingos. Pobrecita, she looks so thin. She's taken it real hard, Roni. I'm surprised you haven't talked to her."

Joe Melendez cleared his throat and frowned at his wife.

"Sometimes it's really hard to talk about—" Pausing, Veronica toyed with the food on her plate, dividing it into neat morsels. "Isabel and Joanna were so close, especially because she was the only daughter—" Her eyes welled.

"Maybe it's better for you not to see Isabel for a while, Roni." Her father's voice was a trifle gruff. "You probably remind her of—everything."

She made herself look at him. "I know I do. But I really care for her, Dad. I shouldn't snub her—especially now."

"You wouldn't be snubbing her." He dug a fork into a chicken thigh.

Sara heaved a sigh. "Hija, it's up to you. The poor woman's still in mourning. 'There but for the grace of God go I,' eh? You almost died, too. It must hurt her to see you when her own daughter's gone."

She winced at her mother's words. "That's why I've backed off. I feel so responsible—"

"You weren't, Roni," Her father said with conviction. "Mira, querida, don't start that again. The Highway Patrol—everybody—said it *wasn't* your fault."

She took a deep breath, trying to ward off those memories. "It's just so hard, Dad. Isabel always asks me tons of questions; she wants to know every detail of Joanna's life. And that hurts *me*, too. Joanna was my *best* friend," she whispered.

"Sara, why'd you bring this up, eh?" Joe handed Veronica a napkin. "Let the poor girl eat in peace."

"I'm sorry, mijita." Sara began to gently stroke her daughter's bowed head.

At her touch, Veronica dissolved into choking sobs. Sara attempted to hug her close, but her daughter edged away. Joe Melendez tossed his greasy napkin on the table, noisily pushed back his chair, and stalked out.

She would always be their "hijita," their "mu-chachita." After the accident, her parents' protective attitudes had intensified; they could not forget they had almost lost her. Over the months, she had grown accustomed to having Frank and Phil as buffers. Without them, she felt too vulnerable in her parents' company. Stifled in their presence, overwhelmed by memories of Joanna, she sought solace in solitude.

Aimlessly, she drove. She found herself on San Vicente Boulevard and followed it westward to the ocean. Its familiar curves, its tree-lined median strip, its luxurious neighborhoods calmed her. In her mood, she preferred its upper-class elegance to the traffic-choked boulevards across the city, though her roots clung to the southern edge of Santa Monica, not on San Vicente where few, if any, Chicanos lived.

She had grown up near the community college, on the margins of the local barrio, close enough to witness its violence. Her hard-working parents had tried to shelter their children from the barrio's harsh realities; Veronica and her siblings had attended parochial rather than public schools. Yet even there, she had known classmates seduced by drugs, crime and sex. She was aware that her studious nature and high grade-point average had offered her an escape route those classmates lacked. But not even those advantages had prevented her from experiencing the loneliness and isolation of being a lesbian in a close-knit, sometimes suffocating, Chicano family.

In the twilight, Veronica parked at the Palisades and slowly walked to the bluff's edge. The sea breeze nipped her bare arms, and she crossed them in front of her, warding off the evening chill. She did not bother to be wary of the homeless people who often slept in the park. A few lovers strolled by—heterosexuals hand in hand. She ignored them and let her eyes absorb the Pacific. The sun had vanished, and the water seemed eerily dark, its white-capped waves the only illumination. She stood near one of the signs warning of possible landslides, and wished the bluff would crumble and swallow her with it.

*

"You're back." Siena stepped aside to let Veronica in.

"What're you doing home on a Saturday night?"

Siena pulled a panel of violet silk from the arm of the leather sofa. "Working on your caftan. You're just in time."

"For what?" Standing beside her, Veronica frowned.

"I need your measurements. I was going by eye, but might as well be precise." Siena peered into Veronica's face. "Oh, my. Don't we look glum."

Veronica set her canvas bag on the smoked glass coffee table. "Take my mind off my parents, please."

Siena grabbed the tape measure from the edge of the table. "What happened?"

"My mother asks too many questions." Veronica pressed fingers to her temples and began to pace.

Siena moved beside her, tugging at Veronica's black crew-necked pullover, rolling it up to measure her waist. "All mothers do."

Veronica gasped at that rather flirtatious action. Whirling around, she stepped away. "Siena, why do you need measurements? Caftans are loose."

"Right, but I need some idea, or you'll drown in it." Siena gestured towards the pullover. "You have to take that off. It's too thick." She gave the top another impatient tug.

Veronica hesitated. Siena had raised the pullover with enough familiarity to arouse her. She remembered tussling with Joanna on their sofa, pushing up her T-shirt to kiss her breasts. Joanna would roll over quickly and dare her to try again, and Veronica would always take that challenge.

Keeping her eyes on Siena's unwavering ones, she raised the top over her head and tossed it on the creme

50

leather sofa. She recalled their morning shower, Siena's alabaster skin, her pink nipples. Veronica's own went taut at that memory.

"That's more like it." Siena approached with the tape measure.

Taking a deep breath, Veronica moved towards her, too. Bare-breasted, she felt reckless—Artemis at the hunt. "Siena—"

She was met with a quizzical look. Without waiting for her response, Veronica leaned forward. Slowly, gently, she drew a finger along Siena's petal-soft cheek.

Siena almost smiled. Then, closing her eyes, she accepted the caress, her lightly freckled cheek joining Veronica's brown hand. Neither woman spoke. Then their lips inched nearer. Veronica's open mouth soon covered Siena's parted one and their tongues collided. They breathed deeply and came closer, not yet embracing.

"I like purple silk," Veronica whispered.

"I know."

Siena dropped the tape measure and it bounced on the unfurled edge of the silk panel. One of her hands strayed to Veronica's breasts. As if unable to decide what to do, she let it rest there and concentrated on the kiss.

Veronica felt delirious. She wondered if she were in a fugue state; her sense of reality seemed obscured. She kept her yearning mouth on Siena's, and her trembling hands were everywhere, in Siena's hair, on her shoulders, feeling her breasts through the scanty tank top, drawing her ever closer. Finally, coming up for air, the women parted.

"Veronica, I've never been kissed like that."

Face hot and flushed, Veronica smiled. "Surprised?"

"Not enough to want to stop."

"Wait." Taking a step backward, Veronica bumped into the sofa. They had so much to discuss first, she thought. Reaching for her pullover, she felt disoriented, but very lusty.

"*You* wait. I still want to measure you." Siena retrieved the tape and efficiently brought it around Veronica's breasts. Whether on purpose or not—she could not be sure—one of Siena's thumbs grazed a dark nipple. Veronica let go of the pullover, her pulse quickening.

"Siena, we have to talk about this—"

"Why?"

Veronica stared, finding Siena's self-composure incredible; as for herself, she felt shaken and bewildered, but wanting more kisses. "Well—don't you have any questions? Isn't this a bit unexpected?"

"Yes. And totally fascinating."

"Look, we both have a lot of emotional baggage and—"

"I told you my secret. Now I know yours." Siena's voice became a whisper. "Veronica, you don't have to explain—"

"That guy at at the restaurant was right: I'm a lesbian." She let the word sink in, but Siena's expression did not change. "I don't want to use you, Siena. I know you prefer men and—"

"I've only been with men."

"I sure don't want to be an experiment." Veronica once again reached for her pullover. She wondered if Siena was bewildered, too, but trying to mask it. "In that case, I'd rather be your friend and nothing else. I'm not looking to be hurt."

"I wouldn't hurt you." Siena's tone was soothing. "I'm sorry if I sounded crazed a moment ago. I don't know how to react—I've never experienced anything like this. But if you felt a need to kiss me—and I felt a need to respond—maybe we should just go along with that.

Maybe this is what we both need—now."

Veronica was wary. "I never do things like this."

"You just did."

"I lost control for a moment."

"It was longer than that." Siena reached over to touch her hand. "It's all right. I loved every second."

"Oh, Siena." She did not look at her. "This is so insane. Now I don't know what to do."

"Let's find out what to do together." Siena squeezed Veronica's hand and held it to her breast.

She felt the rapid thumping of Siena's heart. With a daring movement, she lightly outlined Siena's nipple. And when she did, she saw consent, not revulsion, in those hazel eyes. She leaned towards her again.

"I don't want you to think I'm predatory."

"I don't." Siena lay a reassuring hand against Veronica's cheek. The satiny texture of her palm was so like Joanna's.

Dismissing memories, Veronica let her words tumble out. "I was attracted to you right away, but I don't believe in coming on strong. Besides, you're straight. And last night, when you talked about Gary—"

"Please—I want to forget that."

"Is that what I'm for?"

"No! Last night, we leaned on each other, Veronica. We're friends."

Veronica's words continued in a torrent, and she felt tremendous relief at expressing herself. "When you were crying, I wanted to hold you. It's been so long since I've felt that, but I didn't want this to happen fast. We shouldn't rush—"

"I'm not afraid, and I've never done this before. I trust you and—I want to be with you."

Veronica crossed her arms over her breasts, her nipples

hard buttons. For a moment, she closed her eyes, trying to regain her equilibrium. "This is so strange. I started it, and now I'm the one getting cold feet. I've never seduced anyone. Before—it was always mutual."

"You're *not* seducing me. Don't think that for a minute."

Siena turned and strolled towards her bedroom. In a moment, Veronica followed her.

They kissed obsessively, and Veronica began to caress her, her mouth gradually wandering to those wondrous pink nipples, so different from Joanna's and her own brown ones. She glanced at her arm against Siena's fair skin and again noted the startling contrast. No wonder her mother had dubbed her "la morenita." But she did not want to think about her mother nor Joanna. Instead, she raised her head to view Siena.

She looked so beautiful, auburn hair spread on the eyelet pillowcase, her entire being wanting. Moaning, Siena pulled her closer, fondling Veronica's shoulders. Bending over her again. Veronica concentrated on the sensual sensations and willed herself to forget everything else.

Alternately licking and kneading those lovely breasts, she eventually aimed lower. While her tongue played with Siena's navel, her fingers exploringly parted her soft tuft and found her vulva. It was warm and damp, and Siena gasped with pleasure.

"Yes, Veronica. Yes."

Soon her mouth was where her fingers had been. Siena had a cidery fragrance, a musky taste. Veronica reveled in her. She was relentless, licking, sucking, her mouth and tongue indefatigable. Siena opened her thighs wider, and Veronica swept her tongue repeatedly along her clitoris, liking the way that pink nub rose to greet her. It glistened with moisture, and as she sucked harder, Siena came with a breathless cry.

Veronica moved over her, their mouths joined, and Siena clung to her. Wanting to be pleasured, too, she was reticent about mentioning it. Siena surprised her by wrapping strong legs around her. Veronica smiled when Siena pressed herself against her. She felt her warm moistness, and was further aroused by the touch of her sex-heated flesh. Veronica groaned and undulated against her. Her passion blended with Siena's and she came.

Not satisfied, Veronica continued moving against her. Hair matted against her flushed face, Siena grasped her tightly, meeting each motion with a reciprocal movement of her pelvis. Within moments, they each came again, moaning and crying at once. They lay against each other, Siena's hands glued to Veronica's slippery back. Barely raising her head, she groped for Siena's lips, found them, and did not release them.

"Stay with me," Siena whispered.

"Yes." Veronica rested against her and lazily licked one nipple; it perked up again.

Siena laughed softly. "Why didn't we do this last night?"

"I wanted to. This morning, too—but I didn't want to scare you."

"Veronica, how could I ever be scared of you?"

She gazed into those glimmering eyes. "Some women would be; some would be repulsed. Some would even hate me. I took a risk. You could've thrown me out."

"Never."

"Don't say that. What if Gary comes back?"

"He won't. Even if he did, that's all over."

"What if some other guy comes along? Where would I

be then? Relegated back to 'friend'?"

Siena frowned. "Why are you asking all these questions?"

"I have to."

"Have you had many lovers?"

"Only Joanna."

"The woman in the car?"

Veronica turned away. "Don't ask about her."

Siena tenderly stroked Veronica's shoulder. "What about men?"

"None. I'm not attracted to them."

"Not even curious?"

"Not enough to get involved." Veronica's eyes remained on hers. "I can't function without an emotional attraction, too. I want much more than sex."

"Does your family know?"

"They think I'm a little strange 'cause I write, but they haven't pinpointed anything else. If they have, they probably figure it's safer not to ask questions."

"I wouldn't have guessed."

Veronica smiled and with a forefinger traced Siena's nose, its barely perceptible downward curve a sign of her Italian ancestry. "I don't fit the stereotype."

"Besides, you seem shy, even awkward at times."

"A convenient facade." Veronica was amused by her assessment.

"It works. You're amazing."

"So are you."

Phil glanced up at his aunt's arrival Sunday evening. "You were at Siena's? Too much, Roni. You weren't exactly friendly when she moved in." He set a large bowl of popcorn on the kitchen table and pulled a Pepsi from the refrigerator.

When Veronica noticed he had turned on the lights in Frank's condo, she had reluctantly left Siena. She leaned against the kitchen counter. "Didn't think I'd be criticized for making a friend. Siena and I have stuff in common, which is more than I can say about the boring yuppies who live around here."

Phil's level eyes appraised her. "Jeez, you're touchy."

"Am not." She reached for the copper tea kettle and filled it. "She's coming over in a few minutes. She's nervous about the modelling job, so be nice, Phil."

"Always am." He swigged the Pepsi. "Steve's mom asked a bunch of questions about you."

"Like what?"

"She wanted to know if you're dating anyone."

"Why's she asking *you*?"

"Snoopy, I guess."

"Well, Rita can shove it. I'll go out whenever I'm damn ready."

"Hey, Roni, chill out."

"I'm sick and tired of people butting into my life. I have days when I can hardly move. What do they expect, Phil? Zamora expects me to be a writing machine and now Rita thinks I should go out dancing every night." She tossed a faded potholder across the sink. "I've had it."

The boy munched his popcorn and said nothing for several moments. "Grandma phoned a little while ago."

"What'd *she* want?"

"To apologize. Did you guys hassle again?"

She sighed. "Mom tried to make me feel guilty 'cause I haven't seen Isabel lately. I left, Phil. Sometimes I absolutely can't take your grandmother."

"She didn't mean it."

"Want to bet?" Veronica removed a package of Celestial Seasonings herbal tea and a stoneware mug from the pantry shelf. "Oh. There's the doorbell."

"I'll get it." Phil sprang up before she had a chance.

5

"Hey, there, Siena—what are you going to model? Bikinis?"

"Not a chance, Phil. For a fashion shoot, I'd have to be as slim as Veronica." In jeans and a V-necked pullover, her long hair gathered into a ponytail, Siena presented a subdued appearance compared to earlier. Veronica's pulse quickened at seeing her.

"I think you're just right." Phil grinned and downed a mouthful of popcorn.

"Thanks, but I'll probably model jewelry, hosiery maybe."

"How about nightgowns?" The boy snickered. "Or underwear?"

Veronica cut in. "How about going to your room to study?"

"Aw, Roni. I have all night."

"It's almost 9:00, muchacho. What's the point of taking summer classes if you shirk off studying? You had a fabulous weekend, so buckle down."

At her no-nonsense expression, he gave in, tucking the popcorn bowl under his arm. "Okay, okay. See you in the morning. 'Night, Siena. Good luck with the job."

"I'll need it."

After he left, Siena glanced at Veronica. "Weren't you a little hard on him?"

"If I don't talk to him like that, he'll think I don't care."

"You didn't like his questions."

"Siena, he's a fourteen-year-old with a crush on you. Why encourage it? As it is, the poor kid'll jerk off all night."

Siena giggled. "You're awful."

Veronica laughed, too. "Hey, I'll be doing the same." She wanted to kiss her then, but that would be risky. With Phil home, they had to be careful.

Later, after they had talked for a couple of hours, Veronica watched her from the balcony. Siena blew a kiss and entered her condo. Veronica wafted one back, trudged to the sofa and eased down, her loneliness pervasive. Thin arms crossed against her torso, she felt depressed at the thought of going to bed alone. Being with Siena had been delicious.

Beginning to doze off, she was startled by the muffled sounds of bare feet on the carpet. When she opened her eyes, she saw her gangly nephew in T-shirt and jockey briefs.

"Thought you'd fallen asleep out here again."

"What're you doing up?"

"Had to pee. Too much Pepsi." Phil slumped beside her. "I didn't hear Siena leave." He rested his dark head against the sofa. "Told Steve she looks like she stepped out of a centerfold."

Veronica narrowed her eyes. "She doesn't need a couple of horny kids slobbering all over her. If that's why you're being friendly with her, forget it, Phil. Look, she's trying to get over something, so please don't make a pest of yourself."

He straightened his posture, and his face showed concern. "Huh?"

"The guy Siena was going to marry found someone else, but didn't bother telling her."

"What a geek!"

Veronica was satisfied with his reaction. "She came to L.A. to put all that behind her."

"Bet she slept with him, huh?"

"Philip, I listened to what she wanted to tell me. I didn't interrogate her."

"She must've. Like Joyce used to stay with Dad whenever I was at Steve's."

She rubbed the back of her neck. "That's Frank's business."

"Roni, I know what went on."

"Did it bother you?"

Phil's fingers brushed through his razor-cut hair. "I don't know. Don't even know if I'm going to like living with them."

"It'll be a definite adjustment." Veronica shifted her body to view him better.

"How will I be able to stand all their lovey-dovey stuff?"

"Phil, that's part of the package. Having a teenaged stepson won't be easy for Joyce either."

"Wish she was real friendly, like Siena. Guess Dad didn't have any trouble, though," he added with a grin. He played with the yarn fringe on one of cushions. "Think you'll ever get married, Roni?"

Her body grew rigid. "We're talking about *other* people. Don't drag *me* into it."

"Just wondering. You never go out."

"Don't start that, too. I'm not up to it, that's all." Her annoyance dissipated into agitation. She kept her arms crossed, securing herself from further questions.

"Guess Siena doesn't feel like dating either, huh? I mean, if that guy dumped her—"

"Planning to invite her somewhere?"

"Jeez, Roni. You're really uptight."

"Stick to teenyboppers."

"I like her for a friend, okay?."

"That isn't the whole story, Phil, and you know it. You like to look at her and think about her. Actually, there's nothing wrong with that—just your hormones in high gear."

She struggled to be objective. "What I'm saying is, see beyond her body. Siena's a caring person—that's really what makes her beautiful. And I want you to realize that—not only with her—but with other women, too. Phil, I don't want you turning into a creep who sees women only as available bodies. That's why I'm irked about what you told Steve. I can just imagine you two drooling over her."

"Wait a minute—"

"Let me finish. I know you're better than that. You've been raised to respect women, so don't show off with Steve. Siena likes you, but she might not if she finds out what you've been saying."

"I'm not saying anything that isn't true! Sure, I told him how pretty Siena is. That's no lie. And, yeah, I do like to look at her. But that's it, Roni. Jeez, you make it sound like we're ready to rape her."

"When did I mention the word 'rape'?"

"You're always ready to think the worst. You're such a downer."

At that, she rose, a bit unsteadily. "Well, I won't depress you any more. Be sure to turn off the lights."

*

62

Veronica wept in the bathroom. She had not meant her growing possessiveness about Siena to seep into her conversation with Phil. At least, she consoled herself, he was young, too unsophisticated to delve into her motivations. Yet, she felt exposed, fearful she would be unable to hide her feelings.

She splashed cold water on her face, then stared at herself in the mirror's reflection. She saw a sad-eyed Chicana, her present mood incongruent with that day's bliss. She longed for Siena, but knew she would have to wait.

"I'm really glad you offered to take me to Century City. I'm so nervous I'd probably get lost." Siena studied herself in her compact mirror while Veronica drove.

Two cups of coffee had not obliterated her sleepless night. "Listen, have you had a chance to think about Saturday and yester—"

"Veronica, I don't like to analyze things. All I know is, being with you is so—erotic."

"And impulsive." She avoided glancing at Siena and concentrated on the morning traffic. "I haven't been very rational lately."

"Are you scared?"

"Yes. Aren't you?"

"I'm not sure if I want to find out."

Veronica sighed. Her timing was off. She was too tired to discuss anything, and sensed Siena was too preoccupied with new job jitters. She decided to keep quiet. In a few minutes, she guided the sports car into a brick-paved cul-de-sac bordered with pink geraniums.

Siena grabbed her makeup bag, got out, and leaned into the Z's window. "I'll phone when I'm ready to leave. Already feels like it's going to be a long day."

"Yeah. I'll be working on my story. Good luck, Siena."

"Thanks." With a wave, she disappeared into a sleek high rise, her flaming hair billowing.

For over an hour, Veronica sat at the desk, staring at the typewriter keys, unable to fill the page with an orderly row of paragraphs. The torrent of words she wanted to write about Joanna lay submerged; yet her imagination swirled with images of Siena: beside her, wrapped around her, her lips and body tantalizing, arousing.

Saturday night, she had awakened several times, making sure she had not fantasized being with her. At first, she had been disoriented at finding the sleeping woman next to her. She remembered Joanna had touched her often throughout their nights, securing her proximity. In the months since Joanna's death, Veronica had missed that physical and emotional closeness.

Siena was so new. She was not Joanna—but she was *alive*. Veronica wondered if she would ever love her, and she sensed a relationship with Siena would not be without conflicts.

Abruptly, she rose and pushed her chair against the desk. Peeling off her T-shirt, she changed into a swimsuit and limped outside. Better to exercise than to waste time fantasizing or trying to write.

The swimming pool was deserted because most of the tenants were away during the day. She lowered herself into the water and cautiously swam its length. After several minutes, she raised her head, noticing the stout figure in a flowered housedress standing at the far edge of the pool.

"Mom, how long've you been here?"

"Unos minutos. Don't get too tired, hija." Her mother approached briskly with the towel Veronica had left on a lounge chair.

"I'm not ready to get out. Give me a few more minutes." She rested her damp arm on the pool's flagstone edge. "What's the matter?"

"I decided to stop by on my way back from la tienda." Sara snapped and unsnapped the clasp of her black vinyl handbag. "Did Philly tell you I phoned?"

Veronica nodded and squinted against the morning sun. "Sometimes I just can't take all your questions."

"Pues, lo siento." Her mother folded the striped towel. Her greying black hair, stretched into a tight bun, emphasized her round face and apologetic eyes. Veronica found herself resenting Sara's forlorn expression.

"So do I." Turning, she swam off, hoping her mother would leave, but knowing she would not. At least she had not shown up the day before; Veronica was relieved at that. When she swam the pool's length again, she noticed Sara had pulled up one of the patio chairs and sat primly, the folded towel on her lap. Realizing it was useless to ignore her, Veronica sighed and climbed out of the water. Sara hurried to wrap her in the towel.

"Thanks, Mom. I can do that." She stepped away.

"My independent one." Fondness was evident in Sara's tone. "Roni, sometimes I say the wrong things. I'm not a young-thinking mother like Isabel porque—"

"—you were almost forty when I was born." Veronica supplied that familiar refrain. "I never said you had to be like her. I just wish you knew when to leave me alone."

Sara's plump hands continued fidgeting with her handbag. "I want to be close to you, Roni. Your father and me don't want to lose you, hijita."

"I'm right here—haven't gone anywhere." Veronica

was exasperated. "Look, I just need lots of time by myself. It's nothing personal, Mom. I've been through a lot, and sometimes I just don't feel like being around anyone. I wish you'd understand that."

"You're so different from your sisters."

"None of us are alike." Veronica pulled on the terrycloth robe. "Do you want to come in for a while?"

Sara took on a humble tone. "Only if you're not busy."

"I have a therapy appointment at 11:00, but—"

"I just wanted to see if you're all right. I worry about you, flaquita."

At that pet name, Veronica felt some remorse about her irritability. 'You don't have to. Honest. I'm fine."

"You've changed so much since—"

"Phil says the same thing." Shrugging, she unsuccessfully tried to smile. "I can't help it. Once I'm back in school, I think I'll get back on track."

"Pero, are you ready for that?"

"Sure. Anyway, even if Zamora's rooting for me, the English Department won't hold my slot open forever— Chicana grad student or not."

Sara sniffed at that ethnic connotation. "Ay, that word 'Chicana.' Why do you like to use it, Roni? Why can't you just say 'Mexican-American'?"

Veronica grinned, imagining her mother's reaction to the word 'dyke.' "No political discussions now, okay? Frank's the one who likes to argue over that. Want some iced tea?"

Sara smoothed the lapels of her daughter's robe. "Otra vez, eh? You have things to do. I just wanted to tell you que siento mucho lo que pasó antes. Sometimes your father and me just don't know how to talk to you—but we mean well."

"I know."

Her mother hugged her tightly, and Veronica held her, too, towering over her. As a child, she remembered snuggling against those cushiony breasts, feeling secure in that commodious lap. Would Sara, ever-devoted wife and mother, ever understand her youngest daughter's love for women? Veronica doubted that, and she felt like crying when Sara touched her cheek.

"Mi morenita. Don't get too much sun, eh?"

Veronica kept her voice steady. "I'm going inside. I'll walk with you to the gate."

"I was thinking about you this morning."

"Of course. That's why I called, Lucy." Veronica twirled the phone cord around her fingers after her mother left. For the time being, she abandoned work on the story; talking with her sister seemed a preferable option. "What did your ESP tell you?"

"That you're probably procrastinating about—"

Veronica laughed. "I can't fool you. Actually, writing about being a kid always reminds me of—"

"Am I in your stories?"

"Well, one of them has a certain older sister character who likes to raise a ruckus."

"Ay, Roni! I just hope I won't be too embarrassed when I finally meet Professor Zamora."

"She'd probably want you to write about being a Chicana nun. Camille's really gung-ho on all that."

"I think you like the attention she gives you, Roni."

Veronica leaned back on the sofa. "She knows her stuff. Anyway, Mom left a few minutes ago, so I needed a reality check. You're a lot easier to talk to, but I can't chat long or I'll be late for physical therapy."

"Cómo esta todo?"

"Fine. Getting more limber all the time. And I'm meeting Michi for lunch today."

"Sounds like fun. Well, you take care, hermanita. Keep exercising, and be patient with Mama, okay? Just remember, the other sisters and I are praying for you."

"Thanks, Lucy. I'll call again soon."

At noon, she left with Anna's admonishments reverberating in her ears. Tingling from the strenuous exercises, she stepped from the elevator, her limp less noticeable. She swung her car keys and glanced around.

"My God! Is that really you?"

"Live and in color." Michiko Yamada rolled the *L.A. Weekly* under her T-shirted arm and grinned. Then she clasped her friend's lean frame to her petite one.

Veronica felt close to tears; she wanted to hold Michi for hours. The paper bounced to the floor, but neither noticed.

"Roni, you look fantastic!"

Veronica tousled her friend's moussed crewcut. "You too. When'd you do this?"

The smaller woman shrugged, fiddling with the oblong buttons on Veronica's camp shirt. "Oh, I've been shorn for a while. Pretty slick, huh?"

"Almost didn't recognize you." Veronica savored the sight of her. Michi seemed thinner, but as cheeky as ever.

She bent over to pick up the *Weekly* and tapped Veronica's hip with it. "My new look, Melendez. Let's grab a bite somewhere."

*

The day was overcast, its monotonous greyness dulling the Pacific's azure. Following Michi's dusty white Toyota, Veronica guided the Z past Palisades Park. By day, the park teemed with activity: mothers strolled with their children, senior citizens played cards or dozed in the sun, while homeless women and men gathered near the Santa Monica Pier.

With its panoramic view of the bay, the park was a city landmark. Veronica remembered carefree days beneath those palm trees, playing hide and seek with Joanna and Michi. She would duck from view in the Japanese-styled gazebo, bursting into giggles when they found her. While their families picnicked, the three girls would skip to the telescope located at the park's southern edge; on a clear day, they would even see Santa Catalina Island.

Years of erosion had crumbled the park's majestic bluffs. Warning signs posted on reconstructed fences cautioned visitors of landslides. The Palisades had changed, its wooden benches becoming daily havens for the lonely, the elderly, the homeless. Only on weekends did the park brim again with large families, the Chicanos of her childhood replaced increasingly by Middle Eastern and Eastern European immigrants. Like many Santa Monica natives, Veronica rarely visited there. Yet Palisades Park, with its winding paths and fragrant rose garden, remained one of her favorite places. She veered the sports car left on Santa Monica Boulevard, her memories shifting with it.

At the Boulangerie on Main Street, Veronica cut her cheese and spinach croissant into dainty pieces. Except for Michi's spiky hairstyle and the gnawing absence of Joanna, nothing seemed to have changed between the friends.

"You still doing those stories for Zamora?"

"Three down, three to go." Veronica straightened in her chair and adjusted an imaginary pair of glasses, attempting an impression of Camille Zamora. "Tienes raw talent, sabes? Write about your experiences, your childhood—the accident. Keep disciplined, keep writing. And, por favor, come back to school this fall." She grimaced. "Spare me from over-zealous Chicana professors. I think Camille expects me to be the next Sandra Cisneros."

Michi giggled. "Quit complaining, Melendez. You've got a mentor, which is more than I have." Her smile began to fade. "I'm hoping for a staff job at the Asian-American Center on campus till I decide what to do. I know I should've written, but I've been so scattered." Michi tossed croissant crumbs to the blackbirds fluttering through the patio.

"In some ways, I feel like such a failure—dropping out of graduate school. My parents're thrilled beyond words, as you can well imagine," Michi added. She toyed with the silver cuff on her left ear; a single narrow crystal hung suspended there. "But, through all this, I've learned a lot about myself. I fell in love with a woman during winter quarter."

"Oh."

"Is that *all* you're going to say?" Michi's beringed fingers fanned the air. "Roni, don't be coy. I know about you and Joanna."

Veronica set down the mug to avoid spilling the coffee. "How *could* you?"

"Now that I think back, it was perfectly apparent. But while you were in the hospital, I hesitated to bring it up. You were so devastated. I was mourning Joanna, too, and I could only deal with one thing at a time. Kept hoping you'd tell me."

Veronica closed her eyes and felt a wet trickle emerge from the corner of each one.

Michi did not seem to notice. "Anyway, when I felt attracted to Ingrid, I had you and Joanna as role models. Maybe that's why I've kept a positive attitude about being a dyke. After all, my two best friends were, too."

Veronica looked up then and tried to smile. She could not recover the past; Michi needed her now.

"Roni, I don't know how you've been able to cope without Joanna. It must be torture. I thought I'd go crazy when Ingrid broke up with me. Had to leave Berkeley 'cause we kept running into each other."

"Oh, Mich. I'm so sorry." Her cheeks wet, Veronica reached over to clasp her hand. It was like a child's, not slender and long-fingered as Joanna's had been. She brought it to her lips, not caring if anyone saw. She had to suppress an urge to pull Michi into her lap and cradle her. "Have you talked to anyone else about this?"

Michi seemed to welcome the affectionate gesture. She kept her hand within her friend's brown one. "Are you kidding? The people I knew in Berkeley're more like acquaintances than friends. Roni, you were the only one I wanted to talk with, and you were here—going through your own hell. That's really why I didn't phone or write. I didn't know what to say without spilling my guts."

Veronica continued caressing her. She liked the way Michi's hand fit into hers, its rounded contours melding. "Why couldn't we trust each other, Mich? Why were we so afraid?"

"Really stupid, huh?" With her free hand, Michi scratched her crewcut head. "Yeah, we've both criticized our families for being inarticulate about personal stuff, but we fell into the same trap."

Veronica sighed. With her thumb, she outlined the blue topaz ring on Michi's index finger. "Suppose it's been ingrained in us, no matter how hard we try."

Michi looked at her. "I haven't told anyone in the family. They probably can't even imagine an Asian lesbian, least of all their little Michi. If they knew what'd really happened in Berkeley, they'd probably want to ship me off to relatives in Yokohama."

She took a bite of her croissant. "They're like most Asians—they think we can deal with personal problems without any outside help. You know, we're supposed to be the super minority, zooming through life without anything touching us. Well, I've been touched, and I've been hurt. And that's why I wanted so much to see you, Roni— 'cause you've been, too."

Veronica wanted to forget that ever-present hurt. Instead, she remembered happy times with Joanna. After long hours of studying, they would cuddle on the sofa beneath the Georgia O'Keeffe prints, exchanging kisses. Sometimes they would start making love on the sofa and wind up giggling on the carpet. Other times they would share a bubble bath, nuzzling each other sensuously. Those were the moments she chose to remember, not the accident, not the emptiness. And, there were more recent moments she had found to cherish.

She outlined Michi's bitten cuticles with her fingertips; her friend had resumed that old habit. Her untidy fingernails were a stark contrast to Siena's manicured ones. Veronica remembered the thrill of feeling them brushing against her breasts, surrounding her nipples. She sighed. Finding Michi's eyes on hers, she wondered how long she had drifted off. She had no idea if Michi had asked a question.

Veronica cleared her throat. "The worst part is

missing—her." She hesitated, unnerved to be daydreaming about Siena when Michi expected reminisces of Joanna. She determined to focus on the conversation, no matter how difficult. "Wanting to talk with Joanna, hearing her reaction to my writing—just having her listen and understand—that intimacy is gone, and I don't know if I can ever recapture it, Mich."

Frowning, she chewed another piece of the croissant, not yet willing to share revelations of Siena. "When Joanna died, she took part of me with her. I've changed, and I'd really like to get the old me back. Just don't know how to do it."

Michi nodded. "After Ingrid left, I remember thinking that I finally knew what all those blues songs, those country and western tunes, were all about—people being sacked by their lovers. It's like suddenly being in a different dimension, observing life from an alien perspective. But at least I know I'm a lesbian. For a while, I'd thought I was asexual."

"Mich, I can't believe we're having this conversation. Joanna and I used to wonder if you even cared about a social life. With your personality, it didn't make sense that you hardly cared about dating. We just thought you were too involved with school to be interested in anything else. You were so cute rushing across campus with your long hair streaming. Tell me I'm dreaming all this."

Michi grinned. "You're not. Listen, I owe a lot to you and Joanna. You guys'd been hard-core friends from way back. She's gone, and I'll miss her forever." Michi's lower lip began to tremble. "But you're still around, and I need you, Roni-san. I can't hold all this inside anymore. I just don't know how you do it."

Veronica squeezed Michi's hand again and tried to joke. "Another stoic Chicana, that's all." She blinked away forming tears. "None of it's been easy, though. The time in the hospital was horrendous—I had nothing to do all day but think, replay that last day with Joanna. Even now, I try to remember what we were talking about right before—and I still can't. I only see her looking at me and smiling. Maybe that's why I wasn't even aware of that bastard in the other car. Maybe I was looking at Joanna for too long."

"Oh, Roni." Michi's onyx-dark eyes brimmed again. For some moments, they clasped hands, occasionally sniffling. When Michi stood, Veronica let go of her reluctantly.

"Let's go to the beach, Roni. I need to move."

6

UNBUCKLING HER SANDALS, Veronica sat on the low wall separating the beach from the public walkway. "My physical therapist will love you for suggesting this. She always grumbles 'cause I hate to exercise."

Michi kicked off her Birkenstocks. "You're really lookin' good, Roni. Expected you to be hobbling around with a cane."

"I threw it out in May when Lucy was in town. She used to bring me here, too." While undoing the straps, Veronica noticed how shaky her hands remained. She stuffed the sandals into her canvas bag. "Almost told Lucy everything then, but I chickened out. When I talked to her this morning, I was tempted again—but there wasn't time."

Michi offered a steadying hand as they gingerly tread across the warm beach. "That'd be some conversation—coming out to a nun."

Veronica enjoyed the grainy texture of the sand against her bare feet. "We both have to come out to lots of people. Scares the hell out of me."

"It's weird, but you were the scariest."

Veronica touched her arm. "Why, Mich?"

"I wondered if you'd deny everything. Lots of women in your shoes'd hightail it right back to the closet."

"I owe it to Joanna to be out. Of course, that's easier said than done." She nudged Michi, hoping to redirect the focus of the conversation. "You haven't finished telling your story."

"Leave it to a writer." Despite her teasing tone, Michi's face grew solemn. She rubbed the moussed fuzz on her head and kept her eyes on the ocean. At the shoreline, the sand changed from grainy to damp. Their feet left behind well-delineated prints.

"Met Ingrid in a sociology class. She's a lecturer in the department—Swiss, and attractive in a rather Teutonic way: tall, blonde and opinionated. If I met her now, I'd call her a Nazi, but at the time I really thought she was a bona fide Amazon.

"Sometimes she'd stop me after class and invite me to the Co-op for expresso. You see, she has a thing about Asians, which I didn't know then. I was just so damn flattered by her interest, Roni. She'd tell me about European feminism, and we'd talk about cultural differences. She's fascinated with people of color. Ingrid's very vocal about Native Americans on reservations, and wanted to know everything about racism against Japanese-Americans during World War II and later. When I told her Mom and Dad had been kids in Manzanar, Ingrid probed for details. She was astonished when I said they don't like to discuss it.

"She was the first Caucasian I'd ever confided in about being the child of internees. Before that, I'd only discussed that stuff with you and Joanna. But, with Ingrid, I opened up more than I thought possible with a white person, maybe 'cause she's not American.

"One night we went to a poetry reading, and afterwards to her apartment in Oakland. It was sort of a mutual thing, you know? All of a sudden we were making love, and it seemed so right. I stayed over, Roni. I didn't want to leave, ever. I'd never made love with anyone before, but that didn't matter. I really fell for her."

Veronica leaned closer. "Did you ever question whether you're really a lesbian? Or were you too infatuated for that to matter?"

"It's weird, Roni. It just seemed perfectly apparent, and there was no point in questioning it." Michi frowned. "Maybe I cheated, you know? Didn't have to go through all that agonizing coming out stuff. Maybe the agonizing is what I'm going through now—not about admitting I'm a lesbian, but coping with being dumped."

Veronica winced. "How long were you together?"

"All winter and most of spring. We made love so much there were days I could hardly walk. My mouth would even be black and blue in the morning—no exaggeration."

"But wasn't it more than sexual?"

"Of course. Thought I'd found a treasure, a woman who was not only intelligent, but attractive and trustworthy. Wrong! She started cooling off, quit phoning, hurried off after classes. And pretty soon I started seeing her in the Co-op with another Asian-American woman— same type of body build as me, long hair, the whole bit. Ingrid never explained anything. I guess she figured it was perfectly apparent."

Veronica studied her friend's face. "And that's when you whacked off your hair?"

"Roni, I stormed into this shop specializing in punk haircuts, and told the gay guy to make me look ba-a-ad. He was in seventh heaven, snipping away to his heart's content. I didn't even check the mirror. Just paid and flew out. Buzzed into Mama Bears in Oakland and bought some ear cuffs, about twenty books on lesbianism and stayed holed up in my apartment for about two weeks. All

I did was cry and read. There was no way I could handle staying there after that. I withdrew before the semester ended.

"Then I had to get up the courage to tell my parents I'd dropped out. Major trauma time. Afterwards, I packed my stuff and crossed the bridge to stay with Tami. The family thinks I'm burned out. They don't quite understand it, but that explanation works for now."

"Mich, I wish you would've let me know about this sooner."

"I was too shaky to phone and—I thought you'd be mad 'cause I hadn't written."

Veronica tossed her an exasperated glance, but she had had her own distractions lately.

Michi shrugged. "I've been pretty freaked. For a while, I even thought about staying in San Francisco, but I was homesick for L.A. It's too damn cold up north."

"No one told us life would be this complicated." Veronica surveyed her while they strolled, their feet splashed by the incoming tide.

"They sure didn't. Roni—"

"Hmmm?"

"—we gotta support each other to the max from now on. Coming out to you's been my smartest move all year."

"You sure pulled a fast one. All this time I thought you were a brainy Sansei with dormant gonads."

"Turns out it's the other way around: hypersexed grad school dropout."

They giggled affectionately.

"Roni, do you think you could stand having a room-mate when you move back to your apartment?" Michi kept her attention focused on a nearby flock of California gulls.

For a long moment, Veronica hesitated, her mind churning.

"Earth to Veronica, Earth to Veronica." Michi clenched her fist into an imaginary microphone. "Hello?"

Veronica laughed then. "I'd love having you for my roomie. It's just—"

"I see it only as a temporary arrangement. Soon's I save up some money, I'll get my own place. I'd just rather be with you than stuck in the family home, you know?"

"Mich, you don't have to explain. It'll be great—for both of us."

"You're terrific!" Michi leaped with acrobatic agility, turning a couple of cartwheels, scattering the squawking gulls.

Laughing with her, Veronica wondered how she would ever explain about Siena. And how would Siena react to Michi?

"I've been trying to reach you for over half an hour." Siena sounded impatient over the phone. "Are you all right?"

"Yes." Veronica kept her face averted from the curious Michi who had followed her into the condo. "I had lunch with a friend and it got late. Are you ready to leave?"

"Aren't you even going to ask how it went?"

"Sorry." Veronica rubbed her eyes. "I'm a little out of it. I'll pick you up at the same place."

Siena's voice lost its impatience. "Veronica, is everything okay? You seem so—distant."

"I'll be there in a few minutes." She put down the receiver. Sighing, she turned to Michi, hunched over the Martina Navratilova autobiography plucked from Frank's bookcase. With a smile, Veronica observed her, recalling her own tendency to snatch up any reading material that even hinted at lesbianism.

"Mich, there's something I need to tell you."

"Huh?"

"I'm—sort of—involved with someone."

Raising her head, Michi kept the book in her lap. "Have to admit I'm surprised."

"Because it's so soon?" Veronica slumped beside her.

Michi nodded, brows puckered.

"It just—happened." She twirled a strand of hair around her fingers. "Want to come along when I pick her up from work?"

"If you'd like me to, sure." Michi slowly put the book on the oak coffee table. "Is she—of color?"

"She's Italian-American—very fair-skinned." Veronica decided on more honesty. "Mich, she's straight. And I have absolutely no idea where this is going."

"Oooooh." Michi's almond-shaped eyes widened.

"We have to talk. I won't have much time to tell you everything now, but at least I can start."

She whirled the Z onto Century City's Avenue of the Stars. "So what do you think so far, Mich?"

"I'm not going to say anything yet—maybe not even later. The world's moving too fast for me these days, Roni. Give me a break."

Veronica smiled, showing more confidence than she felt. "Since when have you kept opinions to yourself?"

Michi stuck out her tongue, but resumed a nonchalant demeanor when Veronica slowed the car.

"There she is." She braked, watching Siena skip down

the concrete steps, auburn hair shining.

"She's so—white. A regular Aphrodite. You're too much, Melendez." Michi scrambled over the seat and into the rear portion of the Z. Her small figure somehow managed to fit.

Veronica noticed Siena seemed aghast at Michi's punkish hairstyle. "Hope you didn't have to wait too long." Not giving her an opportunity to answer, Veronica made quick introductions.

Siena twisted in the seat and stiffly offered her hand. "Nice meeting you, Michi."

"Hi." Michi grinned and gripped it. "Don't feel uptight with me here. I'm a dyke, too."

Siena shot a questioning glance at Veronica.

"Michi came out at lunch, so I told her about us."

Siena's voice was cool. "Nothing like an exchange of confidences to make an afternoon fly by."

Veronica chose to ignore that. At a stoplight, she leaned over, caressing Siena's cheek, preferring to discourage an unpleasant scene. "How was your day?"

"Horrendous. I feel like a piece of meat. Modelling is incredibly impersonal. I just want to go home and soak in a hot bath."

"I'll give you a backrub. You'll feel better then."

"Why don't you two spend the rest of the day together? Standing under those hot lights really exhausted me."

Veronica maneuvered the Z westward on Olympic. "Maybe we can have dinner later."

"I shouldn't eat. I have to lose weight." Siena frowned, keeping her eyes on the wide boulevard. "Why are you taking a surface street?"

"It's the same one I took this morning. Besides, the

freeway's worse. Don't worry. I'll get you home soon as I can." In the rear-view mirror, Veronica saw Michi roll her eyes.

She handed Michi the condominum keys and limped after Siena. After the long beach walk, Veronica noticed her calf muscles had begun to ache.

Siena unlocked the door and paused in its threshold. "I'm tired. I really need some space."

"You didn't seem to mind my company over the weekend."

"I'm too tired to argue." Siena tossed her bag on the creme leather sofa and kicked off her Bandolino pumps. She stretched herself along the sofa's length, one leg slightly bent, her short skirt revealing several inches of thigh. Veronica's pulse throbbed at the sight.

"Who's arguing? I just want to know what's wrong." Veronica knelt beside her, bending to kiss her.

"Aren't you even going to say I'm more beautiful when I'm angry?" Siena whispered, as their lips almost met.

"No—because you're not. You're brattier than ever when you're angry." She laughed, then covered Siena's mouth with her own.

Clasping Veronica's shoulders, Siena pulled her closer. She soon slid one hand over Veronica's breasts. "I didn't like waiting so long. And I was worried when you didn't answer the phone. I thought something had happened to you, and I didn't even know who to call. And when you said you'd gone to lunch with a friend—well—"

"You were jealous?" Veronica moved over her and pushed back Siena's hair, fingering its thickness. "Michi's my best friend, Siena. I've known her since first grade."

"You never mentioned her—before."

"Never got around to it. Anyway, she just got back into town, and we lost track of time. At the rate we were going, we could've hiked all the way to Malibu. You can't imagine how exciting it is to find out she's a lesbian, too. She had Joanna and me all figured out. I can't get over it."

Siena touched her cheek. "Why'd you tell her about us?"

Veronica leaned on one elbow and nearly sank into the sofa. "Is that why you're—"

"She assumes I'm—" Siena looked askance.

"I told her you're straight. Though how you can justify that by being with *me* is another story."

"I'll *never* cut my hair like hers."

At that, Veronica exploded with laughter. Imagining Siena with a punk haircut caused her to laugh even harder. She buried her face between her lover's breasts and tried to catch her breath.

"Why is that funny?" Siena struggled to get up.

"You're stereotyping—and being homophobic, too."

Siena glared.

With some effort, Veronica lifted herself and plopped on the sofa's edge. "Michi's *not* trying to look like a guy."

"She could've fooled me."

"You're hopeless." Wiping her eyes, Veronica gazed at her with bemused affection.

"I am not. And I'm not—homophobic, either." She swung her legs over to sit beside Veronica. "I just think she looks extreme."

"For a reason. Why would a lesbian want to attract men? I like the way Michi looks—it suits her cheekiness."

"Would you ever cut your hair like that?"

"Hey, I'd have a great crewcut—a terrific Mohawk, even. My hair's really as straight as hers."

"You're teasing. I see that wild glint in your eyes."

Veronica laughed again.

"You're in a very good mood." Siena slipped a warm arm around her. "Did Michi cause that?"

"You're still jealous."

"I shouldn't be, but after having you all to myself—"

"Listen, I've known Michi as long as I've known Joanna. Today, I found out how much she really knows me, how much we have in common. That makes our friendship stronger than ever."

"What about me?"

Veronica squeezed her near. "You and I are just starting."

"Are you attracted to her?"

She knew that question had been coming. "Siena, I just told you, we're friends. I've never even thought of Michi in a sexual way." At her last statement, she felt uneasy; all afternoon she had viewed Michi in a totally different light.

"In spite of her haircut, she's very cute, Veronica."

"Siena, I can only handle one woman at a time."

"And you do that with great expertise." Siena snuggled closer, temptingly licking her cheek.

Veronica tried not to smile. "I thought you were tired."

"Not too."

Sprawled on the sofa, her fuzzy head propped by fringed pillows, Michi seemed mesmerized by the Navratilova book, but she grinned when Veronica entered. "Weren't you just going to walk her home?"

Veronica felt herself blush. "Had to tuck her in."

"I bet. Feverish, Roni? Your skin looks red-hot."

Veronica hurled a cushion at her, knocking the book aside.

"Rats! Now I've lost my place." Scrambling up, Michi retrieved the autobiography. "Temper, temper."

Veronica laughed and leaned against the sofa while Michi flipped through the book.

"By the way, Phil phoned. He's studying with Steve. Said he's having dinner there, too. They'll drive him home later. Gee, Roni, his voice's gotten so deep."

"And his hormones are raging. He has a crush on Siena."

Michi dog-eared her place in the book. "The plot thickens."

"Nothing serious. Want a soda?"

"Sure. Mind if I hang out a while longer?"

"Suits me fine. We have a lot of catching up to do." Veronica went to the kitchen and opened the refrigerator.

"Did Siena's mood improve?" Michi reached for the 7-Up.

"She's uptight about the modelling. They want her to lose some weight—they just photographed her hands with jewelry, and her legs for shoe ads. Stupid sexists! I hope she doesn't wind up anorexic over this."

Michi said nothing and sipped her drink.

"Do you like her?" Veronica sat beside her.

"Isn't it too soon to tell?"

"You think I'm crazy, right?"

"Roni—" Michi toyed with her ear cuff. "Joanna was my friend. It's really hard to see you with someone else—especially with a—"

"Don't you think it's hard on *me*, too?" Veronica's voice shook. "I *miss* Joanna. Siena's so—different."

Michi squeezed Veronica's knee. "You can't even compare them. Siena's white and straight—I'm not sure

85

which is the bigger hangup."

Veronica smarted from that comment and from the rather rough pinch. Sometimes Michi was better off keeping her mouth shut. Resting her head against the sofa, Veronica glanced at her. "How about some Chinese take-out?"

Michi seemed as eager to dismiss the previous subject. Her expression brightened. "Yeah. We can have an all-night gabfest. I want to hear all of this."

Veronica leaned over and hugged her. "You're on."

Before Michi left Tuesday morning, she nudged Veronica. "Want to tag along to the campus placement center? Have to check the job opportunities."

Veronica yawned and shook her head. "I'd rather sleep in."

"Lucky you. Meanwhile, the family's pushing me to follow the Yamada work ethic. No slacking off in an Asian household."

Veronica leaned over and hugged her. "I'm so glad you're here. Thanks for listening. You're the best, Mich. I really bombarded you with—"

"It *was* a marathon talkathon, but we both needed it." Michi played with Veronica's rumpled curls. "Are you seeing her today?"

"We didn't make plans."

"So you're going to write?"

"I need to."

"Good. See you later."

Without distractions, Veronica found it easier to sit at the typewriter, delving into the past, her concentration unbroken. Talking with Michi, sharing thoughts, and sorting through the ensuing jumble of emotions seemed to have coalesced into a spurt of creativity.

In mid-afternoon, Phil rapped on her open door, a letter in his hands. "Can I bug you for a minute?"

"Sure." Veronica turned off the typewriter.

"Heard from Dad." The teenager sprawled on her bed. "They've been scuba diving and deep-sea fishing. Didn't mention anything about lovey-dovey stuff."

She laughed. "And I'm sure he won't ever." Stretching her arms over her head, Veronica felt the tension settled in her upper back and neck. She was ready for another of Siena's soothing massages.

Phil propped up one of her pillows. "Dad told me to be sure you swim and don't miss any of your therapy appointments."

"Yes, Mr. Watchdog. Who's supposed to be the babysitter, anyway—you or me?"

"Roni, you know how he is." Phil glanced at his watch. "Have to buy some film for class. Need anything from Sav-On?"

"How about some soda?"

"Okay. Know what? Caught Siena this morning by the carports. I need a model for my next photo project. She offered to do it tomorrow night."

"Oh." Veronica shuffled some pages on the desk. "Well, then you'd better make dinner plans, too."

He looked surprised. "Aren't you going to be here?"

"Nope. I'm having dinner with Michi."

"Jeez. Do you think Siena'd like pizza?"

She shrugged. "She's trying to diet. Maybe you should make a salad. There's stuff in the fridge."

"Oh, man. Didn't think I'd have to feed her, too."

7

On a balmy Wednesday evening, Veronica and Michi were lucky enough to find a sidewalk table at Alice's Restaurant on Westwood Boulevard. The street south of the University of California campus teemed with midsummer traffic. Veronica tried to ignore the noise, but its rumbling sounds jarred her nerves.

"So glad you got the job, Mich." She lifted her wine glass. "Now we'll both be on campus this fall."

Michi grinned. She clicked her glass to Veronica's and took a quick sip.

"My parents'd prefer my being in school. But I'll be doing administrative work for a Japanese-American oral history project, so at least it'll be relevant." Michi dug into her salad, selecting slivers of purple cabbage. "You've been quiet tonight, Roni. Still in the writing mode?"

"Sometimes it takes a while to snap back into reality." She rolled some garbanzo beans across her plate. "It's hard to fictionalize something that actually happened. And the more I write about Joanna, the more I miss her."

She turned from Michi, watching a heterosexual couple nuzzling at the next table. The woman's hair was glossy brown, like Joanna's had been. She stared for a moment, remembering, and turned away when the woman's gaze met hers.

"Maybe it's too soon. You get so intense when you're writing. And it's only been eight months since—" Michi's face was uncommonly solemn. "Might be a better idea to write about something else."

"No. I think Zamora's right when she says I need to deal with my feelings now. The first three stories were about childhood; the next three are about adolescence. That's what makes them harder to deal with. But I need to get Joanna's essence on paper, before I forget—" Veronica looked away again.

"You'll never forget her, Roni. I know *I* won't."

Veronica reached across the table and touched her friend with affection. "I'm still dealing with it, but I'm okay." Her caress wound up being a tweak of Michi's pudgy cheek. "Thanks to you, I'm away from the type-writer tonight, even though I've had another distraction lately."

"Yeah. Let me guess who."

Veronica felt herself blush. "Mich, when I'm with Siena—" She speared a cherry tomato with her fork. "—well, it's so physical—sleepless nights, the works. We hardly have anything in common, except making love and being raised Catholic. She's really sexy, and so warm and open-hearted. Maybe I'm stereotyping her 'cause she's from an Italian family. Anyway—you've seen her—she's drop-dead beautiful, Mich. Sometimes I can't take my eyes off her. It's weird 'cause I loved Joanna so much I rarely paid attention to other women. I never expected to be attracted to someone like Siena—I mean, she isn't a woman of color, doesn't even call herself a feminist, much less a lesbian."

"Pure lust, if you ask me."

"Mich, give me a break." She rubbed a smudge off her wine glass. "Tonight, she's being Phil's model. She thought it'd be a good idea to spend some time with him."

"How do you feel about that?"

89

Veronica made a face. "We don't want him to suspect anything." She dabbed her lips with the cloth napkin. "So—tell me about these student films. Zamora gave me a flyer about them last week. She's really trying to lure me back to campus before fall."

Michi perked up. "Can't blame her, Roni. Anyway, after I landed the job, I swung down to the Women's Resource Center to see what's cooking and heard one of these films has a lesbo theme." She wriggled in her chair and leaned forward, eyes alight. With typical zest, she had already found some lesbian culture on campus.

Veronica stared at her. "Do you think Zamora's been reading between the lines? My stories are fairly subtle. Haven't even mentioned the 'L' word in them."

"Beats me. But you're writing about growing up, so—"

"Maybe—"

Michi whooped. "Could Zamora be a dyke?"

"Oh, Mich. That's crazy. Just because she's divorced—"

"Wouldn't that be a trip?"

They laughed uproariously.

Michi did not lose her grin. "Quit sidetracking me, Melendez. Let me finish. There'll be a question and answer session after each film, but we're only interested in the dyke flick, right? We don't have to stay long, especially if you'd rather get home to your sweetie."

"Cut it out, Mich. If I get back too soon, Phil will be pissed."

"He really doesn't suspect anything?"

"I doubt it. He never noticed anything about Joanna and me. Besides, he's wild about Siena. He likes having her around." Veronica squeezed Michi's hand. "Don't be such a worry wart. I know how to be discreet."

*

In the Melnitz Hall screening room, they selected center seats in the fourth row.

"There's Zamora." Veronica nudged Michi. "Right in front."

"Go talk to her."

"Later, Mich."

The friends agreed the first film, a technically superior science fiction spoof, needed editing. While the question and answer session droned on, enlivened by the witticisms of sci-fi buffs, Michi scanned the sparse audience for any trace of campus dykes. She spied some likely candidates in an adjacent row while Veronica watched her with amusement.

Before long, Veronica found it difficult to stay awake. Her sleepless night and long hours of writing caught up with her. She nodded off, curly head propped on Michi's shoulder. Her catnap was interrupted when her friend suddenly jabbed her in the ribs.

"Who is *that*?"

"What?" Veronica frowned and unfolded herself.

"That Latina Amazon who just walked in and brightened the scenery."

Drowsily, Veronica followed Michi's directions and saw a leggy Latina with a stylish haircut: short and sleek on the sides, long and tapering in back. She wore form-fitting Levi's, rust-colored Frye boots, and a turquoise T-shirt with a silk-screened portrait of Mexican artist Frida Kahlo directly over her impressive breasts.

"I think my heart's stopped." Michi sounded breathless, as if gasping for air.

"She's probably straight." Veronica ignored Michi's exaggerated reaction and leaned back again. But she continued gazing at the striking woman, noting her glowing brown skin, black hair and ebony eyes. Keeping her thoughts to herself, Veronica considered the woman a fine mestiza dyke, no doubt with sangre de india. She could not help but stare at her.

Leaving a colorful hemp bag beside her notebook on the discussion table, the Latina paused to exchange joking remarks with Camille Zamora. Then she moved past the two friends towards the projection booth, her long legs covering the carpeted aisle with a distinct dykish stride.

"She's got to be the lesbo film maker," Michi squealed, nearly bouncing off her seat. "Oh, thank you, Goddess!"

"Cool it, okay?" Veronica picked up the one-page program and read it aloud. "The film 'Tortilleras' was directed by grad student René Talamantes." Veronica's mouth stretched into a wide grin. "Zamora told me about her."

"Huh? Did you take a good look at her? Amazon City! Dyke Delight! Aren't you glad you're here, Roni?"

"As long as her film keeps me awake, I'll be fine." Veronica fluffed her hair and stifled a yawn.

"Tortilleras" contained no dialog, but consisted of stark black-and-white close-ups of two Latinas, clad in flowing transparent robes, conducting a silent, but erotic mating dance. Wide awake, Veronica gazed at the screen, mesmerized by the dark-skinned women gliding in stylized movements, nearly touching, tossing their long black hair over their shoulders.

She imagined them to be Joanna and her, advancing and retreating, teasing each other with suggestive motions, eager fingers outlining breasts, hips and thighs.

Alone in their apartment, they had often danced close, moving sensuously to rhythm-and-blues standards, falling into bed together afterwards. Veronica sighed—all those wondrous nights. Seeing those Latinas on the screen made her ache even more for Joanna, gone forever. She heard Michi's sudden intake of breath, and hoped her friend would not hyperventilate. She felt herself tremble.

Communicating visually, the Latinas in the film whirled and twirled, graceful mirror images of one another. At last, they concluded their stylized dance by embracing, their lips touching and melding as the film faded to black. The audience's hushed silence was broken by scattered applause.

"Roni, I'm about ready to faint," Michi whispered. The screening room's lights flickered on and the two friends blinked dazedly.

"I'm feeling kind of woozy myself." She noticed the flush on Michi's face, and wondered if her own betrayed her. The temperature in the room seemed stifling.

They both stared at the willowy Latina standing unperturbed at the discussion table, one brown hand on her hip, awaiting the audience's remarks. A professorial looking man in the front row wasted no time in asking the significance of the film's title.

René Talamantes's smoky voice filled the auditorium. "In Spanish, 'tortillera' literally means a woman who makes tortillas. In the film's context, I use 'tortillera' to suggest tribadism."

Veronica felt a titillating shiver course along her spine. Talamantes's words had a Southwestern tinge, a slight drawl uncharacteristic of local Latinas. Veronica imagined the dark women in the film rubbing their bodies together like warm tortillas gently molded in a Chicana's hand. She could not take her eyes off the self-assured film maker.

"She actually said 'tribadism,'" Michi murmured in awe.

"I wonder if everyone here knows the definition." Veronica could not recall having been so affected by any other film, and tried to modulate her tone. "Some of those guys in front look absolutely mystified."

"Ask her something," Michi urged with a nudge.

"*You* ask her." She edged away and rested her chin on her hand. "I dare you, Mich, since you're creaming all over the place."

Suppressing a giggle, Michi accepted the challenge. Her right arm with its multicolored yarn bracelets shot up. Determined to be noticed, she even stood.

The film maker cooly pointed to her.

"I was just wondering why you decided to shoot in black and white." Michi's voice sounded an octave higher than usual.

René Talamantes grinned at the question. "Two reasons: First, I wanted to focus on the women's mutual sexual attraction. Color would've distracted from that, and it really wasn't necessary anyway, because both women have the same skin tones. I think black and white emphasizes their similarities. If I had wanted to show their dissimilarities—for example, if one woman were Latina and the other white, color might have worked better. For my purposes, black and white worked just fine. My second reason was purely financial. Color film and processing is expensive."

The film student's frank answer prompted some murmuring and laughter. Camille Zamora half-turned in her seat and smiled at Veronica; she nodded automatically. While the film student responded to a more challenging question, Camille became attentive to her again.

Michi glanced at her companion. "Isn't she fabulous?"

Veronica frowned, recalling her day's labor at the typewriter. "Get real, Mich. Words are my game. What if everyone decided not to use dialog? As much as I like her film, I'm uncomfortable with its silence."

"Tell her so." Michi gave her a teasing pinch.

Wincing from the sudden pain, Veronica moved her arm reflexively, just in time for the film maker to point to her.

"Michi, I'll kill you someday." Veronica glared at her amused friend and quickly formed a question. When she saw Camille whirl once more in her chair, she tried to steel herself. Although Veronica felt her heart slide into her throat, her words tumbled out without obstruction.

"I'm curious about the lack of dialog—and even of music. I think the film is unique as it is, but silents aren't too common these days. Most current films, it seems, have superfluous dialog—not like the well-crafted scripts of the classics. And recently there's been so much emphasis on technique. Was eliminating dialog and music a budgetary decision, too? Can you elaborate on your reasons for making a silent film?"

With a droll expression, the Latina appraised Veronica before answering. Her drawl became more pronounced. "For a film student, almost everything boils down to budgetary decisions. Despite that, I really wanted to show that when a definite sexual message occurs between two people, only the basics count—eye contact, facial signals, body language. I decided to pare everything down to the bare essentials—eliminating color, dialog, and music." She paused. "You seem to know a lot about films. Do you think my technique worked?"

Veronica's heart threatened to pop out of her cotton shirt. "Well—yes."

"Bueno. Quiero hablar contigo después. Espérame."

At that personalized request, Veronica blushed, noting Camille's look of satisfaction. She was even more embarrassed when several audience members turned to gawk.

"Roni, you're terrific!" Michi snuggled closer, one hand on Veronica's knee. "What did she say?"

"She wants to talk with me afterwards."

"Sounds like a 'definite sexual message.'" Michi pressed Veronica's knee. "Let's ask her out for cappuccino."

"If I don't murder you first." She pretended to be annoyed; yet she could barely hide her eagerness—and apprehension. "I don't even know what I said."

"Words just poured out of your eloquent little mouth."

"Michi, you're so full of it."

Before the next film began, Veronica and Michi scurried out of the auditorium. René Talamantes stood in the film department's narrow lobby, conversing with Camille and a ponytailed Chicano. Stuffing her notebook into her hemp bag, she glanced up when the two friends appeared.

Veronica lagged behind, trying to maintain her dignity despite her nervousness. Memories of Joanna flooded her, but she did not want to think of her at that moment. She did not want to remember anything about Siena either. She felt disloyal towards both, but aimed for a calm attitude in spite of her conflicting emotions. Without a doubt, she considered René Talamantes the most tantalizing woman she had ever seen, much less met. Appearing more casual than she felt, Veronica leaned against the corridor wall, waiting.

The film student seemed engrossed in a technical discussion with the Chicano. Camille glanced over, sensitivity antennae on the alert. She murmured something to Talamantes, who hardly noticed, and came over to Veronica and Michi.

The professor looked spiffy in a well-tailored beige linen suit. "Veronica, you raised important points in your question. I'm sure René will want to discuss them with you further." She touched her student's arm lightly. "Que talent, verdad? I'm glad you decided to come."

Veronica nodded, wishing Zamora would leave. "Michi didn't want to miss the screening."

Accustomed to outlandish campus styles, Camille seemed unfazed by Michi's current look. She chatted with her for a few moments before redirecting her attention to Veronica.

"You left so quickly last week. I forgot to give you this." She propped the edge of her briefcase against a water fountain and removed a pink and lavender paperback. "It's my extra copy."

"Camille—" Veronica found herself staring at an elaborate purple moth on the book's cover.

"For the inspiration." Camille handed her a Chicana author's collection of short stories, then strolled through the glass doors of Melnitz Hall.

Veronica groaned, sticking the paperback into her canvas bag. "That woman and her damn motivating ways!"

"But she's sooo fine, Roni," Michi remarked, eyes on Zamora's departing figure. "Thought she was going to do the intros, but we're on our own. Who's the dude?" She nodded towards the Chicano conversing with Talamantes.

"No idea." Veronica began to question her own reasons for lingering. "Mich, I don't want to hang around all night."

"Shhh. He's shoving off."

"Ándele pues, Jorge." Talamantes slapped the swarthy man's back. "I'll see you in the editing room el sabado."

The Chicano high-fived her and darted off, his thick ponytail bobbing against his husky back.

Talamantes smiled and waved Veronica and Michi over. "Thanks for your comments, mujeres. I had a feeling I'd be crucified in there. Did you hear that one pendejo ask why there were no men in my film?" She laughed, her teeth large and white.

"I guess the subtleties were lost on him." Veronica shrugged, hands in her jeans' pockets. She pressed her stiff body against the hard wall; she ached from sitting so long. She forgot her physical discomfort when she noticed the Latina was about three inches taller than her and even more attractive up close.

"De veras." Those deep-set dark eyes surveyed hers. "Vienes de aqui?"

"Born and raised in Santa Monica." Veronica suddenly wished she had used the proper Spanish pronunciation of her home town; she was unaccustomed to switching languages in midstream and uneasy about her rusty Spanish. She hoped the film student would not insist on speaking it; some Latinas did as a matter of principle. Besides, Veronica did not want Michi to be left out of the conversation.

"Yo soy Tejana, nacida en El Paso. Eres Chicana?"

Veronica nodded, not trusting her voice.

Michi cut in. "We're going for cappuccino. Would you like to join us?" Next to the Latina, Michi seemed smaller than usual.

"Sure." The film student offered one lean brown hand to each. "Didn't catch your names."

After they introduced themselves, they stood awkwardly in the empty hallway, still clasping each other's hands.

The Latina squeezed Veronica's fingers. "So you're Chicana, too. Que suave! I got jazzed seeing you in the audience. Usually I'm the only brown woman in sight."

"I know the feeling." Veronica met her compelling gaze again and did not look away. René's fingers were warm and electric.

"It's a bitch, huh?"

"Happens a lot on this campus." Veronica did not want to let go of that encompassing hand.

"Sure does. Saw you talking with Camille and—"

"I'm one of her grad students."

Her free hand smoothing her moussed head, Michi fidgeted.

At once, Talamantes noticed Michi's impatience and alternated her gaze between them. "Perdóname. Are you two lovers?"

"Friends," Veronica sputtered. She was taken aback at that candor, but also grateful for the question.

"Since first grade," Michi swiftly added.

"Hey, that's cool." René released their hands finally, slinging the hemp bag over her wide shoulder. "Want to go off campus or over to the Kerckhoff coffeehouse?"

"Kerckhoff sounds fine," Veronica said with a sudden smile.

"So what brought you two dykes to my film preview?" René Talamantes stretched her long legs and waited for her cappuccino to cool.

Michi raised her brows. "Are you always this blunt?"

"Why not, huh?" The film student's even teeth gleamed.

"Roni, you're blushing," Michi teased.

"That's just the reflection of my red shirt against my brown face." Veronica toyed with a strand of her curly hair.

"Yeah, and my eyes're slanted 'cause I'm squinting from the cappuccino steam." Michi impishly wriggled her brows.

Amid Talamantes's raucous laughter, Veronica tried to maintain a serious demeanor. "Let's get back to René's question. This Munchkin," she continued, gesturing towards the grinning Michi, "lured me over to Melnitz by mentioning your film. And, even though I split hairs over the lack of dialog, I really am impressed with 'Tortilleras.' It's sensual and erotic—and it works."

"For her to say that is a major compliment," Michi interjected. "She's a writer, you see."

"Oh, yeah?" Talamantes leaned forward, one round breast brushing the table. "Grad student stuff, or something I'd be familiar with?"

Veronica tossed Michi a peeved glance. "When I was an undergrad, I wrote articles for some of the campus publications: *Westwinds*, *Together* and *La Gente de Aztlan*."

"Maybe that was before my time. I'm in my second year here in Film. Have you done anything lately, like for *Ten Percent*?"

Michi seemed to sense Veronica's discomfort at the mention of the gay and lesbian students' quarterly newsmagazine. She cut in. "Tell her about your stories, Roni."

"Stories?" At that, Talamantes set down her cup, elbows on the table.

Veronica blew on her cappuccino to avoid looking up. "I'm working on some short fiction, thanks to Zamora's goading."

Talamantes smirked. "About tortilleras?"

Veronica felt herself blush again. "Let's just say I'm starting to head in that direction. My work has a Chicana slant, but the lesbian subtleties are surfacing." She finally took a sip.

René's gesticulating hands spoke a language of their own. "Listen, we ought to collaborate. To be honest, Verónica, my weak point is structure. I do great camera work, but when it comes to structuring a story, I really have to buckle down and map it all out. The writing doesn't come easy. I'd sure like to get some tips from you."

Veronica studied her, liking the way Talamantes had pronounced her name in perfect Spanish. Veh-roe-nee-ka—a verbal caress. Accustomed to her childhood nickname, she had forgotten the Latina beauty of her actual appellation. She felt herself smile.

"Well, I'll be back on campus this fall. Right now, I'm committed to finishing these stories for Zamora. I'd like to help you out, but I've only taken one screenwriting course."

"Hey, I'd be satisfied if you'd just take a look at one of my screenplays." René reached for her hemp bag and fished inside for her combination calendar/address book. "What's your phone number?"

Veronica heard herself stutter. "395-6496. Pretty soon, it'll be 450-1868—Michi's number, too. She's moving in with me."

"We're both in states of transition, and decided we needed mutual support," Michi explained.

"Tell me about it. I could use some supportive friends myself. I'm the token Chicana dyke in the film department, and sometimes it gets damn lonesome." René threw the book into her bag and downed more cappuccino. "Besides, earlier this year I made the mistake of getting involved with a theater arts major. She thought I'd make her a star."

"One of the women in the film?" Michi probed.

"Hell, no. That's what caused all the mitote. She's white, and couldn't understand why I wouldn't use her in 'Tortilleras.'" Talamantes pushed her coarse black hair from her face. "Are you two single?"

Michi played with her ear cuff and nodded.

Veronica's voice was quiet. "I'm seeing someone."

She did not want to offer any details. Keeping her eyes downcast, she was unwilling to face Talamantes at that moment, recalling the previous evening with Siena. Her mind clouded, her body aroused, Veronica eventually tuned back into the conversation, in time to hear Michi tease René into getting together that coming weekend. René agreed, not skipping a beat with her banter. Listening to them, Veronica felt detached, remote. Michi was outgoing; no wonder René had changed focus. Veronica and René had more in common—both Chicanas, both creative. Was it only because she had admitted to "seeing someone" that René had turned away?

Veronica wished she knew how to function as a single lesbian. She and Joanna had grown up together, inseparable from first grade through college. As a result, she felt socially inept during the rare times she found herself in the company of other lesbians. And with the added complication of Siena, she felt depressed as well, missing out on a chance with René Talamantes.

Michi chattered away. "Listen, René, we have to celebrate my new job. Let's have dinner out and hit the dance spots. Any suggestions?"

"There's a dance this Saturday in Santa Monica—one

of the dyke organizations is sponsoring it. Let's liven it up." René pulled a crumpled flyer from her hemp bag. "It's at the Union Hall on Second Street."

"Sounds great. You have to come, too, Roni."

Veronica sighed. "I'll see what Siena's plans are."

"You sure turned glum all of a sudden." Michi glanced across the car after they had left René. "What's up?"

"Just being my regular moody self." Veronica guided the Z out of the campus parking structure.

"Look, just 'cause René's meeting me at the dance doesn't mean anything. She's really attracted to *you*, Roni."

"Mich, don't start in."

"It's perfectly apparent."

"More like a professional interest." Veronica drove slowly through the darkened campus. "She doesn't meet another Chicana artist every day."

"My ass." Michi fiddled with the tape deck and rewound Cris Williamson's *Strange Paradise* cassette. The title track's dissonant sounds were not the distraction Veronica needed, and Michi would not let her off easily. "You *will* come along Saturday night?"

"If I can talk Siena into it."

Michi propped her chin on one knee and faced her. "Who says she has to tag along, anyway? It'll be good for *you*, Roni. I mean, we really have to start being 'out.' What're you going to do when your stories are published—stay in the closet?"

Veronica tossed her a skeptical glance. "You mean, *if* they're published."

"There's no reason why—" Michi turned down the stereo's volume. "You think I'm pushy, don't you?"

"I *know* you are. And sometimes I just don't move as fast as you. I need to slow down a little."

Michi took on a gentler tone. "Just keep reminding me. But aren't you glad you came along tonight?"

Veronica chuckled and drove her talkative friend home.

"How was your photo session?" She found a sleepy-eyed Siena and wide-awake Phil watching *Invasion of the Body Snatchers* on video.

"I used two whole rolls, Roni."

"He made me do everything but stand on my head." In black shorts and pink tank top, Siena could not be more unlike René Talamantes.

Phil laughed. "She's exaggerating."

"That's what you think." When he looked aside, Siena winked at Veronica and adjusted the fringed pillow behind her head. "You were gone for hours."

Veronica yawned. "Michi invited one of the film students for cappuccino afterwards."

"Michi asked a guy out?" Phil cut in, all ears. He turned off the VCR.

"This particular film student is a woman."

"Probably made some weird experimental flick about a female takeover of the world, huh?" He grabbed a handful of popcorn from the huge bowl on the coffee table.

Veronica aimed a cushion at him. "It's long past your bedtime, kid."

He ducked and the cushion bounced off his arm. "Roni, you're such a sorehead." He tossed some popcorn in the air, catching it in his mouth.

She let out an exasperated sigh. "Has he been like this all night?"

"He's been fine." Siena smiled. "Phil, you do have an early class."

"I get the message." He sprang up and bowed extravagantly. "'Night, ladies."

When he was out of earshot, Siena gestured for Veronica to join her on the sofa. Veronica snuggled there.

"What's this about a film student?"

"Michi's developing a crush." And so am I, Veronica thought. Trying to dismiss that, she fondled Siena's hair. Its silky texture reminded her of Joanna's, but it was totally unlike René's thick black strands. Joanna and Siena were femme types—while René Talamantes definitely was not. Veronica considered her own outlook and appearance as androgynous. Maybe her attraction to different types of women proved that; that idea intrigued her.

"On who?" Siena's fingers coursed along Veronica's cheek.

"Oh—on René Talamantes." She blurted out the details. "Michi was all agog and asked René out this weekend. They want to make it a foursome."

"Meaning you and me?"

"No, Gertrude Stein and Alice B. Toklas." She gazed at Siena. "Want to go?"

Those hazel eyes were evasive. "Do you?"

"It'd be fun, Siena—something different."

"What's she like—this René?"

"Creative, candid—and funny."

"What's she *look* like?"

"She's Chicana—browner than me." Veronica heard her own impatience. "Look, if you don't want to go, just say so."

"Don't get huffy." Siena soothingly slipped an arm around her.

"I'd rather get huggy." Veronica tried to maintain a

stoic expression, but she was already aroused by Siena's nearness. "If you're staying tonight, we have to be careful 'cause of Phil."

"I know. My things are already in your room."

"After that," Siena whispered against her, "I'll go anywhere with you. Did you and Joanna go to dances?"

Veronica kissed her again, and her voice acquired a nostalgic quality. "We grew up watching Bandstand, so we'd danced together for years. Once in a while, we'd go to a lesbian dance at the Union Hall, but usually we were too busy studying." She leaned against the furrowed pillows. "Maybe Michi's right. She said I really need to get out more. Here I am, planning to write about being a lesbian teenager, but I'm closeted. Doesn't make much sense."

"Why advertise being—gay?"

She met Siena's gaze. "Why should I hide? Would you be content with keeping—this—a secret? That's a very restrictive way to live."

Siena said nothing.

"René seems secure with her identity, whether anyone likes it or not. Some guys in the audience tonight were downright hostile, but she handled them. Michi said I turned moody—probably 'cause I was comparing René's upfront attitude with my own."

Siena glanced at her across the pillows.

"René's out to her parents; they're divorced. She's a working-class kid, the first college graduate in her family. She won a film award at the University of Texas before winding up here. She has lots of guts—and talent."

"You sound sold on her yourself."

"She's a survivor, Siena—like you, like me."

Siena cuddled nearer then, welcoming her kisses. But Veronica continued to think of that long-legged, smoky-voiced Tejana dyke.

Veronica developed a daily regimen of morning and afternoon swims, spaced between hours of plotting and drafting another short story. She was determined to be limber for Saturday's dance.

According to Phil, he was the envy of his photography class. His shots of Siena showed promise. He gave several photos to her, kept some in his portfolio, and tacked the rest to the corkboard in his bedroom. Enthused with his success, he and Steve Martínez planned to gather nature shots for their next class project. Veronica was relieved he would be occupied over the weekend.

8

PARKING NEAR JOANNA'S grave, Veronica stayed in the Z and watched a burial ceremony in progress. The mourners, an extended Latino family, repeatedly stroked the small casket's mauve surface and left blossoms atop it at the conclusion of the service. Sheltered from them, Veronica wept alone, an anonymous mourner. She had not even witnessed Joanna's burial, never consciously seen nor touched her one last time.

When the Latinos scattered, she took deep breaths to discourage further sobs. Bouquet in hand, she slowly trudged up the slight knoll, skirting granite and marble tombstones. With studied precision, she arranged the bouquet, removing some carnations from the outermost edges and placing them in the center. Then she knelt and stared at the gravestone, her fingers tracing the carved words: "Nuestra Hija Querida, Joanna Maria Nuñez."

That brief inscription summed Joanna's lifespan into one succinct phrase; but so much remained unsaid, untold. The summer gusts whipped Veronica's hair into a curly nimbus. Alone with Joanna, she spoke softly.

"This Siena thing—I hardly know her. Joanna, sometimes I can't believe I got myself into this." She blinked rapidly in the harsh sunlight. "Having Michi back knocks me into reality. They don't seem to like each other. I think Michi's disappointed in me—and that hurts. Most of the time I feel like I'm drifting, and don't know how to stop."

She hugged herself and rocked, tears splashing on the rose granite stone.

"Buenos días, Roni."

Looking up, Veronica saw Joanna's mother. Contrary to Sara Melendez' description, Isabel Nuñez did not look drawn and thin. Twenty years older than Joanna, she possessed a delicate beauty, reminiscent of her daughter. Isabel's sepia eyes moistened when the younger woman rose and spontaneously hugged her.

"How've you been, honey?"

"Feeling better. It's been a while since I've seen you."

Isabel loosened her hold on Veronica. "I've been keeping to myself. And guess what? I'm going to take some classes at Santa Monica College. With my boys in high school, there's no need for me to be home all day. At first, I thought I'd go back for Joanna, but now I think I'm doing it for myself."

"I'm really glad." Veronica had not realized how much she had missed her. "What are you majoring in?"

"Give me a chance, girl. Making the decision to go at all was hard enough." Isabel laughed, smoothing Veronica's windblown hair. Her voice grew gentle. "How're you *really*, Roni?"

"It varies from day to day, but lately I've been great."

"Good. Still at Frank's?"

"I'll move to my own place before school starts."

Sighing, Isabel studied her. "It won't be easy to live there—by yourself."

"Can't lean on the family forever."

"You haven't done much of that—not that I've seen, anyway." She patted Veronica's shoulder, then turned her attention to the grave. Kneeling, Isabel placed her own bouquet beside Veronica's. For a moment, she remained silent, her head bowed. Then she spoke again. "I've finally started going through Joanna's things. I've set some aside for you."

Veronica said nothing.

"I found the letters you wrote her from Mexico." Isabel's eyes brimmed. "If you want them, Roni, they're yours. No one else has seen them."

Veronica did not know what to say. Two summers before, while Frank worked as a structural engineer for a Mexico City hotel project, she and Phil had tagged along, exploring museums and historical sites; but the excitement of being away from home had not kept her from missing Joanna.

"You loved her very much."

"I still do, Isabel." Feeling dizzy, Veronica knelt beside her.

"I hadn't realized how *deep* you—" Bafflement appeared on Isabel's otherwise calm face.

She sensed the older woman's unease. "You read all the letters?"

Isabel nodded.

"We didn't want to shock anyone. It was between *us*—no one else."

"I was going to keep quiet and burn them." Isabel's eyes moved again towards the grave. "But then I felt I had to talk with you. I wasn't sure how you'd react, Roni. I know how private you are."

Veronica rested shaky hands on her thighs, her palms damp. She kept her voice monotoned. "You're her mother. I can be honest with you." She paused, searching for appropriate words. "Joanna would've told you eventually. We used to wish someone would just ask us—it would've been easier. It's a miracle my mother hasn't asked either—she'd never understand."

"Roni, I'm not so sure *I* understand. I had favorite girlfriends, too. We just never—"

"Joanna and I were so close that loving each other came easily, too."

"I remember how you girls could practically read each other's minds. It used to amaze me when you'd come over for dinner. Joanna would start a sentence, and you would finish it. I thought that was friendship, nothing else. I—" Shaking her head, Isabel wiped her eyes hastily. "I'm sorry. Talking about her always makes me cry." She took a deep breath. "Tell me—had she ever been with a man?"

"No. Neither of us." Veronica let her absorb that. "Joanna wasn't interested in men in a sexual way. How could anything compare with what we had?"

Isabel did not even notice the dry grass sticking to her linen slacks; it made criss-cross patterns on the ivory fabric. "You knew her better than anyone else; I'm positive of that now. I want you to tell me the truth, Roni. Was this a passing thing, or do you think she would've always—"

Veronica gazed into those probing eyes. "We used to ask ourselves that all the time. At first, we thought we were going through a phase, experimenting with each other before getting involved with men. We both tried dating, but we realized right away we were much more comfortable with each other. We had a good excuse not to date—we were too busy keeping our grades up. We were in love and wanted to be together for the rest of our lives. So, when I found out Joanna was gone forever—" Her voice broke. "—I wanted to die, too. I really wanted to tell everyone why and how I miss her, but I just couldn't. I was afraid. I especially wanted to tell *you*, Isabel, but you were heartbroken enough already."

Isabel's voice quivered. "I never thought of you two—

that way. I knew Joanna and you were always together, and had been for years, but I thought she was close to you because she didn't have a sister." She rubbed her eyes. "I only wish she would've trusted me enough to—"

"Isabel, do you know anyone in either of our families who has positive feelings about lesbians?"

Isabel cringed at that last word.

"Of course, you don't. Our love was between *us*. We didn't think anyone else had to know."

"But you girls weren't really—"

"Yes. Joanna was a lesbian, and so am I."

"But you don't—"

"—look any different from other women?" Veronica could not resist smiling. "Isabel, I don't want to look like or be a man. Neither did Joanna. We just happened to be emotionally and sexually attracted to each other."

"Do you think it was because of something *I* did?"

"No." Veronica touched her hand. "What matters is, she and I loved each other. We were very happy, and I'll never forget her, no matter how old I live to be. I still love Joanna very, very much," she added in a whisper.

"Ay, Roni, I know." Sniffling, Isabel grasped her, as if steadying them both. "But now that she's gone—"

"I don't want to change. Isabel, changing would mean everything Joanna and I shared was illegitimate. It wasn't. It was very real." She closed her eyes, recalling her lover's ready smile, her tenderness, her passion.

When she looked at Isabel again, she spoke with a firm voice. "My family will probably have a collective nervous breakdown over this issue; it's a religious and cultural taboo. But I refuse to get hung up on that. I know who and what I am. I'm woman-identified. I'm a lesbian."

Isabel took on a persuasive tone. "But, Roni, you get

along with Frank and Phil so well. It doesn't seem like you have anything against men."

Veronica sighed. Why did heterosexual women seem to focus on the anti-male angle? "Neither did Joanna. Isabel—how can I say this? Men are all right, but I prefer women. That's the most simplistic way I can explain it."

"I still have trouble understanding it."

"Most people do." She leaned closer. "All I want to know is this: does knowing the truth change your feelings about me?"

Isabel answered at once. "All the time you girls were growing up, I was always glad Joanna had you for a friend. You're such a good student, a nice quiet girl—never in trouble."

"You have to watch those quiet ones," Veronica quipped.

Isabel ignored that modest attempt at levity. "I thought you were a good influence on her."

"Do you still think so?"

"Who started it?"

Veronica tensed at that abrupt question. "It was—mutual. Like I said, we thought we were going through a phase. We just never outgrew it." She ran a nervous hand through her hair, wishing Joanna could help her through this conversation.

Isabel rearranged the bouquets to seem as one. "Do you want the letters back?"

"Yes." Veronica placed a tentative hand on the older woman's wrist.

Joanna's mother met her gaze again, questioningly.

"Isabel, I'm sorry you found out this way. We really should've told you ourselves."

"I would've liked to talk with her about it. That's why

I wanted to tell you, Roni—you're as close to her as I can get. She was a wonderful daughter. She never disappointed me."

"Not even now, knowing about—?"

"Not even now." She rose slowly. "Roni—"

"Yes?" Veronica also got to her feet.

"Ten cuidado, okay? Don't decide too soon about keeping up this kind of life. Maybe you'll never love another woman like you loved Joanna. Give yourself a chance. Think about your parents. And what about your future? Don't you want kids someday?"

With some misgivings, Veronica wondered what Isabel would say if she knew about Siena. Would she label Veronica an incorrigible pervert? She tried to shake off those troubling questions and aimed for a confident tone.

"Being with women is what I want. Joanna helped me discover that. I've thought about this a lot since she's been gone. I miss her very much, but I'm going to be all right."

Isabel wiped her eyes, as if signalling her need to end the conversation. "Drop by soon. I have—things—to give you." As she left, her fingertips lightly brushed Veronica's shoulder.

"Isabel's a neat woman, Roni." Poolside, Michi lay on a chaise longue near Veronica. "Do you think she'll adopt us? Sounds like you could tell her stuff you'd never tell your mom."

Drying herself off, Veronica was a bit breathless from her swim. "Maybe. I should've asked if she'll tell Rubén. He'd be devastated."

"Yeah." Michi sighed, reality setting in. "Joanna's dad's a pretty traditional guy."

For seconds, Veronica was silent, recalling Rubén

Nuñez's initial objections to his daughter and her sharing the Amherst Avenue apartment. Veronica's brother Frank was the one who had persuaded Rubén that the two college students needed their own space to study.

"Roni, what was in those—"

"They're love letters, Mich. Since I shared the hotel suite with Frank and Phil, I couldn't really phone Joanna so I wrote instead. Joanna treasured those letters, kept a ribbon tied around them. Suppose that's what caught Isabel's eye."

"Maybe it's better this way. Everything's spelled out, Roni. Isabel already knew the facts before she ran into you."

Veronica shrugged. "We can speculate all we want. It's done." She grabbed a tube of Coppertone and smoothed the lotion on her legs. "I'm just glad *you're* around. Couldn't get by without you."

Michi grinned. "And without me, you never would've hung around and met Talamantes."

"Mich, come on. Don't you think Zamora set that up?" Veronica put down the tube and reclined again. "Her intuition's in overdrive. She'd even mentioned René as someone I ought to meet."

"Want me to find out when I talk to René?"

"No. Let it lie."

"Rats, Roni. So when are you picking up the stuff from Isabel?"

"Should've done it this morning. But I needed space after talking with her. I felt rattled." She glanced at her friend again. "You're going to talk to Talamantes?"

"Tonight. I like to schmooze with her."

Veronica cast her a sly look. "You'd like to smooch her, too."

"Speak for yourself, Roni."

"I have Siena, remember?"

"I'd just as soon forget."

After lunch Saturday, Veronica turned the Z onto Rochester Avenue, a side street intersecting Westwood Boulevard, passed several apartment buildings, and parked near a condominum project under construction.

Siena pushed her sunglasses atop her head. "Taking a look at model condos?"

"Nope. You're going to get a crash course." Veronica slammed the car door and gestured for her to follow.

Looking wary, Siena accompanied her across the street and into the narrow, glass-paned doorway of Sisterhood Bookstore. Veronica led her among browsing customers, past the revolving racks of feminist-titled paperbacks, past the display table of current hardcover releases, past women-themed greeting cards, records and music cassettes, past the well-stocked display cases of feminist jewelry and pottery, past the growing numbers of books on Third World women.

Near the rear of the store, she paused and gestured towards the south wall. Her eyes shone as she pointed out well-remembered titles—novels by Katherine V. Forrest, Jane Rule and Ann Allen Shockley; poetry by Judy Grahn, Audre Lorde and Adrienne Rich; non-fiction by Gloria Anzaldúa and Cherríe Moraga.

Siena gazed at the rows of lesbian publications. "I never imagined there'd be this many."

"Starting in the late sixties, the silence was broken. If it hadn't been for the women's movement, lesbian literature would still be hidden." Veronica's eyes never left that book-lined wall. "Whenever I feel discouraged, alienated,

I stand here and look at all these books, remember these writers—and my spirits rise. I want to be part of this."

Siena did not look at her. "You're not afraid to go public?"

"I'm terrified. But hiding, keeping silent, won't solve anything. I'm a writer—and I have to write what I know. That's what I'm trying to do, and I hope to do it for the rest of my life. Someday, I have to take the risk of being public. I want you to be aware of that. Being with me means being out—maybe not right at this moment, but definitely in the future."

Siena said nothing. She climbed two adjacent steps, rounded the corner to the art book section, and browsed amidst photography volumes and biographies of women artists.

Veronica marveled at her own uncharacteristic enthusiasm. No doubt Michi's influence—not to mention Talamantes's—had begun to rub off. She ran her fingers along the spines of several books, and finally removed one. Pulling over a rattan stool, she sat and began to read.

In a crowded Santa Monica meeting hall they stood, Cokes in hand, while women gyrated around them to booming rock music. Michi's mousse-drenched spikes pressed against the soft folds of her violet scarf, tied samurai-style, around her head. The auditorium's flashing strobe lights accentuated the metallic threads woven into the scarf.

"René said she'd meet us here," Michi reminded Veronica for the fourth time. "Guess she's like you—working on a project and losing track of time. She's probably holed up in an editing room, snipping film."

"Well, you saw her yesterday." Veronica sensed Michi's growing apprehension. "I doubt if she's forgotten."

While talking with Michi, Veronica kept her eyes on Siena. She appeared ill at ease among that lesbian crowd. Women of all ages and descriptions milled about, and some stared at Siena flirtatiously. Standing close to Veronica, she wore a mint-colored jumpsuit. Her auburn hair cascaded to her shoulders. She was exceptionally quiet.

"Go ahead and dance," Michi said. "I'll be right here."

"Want to, Siena? It's slow and mellow right now, just my speed." Smiling, she reached for Siena's hand. "Thanks for being here—" They swayed to that golden Johnny Mathis oldie "Chances Are." "—even if you looked freaked by all this—"

"Actually, I'm fascinated." Siena's cheek was soft against Veronica's. "The bookstore kind of prepared me— I didn't know what to expect." She glanced around. "Some of these women look ordinary, others are gorgeous, and lots are really—obvious. Am I staring?"

"Not any more than I am. I like getting an eyeful, too. I just wish René would show. Michi's rattled."

"Doesn't look like it."

Veronica turned in Michi's direction. "Oh, wow— she's found an Asian-American dykette! She's been complaining about not knowing any in L.A." Grinning, she waved to Michi. She admired her friend's lack of shyness in meeting women.

Michi danced close with a small woman. Her scarf sparkled. Despite her romantic pose, she mugged at Veronica outrageously.

*

"Buenas noches, compañera." In black jeans and matching satin shirt, René Talamantes touched Veronica's shoulder. The warmth of her fingers permeated through the polo shirt's thin knit.

"We were about to give up on you."

"Porqué? The night's still young, Veronica." Her large teeth flashed. "Is this your—"

Self-consciously, Veronica introduced her to Siena.

Talamantes accepted the rather restrained handshake. "An unusual name. By any chance, are you Latina?"

"Italian-American." Siena's hazel eyes met René's ebony ones. "Veronica said she enjoyed your film the other evening."

Lithe and sexy in her flashy shirt, Talamantes nudged Veronica. "Yeah? Her critique sure stands out in my mind."

Veronica downed the last of her Coke to avoid looking at René. Her presence was too provocative.

Talamantes continued to stay near. "I really want to collaborate with you, mujer."

Veronica arched a brow. "On what?"

"I'll tell you while we dance." With a vise-like grip on Veronica's arm, she lurched her up and away.

That sudden action caught Veronica off guard. She glanced at Siena and shrugged while struggling to keep up with René's long strides. She could have pulled away, but chose not to. Siena looked bewildered.

"That hurts, René." She at last protested the firm grip.

"Sorry. I've wanted to be alone with you since we met, mujer. You sure don't make it easy."

"What're you talking about?" Veronica was un-accustomed to strong-arm tactics. They reminded her too much of macho Latinos. When René's arms went around her during a Linda Ronstadt ballad, Veronica hated to ad-

119

mit how attracted she was to this impetuous woman.

"You know what I'm talkin' about."

"You ought to dance with Michi. She's been waiting for you."

"Take it easy." Talamantes' arms remained securely around her. "I just saw her outside. Somos amigas, mujer. I told Michi I'd meet her here. She didn't expect anything else."

"Look, I'd better get back to Siena—"

"She's fine." René's strong hands continued to hold her near. "Michi says the redhead's your neighbor. That's damn convenient."

"Meaning?"

"You're too busy writing to go out and meet women, so it's pretty damn convenient to find a lover who lives practically next door."

"That's none of your business," Veronica snapped. She started to pull away, but Talamantes would not let go.

"The music isn't over yet, Verónica."

"It is for me. Let me go. Now."

"Cálmate, okay? Michi told me the whole story— about your lover who died—"

"She had no right!" Veronica stared at Talamantes in disbelief, but how else could she have learned about Joanna? How could Michi have confided in this obnoxious stranger?

"Hey—don't blame Michi. *I* asked her about you. I knew there had to be some reason why you spaced out the other night. I guessed you'd either been hurt bad, or you're in love. I didn't figure it'd be both." Talamantes' tone softened, but she did not ease her grip. "Yo sé que I'm not the most subtle person in the world—"

"Obviously. Let me go. René, I mean it."

"I want to get to know you, Verónica. And I want to

be more than friends. I want to be your lover."

Veronica trembled. "Not a chance." She made herself look directly into René's eyes. "If you don't let go of me this instant, I'm going to kick one of your skinny knees right out of its socket."

René released her with a grin. "Éjole! Will you lighten up?"

"No! And if you were ever serious about collaborating, you can forget it." Her voice shook in its intensity. The more she envisioned Michi and René discussing her, the angrier she became. "There's no way that will ever happen."

Talamantes shifted her hips and stuck her thumbs in the jeans' belt loops. "And why's that? Are you only into fucking straight white women these days?"

Veronica stalked back to Siena, her whole body rigid.

"Are you all right? What's her problem, anyway?"

"I'm not going to bother to find out."

In a shadowy corner, Michi sat with her new-found friend. Shorter than Michi, the woman sported preppy-styled clothes and wore her shiny black hair in a pageboy; she seemed entranced. Approaching them, Veronica struggled to keep her temper in check. She could not recall ever being so angry with Michi.

"We're leaving."

"So early? Have you talked with René?"

"That's why we're leaving."

"Roni, what happened?" Michi came over and touched her arm.

Veronica pulled away, her voice hoarse. "Damn it, I thought *you* were my friend. What the hell did you tell her about me?"

121

Michi's pudgy face slackened. "I only told her about—"

"That's none of her business, Mich. You're just too damn friendly for your own good."

Michi winced. "We need to talk, Roni. I want to explain."

"This isn't the place," Siena interjected.

"If you want a ride with us, let's go." Veronica turned and headed towards the exit.

"I'll get home on my own," Michi called after them. "And I'll phone you tomorrow."

9

Siena took the car keys from her while they crossed the street. During the drive home, Veronica was quiet. Her head began to throb as she replayed the evening's happenings. Nothing was the same with Joanna gone. She remembered the years of friendship they had shared with Michi, with some misunderstandings—but never anything like tonight.

"I don't understand what's gone wrong." She spoke rapidly, shakily. "A few days ago, I was so glad Michi'd come home. Now I can see she's really changed and—I don't know who the hell René is. Maybe I'm not ready to be out yet, Siena. I feel so mixed up—and so furious with them."

Siena drove steadily. "What else can you expect? Your emotions are right on the surface. You've opened yourself to me, you've talked with Michi and Isabel—all this in a few days' time. It takes a confrontative person like René to prove how vulnerable you are, Veronica. To be honest, I don't like her. I don't care how talented she is. I'm not sure how I feel about Michi, but I don't like seeing you hurt like this."

Swallowing sobs, Veronica stared into the moonless summer night, embarrassed by her emotional upheaval, yet comforted by Siena's words.

"You've been through hell—and you've faced it alone, Veronica. Until lately, no one'd recognized the depth of your pain. So, of course, you feel betrayed that Michi told a complete stranger about it. That's one reason why I was upset about her knowing about *us*. For all I know, she's probably told René all about me, too."

Veronica wiped her eyes with the back of her hand. "Michi only knows we're—seeing each other. I didn't tell her about the abortion—God, I'd never do that. And whatever she said to René, I'm sure she didn't do it maliciously. She just didn't think. Even so, it really hurts. And I feel like a fool for misjudging René."

"Veronica, you like to think you have an uncanny ability to read people—"

"I'm not usually this wrong." She frowned, at last looking at Siena. "Look, I'm sorry I got you into this."

Siena put her hand over Veronica's. "No wonder you and Joanna kept to yourselves."

"I don't want you to get a negative impression about lesbians. Sometimes we hurt each other. We're as human as anyone else."

Not answering, Siena swung the Z into the carport. She shut off the engine and handed Veronica the keys. "I'm too tired to talk any more."

Veronica nodded. "I'm sure glad Phil's staying at Steve's. I really need cuddling tonight."

"Just hold me." Veronica felt her knotted shoulder muscles relax when Siena's arms surrounded her.

Gently, Siena kissed her. "Come sit with me."

"We really should go to bed."

"Not yet." Siena led her to the sofa, easing beside her. There she opened her arms again, welcoming Veronica as she would an injured child.

Closing her eyes, she relished Siena's hands first on her

124

shoulders and arms, eventually on her breasts and lower. "Is this what you really have in mind?"

"The most wonderful antidote to pain." Siena unzipped Veronica's white jeans, her nimble fingers enticing. "Nice and wet."

Veronica moaned at the intimate contact, the arousing edge of Siena's manicured thumbnail on her clitoris. Although her sexual excitement had begun earlier in the evening, she hoped Siena would not ask about that. And Siena did not disappoint her. She continued stimulating Veronica, long fingers inside.

Soon they sprawled on the sofa, Veronica above her, thighs spread, their mouths passionately glued together, too obsessed with each other to realize they were no longer alone.

"Steve said you're a fucking dyke—I called him a liar, Roni. And all the time, he was right." Fighting tears, Phil spoke in breathy gasps. He stood in the middle of the living room, his lankiness pathetically child-like in T-shirt and shorts.

Veronica pulled herself up in one concentrated motion, yanking down her shirt, pulling up her jeans. Her mind became alert, her heart leaden. In the far corner of the sofa, Siena slumped, dishevelled head bent, hands shielding her eyes.

"Philly, I—" Veronica faced her panting nephew.

"You did this with Joanna, too, didn't you?" Outrage and revulsion permeated his words. "You're really sick."

"If you want to yell at me, Phil—go ahead. Get it out of your system. But, afterwards, I want to talk to you. Will you at least allow me that?"

"I'm getting out of here before I puke." He hurried towards the door.

"It's past midnight—" Limping after him, Veronica

paused when he stood in the threshold.

The boy's face was contorted by withheld tears, his voice anguished. "You should've died with Joanna. I hate you, Roni!" Sobbing, he stumbled down the stairs.

"Philly, please—"

He scrambled through the wrought iron gate, swallowed by the night. Leaning against the door frame, Veronica wept, unconsoled by Siena's touch.

"I have the car keys," Siena whispered. "Let's find him."

"Tell me where to go." Her voice unnaturally flat, Siena stared across the car. "You can cry later. He's in no state to be out by himself. Where do you think he's gone?"

Through her tears, Veronica shook her head, at a loss to answer. She could not forget the revulsion in his eyes.

"Is there a park he'd go to? Steve's or some other friend's house? Give me some suggestions, damn it! We can't just sit here."

Wiping her eyes on her arm, Veronica took a deep breath. Siena's sharp words were justified. Phil was somewhere in the night, and there was no time for agonizing.

"Go down to Ocean Park Boulevard. He may've headed to the baseball field. I don't know why, but—"

"It's better than nothing." Siena recklessly backed the Z out of its stall.

Not finding him at the deserted ballfield, they spent long minutes exploring side streets nearby. They hardly spoke, too traumatized to share their thoughts. Staring into the inky night, Veronica prayed. Where was Phil? What if something had happened to him? He had always turned to her in times of confusion and disappointment. Now he had nowhere to turn.

She wished she had not listened to Siena. If they had gone to the bedroom, the boy would not have seen them. Why had she become involved with Siena anyway? She would have been better off grieving Joanna and concentrating on writing instead of becoming sexually entangled with this new neighbor.

Siena's next question jolted her. "Do you think he went to your parents'?"

"When we see a phone booth, I'd better call. God, I just hate to worry them."

"Has he ever run off like this?"

"He's never had a reason to."

At 28th Street and Ocean Park Boulevard, Siena pointed to a public phone outside a mini-mart. She was about to veer into the parking lot when Veronica grabbed her arm.

"Wait. Look up the street. Paramedics."

Before Siena halted the car, Veronica had leaped out. She dashed into the street and saw her nephew's still body being strapped to a metal stretcher.

"Miss, you can't—" A burly paramedic blocked her headlong approach. Several feet away, a uniformed police officer, scribbling an accident report from a distraught elderly man, paused to look at her.

"He's my nephew," Veronica screamed. "Oh, God—Philly!"

The boy did not move—was he dead? She clawed frantically at the paramedic's husky arms. Not again, she prayed. Please, not Phil, too. Through her panic, she heard Siena's voice.

"His name is Philip Melendez. Is he going to be all right?" She eased Veronica away from the paramedic. The officer strode over, clipboard in hand.

"We've immobilized his right arm," the paramedic

said. "He was conscious until a few minutes ago. We're taking him to Santa Monica Hospital. Just follow us."

"I want to ride with him." Veronica moved forward and tried to shake off Siena.

"He won't know if you're there or not, miss." The paramedic helped his partner load Phil into the back of the van. They slammed the rear door. Turning on the siren, they sped away.

The nightmare had started all over again—someone Veronica loved was hurt because of her thoughtlessness. How much more could she endure? Through her tears, she saw the elderly man, pale and still beside his late model Dodge. She did not trust herself to say anything to him.

The Anglo cop strode over, all business. "Why was your muchacho out so late? He's about fifteen, right? Is he in a gang? Was someone out to get him? Did his homeboys take off and leave him? The gentleman driving the car says the kid came out of nowhere, running like hell—"

Veronica turned reddened eyes on him. Because Phil was a Chicano, this cop suspected he belonged to a gang. Her voice was frigid. "If you want to ask me anything, do it at the hospital. That's where I'm going."

"I'll see you there." He nodded, letting the women pass.

"If he dies, I'll kill myself."

"Phil's not going to die. Please calm down, Veronica. We have to phone your parents when we get to the hospital. Your mother might get hysterical if she hears you crying."

"Will *you* talk to her? I'll completely fall apart if I have to tell her."

Siena sighed, looking worn out. "Sure."

"It's all my fault," Veronica sobbed anew. "If—"

"We had *no* idea Phil was home. And we can't blame ourselves for his being hit by that poor old man's car either."

Veronica stared at her. "What're you talking about? If Phil hadn't seen us, he'd be home in bed right this minute. He hates me now and—I can't bear that. There's no way in the world I would've deliberately hurt him." She buried her head in her arms and sobbed. "How am I going to tell Frank about this? I was supposed to be taking care of his son. I really know how to bungle things."

In a molded plastic chair in the Santa Monica Hospital Emergency waiting area, Veronica fidgeted while Siena phoned the Melendez home. Relaying medical insurance information to the admitting clerk and answering the police officer's questions, she had functioned automatically. She was relieved the cop had accepted her story about a family quarrel. Maybe the condominium's upscale address had convinced him. Dreading her parents' arrival, she doubted if they would fall for the same line.

Awaiting Siena, Veronica centered her thoughts alternately on Phil's trauma and her own escape from death months ago. She remembered her groggy awakening after being comatose for days, only to be told of Joanna's death. She had wished for death then, too, as Philip had echoed tonight. Willing those morbid thoughts aside, she looked up at Siena's approach.

"Your mouth has traces of my lipstick." Siena handed her a kleenex. "Your parents will be here as soon as they can. Your father answered the phone."

"How did he react?" Veronica wiped her lips quickly and discarded the kleenex in an adjacent ashtray. Her hands shook and she sat on them to hide the tremors.

"Calmer than I expected. He asked about you right away. He sounds like a nice man." When Siena held her, Veronica felt her quiver, too.

Her voice was muffled against Siena's shoulder. "What'd you tell him?"

"That Phil's being x-rayed, and I'm the neighbor who drove you here."

"I can't tell them the truth."

"What if Phil does?"

"He could, I guess—out of spite. He's really angry and he knows how conservative they are." Leaning against Siena, she sighed. "Right now, all I care about is whether he's going to be fine. I wish they'd let me see him. It seems like we've been here for ages."

"Ms. Melendez, I'm Dr. Howell," announced an elegant black woman with a short, greying Afro, a little later. "Philip will have to stay here a couple of days for observation. He's in the second cubicle to your right. We'll take him to his room in a few minutes."

"Is he—?"

"A little worse for wear, covered with bruises—and very fortunate." The doctor smiled, mahogany eyes tired but friendly behind tortoise-shell glasses. "He has a concussion, a fractured arm, and a couple of cracked ribs. We've just fitted him with a cast and taped his ribs. Just between you and me, I hope tonight's the last time he decides to take a midnight jog."

"Me too." Veronica whispered a prayer of thanks and followed the doctor.

*

In a wheelchair, his right arm shielded by a thick cast, his head bandaged, Phil sat alone. He wore a flimsy hospital gown, his back to the door.

"Philly—"

He seemed to stiffen and did not respond.

Seeing him safe and sound, Veronica leaned against an examining table and tried not to weep.

The fingers of his left hand tapped the metal spokes of the wheelchair. "I'm not dead, Roni."

"I was so scared you'd be." Veronica was unable to keep the tremor from her voice. "Phil, I'm really sorry about—tonight. If I—"

He would not look at her. "Don't want to talk about it."

"We have to—maybe not right now, but we do have to. And—I'm going to tell Frank."

Phil at last raised his head. He had a large contusion over his left eyebrow, and a bruise on that cheek. "Why?"

"It's about time I start being honest."

He shook his head slowly and looked away again. "Is she out there—your girlfriend?"

Veronica nodded. She knew he felt betrayed by Siena, too. "She's worried about you."

"I bet. You're the one she cares about."

"Siena cares about you, whether you want to believe it or not. Phil, if it hadn't been for her—well, we wouldn't have known what'd happened to you till hours later." She stepped closer and squatted before him. Tenderly, she placed a hand on his bony knee. "I love you, Philly."

He erupted into sudden sobs, and bent his bandaged head even lower. She held him, mindful of his taped ribs and fractured arm. His sobs wracked her, and she bit her lips hard to keep from crying, too.

He took a shuddering breath. "Steve said—all this

shitty stuff about you, so I got really mad and came home. I didn't even know why he said it and—I didn't believe him. But then I saw it for myself. Roni, I—I just don't get it."

"Honey, I don't either. That's just the way it is." Lifting his bruised face with utmost care, Veronica met his wet gaze. "I never meant to hurt you, Phil."

He said nothing, still sniffling. With the edge of his cotton gown, she wiped his bewildered eyes.

"Your grandma and grandpa are probably here by now."

"Don't tell them, Roni."

She was surprised at the assurance in her voice. "I have to."

"Not now. We'll make up a story—"

"You're not going to cover for me, Philip Melendez."

"Don't want you to get in deep shit with them. Look, you already said you're going to tell my dad. Let him decide what to do."

"We always let Frank make the decisions." Veronica rose when her legs began to stiffen. "I wonder if they've already phoned him."

Phil ignored her remark, grimacing as he touched his bandaged head. "I'll say we fought 'cause I came home late instead of staying overnight at Steve's. I'll say I walked home 'cause I was mad at him—they know what a geek Steve is sometimes—and that you were shook up 'cause I was out so late by myself."

"Phil, I don't like this at all." Veronica paced the narrow examining room, hugging herself to keep from shivering.

"That's what I'm going to say, Roni. I got really mad at you 'cause you yelled at me, and I ran out."

She shot him a skeptical glance. "Since when've you

had temper tantrums?"

His voice was determined. "That's what I'm saying."

Accompanying the taciturn orderly wheeling Phil towards the elevators, Veronica spotted her parents speaking with Dr. Howell at the far end of the corridor. Siena sat apart from them in the waiting area, paging through a crumpled magazine.

"Ay, pobrecito mijito," Sara crooned when she scurried towards her grandson. Joe Melendez strode beside her, his rough-hewn face brightening at the sight of his daughter and Phil.

"Roni, I'm ready to crash," the boy confided, watching them.

"Let them get their hugs in. Then you can have your rest." She stepped aside as her parents engulfed him. Dr. Howell soon interrupted the emotional reunion, and disappeared with Phil into the elevator.

Sara embraced her daughter. "Ay, Roni. I prayed so hard you weren't hurt, too."

"Mom, you're cutting off my circulation."

Her mother contented herself with grabbing one of her daughter's hands and rubbing it between hers.

"Que pasó, Roni?" Joe Melendez pressed. He frowned and kept his large workingman's fists deep within the pockets of his blue windbreaker. "Your neighbor didn't explain much. I want to know what to tell Frank."

"Why don't you wait till morning to phone him? There's no point in worrying him now. Did Dr. Howell explain about—"

"Yeah. Pues, dígame, hija."

Veronica released herself and leaned against the wall next to the bank of elevators; the hard surface felt strangely comforting. "Everything happened so fast." She paused and rubbed her eyes. "Phil was supposed to stay overnight at Steve's. They've been working on their photography projects. From what I've been able to piece together, they had a tiff. I got mad at him for not patching things up with Steve, and for walking home in the dark. I kept thinking he could've been jumped by a gang or something. I suppose I overreacted. Then he got huffy, and the next thing I knew, he ran out. My neighbor came with me to look for him—and when we found him—" Her voice threatened to break. "—he was lying in the middle of Pearl Street. I thought he was dead," she cried, rushing into her parents' arms, and all three wept together.

"It brought everything back—from months ago," Veronica explained through her tears.

"Roni, you should come home with us tonight."

"We should be together esta noche," her father agreed.

"I'll be fine—really. I just need to sleep. My poor neighbor's been waiting around all this time. We'd better get going." Veronica began to move away. They let her go, but continued to hold each other. "I'll be here with Phil tomorrow. See you then." She blew them a kiss and walked towards Siena.

"All that waiting reminded me of—" Siena kept her troubled gaze focused on the deserted streets. "I guess neither of us reacts positively to hospitals."

"Too many bad memories." Veronica caressed Siena's thigh. "Thanks for being with me. I couldn't have faced this alone."

"You wouldn't have had to. How is Phil handling it?"

"In an odd sort of way, he's being protective." She ran a nervous hand through her curly hair. "I've been his security blanket most of his life. He's worried about what'd happen if the truth came out. I am, too. Feel like such a hypocrite."

"Under the circumstances—"

"I know. I just don't feel good about myself right now."

"You did what you had to." Parking the car, Siena gazed at her. "Your place or mine?"

"Mine—in case someone in the family phones."

10

NEITHER OF THEM slept much. Every time she closed her eyes, Veronica was haunted by violent images: Joanna's lifeless body beside her in the crumpled Rabbit; Phil's lanky form, caught by stark headlights, bouncing off a hastily braked Dodge. Rolling over, she found Siena awake, eyes red-rimmed.

"I keep thinking about how young he is, Veronica. How is finding out about us going to affect him?"

"He wouldn't even mention your name. He referred to you as my 'girlfriend.'"

Weeping soundlessly, Siena allowed Veronica to hold her. Her silent tears soon evolved into shuddering sobs. "I thought it was sexier to make love on the sofa. I was so sure we were alone—"

"Siena, when we got home from the dance, I just wanted to forget about Michi and that bitch René—I knew you could make me forget." Veronica sighed. "No matter how terrible we feel about all this, we'll have to put it aside for the time being. What matters is, Phil's alive—that's really a miracle. He's so coherent—he seems more concerned about me than about himself. I wonder if that's healthy. Maybe he feels he can't afford to get angry with me again."

A frown flickered across Veronica's face. "What really worries me is the rest of the family. Sooner or later I have to be honest with them. And I'm not sure how Frank will react—I can't ever lie to him. Frank deserves the truth."

The jangling phone awoke her.

"I just talked with Dad, Roni."

Instantly alert at hearing her brother's terse voice, Veronica cleared her throat. "Frank, Phil's going to be—"

"I know. I'll be home tonight. Meet me at the airport."

"Sure." She grabbed a notepad from the bedstand and scribbled his flight number and arrival time. "What about Joyce?"

"She'll be flying back in a few days. I want to know what happened."

Veronica shut her eyes tightly and groped for words. In drowsy curiosity, Siena's auburn head emerged from beneath the sheet.

"Roni, what the hell happened?" Frank's voice was gruffer than she had ever heard it.

She kept her eyes closed. "It's too personal to discuss now. I'll tell you when I see you."

"Is Phil into drugs?"

"No! It isn't that at all. It has to do—with me, Frank."

"Honey, you know you can tell me anything."

"Tonight. Please."

Her brother agreed with some reluctance. "Tonight, kid."

They made love tenderly. Veronica felt safe in Siena's arms. Alone with her, Veronica wanted only to love and be loved. When Frank arrived, their privacy would be over. She wanted to postpone confronting reality for a few more hours.

*

137

From the patio table on the terrace, Veronica saw Michi enter the wrought iron gate downstairs. Her friend wore a lavender tank top and purple shorts, and her spiked hair glistened in the sunlight. Siena got up to let her in.

Moments later, an astonished Michi sank into a chair opposite Veronica. "Phil's in the hospital?"

Veronica nodded. She wanted to forget the previous night's anger. "It's been a hell of a weekend." She offered Michi a cup of coffee.

"No lie."

Chin in hand, Michi listened to the unfolding of events. "No wonder I couldn't reach you. I really felt bummed out after you left, Roni. When you didn't answer your phone, I figured you were at Siena's—but I didn't have her number."

Veronica rolled up the sleeves of her terrycloth robe. She was still damp from her morning swim, but the sun had warmed her. She shook her head, and her wet curls caused a faint drizzle. "I'm not sure what time we left the hospital."

Siena dunked the end of a cinnamon roll into her coffee. "The wait seemed endless."

"Oh. Well—I really came over to apologize—about mouthing off to René. I'm sorry, Roni. You, too, Siena. I never should've blabbed."

Veronica noted the color rising in Michi's round cheeks. At that moment, she found her irresistible. She pulled her repentant friend into her lap, and Michi squealed in delight. Even Siena laughed at that unexpected action.

Veronica noisily kissed Michi's cheek. "I can't even stay angry with you. After everything else, that seems so trivial."

Seeming satisfied, Michi grinned and leaned against

Veronica's shoulder. "Do you forgive me, too, Siena?"

Stacking dishes, Siena did not look up. "From what I've seen of René, she's an expert manipulator. I wonder why you didn't catch on to that."

Michi cast her a sidelong glance. "At least she doesn't beat around the bush."

Veronica groaned in exasperation, but Siena made no comment. Veronica sensed the tension between the two women.

"So—" Michi pinched her friend's chin. "Quite a night. And poor Phil. Have you talked to him today?"

"He was asleep when I phoned. I'm going to see him in a little while."

Siena picked up the empty cups. "I doubt if he's ready to see me."

"Well, it's a touchy situation. Would you mind if I tagged along, Roni?"

Veronica's voice was quiet as she watched Siena leave. She wished her lover would give Michi a chance. "I could use the company, but I want to be alone with him first."

"Sure. Has René phoned?"

"No." Veronica frowned. "Why?"

"She thinks she was a total ass last night."

"For once, she's right." She gave Michi a hinting shove and stiffly rose. "If she's going to phone, I'm getting out of here fast."

Chattering away, Michi drove her trusty Toyota towards Santa Monica Hospital. "Anyhow, I'm going to dinner with Beth—the woman I met at the dance."

"Great. Sounds like one good thing happened last night." Veronica marvelled at how relaxed she felt with Michi; she was relieved her animosity had faded. "Is Beth in school?"

"She's a dental hygienist—kind of shy. Says I have dazzling teeth." Michi grinned.

"She's a cutie."

"You would notice that, you slut."

Laughing, Veronica gave her a playful nudge, then instantly sobered. "Mich, I have to tell Frank tonight."

Her friend made a right turn on Arizona Avenue. "You guys have always had a fabulous rapport."

With a sigh, Veronica removed her sunglasses and rubbed her eyes. "He doesn't see me as a sexual critter, though. I'm his smart kid sister—the nerdy bookworm—not an active dyke."

"And you've been pretty active these days," Michi teased. "Siena's crazy about you and—René thinks you're dynamite."

"Enough about René, all right? She almost broke my wrist last night. Is she into S/M or what?"

Michi shrugged. "She's used to being irresistible. She figured you'd dump Siena and go home with her instead."

"She actually told you that?"

Michi nodded. "I doubt if you've heard the last of her."

"It's about time you got here." Propped in bed, watching a Dodger game on the overhead TV, Phil flashed a relieved smile. "Grandma and Grandpa're coming over after Mass. They phoned Dad this morning—"

"And I'm picking him up later." Veronica nuzzled his forehead, then set the Sony Walkman and several cassettes on his bedstand. "Muchacho, your bruises are unmistakable in daylight."

"I'm one big ache, too. But at least I'm not in traction

like you were."

"Thank God for that. Phil—" She seated herself on the edge of his bed and took his left hand in hers. "—it's going to take some time for you to mend. We both know that. But what're you feeling inside—about me, about what you saw?"

Hesitantly, the boy raised his eyes to hers. She saw utter confusion there.

"Can't we just forget it?" His voice cracked halfway through the question.

"No. We're part of each other's lives. We can't sweep it under the rug. Besides, you and Steve argued about it, too. He's been your best friend for years. Does he even know you're here?"

"Don't feel like talking to him. He doesn't have to know anything about you either."

Veronica squeezed his hand tighter. "What did he say last night?"

The boy focused his gaze away from her. "That you're a—bulldyke." He whispered that final word.

She flinched and made herself ask another question. "What brought that on?"

Phil sighed and flicked a tear from his cheek. "We were looking at some of the photos."

"Of Siena?"

He nodded. "And I said how great it was that you'd made friends with her. I said something else about Michi being back and how different she looks. I don't know—I was just telling Steve that you're starting to go out with friends again. And all of a sudden he said, 'How come they're all girls? Is Roni a lezzie?'" At that, Phil began to cry.

Tenderly, Veronica drew him close, letting him weep against her. "And then what, honey?"

The boy sought control over his voice. "I said he was crazy. He started horsing around, kind of bouncing a-round the room—just goofing off, you know—throwing punches at me, and saying how come you have all these good-lookin' girl friends—Joanna was really pretty, too—and how come you don't date guys, and neither do your friends. And how come your girl friends stay overnight a lot." Phil took a shuddering breath. "So you must be a—bulldyke—and you act like a man when you're with them. He said a lot of gross stuff, Roni—and I got pissed off and walked home."

"Then you found out he was right about most of it." She lifted his chin and studied his misty eyes. "Phil, I *am* a lesbian. But I'm not into role-playing—I don't want to be a man. I'm very content being a woman, and I happen to be attracted to women instead of to men. That's hard to understand, but it's true. I hope it doesn't affect how you feel about me. You have to tell me if it does. Couldn't handle it if you turned against me 'cause of this."

"I'd never do that, Roni." He bit his trembling lower lip. "I'm sorry for wishing you dead—I didn't mean that. I just—wish I understood all this stuff. How do you *know* it's true?"

Phil's bewilderment unnerved, yet touched her. She tried to maintain her composure. "I was in love with Joanna. For a while, I thought I would only feel that way about *her*. But now—I'm involved with Siena. Phil, I've never felt like this about a man—in fact, I can't even imag-ine it."

"Do you hate men?"

"No!" Why did everyone ask her that? "You know I love you and Frank and Dad. I just don't have sexual feel-ings towards men. I don't mean that as a put-down. There's just no point in trying to fake it. I mean, why should I hurt some nice guy by pretending to be attracted to him? What would be the point?"

He sniffled again. "How can you be so sure you like women better?"

"I was in love with Joanna for years—since grade school. I don't know if I'll ever love anyone that much again." She paused. "I care for Siena—but it's different."

He took a deep breath. "Did her boyfriend really jilt her?"

"I didn't lie about that, Phil. I just wasn't willing to be truthful about everything else. I'm sorry." She wiped his cheeks with her fingertips. "You've liked her from the start. How do you feel about her now?"

His dark eyes delved into hers. "I think—" He swallowed. "—maybe she was friendly with me to get to know you."

"No." She wanted him to believe her. "Siena isn't like that. When you helped her move in, she didn't know anything about me."

"Roni, she sure asked lots of questions."

"Probably 'cause we're close in age—nothing else." She still held his hand, noting its coldness against her own clammy one. "Phil, she'd like to see you, but she isn't sure how you feel about her."

He grimaced. "Maybe when I'm home, Roni—not yet. I don't know what to say to her." He blinked quickly. "When I saw you with her—I kind of went crazy, you know? The way you were kissing each other—"

"We kiss like everyone else does."

"Roni, you're both girls."

"Do you think lesbians shouldn't be allowed to love each other? Should we be denied that opportunity 'cause people think we look weird together?"

"I *didn't* say that. I'm just not used to seeing—I don't

know—it was like watching a movie, like it wasn't really happening. Maybe it's 'cause I've never seen you kiss anybody that way. It was kind of—"

She cut in. "Shocking?"

He nodded.

"Phil, just 'cause you've never seen me act out my feelings doesn't mean I haven't had them. Listen, you have to remember Siena and I thought we were alone. You weren't supposed to be home. There's no way you would've seen us otherwise. One of the reasons why I want to tell Frank is 'cause you and he need to discuss this. You guys've talked about sex before. I really think you should discuss this, too."

Phil leaned against the pillows. "Dad can be kind of macho sometimes. What if he flips out?"

Veronica patted his hand. "I'll find out when I see him tonight. In the meantime, I want you to know I love you. And I never, ever intended to hurt you. I shouldn't have let you leave when you were so shook up."

"You couldn't have caught up with me," he said with a trace of boastfulness. "Don't you think I knew that? Yeah, I shouldn't have run off in the dark—it was crazy. I really lost it—partly 'cause Steve was right, partly 'cause I was blown away by seeing you, partly 'cause—"

"Of your crush on Siena?"

He stared at the channel selector by his bed. "Huh? Get real, Roni."

"You sure fooled me."

He looked away again, in time to see Michi saunter in, carrying the latest edition of *Mad* magazine. Veronica's parents accompanied her, and they immediately surrounded Phil's bedside. He seemed relieved to see them.

"Cómó estás, mijito?" With a flourish, Sara produced a couple of homemade beef and bean burritos from a tidily folded sack.

"Hey, Grandma, you're all right!" Wasting no time, Phil bit into the tasty snack.

"Sabes qué? Last time I was in the hospital, I almost got sick from la comida. Tan horrible." Sara rearranged her grandson's pillows. "We don't want you getting más flaquito. Did Roni tell you Frank's coming home?"

"Yeah." He munched the burrito with enthusiasm. "Do you think Dad'll talk the docs into letting me leave?"

"La doctora Howell said one more day, eh?" His grandfather assured him. "She wants to be sure your cabeza's in good shape. How do you feel today, mijo?"

"A little dizzy sometimes. And I'm really sore. Otherwise, I'll live." Phil swallowed a large chunk of burrito. "Hi, Michi. What'd you bring?"

"Your favorite, what else?" She grinned, handing him the magazine. "Can you believe your grandparents didn't even recognize me? I was using the phone in the hallway when they strolled by. I was waving like mad, and they went right past me!" She wriggled her eyebrows in consternation.

Veronica's parents laughed uproariously. "You crazy girl," Sara chided. "How could we recognize you? Cutting off all your hair! What'd your poor mother say about that?"

"She hasn't gotten over it yet. Dad's really happy 'cause he was always complaining about globs of hair in the bathtub drain."

Joe nodded knowingly. "When our three girls lived at home, I had to snake out our pipes all the time."

Sara continued fussing over her grandson, and for once, he allowed her. "Well, did you and Roni make up?"

The boy took on a chastened air. "Sure, Grandma. I was a jerk last night."

145

"Next time you listen to Roni, okay?" Joe advised sternly. "Mijo, it's too dangerous to be out late by yourself. Suppose somebody'd taken a shot at you while you were walking home, eh? The gangs're all over town these days. And don't be so ready to run out when Roni's trying to talk sense to you. You could've been killed."

"I know, Grandpa." Phil kept his eyes lowered. "Is Dad mad at me?"

"More worried than anything else. Didn't he phone?"

"If he had, he would've missed his flight," Veronica explained, feeling hypocritical.

"Pues, si." Satisfied Phil was comfortable, Sara seated herself next to his bed. "After we talked with Frank, we called your Tia Angela in Arizona—and your Tia Lucy in Santa Barbara, to let them know you're doing fine. They both sent their prayers, Philly. Then I phoned Rita Martínez. Apenas se puede creer—she didn't even hear you leave last night."

Phil looked uneasy at that disclosure. "Steve and me were watching TV in the den, Grandma. I went out the side door."

"The Martínezes should've been keeping an eye on you boys. They should've at least given you a ride home," Sara added with indignation. "And what were you y Steve arguing about?"

"Some girl," Phil murmured.

"Ay, que muchachos! You're too young for that, Philly."

"Sara, he's old enough to shave." Joe offered his grandson a conspiratorial smile. "Just be careful next time, Phil. The Martínezes feel bad because they didn't know you'd gone home. They're probably giving Steve hell right now."

At that, the boy's eyes widened, but he said nothing.

Feeling queasy, Veronica brushed her fingers against his hand.

"Phil's such a great kid." Michi swung the Toyota towards Wilshire Boulevard.

"I don't like all this lying, Mich. It really bothers me." Veronica watched the clumps of Sunday afternoon traffic headed westward. She envied those beachgoers with nothing else on their minds but suntans and cold drinks. She would have gladly changed places with any of them.

"Roni, who says you have to give your parents the gory details? Telling Frank makes sense—he's Phil's dad and the person in the family you're closest to. But your parents are like mine—really traditional. So what're you supposed to say—that the kid caught you in flagrante delicto with your girlfriend, and that's really why he ran away?"

"They wouldn't even know what that means, show-off." Veronica grinned, in spite of herself. Michi had a knack for simplifying complicated situations.

"Give yourself a break, Roni. There's no way you can tell them the whole truth. You have to stick with the decision you and Phil made, even if it isn't easy."

"I feel so overwhelmed." Veronica rubbed the back of her neck; it was stiffening again. "You know something? A few weeks ago, life was a bore. Right now, I'm actually feeling nostalgic for boredom."

"Just a temporary setback, cookie." Michi halted the Toyota behind Frank's car. "Oh, before I forget—did I leave my comb in the Z last night?"

Getting out, Veronica saw the metal comb in the Z's back section. She retrieved it, then noticed a folded piece of paper beneath the windshield wiper.

"I'm so sick of finding stupid flyers on here." She handed Michi the comb with one hand and grabbed the paper with the other. Unfolding it, she saw an unfamiliar scrawl:

Verónica,

I phoned you mil veces, but you either weren't home or didn't want to answer. I was a pendeja last night, and I beg your forgiveness.

I won't ever be sorry for believing you're la más suave, más inteligente mujer I've ever met. Why am I so sure of this? Because I went to the Research Library before going to the dance to look up your stories and articles.

You make me proud to be Chicana. I know I was more than blunt last night, and more forceful than I intended, but mis sentimientos remain the same. I want to be your lover un día—soon, I hope.

Con mucho cariño—R. Talamantes

"What is it, Roni?"

Crumpling the note, Veronica kept her voice monotone, but her heartbeat accelerated. She remembered her undeniable excitement on the dance floor with René Talamantes.

"A mash note from that idiot film freak."

"What? Let me see." Michi grabbed the paper, partially tearing one of its wrinkled edges. "Oh, my. She really has it bad. That dyke is hot to trot."

"Mich, if you say another word, you won't have a hair left on your fuzzy little head."

"My lips're sealed." She giggled, locking them with an imaginary key and elaborately tossing it away.

Veronica tried not to smile.

148

11

THE SULTRY NIGHT WAS moonless, illuminated only by the runway lights. Veronica watched the landing aircraft taxi, rehearsing what she planned to say. However, when the passengers began to spill out, she panicked. Her well-chosen words faded when her broad-shouldered brother elbowed his way towards her. Frank looked casual in jeans and a polo shirt, and his brown face had a weary grin.

"How's my little sis?" Before she could answer, he swept her up and twirled her around. "Been in the sun, huh?"

She nodded and hugged him tightly. "How was your flight?"

"Too long. How's my kid doing?" He put Veronica down and appraised her.

"Phil wants to come home, but they're keeping him one more day. He's pretty banged up, Frank." She took his offered hand, and they walked together.

"Typical Melendez. He never wants to stay down." He slowed his long strides for her. "You're not limping much, Roni."

She let herself smile. "So it's noticeable?"

"Sure. I take it you've been going to therapy."

"Phil nags me if I don't."

"That kid's one in a million." Frank swung her hand as they headed towards the baggage claim. "So when're you letting me in on this mystery accident?"

149

Her hand felt clammy in his large one. "When we get home."

"You said it's 'personal.'"

She nodded and wished she could avoid his gaze while they emerged from the long corridor into the pandemonium of the baggage claim area.

He did not pursue the subject, but continued studying her. "Roni, you're still the best looking Melendez girl—"

"You're so full of it," she groaned.

"—even if you do have that big Aztec nose." He chuckled.

"I should've known you'd add that."

Laughing to postpone her anxiety, she watched with affection while he stood at the baggage carousel. Taller than their father, Frank was ruggedly handsome, tautly muscled. As a shy child, Veronica had idolized him for his easy charm, his professional success, and most of all, because of the special attention he had always given her. He was one of the few people who remained untarnished in her adult eyes. She wondered how he would feel about her before the night was over.

"The car's running real smooth." He insisted on driving home; she sensed his need to be in control of that, at least. So far, he had not gotten anywhere with his questions. "And it's clean, too," he said with an appreciative grin.

"I had it washed yesterday." She tuned down the radio. "How's Joyce?"

"Terrific. She wanted to fly back with me, but the best thing is for her to close up the house we were renting. My work's done. We could've come home a week ago."

"But you were supposed to stay two months. I

thought you were just flying in to see Phil, then going back." She wondered if his marriage was still intact.

"How could I enjoy my honeymoon when my kid's been hit by a car? I'm not heartless, Roni. Besides, getting used to Joyce will be hard enough for Phil. I think a few days alone with him will be good for both of us." He accelerated and changed lanes, passing slower moving vehicles. Reflexively, Veronica clutched the edge of the bucket seat.

"Anyhow, I can only relax for so long. After I finished my part of the hotel project, Joyce and I went snorkeling and deep sea fishing. It was fun, but what can I say? I love being with my wife, but I'm no beach bum. Dad raised me to work, and that's what I'm used to. I'm back to stay."

Veronica touched his arm; its muscled, hairy texture felt foreign. But Frank was solid, the most reliable person in her life. She wanted only the best for him. She could not help remembering their parents' reservations about his marriage to a younger Anglo woman. She hoped everything would turn out all right for him and the woman he loved.

"Has there been trouble between you and Joyce?"

He grinned. "I see that scrunched-up look of yours—imagining all kinds of major problems. Roni, Joyce and I are fine—really."

"Just want to be sure." She stared at the upcoming Santa Monica Freeway interchange sign. "There's been enough hassle around here already."

She filled his personalized stein with Lowenbrau, grabbed a 7-Up for herself, and nervously joined Frank in the living room.

"Ah." He took the beer with satisfaction. "I trained

you right. A cold beer for a tired man. Roni, you're great."

"Sexist." She collapsed into the easy chair opposite him.

He winked, took a large gulp, and leaned back on the sofa. "Well—I'm all ears."

For several seconds, she eyed him speculatively. She felt as if she were going to vomit. His dark eyes never left hers, and he offered an encouraging smile.

Veronica inhaled deeply. "Frank, I'm a—lesbian."

"I know."

She almost choked. "What?"

"I've been around the block a few times, Roni. I can size up women pretty well. Little sis, I've watched you grow up—I've seen the clues." He downed more beer. "What's this have to do with Phil?"

"Who else knows?" She ignored his question, a wave of nausea sweeping through her.

"Joyce."

"Oh, God. Did you tell her?"

"She asked."

At that, her anxiety turned to annoyance. "Thanks a lot for telling *me*, big shot." On impulse, she whizzed her plastic coaster at him, aiming at his head.

Frank ducked. The coaster bounced off one of the bookcases with a sharp thud. Her brother took on a serious expression and leaned towards her.

"Let's be cool through this, okay? You know I hate violence. It's taken real guts for you to tell me this because you didn't know how I'd react. Roni, I figured you'd tell me someday—I wanted *you* to decide when. Besides, I know how hard losing Joanna has been for you."

She stared at him, wondering whether to laugh or cry.

He kept talking, as if realizing she needed reassurance.

"I first suspected when you moved in with her. Afterwards, when you were in the hospital, I helped Isabel and Rubén take Joanna's things from the apartment. They were in such grief I doubt if they noticed anything.

"The room with the double bed—your bedroom—was the one that was lived in. Anyone could see you two slept together. The nude prints in the bathroom, the lesbian novels on the shelves—the evidence was all there, Roni. But, you know something? People see what they want to. Isabel and Rubén were so broken up—they were crying the whole time we were there. Either they were mourning Joanna too much to see, or they denied it all."

Veronica heard herself speak. "Isabel knows. I don't know if she's told Rubén yet." Her nervousness eased somewhat, but she still had to talk about Phil—and Siena. She decided to follow Frank's lead. "Isabel found the letters I wrote from Mexico."

"I take it they said a lot. How's she dealing with it?" He took another sip of beer, and she admired his self-possession.

"Better than I thought."

"Isabel's some lady." He patted the sofa cushion next to him. "Get over here, hermanita. You're sitting there looking like you're going to melt into that chair."

With no hesitation, she stepped over his long legs and snuggled beside him. Sighing, she rested her curly head on his broad shoulder. "Does it matter to you, Frank—about me?"

"No." His voice was gentle. "Did you think it would?"

"I wasn't sure. Phil didn't want me to tell you."

"Now I get it. He knows."

"That's how all this turmoil started." Gesturing often, her voice bordering on tears, she began to describe Phil's unexpected discovery and the accident.

Frank listened without interrupting. At last, he asked, "You've explained things to him?"

"Yes. But he needs to talk with you, too. You see, he has a crush on Siena." Her eyes met his. "Poor unsuspecting Philly, mooning over her, even bragging about her to Steve—and it turns out she's interested in *me*, not him. I don't want him to think I've stolen her away."

Frank rubbed his chin. "But you have, Roni. Sure, he's hurt—finding out about you, seeing you with her. That's bound to affect him. But he's also lost that special something he thinks he had with her. He probably isn't even thinking about the age difference. Phil's real sensitive." He patted her knee. "Like you."

She nodded. "Frank, I never meant to hurt him. He could've died."

"But he didn't. Don't take on any more guilt, Roni. You're already shouldering enough about Joanna—and that wasn't your fault either. Honey, I know what guilt can do. Don't let it eat you up."

She leaned against him again, feeling his muscled arm around her, listening to him. "When Connie was diagnosed with the spinal tumor, I had lots of guilt. She'd complained about her back hurting for months, saying Phil was too heavy for her to carry. I shrugged it off and told her to use the stroller. Afterwards, I felt so responsible because she hadn't seen a specialist right away. And, all that waiting around, putting things off, made it too late for the surgeons to remove the tumor." His voice wavered.

"Now that I'm older, Roni—I can see I wasn't responsible for her dying. For a long time, though, I felt guilty about being alive when Connie—the mother of my baby—was dead. I know you feel the same about Joanna.

You were driving the car—but she's the one who died. Roni, it was meant to be, that's all. And the fact that Phil saw you with your girlfriend—you didn't arrange for that to happen. Hell, he almost caught Joyce and me once. We were on the couch, too, and he got up to raid the fridge. This was at midnight, mind you. Luckily, he sneezed in the hallway, and we heard him. I took Joyce home fast."

She gazed into his level brown eyes. "You're not angry with me?"

"For being human? For wanting some love in your life? Hell, no. Roni, I'm glad you're feeling well enough to *have* a girlfriend. When Joyce and I got married, you were still pretty much in a slump."

Veronica's tone was affectionate. "For a man, you're damn perceptive, Frank Melendez."

"What do you expect from your only brother?" His voice was low, intimate. "One of the reasons why I wanted you here is because it's a calmer environment. Ma drives you crazy, I know. Sometimes when I went over to see you there, I could tell you were just about at the edge. I was afraid you were thinking of suicide."

She felt her eyes mist. "It did cross my mind."

"I thought so. Knowing how much you love Phil, I figured it was better for you to be with him. I knew you wouldn't knock yourself off with him around."

Her voice was quiet. "You took a big chance, Frank."

"I trust you." He took her hand in his. "I never told anyone but Connie about this—"

She heard the sudden catch in his voice. "What?"

"When I was an undergrad, I knew this guy named Eddie. He was in some of my engineering classes, and we'd have lunch together, bone up for exams. He was doing fine in school, but he was unhappy. He'd never go into detail about it, but it was always there."

155

Veronica saw the pain etched in Frank's face, and she steeled herself against him.

"Afterwards, I heard Eddie'd fallen in love with his roommate, and the kid had gotten all paranoid and told him to move out. My friend Eddie had no one to turn to. He hung himself because he was gay."

Veronica shivered at his whispered words. When Frank wiped his eyes with the palm of his hand, she reached up to caress his cheek. She did not want him to think suicide loomed in her future; over the months, she had decided she had too much to live for. Their eyes met, and Frank nodded as if he understood.

"Connie was pregnant then, and I remember promising her that if I ever knew anyone else like Eddie, I'd be there—to talk, to listen—whatever." His eyes were sad, but he smiled at her. "I didn't have too far to look."

"Siena, I'm going to be tied up with family stuff today," Veronica announced over the phone the next morning. "I'm dropping Frank off at the hospital, then going for my therapy appointment. After that, I'll go back to the hospital. And tonight, we're having dinner at my parents'. I may not see you till tomorrow."

"Stop by tonight, even if it's late. I want to see you, hear what's happened."

Hearing the urgency in Siena's voice, Veronica gave in. "How about now?"

"I'm waiting, Veronica."

"While you were at Siena's, I phoned Phil." Frank filled his sister's coffee mug. "He's raring to get out, so I put a call in to his doctor." He gazed across the breakfast table at her. "Roni—"

"Hmmm?" She unfolded the *Times* "View" section.

"Do you love this woman?"

She met his steady eyes.

"If you're planning to tell Mom and Dad about her, you need to be sure. Otherwise, don't say anything." He poured himself more orange juice. "On the other hand, if you decide to live with Siena—"

Veronica realized he had given the matter some thought earlier while she had been with Siena. He had often said he did his best thinking while shaving. She decided to ease his worries; he had enough on his mind already.

"Frank, I just met her. We've never even discussed living together. In fact, Michi's going to be my roommate this fall." She tipped some milk from the carton into her coffee. "I haven't made any commitments—mainly because it's too soon. Not only that, but Siena doesn't identify herself as a lesbian. For all I know, she could start dating men tomorrow. You see, I plunged into this on impulse."

"She's basically straight?" He passed her the box of Quaker Natural Cereal.

"She was supposed to be married in December." At his wary expression, she quickly explained. "Her boyfriend took up with someone else. I had nothing to do with it."

He added milk to his cereal. "Who's René Talamantes?"

Veronica put down her spoon and felt her heart flutter. "She phoned?"

"Said she'll call back. She's real friendly. Asked how Phil's coming along."

"Damn. She's been talking to Michi again."

"Guess you haven't been vegetating." Frank's dark eyes were amused.

She pursed her lips at his expression. "Lay off, okay? René Talamantes is Ms. Assertive Dyke of the Year, and I *don't* want to speak to her."

Leaving the physical therapist's office, she was pleased with herself, basking in one of Anna's rare compliments; the therapist had noticed her client's increasing flexibility and stamina. Veronica got out of the elevator on the first floor and entered the small pharmacy. The only other customers were two elderly women, whispering together among the feminine hygiene products. In the shampoo aisle, she browsed, searching for hair conditioner.

"Alone at last."

Veronica's shoulders tightened on reflex. With a quick sideways glance, she saw René Talamantes strolling towards her in faded jeans, an embroidered Mexican blouse, and brown leather sandals. She wore a shiny silver labrys around her neck.

"You followed me." Veronica faced her with defiance, but she was already ensnared by those hypnotic ebony eyes.

"Sin duda, mujer." Talamantes' eyes lingered on her. "Como te sientes? You were upstairs a long time."

"My physical therapist is in this building, you snoop. What do you want, anyway?"

René grinned, one hand on her hip. "You know what, but I'll settle for taking you to lunch."

"Give it up, Talamantes."

"No way. I thrive on challenges."

Grabbing a bottle of conditioner, Veronica moved on.

"Verónica—"

With impatience, she turned around to find René kneeling in a supplicant's pose, hands crossed madonna-like over her breasts, dark head bent. "I beg forgiveness, Señorita Melendez."

Veronica felt her lips twitch into a smile, but she was determined to ignore her. She could have if the two elderly women had not rounded the aisle and nearly tumbled over René's legs.

"Really, young woman, you should be more considerate!" one of them huffed in annoyance. To regain her balance, the old woman clutched her friend's needlepoint handbag and almost toppled her as well.

"I'm atoning for my sins, ma'am," René said, not budging.

"Street people are everywhere these days," the other woman grumbled. They primly straightened themselves and brushed past.

Veronica could not stop herself from laughing. "You cause a ruckus wherever you go. Get up before you get thrown out."

Talamantes remained kneeling. "Only if you forgive me for Saturday night."

She was exasperated. "Loca, you're forgiven, okay?"

"You have to come over here and put your hand on my head when you say it. Otherwise it doesn't count."

Veronica backed off, hating to be manipulated. "Forget it."

"Por favor."

By this time, the bespectacled pharmacist had leaned out of his glass-enclosed cubicle and blinked at them. Embarrassed, Veronica hesitated.

"Te estoy esperando, mujer."

"You're such a pest." Trudging towards René, she reluctantly placed one hand on that bent dark head; the texture of Talamantes' hair was coarse, thick, so unlike the feathery feel of Joanna's—or Siena's. Veronica pulled her hand away.

"I suppose I can let bygones be bygones this time because it's just not worth the hassle. Get up, will you?" She glanced over her shoulder at the pharmacist. He continued to stare.

"A sus órdenes." René gave her a satisfied grin. Rising, the film student clasped Veronica's hand and kissed it with a flourish, her lips fiery on her cool skin.

Veronica felt herself blush and nudged Talamantes away. "You're so damn outrageous."

René slipped a determined arm around Veronica and guided her towards the cash register. "So they tell me. Now let's do lunch."

"Melendez's Bar and Grill," Frank joked when Veronica rang her nephew's room from the hospital lobby.

"You maniac." She cleared her throat, hoping to unclog her brain as well. "Listen, your car's parked on the second level on 15th Street—the ticket's on the dashboard and I'm—"

"What's going on?"

She wondered if she sounded as rattled as she felt. "René's been following me. In fact, she's waiting outside."

"Take the Z and make a fast getaway."

"Frank, she's not a kidnapper." She sighed. "Look, if I have lunch with her, maybe she'll be satisfied and—"

"The reverse is probably true, Roni."

She was too edgy to acknowledge that. "Tell Phil I'll see him later."

12

DOUBLE-PARKED IN HER RED VW van, René leaned over to open the passenger door, and Veronica slid in.

"Fasten your seat belt, mujer. We're headed for a bumpy ride."

Veronica's hands shook as she secured the strap. "Bette Davis you're definitely not."

"That's what I really like about you—those snappy put-downs." Whirling the van into a two-wheeled U-turn, Talamantes tore down 15th Street, making a neck-twisting right on Santa Monica Boulevard. "Aren't you glad you're buckled in?" She tossed Veronica a triumphant glance.

"Otherwise I would've been hurled through the wind-shield." Veronica decided not to ponder that. She noticed René looked even better in daylight; her skin was brown and smooth—and very touchable. Trying to put that out of her mind, Veronica nestled closer to the door. "Where are we going?"

"La Cabaña—for freshly made tortillas de maíz."

"By any chance, are you a tortilla freak?"

"I'm a tor-ti-llera." Talamantes sang off-key and raucously, to the tune of the Beatles' "I'm a Loser." "'And I've found the one who's dear to me.'"

Veronica wondered if the original lyrics were more appropriate, but she kept that to herself. Guiltily, she thought of Siena, at that very moment eating lunch among strangers in Century City.

"Preciosa, don't fade on me." Punctuating her words, René tapped the steering wheel and sang, "'Love, love will not fade away.'"

Veronica liked how René's ebony eyes gleamed in amusement, and the way her black hair shone in the sunlight. But she could not help herself from being sarcastic. "Are you on drugs?"

"Just high on love, my little chickadee. Who needs chemical elixirs when my love's beside me?"

Ignoring René's grin, she faced the window and wondered what madness had possessed her to accept this invitation.

Careening onto Rose Avenue, René aimed the van into a narrow driveway and deftly veered it in front of La Cabaña, a small stucco restaurant with a tiled roof. On shaky legs, Veronica disembarked. Talamantes rounded the VW and hurried to escort her.

"René!" A distinctly male voice shouted when they entered the cavernous interior.

"Carlos!" She yelled back, grabbing a tiny pot-bellied Chicano in a hearty abrazo. "Cómo estás, carnal?"

"Magnífico, querida. Cómo está tu mama?"

"Trabajando como siempre."

Veronica disregarded their banter and studied La Cabaña's decor. Framed photographs of Emiliano Zapata and Pancho Villa vied with Mexican pottery, serapes and sombreros amid the rough stucco walls. Maybe the owners had overdone the traditional decor, but Veronica could not deny the restaurant's charm. A Mexicana in a scoop-necked embroidered blouse and gathered skirt knelt near a stone hearth and meticulously patted tortillas into shape.

The intimate way she handled the maize, coaxing it into rounded forms, reminded Veronica of the imagery in René's black-and-white film.

"Carlos, quiero presentarte a mi compañera, Verónica Melendez."

Veronica hoped the dim lighting hid her sudden color. Shyly, she extended her hand. "Mucho gusto, señor."

"Carlos Barajas a sus órdenes, señorita." He looked elfin compared to Talamantes' height.

René seemed tickled that Veronica had responded in Spanish. She nudged Carlos. "Queremos una mesa atrás, por favor, Carlitos."

Bowing, he guided them to an isolated corner nook, leaving them with menus before he vanished.

Veronica slid into the booth and planted her canvas bag between them. "Do you speak Spanish often, René?"

"Have to. My mother doesn't speak English." She grabbed the bag, set it on the shelf above the booth, and edged closer. "I'm first generation Chicana."

"I'm third." Veronica decided against retrieving her bag.

René spread a long arm behind her companion's head. "Thought you were more like sixth."

"I'm a little sensitive about that—some Chicanas on campus have criticized me for behaving 'too white.'"

"They've probably suspected you're a dyke, so they've put you down for being a 'coconut'—brown on the outside, white on the inside. Hell, I can't believe that." René brought her ebony eyes nearer. "I bet your insides are rojo y sabroso."

Veronica grimaced and reached for the glass of iced water Carlos had left. She had not expected that response.

René leaned back and chuckled. She kept her arm behind Veronica's head. "How's your girlfriend, anyway?"

163

"None of your business."

"That's what you think." René's eyes flashed. "When that redhead goes back to the straight life, you're going to need someone to cushion your fall. And you're looking at her, mujer. *I'm* the one for you."

"Such an egotist."

"If I don't believe in myself, who will?"

Veronica picked up the menu.

René opted for a safer topic. "How are your stories coming along? Camille can be tough to deal with, but I hear she's one of your boosters."

Veronica continued studying the menu. "I haven't written anything since Friday."

"Writer's block?"

Veronica shook her head. "It's all this family turmoil—my nephew's in the hospital and my brother's back home."

Talamantes did not miss a beat. "Plus your lover demands a lot of your time."

"That really doesn't concern you, René."

"Like hell it doesn't. You and I would have the perfect partnership. There's no way on earth I'd keep you from writing. Mira, I'd really like to show you some of my screenplays." She hardly took a breath. "As a feminist, don't you think women need to help each other in all kinds of ways, including creatively? Veronica, you're the only Chicana writer I know—and a dyke besides. Couldn't you make time to look at another struggling Chicana's work?"

The hints at feminism, combined with references to ethnic solidarity pinched Veronica's sensibilities. She was half amused, half annoyed by René's comments.

"I suppose I can look at *one* screenplay—but I can't promise more than that."

"You won't be sorry." René grinned. "Just happen to have one in the van."

"I really thought you and Michi'd get together." Veronica gingerly held her chicken taco and bit into it. As much as she craved tacos, she wished she had ordered something else; this one seemed about to fall apart. "You both tend to be irreverent."

"Cómo eres, Verónica. Hey, I'm way flashier than Michi." Talamantes took a sip of Dos Equis. "She's a trip, that's for sure—but she's looking for an Asian-American dyke." She pulled the corn husk from one of her beef tamales. "You still mad at her?"

Veronica shook her head. "If you ask Michi anything, she'll wind up giving you lots of details. She loves to talk, so sometimes she gets a little carried away. From now on, if you want to know about me, come to the source."

"All right." René pushed her plate aside. Lightly, she touched Veronica's hair and leaned nearer. "Do you think I'm sexy?"

Veronica swallowed, then smiled. "I guess I asked for that."

"You sure did. What's your answer, huh?" Talamantes's eyes were ebony magnets.

Veronica tried to avoid them. She focused on the embroidered pastoral scene on René's blouse and imagined the dark nipples beneath. "You're dynamic—in an offbeat sort of way."

"And sexy?"

"Well—yes." Boldly, she met her gaze.

"So why're you hanging around with that redheaded gabacha?"

"I'm monogamous."

"Do you think I'm not?" Talamantes scoffed. "Since meeting you, I haven't even thought of any other mujer. Hell, Veronica, just being next to you makes my clit hard."

She blushed at René's outspokenness, and remembered her own sexual excitement at the dance. It flooded her again, making her dizzy.

"I'm not lying. The real reason you've been giving me the brush-off is 'cause you're not sure you can handle me. I'm a wild woman from El Paso—like 'Texas Ruby Red' in the Cris Williamson song. I think that scares the hell out of you since you're so civilized and citified." Her index finger tapped Veronica's shoulder. "What do you think of that?"

Veronica's equilibrium returned. "Not much." To her chagrin, she noticed that the taco at last began to crumble.

Scooping up the disintegrating tortilla, René piled on a combination of beans and chicken, offering it. Veronica hesitated, but René's determination persuaded her otherwise. With steady fingers, Talamantes held the tortilla to Veronica's mouth. Slowly opening her lips, Veronica allowed her to feed her. At the same time, her tongue lightly stroked those delicious brown fingers.

While René's smoldering eyes watched, Veronica felt her entire being become as pliable as her crumbled taco. René's other hand crept under the plastic tablecloth and ever so deliberately parted Veronica's thighs.

Sighing, she did not resist. That elusive hand discovered the damp crotch of her jeans, and stayed there, knuckles exerting pressure.

"René—" She breathed.

"Look at you. You can't even hide how much you want me." Talamantes' face glowed with a coppery hue.

She pressed against Veronica once more, and gradually moved her hand away. "Si quieres más, you know where to find it."

Abruptly, she pushed back the table, left the booth, and strode towards the rear of the restaurant.

Flooded with desire, Veronica struggled to regain her composure. She closed her eyes and wondered if René had left her stranded. She sat still, waiting for her heartbeat to resume its normal pace. She did not know what to do next. Her appetite for food was stanched, and she longed again for that arousing hand pressed against her. When she at last opened her eyes, she saw Talamantes's leggy form hovering above her.

"Where were you?" Veronica reached for the water glass.

"In back—taking care of myself." René's voice was harsh.

She stared, noting the anger in Talamantes' eyes. "You're insane."

"*You're* the loca, mujer." René did not move, but continued glaring. "I could've made you come right here. You were ready. But I'm not giving you that satisfaction. If you want me, compañera, it's got to be *me* and no one else. When you're ready to give up that redhead, let me know. Otherwise, no dice."

"René—"

"What?" Talamantes spoke curtly and removed her wallet from her jeans' pocket.

In no mood for a confrontation, Veronica slid out of the booth. "Never mind. Will you drive me back to the hospital?"

"Vámonos."

*

167

"It isn't true," Veronica began on the way to Santa Monica. Talamantes's sullenness unnerved her. She preferred the joking René, not this brooding woman.

"What's that?" Talamantes' smoky voice was brusque.

"Your comment at the dance—about my being into white women."

"Don't you stick your brown fingers inside esa gabacha?"

"Look, if you're angry with me, just say so." Veronica studied the stalled traffic clogging Lincoln Boulevard.

René hit the rim of the steering wheel with her palm. "I'm not mad at *you*—I'm mad at the situation. It's a no-win deal." She swerved around a bakery truck and cut sharply into a side street. "What were you saying about the dance?"

Veronica winced at her recklessness. "I'm not with Siena because she's white, but because she's kind and giving and—"

"Available—not to mention a real looker."

"That's incidental. Joanna was beautiful, too—and Chicana."

"Michi told me." Talamantes kept her eyes on the traffic merging from Colorado Avenue. "A lot of your confusion has to do with Joanna, mujer. Don't you think I'm aware of that?"

"I *really* loved her," Veronica said softly.

"'The love between women is a circle and is not finished.'"

She felt her eyes mist at hearing that favorite quotation. "Judy Grahn."

"Yeah. Can Siena quote lesbian poetry?"

"You've made your point."

"Think about it."

*

Drained, Veronica wanted to erase any lingering thoughts about René Talamantes. She took the hospital elevator to Phil's room.

"Hi, muchacho." She pressed her lips to her nephew's bruised forehead. "Where's Frank?"

"Talking to the doc." Phil put down his creased copy of *Sports Illustrated*. "Take a load off your feet, Roni. Guess who sent me those?" He pointed to a cluster of rainbow-hued balloons, their trailing ribbons wrapped around the chair's wooden arm.

She raised her brows and sank into the chair.

"Siena. Didn't she tell you?"

"She probably called in the order from work." Veronica rubbed her eyes. No question about it, she needed sleep—a necessary escape from reality. "That was sweet, Phil."

He shrugged. "Dad said not to hold anything against her."

She smiled at his grown-up attitude and wondered how much he mouthed his father's advice. "Well, you have to go with your feelings. What happened to your head bandage?"

"It's in the trash." He grinned. "Skull x-rays were negative. The brain is intact."

"Terrific. You're pretty chipper today—'cause Frank's back?"

"Guess so. I missed him."

She curled the balloons' ribbons around her fingers. "He's really happy you're doing fine."

"And he's in love." He rolled his eyes theatrically.

"Well, that, too. It's good for him, Phil."

Her nephew responded with a deadpan expression,

169

and at that point his father sauntered in.

"Tomorrow we get to bring this rascal home, Roni. Ready for him?"

"We'll manage." Yawning widely, she covered her mouth.

"Let's go, sleepy time gal." Frank patted her shoulder. "You look ready for a nap."

Not about to argue, she got to her feet. "We'll see you mañana, Phil. We're going to dinner at—"

"I know. Grandma brought me chile rellenos for lunch. But I have to eat that yucky hospital food tonight." In mock agony, he crossed his eyes and stuck out his tongue.

Laughing, they kissed him and left.

Frank glanced at her as they crossed the street. "You look pretty down in the mouth."

"René wants me to read one of her screenplays." She pointed to the binder protruding from her canvas bag. "She wants help with dialog."

Frank took out his car keys. "She's picked the right woman."

"Whose side are you on?"

"Honey, I just want you to be happy. You seem bummed out."

Veronica yawned again. "I'm exhausted, and sure don't feel like having dinner with—"

"No backing out, Roni. Take a little nap. We don't have to be there till 6:00."

She fell into a heavy slumber and dreamed of Joanna. Dressed in white, her lover stood atop the Pyramid of the

Sun in Teotihuacan, her shoulder-length hair buffeted by arid Mexican winds. Below her, Veronica climbed the narrow steps of the pyramid, crouching often to avoid being blown off. She called to Joanna for help; the wind obliterated her words, and her lover remained motionless. When she at last reached the summit, hot and exhausted, Joanna was gone. A thin Mexicana, vaguely resembling René, sat there crosslegged, molding tortillas and laughing.

Veronica twitched at feeling a strong hand on her shoulder. Groggily, she opened her eyes and saw her brother. It took seconds for her to realize she was in his condominium, not in the torrid desolation of Teotihuacan.

"Did you say something, Frank?"

"Siena's here."

She sat up stiffly. Blinking, she recognized her typewriter and the manuscript pages next to it. She felt unfocused, scattered. Why had Siena been absent from the dream?

"Are you okay, Roni?"

"Weird dream."

"Well, take your time." He squeezed her shoulder. "You're going to think this is a sexist remark, but—you have fantastic taste in women. I'm dying to see what René looks like."

"You and your compliments." Pinching his close-shaven cheek, she gave him a brief smile. Then she smoothed her clothes and limped out of the bedroom.

"I hear Phil liked the balloons."

"Proves he's still a kid."

It seemed so long since she had held Siena. Veronica relished her nearness and inhaled the fragrance of her hair.

Everything about her was so different from René Talamantes.

"I missed you." Siena drew her closer and their lips met. Veronica wished they would only kiss, not talk, but Siena broke the spell. "Will you stay with me tonight?"

She stepped back. "I'm not sure what time I'll be home."

"I'll wait up. I'm almost finished with your caftan. You'll have to try it on."

"Siena—"

"Yes?" She nuzzled Veronica's cheek.

She made herself ask the question. "Do you think you're a lesbian?"

"I just know—I love making love with you."

Veronica sighed. "How was work?"

Siena hardly seemed to notice the change in subject. "Boring. They treat me like a mannequin. 'Stand here. Stand there. Pout. Don't smile. Be sexy.'" She moved to the bookcase, scanning the titles. "I don't know how long I can keep that up."

Frank entered the livingroom, carrying a stray coffee mug on his way to the kitchen. Veronica realized his curiosity was boundless.

"Excuse me," he said, over his shoulder. While he rinsed the mug, he kept talking. "Siena asked if it'd a good idea to visit Phil tonight. What do you think?"

Veronica did not want to offer an opinion. She still felt disoriented and noticed Siena seemed distracted, too. "You talked with him, Frank. Is he ready for it?"

Her brother leaned on the kitchen side of the counter, alternately looking at them. "If he isn't, he'll probably say so. It's fine with me if you want to keep him company tonight, Siena."

"I'll do it then." Her manicured fingers traced the

spine of one of his art books.

Frank seemed pleased with her offer. Allowing them some privacy, he bid her good-night and headed back to his bedroom.

Siena smoothed her hair from her forehead. "Your family's special, Veronica."

"You haven't met the rest of them." She walked with her to the door. "Well, see you around 10:00."

"When're you going back to work, mijo?" Joe Melendez offered his eldest another beer.

"Depends on how well Phil does at home. I phoned the office today. They couldn't believe I'm back. I might go in next week, or the week after. Joyce'll be home soon, and I have to help her get settled, too."

"But what about Roni?" Sara interjected.

"I'll camp on the beach till my apartment's ready." Veronica casually met her mother's worried gaze and hoped the sarcasm would prevent Sara from asking her to come home for good.

Frank cut in. "Roni can stay put for the time being. Manuel only needed her apartment for a few months. I'll phone him tomorrow and see if he's found his own place yet." He served himself another heaping portion of spicy chile rellenos. "Sure missed your cooking while I was in Saint Croix, Ma."

Sara puffed up. "Do you think la Joyce will want this recipe?"

"Not if you have that green-eyed monster look on your face when she asks," he quipped, making Veronica giggle.

"Joe, when these two get together, nomás se burlan de mi," Sara complained.

"Kids, quit teasing your mother." Joe's brown eyes crinkled at their corners. "Pues, has Steve been to see Phil yet?"

Frank shook his head. "I don't know what's with that kid. I'm going to talk to him myself. I don't want them feuding."

Veronica kept an uncomfortable silence and filled her glass from the pitcher of beer.

"Boys will be boys, eh?" Sara daintily gestured with her fork. "Gracias a Dios que Philly wasn't hurt worse. Pobrecito. At least his cast will be off before school starts." She looked across the table at her quiet daughter. "Roni, quieres más?"

"I'm fine, Mom. Thanks."

"Lucy asked about you when I talked to her esta mañana. You still haven't taken her offer to visit the convent. I think her feelings are hurt."

Veronica rolled her eyes. "She's probably trying to recruit me. Lucy'd like to hold me hostage, shave off my hair, and throw a Carmelite veil over my head."

When Frank and Joe guffawed, Sara showed her displeasure by pursing her lips and shaking her index finger. "Te va castigar Dios por eso, muchacha. You should feel privileged to have a sister who's a nun. Instead, you exaggerate and make jokes. And you men shouldn't encourage her, either. This girl has such a smart mouth."

Frank winked at his sister.

"I'd never make fun of Lucy." Veronica was unable to keep a grin off her face. "I just don't have any inclination to spend a lot of time with nuns."

"You could go there to meditate and be alone—like a religious retreat," Her father suggested, suddenly serious. "You've been through a lot, hija. Tu vida está cambiada. You've said that yourself. Maybe Lucy has the right idea.

Getting away for a while might be the best thing."

"What is this—a conspiracy to get rid of me?" Veronica tried being flippant, but her father's words struck a responsive chord.

"Sounds perfect to me, Roni," Frank remarked. "Suppose Manuel isn't ready to move out of your apartment yet? You could take your typewriter to Santa Barbara and work on your stories without any interruptions."

"Well, I don't know if Lucy wants her to *write* while she's there—" Sara sputtered.

"What *else* would I do? Stay on my knees and pray all day?" Veronica was continually exasperated by her parents' attitude towards creative writing.

"Your typewriter's so noisy, and you're so irritable when you write. The nuns are muy silencitas—at peace," Sara reminded her. She looked flustered at Veronica's change in attitude.

"I'll phone Lucy myself—and maybe I'll take her up on it." Veronica felt excited by the prospect of unlimited writing time.

"If you go, behave yourself." Sara got up and began to clear the table. "For one thing, you'll have to watch your mouth."

"Mom, I wouldn't be sassy and embarrass Lucy. I'd probably just keep to myself." Veronica rose to help her.

Her mother appeared to regret she had even broached the subject.

Siena traced the lean outlines of Veronica's body. "You have such a dreamy look in your eyes."

She relaxed against the pillow, unwilling to admit that her actual thoughts—even while making love with Siena—had centered on the unconventional, but tantalizing,

175

René Talamantes. René was unpredictable, in an exciting, almost dangerous way. For unexplicable reasons, Veronica found herself attracted. She certainly did not wish to share those thoughts; nor did she wish to reveal her growing need for solitude or mention the possibility of accepting Lucy's invitation.

She shifted to face Siena. "My head's full of unwritten words."

"Get up early and write before Phil comes home." Siena sensuously stretched and cuddled close again. "When I got to the hospital tonight, we had some awkward moments, so I didn't stay long."

"If Phil were older, would you go for him?"

Siena's eyes widened. "What a thing to ask."

"You said he's nicer than most men you meet." Veronica shrugged. "My question's a logical extension of that."

"I don't even want to think about men." She caressed Veronica's cheek. "The ones I've dealt with lately sure haven't upgraded my opinion." Her wandering fingers traveled from Veronica's shoulders towards her breasts. "Speaking of men, how'd you explain to Frank about coming over here?"

"Just said I was staying overnight." Veronica smiled. "My brother thinks I have great taste in women."

Siena giggled. "You do."

"Then come closer and let me have another taste."

13

VERONICA TIPTOED PAST FRANK'S bedroom towards her
own. She changed into a baggy T-shirt and shorts, unplugged the telephone, and reread her manuscript. When
she finished, she leaned back and frowned. How could she
construct fiction when her own life seemed in shambles?
Maybe she should consider this stage of her life a first
draft. She smiled at that.

From the window, she could see some neighbors in the
pool, but her own swimming would have to wait. She had
no time to whine about her indecisiveness about Siena either, especially after spending a passionate night with her.
Yet ever since meeting René Talamantes, Veronica had felt
increasingly ambivalent about Siena; and Talamantes, it
seemed, was perceptive enough to notice.

Veronica stretched and yawned, listening to her bones
and jaw creak in protest. She was probably on her way to
becoming arthritic—another depressing thought. Shrugging that off, she rolled a blank sheet of paper into the
typewriter. Just work, she told herself—don't think about
anything else.

His hair tousled, Frank leaned in the threshold and
knotted the belt of his burgundy robe. "Isabel's on the
phone and sounds pretty shook."

Veronica followed him into the living room. She tried

to sound nonchalant when she picked up the phone.

Joanna's mother's voice was tense. "Roni, I need to see you. Does Frank know about you—and Joanna?"

"Yes. Why?"

"I'll be right over."

Veronica replaced the receiver. "She's on her way, Frank."

"Make some coffee. I'll get dressed."

"If you two'd rather be alone," Frank began when Isabel arrived.

Veronica did not want him to leave and hoped her eyes conveyed that message.

"Frank, this concerns you, too." Isabel sat on the edge of the sofa, attractive but subdued in a blue shirtwaist dress. "I heard about Phil's accident. How is he?"

"Indestructible, I guess. He'll be home today. Want some coffee?"

"Ahorita no, gracias." She gestured towards them. "Sit down, both of you."

Veronica's head began to ache, but she did as she was told.

Isabel studied the cover of the Los Angeles architecture book on the coffee table. "Yesterday my boys fought with Steve Martínez."

"Jesus," Frank muttered.

Veronica stared. "Are the kids all right?"

"Larry has a black eye. Teddy has a cut lip, some bruises." Isabel sighed, her gaze moist. "Steve's been spreading rumors about you and—Joanna."

Veronica felt nauseous.

"Where did this happen?" Frank interrupted.

"At the Will Rogers' School playground. The boys

were playing basketball. Between games, Steve pulled out a magazine—"

"A *Penthouse* spread—with two women." Frank grimaced and set his mug on the coffee table.

Both women turned to him in astonishment. In her corner of the sofa, Veronica rubbed her temples and yearned to disappear.

"Steve showed the same magazine to Phil, Roni. He didn't want to tell you that." He explained Saturday's events to Isabel, omitting any mention of Siena. "Have you talked to Steve's parents?"

"Rubén was ready to drive his truck through their living room wall last night," Isabel said, her voice querulous. "I'd rather talk to Rita alone, without our husbands around."

"So you've told Rubén—about us?" Veronica whispered.

"How could I keep it from him any longer?" With agitation Isabel wiped her eyes. "I wish my boys hadn't looked at those filthy pictures."

Veronica cringed at her choice of adjective.

"You can't expect your kids to ignore skin magazines. It's natural male curiosity, Isabel. But I suppose Steve really laid it on thick," Frank added, shaking his head.

"While they were looking at the magazine, Steve said Joanna used to—do that, too." Her mouth trembling, Isabel averted her eyes.

"Let me get you some coffee." Frank patted her knee as he rose. Numbly, Veronica watched him go into the kitchen.

What could she say to Joanna's mother? As for herself, she felt violated. A dirty-minded kid had twisted her love for Joanna into a taunting gibe, a cruel weapon with which to hurt Phil and the Nunez boys. She saw the pain in

179

Isabel's face and felt helpless. Huddled in her corner, Veronica spoke hoarsely, tears streaking her face.

"Isabel—I'm so sorry about all this."

"Oh, Roni. It isn't your fault. You and Joanna loved each other in an innocent way. It wasn't like—in that magazine."

Had Isabel forgotten their conversation at the cemetery, the contents of the Mexico City letters? "Isabel, Joanna and I *loved* each other, emotionally—*and* sexually. Don't you know what that means? We lived together for almost four years. We—"

Isabel's voice grew harsh. "Don't say anymore—please. You're talking about *my daughter.*"

"Yes. The woman *I love.*"

Isabel's eyes were cold. "Steve said you have another woman now."

Although Veronica said nothing, she refused to look away. She felt herself tremble, and her palms were clammy.

Isabel caught her breath and went on. "I care about my daughter's reputation, Roni. Do you think I like hearing a foul-mouthed boy ripping Joanna to shreds—laughing at her, calling her disgusting names? She's not here to defend herself. If *you* don't care—"

"I *care.*" Veronica leaned forward in her intensity. "And I will never deny that I loved her and still do. If she were alive, we'd be together. I'm convinced of that. We didn't 'go public' because we didn't want to hurt our families. That's damn ironic, isn't it? If we'd been honest about our relationship in the first place, we wouldn't be coping with this mess."

Frank returned with the coffee and cast his sister a cautioning look.

"What do you mean?" Isabel frowned and took no

notice of his presence.

Veronica sighed. "Lesbianism has shock value because it's taboo, secret. People are afraid of what they don't know. They form negative opinions about us—they either condemn us or crack jokes about us. They might even consider lesbians and gays a totally different species, like subhuman—"

"Roni—"

"Let her talk." Frank kept his eyes on his sister.

"—but the only genuine difference is our attraction to our own sex. Isabel, all we want is to love and be loved. What's wrong with that? Did Joanna and I ever hurt anyone by loving each other? Think it over. Steve's the one who's causing harm—not me, not Joanna. If Larry and Teddy had known the truth, they could've stood up to Steve. They could've said, 'yes, my sister was a lesbian. So what?' Instead, they got into a macho brawl, defending Joanna's 'honor.'"

No one spoke for several moments. Frank absently twirled his wedding band around his finger. Veronica watched him and Isabel, wondering who would respond first. She had thought of Joanna's mother as an ally—now she could no longer be sure.

Isabel wiped her eyes. "One of the boys at the playground was Jimmy Gomez. He lives next door to your parents. Sara and Joe will find out about this."

Veronica's head throbbed. "I've thought long and hard about telling them. Guess I'm going to have to."

"Think about it some more, Roni," her brother urged.

"How do you think your parents will feel when they hear the rumors? They're so active in the Church. Think about *them*."

"Don't pressure her, Isabel. It's *her* decision."

"I'm speaking as a mother."

"I'm not arguing with you. All I'm saying is, my parents gave me a hell of a time when I decided to remarry; religion sure didn't make them very charitable towards Joyce, so I can't see them being too receptive to Roni's news either." He picked up his coffee mug and took a quick sip. "As for Steve, I don't know if his parents are even aware of what he's been up to, but it involves my son and my sister. That kid needs someone to turn him around. You're welcome to come with me when I go talk to him."

Isabel sighed. "When?"

"Soon as I bring Phil home. After listening to you, I don't want to put it off any longer."

Isabel reached for her handbag, ready to leave. "I'll talk to Rita on my own."

"Frank, I really wish—" Veronica cut herself off. Too exhausted to argue, she was determined to remind him later that not only parental and religious issues were involved in the situation, but also homophobia and sexism. At the moment, she was unsure of where she stood with Isabel and preferred to lie low.

"Steve's dealt with me before, Roni—he knows I mean business. He just can't keep shooting off his mouth."

"Guess Dad's really going to let Steve have it." Phil leaned on Veronica while she laboriously helped him to the terrace. Bored with being cooped up in the hospital, he had looked forward to soaking up some afternoon sunshine at home.

She eased him into a chair. "Do you think Steve's parents know what's been going on?"

"Naaa." The boy unwound the headset wires of his

Walkman. "The whole thing gives me the creeps."

Veronica sat beside him, René's screenplay in hand. She felt uneasy about letting her brother deal with Steve Martinez, and angry with herself for again neglecting to ask Isabel for the Mexico City letters. "I should've gone with Frank."

The boy selected a cassette and popped it into the Walkman. "Roni, Dad wanted to handle it himself."

She propped her stiff leg on an opposite chair, knowing she definitely had to get out of the habit of relying on Frank. He liked the caregiver role and family members were willing to acquiesce, but he needed reminding that he had his own family unit to be concerned about these days.

She opened the screenplay to its first page and glanced at Phil while he adjusted his headset. "Why didn't you tell me about the *Penthouse* pictures?"

He looked uneasy. "I thought you'd get mad."

"Phil, it would've made more sense if you'd told me." She tapped a pencil against the three-ring binder. "I couldn't understand why Steve'd suddenly started talking to you about me. Now it all falls into place. Don't ever be scared to tell me anything."

"Do you hate Steve?"

"No. He tries to be such a know-it-all, but he really doesn't know much. How do *you* feel about him?"

He grimaced. "He's a geek. It was bad enough what he said about you. He didn't have to tell Larry and Teddy about Joanna—especially in front of other kids. No wonder they jumped him."

She squeezed his skinny knee. "At least you didn't try that."

"You think I'm crazy? He could clobber me. Anyhow, Dad raised me to be non-violent," he added in an apparent afterthought.

Veronica tweaked his cheek and opened the screen-play. "Tell me if you need anything, Philly."

He readjusted his headset. "Gotcha."

The telephone summoned her inside.

"Is your crotch still wet?" René joked.

"Yours probably is." She tingled at hearing that smoky voice, imagining the suggestive gleam in those ebony eyes.

"Do you want to find out?"

Veronica decided to be brusque. She had to remind herself that she had made love with Siena that very morning, and she was not about to let René Talamantes bulldoze her. "Why are you calling, anyway?"

René chuckled. She did not seem surprised by Veronica's attitude. "I'm editing some footage in Melnitz. Want to see a flick tonight?"

"No.

"Why not?"

"I'm busy, René. Anyway, I thought you wanted comments on your screenplay. I've just started reading it—never expected it to be a Western."

Talamantes seemed willing to play along. "From a Chicana's point of view, preciosa. It has a contemporary Southwestern flavor. I write what I know, city girl. You like it so far?"

"Haven't read much yet."

"So take a break with me tonight."

Veronica toyed with the phone wire. "I'd rather pass on that."

"Cómo eres, Verónica."

"Phil's just back from the hospital." She picked up a pencil and began to doodle.

"So? His papacito's home. Why do you have to hang around, too?" She paused. "Never mind—I get it. You're 'busy' with Siena." She let out an exasperated sigh. "Listen, you're not married to that gabacha. Exactly how long've you known her?"

Not answering, Veronica drew a labrys on the notepad.

"I'll pick you up at 7:00."

"René, I'm not going."

"Hasta luego." Talamantes clicked off.

Hurling the screenplay across the livingroom, Veronica vented her frustration further by breaking her pencil in half.

As he unlocked the door, Frank ducked when the vinyl binder crashed into the wall inches from his head. "You have to break that habit, Roni. Too dangerous to my health."

"It's your own damn fault for walking in." Grudgingly, she retrieved the binder and smoothed its crinkled pages.

He paused on his way to the kitchen. "Phil giving you a hard time?"

"No. It's that idiot René. She asked me out tonight."

"That's why you practically decapitated me? Why don't you go? You're a free agent. Do you and Siena have any plans?"

She glared.

"By the looks of you, the answer is 'no.' Do me a favor and split. Phil and I need some time together."

At the dinner table, the three of them hunched over their pizzas.

"Steve stood right in front of me and denied everything. Said he'd never spread any rumors about you, Roni. Said Phil left on Saturday without even telling him. I looked him straight in the eye and said he was lying."

Phil gulped. "What'd his Mom say?"

"She called me a bully and told me to quit picking on him. Can you believe that?" Frank shook his head and grabbed another slice.

"Doesn't really surprise me," Veronica said. "Remember that time Steve broke the bathroom window and tried to blame it on Phil? The fool didn't realize I'd seen him throw the baseball. He never did pay Mom and Dad for the damage. And you were willing to take the rap, Philly."

"I was kind of a dumb kid," He admitted.

His father gazed at him fondly. "No, you're big-hearted, that's all. What you need to learn is how to gauge who to open your heart to. A kid like Steve takes advantage, Phil. Hell, why shouldn't he? His parents back him up all the way." He sipped more Lowenbrau. "I wonder what Rita'll say when she hears Isabel's version."

"She'll be true to form." Veronica touched his arm. "Frank, at least you tried."

"Did my knight in shining armor bit." He sighed. "What's your verdict, Phil?"

The boy studied the cartoons and doodles on his cast-bound arm. "Steve isn't really my friend any more, and—that makes me sad."

His father patted his shoulder consolingly.

"Hi. Where are you?" Wincing, Veronica heard the false vibrancy in her own voice.

Over the phone, Siena sounded oddly unanimated. "Still at work. My dad's friend Jack invited me to dinner. I

186

really can't refuse since he got me this job. I'm not sure when I'll be home. Veronica. Wish I could talk longer, but I have to run. Bye."

Veronica hesitated, then put down the receiver. Siena's hurried tone bothered her enough to cause a quick decision. "Frank—"

He looked up from tidying the dinner table.

"You'll get your chance to meet René. I'm going with her, after all."

"I always wanted un hermano mayor," Talamantes said. They sat in her VW van, waiting for the traffic light to change. "Frank seems like a cool dude."

"I rely on him a *lot*."

"Isn't that what brothers are for?" For a change, René drove less recklessly. She took the residential route along Ohio Avenue to the campus. "You don't seem too feisty tonight. Qué pasó, eh?"

Veronica was too emotionally fatigued for verbal sparring. Isabel's morning revelations and Siena's sudden dinner invitation had disturbed her, but she was not about to confide that to Talamantes. "Sometimes I wish I was a hermit."

"So you'd have more time to write? Preciosa, if you and I were together, you'd have plenty. I'd be working on my own stuff, off shooting somewhere, maybe doing some editing, and you'd be doing your own thing. When I'd get home, we'd spend all night—"

"I get the picture."

"Doesn't that appeal to you?".

"I'm thinking about going away."

"Have a lot on your mind, huh?" René looked at her with concern. "Á dónde vas?"

"Santa Barbara. My sister Lucy's a Carmelite and she's invited me to her convent."

"*You* in a convent? Ay, Dios! The nuns'll be as horny as diablitas."

Veronica found herself smiling. "You're crazy."

"That usually makes me irresistible." Talamantes offered a toothy grin. "But it hasn't worked too well with you."

Veronica noticed René had driven past several Westwood movie theaters. "What are we—"

"We're seeing a private screening of *Lianna.*"

"Where?" She looked at her suspiciously.

"In one of the Melnitz screening rooms—just you and me."

"No."

"Yes."

"So help me, René—I'll jump right out of this van." She grabbed the door handle, but lacked the nerve to turn it. She despised being manipulated, though she could not deny how much la Tejana excited her.

Talamantes gently touched Veronica's arm. "And risk breaking more bones? Don't be an idiota."

Veronica did not pull away. "It just isn't fair that you keep luring me—"

"Who's luring? Did I force you into my van? Mira, que loca es esta mujer!"

Veronica would not allow herself to laugh. "Quit turning into Ricky Ricardo. Just tell me why you're doing this. I suppose you think I encouraged you yesterday."

"Didn't you?"

Veronica decided not to answer. She kept her eyes on the winding campus road.

René zoomed the van past the Law School and around the bend. "Hey, don't get uptight. I just want to see the film with you. Come on, mujer. When's the last time you saw it?"

Veronica's voice was quiet. "Joanna and I saw it together—and it hurts too much to remember that."

"Oh." René turned the van into the north campus parking structure and found a spot near the entrance. "Por favor, no llores, preciosa."

Veronica exhaled slowly, trying to will her tears away.

Talamantes seemed at a loss, but eventually broke the silence. "Would you rather see outtakes from 'Tortilleras'?"

Veronica met her questioning eyes. After a moment, she relented. "Sure. I'm sorry—about the other."

"Hey, don't be. There's lots of footage I didn't use. You're the only one who'll ever see it."

They sat side by side in the projection room, and Veronica remained ever conscious of Talamantes's presence. She enjoyed watching René in her element, selecting the film, threading it through the projector. She especially liked how easily René had compromised, something Veronica had not expected. That willingness had offered an intriguing glimpse of another side of la Tejana.

When René flipped off the lights, Veronica sipped a Coke and began to focus on the outtakes. The Latinas in the film were dark and lovely.

"Where'd you find them, René?"

"They're both dance majors on campus." She took a swig of 7-Up. "Rosalinda y Beatriz. I dated one for a while."

Veronica was not surprised. "Which?"

"Rosalinda—la chaparrita."

"You mean, the prettier one." She smiled when René

did not deny that. Veronica stared at the screen, captivated again by the women's stylized movements. Their graceful bodies and sultry faces exuded sexuality, and she recalled the excitement she and Michi had experienced the night they had seen "Tortilleras." "Where is she now?"

"Back in Albuquerque."

"Are you over her?"

"Huh? Hey—it wasn't serious, preciosa." Talamantes glanced at her. "What's with all these questions?"

"You've asked *me* plenty."

René laughed. "What *else* do you want to know?"

"Well, I was wondering—who made their costumes?"

"Mi mamá. She works in the garment district downtown." René clicked her soda can to Veronica's. "She'd like you."

"How does she feel about your—girlfriends?"

"She usually likes the Chicanas."

"I suppose there've been lots."

"You're the one I've been waiting for."

Veronica decided to ignore that. She tried to focus on the outtakes. "I can see why you didn't use this footage. It's jerky in parts."

"Probably 'cause I started dancing while filming. I got a little carried away." René put down her soda. "Did you get a chance to finish reading 'Adobe'?"

"Not yet. I wasn't about to drop everything for it." She leaned back. "I really like the old woman narrator, though. She adds an authentic touch."

"She's based on mi abuelita." Talamantes hesitated. "She died right before Mamá and me moved to California and—"

"You were close to her."

"Yeah." René's voice quivered. "Sorry. Haven't talked about Nanita in a long time."

"I understand." Veronica found herself wanting to hold her, soothe her.

"I know you do." Talamantes sighed. "You don't talk about Joanna much either. I hear she was really something."

"The subject was your grandmother, not—"

"Verónica, you can trust me. When you're ready to talk about Joanna, I'm right here. And when I'm ready to talk about mi abuelita, I hope you'll be around for me. I can be a real pendeja sometimes, but give me a chance, okay? I'm on your side, and I know it can't be easy to be as closeted as you are. Once in a while, you need to lean on—"

"No. I need to stand on my own, René."

"So why's that redhead around?"

"If you're going to start that again—" Veronica stood up abruptly.

"Cálmate, mujer." René got up, too, standing close. "I just don't get it, that's all."

"I don't have to explain anything to you."

"De veras. Siena's just—not your type."

Veronica started to move away. "I'm taking the bus home."

"Wait a minute." Talamantes reached the door first and leaned against it. "I'll drop it, all right?"

Veronica faced her. "I don't know why I waste time on you. You never mind your own business, and you're such—"

"An incredibly sexy, talented Chicana film maker." René's ebony eyes sparkled.

"Sure. That's why Rosalinda went to Albuquerque."

"Low blow, Verónica."

"You asked for it."

She touched Veronica's hand with her fingertip. "How

about a truce, huh? We were talking about 'Adobe' and really got sidetracked—éjole! I'm going to have to rewind the film. It's almost to the end, and you're not even watching it." She quickly went back to the projector.

With some reluctance, Veronica slumped into her seat. As frustrating as René could be, she was not maddening enough to make an evening bus ride seem appealing. Veronica watched her concentrating on her task with the same intensity which characterized her other actions. Though exasperated, Veronica could not help but be intrigued by that single-mindedness.

"Do you live with your mother, René?" she finally asked.

Talamantes looked up and seemed relieved at the question. "Have to. I'm a poor student, remember? We found a house in Venice that has a separate entrance. That helps. Mama's not too crazy about mujeres staying over." Although the film rolled again, Talamantes did not remove her eyes from Veronica's. "You and Joanna had your own place, I hear."

She nodded. Michi had been at it again. "Joanna's parents paid half the rent; Frank and my parents paid the other half. They didn't want us to work our way through college. Sometimes I feel guilty about that."

"Well, don't. How about your sisters? Did they get the same deal?"

"No. Lucy went into the convent right after high school. Angela went to Santa Monica College, which is practically free, then got married. Frank and I are the UCLA grads."

René stepped away from the projector. "You're not watching the film, Verónica."

"'Cause I'm looking at you."

Talamantes came nearer. "And what do you see?"

Veronica felt as if she could study that compelling face all night. "A Chicana virago."

René was amused. "What else?"

"A talented woman with vision—sometimes charming, mostly maddening. And whether I've wanted to or not, I've thought about her constantly since yesterday—"

"Really? You sure didn't say so a little while ago." Talamantes' deep-set eyes grew more sultry. "Gave your libido a workout, huh?"

Veronica was grateful for the room's dimness because she felt herself blush to her roots; but her eyes remained riveted to hers. René sank into the next seat, lanky legs spread before her in their faded jeans and scuffed boots. For a long moment, Veronica looked at her.

"Will you just listen?" She touched her index finger to Talamantes' slightly parted lips. "Somehow, whenever you're around, I wind up asking myself questions—about everything. And I'm beginning to think I need to do more of that."

"Sure can't argue with that, preciosa."

Slowly, Veronica reached over and slid her hand atop hers. She liked the warmth of those slender fingers, the almost identical shade of brown of their hands. Very naturally, it seemed, Talamantes placed her other hand over Veronica's, covering it. Leaning closer, René's mouth beckoned. Still holding hands, they kissed, more tenderly than Veronica had ever imagined. Their soft lips parted and their tongues met shyly. René's long eyelashes grazed Veronica's cheeks, fluttering at that delicious contact.

"I thought you'd be different," Veronica whispered.

"How?"

"Rough—I don't know."

"Michi said you figured I was into S/M."

"Are you?"

"No, preciosa."

"Right answer."

"You really thought I was?"

Veronica traced those brown fingers again. "René, I never know what to expect from you, but I love the way you kiss."

"De veras. Things've been rough enough for you, Verónica. You don't need any more of that from me, too." She smoothed Veronica's curly tendrils from her moist forehead. "It's really warm in here."

"I don't care. Let's stay awhile. There's so much I want to tell you—months' worth."

"Tell me everything."

After hours of non-stop conversation and intermittent kissing in the screening room, Veronica turned to her when René halted the van behind the condominium complex.

"I think—I want to see you when I come back from Santa Barbara."

"Yo quiero lo mismo, but I guess you've known that for a while."

"You haven't kept it a secret."

"Not exactly." René pushed back her black hair and smiled. "Don't forget to phone Sister Lucy tomorrow. Is it okay if I call you at noon?"

Veronica nodded and touched Talamantes' hand. "I'd like that. Good night."

With no hesitation, René held her once more and they kissed gently, briefly. "Buenas noches, preciosa."

Reluctantly, Veronica left the van and blew her another kiss. When she passed the carports, she noticed Siena's Accord was gone. Somehow, that did not matter. She unlocked the gate, waved to René once more, and stepped inside.

14

V ERONICA LAY STILL, listening to her steady but rapid, heartbeats. Not ready for sleep, she allowed her fingers to course along her body, tracing its familiar angles, its feminine secrets. She wished René would touch her so, to know her intimately, and she wanted to probe Talamantes' inventive mind, to love her long brown body. She remembered the magical touch of René's lips, passionate yet tender, and she knew she was falling in love with that quirky, magnetic mujer. But why? René lacked Joanna's serenity, her tactfulness, her levelheadedness. Yet she pulsed with energy, ideas and humor, sharing visions of Chicana creativity. In that, Veronica knew she had found a soulmate.

In the screening room, René had behaved differently, less aggressively than she had at La Cabana. Alone with Veronica, René had been willing to show her vulnerability, her tenderness—but not for too long, it seemed. She preferred to use humor and candor to shield herself, but Veronica was learning to see beyond that. Smiling, she remembered Talamantes' self-description: wild woman from Texas. That she was—tantalizing, unnerving.

Veronica's thoughts drifted to Siena. Would she stay out all night? Had she sensed Veronica's increasing disinterest? From the beginning, Veronica had recognized Siena's heterosexuality, but the possibility that she had acted on that caused less disappointment than anticipated.

One thing was certain: Veronica had to talk with her soon.

Unwilling to contemplate that, she closed her eyes and continued fingering herself, fantasizing about René. She imagined her near, joking, teasing kisses eventually becoming ardent, her hands thrilling. And, at last, satisfied, Veronica slept.

She phoned Siena in the morning; there was no answer. Without pausing, Veronica dialed the Convent of St. Teresa. Following a laugh-punctuated conversation with Lucy, she felt rejuvenated and headed for the pool.

The crisp morning air belied mid-July. Veronica enjoyed the solitude of her early swim. The warm water melted her customary stiffness; the resulting pliability of her body matched the increasing flexibility of her heart and mind. Panting but refreshed, she bundled into her terrycloth robe and hurried upstairs.

"Buenas dias." Her cheery greeting seemed to startle Frank and Phil when they drowsily wandered into the kitchen. "How about flapjacks for breakfast, hombres?"

They looked skeptical, accustomed to her morning testiness.

"What's in the pool—PCP?" Phil quipped.

She laughed and pinched his cheek. "Nope. I'm leaving for Santa Barbara on Sunday. Lucy says there won't be a room available till then." She flipped a pancake on the griddle.

"We can drive you there, Roni."

"Big brother, your wife'll be here tomorrow. You need to stay home. Anyhow, I've already figured out the transportation."

When Frank gave her a sly look, she blushed.

"Can't believe you're really going." Phil took a stack of hotcakes from her. "Won't you get bored?"

"Not if I can finish the next three stories there. I want Zamora off my back." She doused her pancakes with a generous flow of maple syrup. "Of course, I'll have to spend some time with Lucy, too."

"Yeah, don't forget about her," Frank drawled. "I'm really glad you've decided to get away. Who knows what'll happen with this Steve Martínez jazz? It could all blow over, or the whole town could wind up gossiping."

"Do you think Steve'll keep on spreading rumors?" Phil frowned. His facial bruises had begun to fade.

"They aren't rumors." Sometimes Veronica wondered if her whole family suffered from collective denial.

"He said you sleep with all your girlfriends and—"

"I *am* a lesbian, Phil. If Steve confronts you again, I don't want you to lie. I never should've let you cover for me in the first place."

"Let's take it easy here," Frank interrupted. "Both of you did the right thing by not giving Mom and Dad all the details. Roni, whether or not you tell them is *your* decision. You can't expect us to tell them or anyone else for you."

"I just don't like the lying." She stabbed a pancake sliver with her fork.

"Then the question is: are you willing to face up to the responsibilities of the truth?"

Her eyes met his. "That's one of the reasons why I'm leaving—to find out."

When René telephoned at noon, Veronica set aside the screenplay and sprawled across the bed, receiver in hand.

"Let's work tonight. I'm leaving for sure on Sunday."

"How long will you be gone?"

Veronica rolled over, stretching her stiff leg. "A few weeks. I plan to get lots done there, and I sure don't want to come back and stay with the newlyweds. I'll need my own space again."

"Oh." Talamantes cleared her throat; she stayed silent for a few seconds. "Well—what'd you think of 'Adobe'?"

"I have tons of ideas about dialog changes—a whole sheaf of notes for you."

"Didn't you like *any* of my dialog?" René sounded a bit defensive.

"Talamantes, I'm not going to discuss it now." Veronica curled her bare toes and tried to imagine the expression on René's face. "I'll tell you one thing: the storyline is marvelous."

La Tejana's laugh was full of relief.

"You don't have to take all my suggestions either."

"Who said I would? But I'm damn curious to hear them. Verónica—"

"Yes?"

"I'll never forget last night."

Suddenly, she felt shy. "Listen, come over around 7:00. Frank and Phil are going to my parents' to watch the ballgame. You'll behave, won't you?'"

"I keep my promises, preciosa. Hasta luego."

Veronica remained reclining, her mind alive with images of René. Her brother's abrupt rap brought her back to earth, and she limped to the door.

"Didn't hear your typewriter so—"

"You want to talk." She was not surprised. "Where's Phil?"

"Would you believe taking a nap? He's bummed out." Frank moved the screenplay and sat on the edge of the bed.

"You'd be, too, if you'd just lost your best friend, your favorite aunt admitted to being a lesbian, and your brand-new stepmother was flying in tomorrow. Not to mention whatever he's feeling about Siena."

Frank reclined against the pillows. "He's rattled about your going, too."

"He figured I'd be around when Joyce flies in. He has to get used to her, Frank, sooner or later."

"He doesn't realize she's just as jittery as he is."

"Tell him that."

"We've talked a lot since I've been back." Dressed almost identically to his sister, in shorts and a T-shirt, Frank changed into a sitting position. "Roni, I don't want you to get the wrong idea, but I'm relieved you're leaving."

"Get the trouble-makin' dyke out of town, huh?"

"Maybe it seems that way, but the fact is I'm being selfish. I want Joyce, Phil and me to get off to a good start. Right now, I'd like him to concentrate on Joyce, not you." Frank's manner was earnest, but Veronica did not like the direction he took. "He loves you, Roni. There's no question of that. But he's seeing a different side of you, and it's going to take some getting used to. You're right about Siena. She's played a big part in this. The kid's been hurt, in more ways than one. He needs some time to heal."

Her shoulders tense, Veronica picked up the screenplay and plopped it on the desk. "I want my apartment ready by August 1."

"Roni, I'm not trying to get rid of you."

"You just said you're relieved—"

"Look, I've been more than fair. Give me the same treatment, all right?" His dark eyes remained intent on hers. "You're just as hardheaded as Mom. No wonder you two butt heads all the time."

"Don't yell at me." Turning her back, she stared out the window at the shimmering pool. At that moment, she wished she were underwater, away from his candor.

Rounding the bed, he stood near and touched her shoulder. "I'm not yelling, honey."

"*Don't* call me 'honey.'"

"Will you look at me, at least?"

Grudgingly, she faced him. "What?"

"I admire your guts."

"What're you talking about?" She wished he would leave her alone.

"You're not waiting as long as I did to find someone to love."

She softened a bit. "Frank, you had Phil to raise. You couldn't exactly—"

"Mom and Dad brought him up. I was on automatic pilot for years. I don't even know how I functioned. But you—you're not wasting any time."

Her hackles rose again. "Are you implying that you loved Connie more than I loved Joanna?"

"Will you get rid of that damn chip on your shoulder? Jesus! I'm not implying anything. Just listen to me." His eyes bored into hers. "You're tough. You fought death by coming out of the coma. You've been through months of physical therapy. And all through that, you've pushed yourself, over and over again. Hell, I wish I could be as tough as you."

She felt close to tears at hearing the admiration in his voice. "I couldn't give up because—I didn't want to disappoint you and Phil."

"You haven't, Roni. And you never will as long as you're true to yourself."

*

201

From the bedroom doorway, she noticed Phil had removed Siena's photos from his bulletin board. Flat on his back, his fractured arm outstretched, the dozing boy seemed vulnerable in a tank top and Hawaiian print shorts, his thin legs dotted with bruises. He moaned in his sleep, about to roll over, but impeded by the awkward cast. Veronica moved toward him on reflex, and he awakened.

"Thought you were going to hurt yourself."

"What were you staring at?" He sounded grouchy.

She smiled, mindful of his mood. "Sometimes I forget how much you've grown. You're almost too long for this bed."

When he tried to sit up, she rearranged his pillows.

"Roni, why do you have to leave town?"

"To do some work, for one thing. And to give the three of you some privacy." She touched his knee. "I'm not abandoning you."

"You're running away."

She sighed. "I guess it looks like that, but Lucy's offer came at the perfect time." She raised her eyes to his; they were as candid as his father's. "If you were me, what would you do?"

"I'd be scared."

"So am I. And I think Siena is, too. I haven't seen her since yesterday morning."

He did not reply, his brow furrowed.

Veronica decided to share his honesty. "I think you're scared, too, Phil."

His mouth twitched. "Lay off, okay?"

"I mean—about Joyce. Do you want to talk?"

He shook his head, looking away.

"If you change your mind, I'll be here till Sunday."

"I know." He rubbed the rough surface of his cast. Decorated with family signatures and cartoon characters drawn by Michi, its colorful appearance contrasted with his somber expression.

She moved towards the door. "Frank's in the pool. Yell if you want anything."

He nodded, and she edged away, troubled by his broodiness.

After an hours-long burst of productivity, Veronica turned off her typewriter. Within minutes, she moved rhythmically in the pool, her slender arms and legs propelling her along its length. She left personal and family problems aside and immersed herself in the serenity of the turquoise water. Yet she remained alert enough to hear the abrupt swing of the wrought iron gate and the rapid click of high heels on the flagstones.

"Siena—" Veronica caught her breath and slowly raised herself to the pool's rim. "—do you have a minute?"

"Of course." She paused halfway to her condo's entrance, provocative in a clingy mini.

Tugging on her robe, Veronica approached. She did not look forward to their conversation, but there was no point in postponing it. "I phoned you this morning."

Siena's face colored and she dropped her housekeys. With some effort, Veronica bent to retrieve them. She unlocked the door, letting Siena enter first.

Siena tossed her tapestry satchel on a nearby chair and whirled to face her. "I didn't come home."

"I noticed your car was gone when René dropped me off."

"René?" Her fair complexion retained its sudden flush. "Yes."

"I see." Siena bit her lower lip. "Well, I can't lie to

you. I was with—a man."

"I thought so."

"You don't even sound angry! I'm *furious* with myself for being so stupid! You'd think by now I would've learned something. I wasn't even prepared." She sank to the sofa, holding her head in her hands.

"Oh." Veronica grasped her meaning, but felt detached. She sat on the sofa's arm and wiped one foot with the hem of her robe.

"I don't even have a doctor in this shitty town."

Veronica wished she were back in the pool. She sat quietly and did not know if she could cope with another crisis.

"Oh, Veronica." Siena looked up. "I'm so—sorry."

Veronica moved to kneel beside her. "Was it because of—Saturday?"

Siena's hazel eyes were tear-filled, and she spoke in breathy gulps. "I can't forget the way Phil looked at us that night. I wake up and see his face, the horror on it. And at the hospital on Monday, he was so uncomfortable with me." She wiped her eyes with her fingertips. "I love being with you—but I don't know if I could ever get used to—it. You thrive in that woman-only environment—you belong there. I don't." She sobbed, choking on her words. "I don't know where the hell I belong."

Veronica held her, unwilling to interrupt.

"I slept with the first man who was nice to me—my father's friend, for God's sake. I feel awful about it—and Jack's a decent guy, too."

"You needed male approval after what happened Saturday."

"Veronica, will you quit analyzing me?" Flustered, Siena rose and stalked across the room. "He wanted to fuck, and I went along."

Veronica flinched. "Did he rape you?"

"Of course not. You know how I am about sex. Once I get started—"

"I don't want any details." Veronica got to her feet.

Siena continued pacing. "As usual, I wasn't thinking."

Resuming her seat on the sofa arm, Veronica wondered if Siena had turned to her in a similar fashion— because she "wasn't thinking"? She tried to dismiss that; it reminded her of her own impulsiveness. "Are you going to see him again?"

"Every day at work. I can't exactly avoid him." Siena kicked off her pumps and sank into the leather chair, averting her eyes. "So—is it over—between us?"

Veronica tightened the belt of her robe. "I came to tell you I'm going away."

"What?"

"Lucy's invited me for a visit. My mother thinks I'll wreak havoc in the convent. René's opinion was a little more graphic."

Siena's tears were still evident. "You told *her* before telling me."

"We talked about a lot last night."

"Did you sleep with her?"

"No." Veronica looked at her. "Not that I didn't want to. I just felt it was better to wait. I wanted to settle things with you—and I didn't want to plunge into anything else."

"How gallant." Siena wiped her eyes. "You were attracted to her right away. I don't understand why."

Veronica crossed her leg and rubbed its scar, remembering how Siena had never commented on it. "I'm trying to figure it out, myself. Maybe it's because we're both Chicanas." She wound one end of the terrycloth belt around her fingers. "Anyhow—going away makes sense.

I need time to finish my stories—and to think. In the meantime, I'm putting everything here on hold."

"Including me."

"No. Siena, I *don't* want you to wait for me. You need to find out what you really want. I can't help you with that, but I value your friendship, and always will."

Siena reached out to touch her, and Veronica was still moved by those familiar fingers.

"I remember the first time you kissed me. It was such a glorious experience—so unexpected, so right. I've always felt safe with you, Veronica," she added, her voice breaking.

Eyes moist, Veronica attempted to smile. "*You* held me together the night of Phil's accident. And if you could do that for me, you can do it for yourself, too."

Needing solitude, she swam the pool's length again, her tears coalescing with the calm water. The daily exercise had firmed her strokes, invigorating flaccid muscles. With increased stamina, she was able to prolong the swim, allowing herself precious moments to feel as one in mind and body. Never much of an athlete, she had gained confidence in her improved muscle tone, her burgeoning physical strength. She wondered if she had gained emotionally as well.

After months of grief and pain, Veronica could not forget how easily she and Siena had come together. Had that happened because Siena had been as needy? Desire had obliterated Veronica's fleeting doubts about becoming involved with the new neighbor. From the beginning, Siena had aroused her sense of protectiveness; only Joanna had previously provoked that. Veronica had experienced such feelings towards René only once—when Talamantes had spoken of her deceased grandmother. Otherwise, the film student had given the impression of being able to take care of herself; Veronica found that tremendously attractive.

But she pushed thoughts of René aside; the evening would be time for that. Instead, she contemplated Siena's confusion and tendency to engage in self-destructive behavior. Veronica was no psychologist, but she realized homophobia explained much of Siena's motivation. Yet she remained grateful to her, remembering her warmth and playfulness. Without that vital connection, Veronica knew she would have been unprepared to cope with the emotional challenge of René Talamantes.

She showered and primped. Facing the mirror, she wondered what Talamantes found appealing. She stood on tiptoes, wishing she were taller, noticing her perm needed recurling. She tried to fluff it, to give herself an extra inch of height, but her hair remained uncooperative.

In disgust, she gave up and puttered through the living room, punching sofa pillows, straightening books on the shelves, plucking yellowed leaves from the scrawny philodendron. On impulse, she dialed Michi's number, needing to hear her jokes, only to be told by Mrs. Yamada that her daughter was out for the evening—with the dental hygienist, no doubt. Veronica thanked her and hung up.

Noting smudge marks on the glass-topped coffee table, she decided to respray it. Intent on that task, she jumped at hearing the doorbell. She stashed the Windex bottle and paper towel beneath the sofa, smoothed her white cotton shorts and "Zoot Suit" T-shirt, and went to the door.

"Que linda te ves." René handed her a pint of Baskin-Robbins chocolate raspberry truffle. In khaki shorts with numerous pockets, a safari-type shirt and huaraches, she carried a notepad and the inevitable hemp bag dangled from her shoulder.

"René, I thought we were going to work."

"We'll need at least one break." Finding her screenplay spread on the coffee table, she settled herself on the sofa.

Veronica was determined to relegate self-consciousness to the background and concentrate on the work ahead. She flipped open the screenplay and gathered her notes. Talamantes's smoldering eyes never left her face.

"Quit staring and focus on what I'm saying," She uttered in exasperation a few minutes later.

Laughing, René held out her hands. "I'm used to looking at whoever's talking to me. And I *am* focused, mujer."

"So what did I say?"

"La viejita sometimes sounds too contemporary—her speech ought to be flavored with Southwest colloquialisms." It was Talamantes's turn to be exasperated. "If I go that route, I'll wind up with a bilingual screenplay."

"That's a definite possibility. What's wrong with that? Zamora's always after me to write bilingual dialog."

"Was hoping to be a little more commercial this time."

"The old woman's English would be strongly influenced by Spanish, Ms. Tejana." Veronica tapped the page with the pencil. "That's my opinion."

René shrugged. "It's valid. I'll think it over."

"Okay. Next item—the transition into the first flashback."

"Now I'm really in for it." Talamantes slumped, long legs outstretched. "Fire away."

And so it went that evening. They challenged each other's perceptions and argued over fine points of dialog and plot development. Veronica thrilled to the verbal frays, the creative wrangles. With equal gusto, René held her ground, never losing sight of her original premise.

Throughout, Veronica recognized that beyond the sexual attraction lay the strong likelihood of collaborative writing; she felt ecstatic—and terrified.

15

"ARE YOU AND SIENA still friends?" At The Sizzler, Phil leaned back while the waitress served his steak and shrimp platter.

"I think so." Veronica paused, waiting for her order of hibachi chicken. She noted her nephew's awkwardness with the utensils. Moving the Pepsi out of his way, she watched his patient attempts at cutting the steak. "You're becoming a pro at that, Phil."

"Takes practice." He grinned, at last munching a morsel.

"So you want to hear about Siena?"

"Sure."

"I knew from the beginning she was lonely—and so was I." Veronica spread gobs of sour cream on her baked potato. "It's hard to explain, but I think I needed to be connected with another woman in order to start putting Joanna behind me."

She wondered if it were foolhardy to open herself to Phil; she did not want to give the impression of flitting from one woman to another. Yet she wanted to be honest with him, to at last be herself.

"Siena needed me as much as I needed her." She watched him fumble with the utensils again. "And now— I guess our needs have been met, and it's time to move on."

"I don't get it, Roni."

"Relationships can be very complicated. When you start dating, muchacho, you'll find out."

"Sure have a lot to look forward to." He smirked and gazed out the window. A couple of long-haired skateboarders zoomed by. "I really liked Siena."

"There's no reason why you can't still be friends with her. She cares about you, Phil."

"Feels weird to be around her."

She leaned closer. "Do you feel that with me, too?"

"Sometimes." He picked up his Pepsi and kept his eyes on the noontime traffic and the office workers crowding into Carlos and Pepe's across the street. "With Siena, I feel—I don't know."

"Maybe you feel—betrayed—that she was involved with me."

He shrugged, intent on his meal. For several minutes, they ate in silence. She knew better than to prod him.

He jabbed a potato skin with his fork. "How will I ever know if a girl I like is—a lesbian?"

"Phil, I can only speak from my own experience." She did not want to lecture him, but was not about to dismiss his question either. "Teenagers have a lot to face at once—body changes, peer pressures, sex. Gay and lesbian kids really have trouble fitting in, so they might try to hide their feelings and act like everyone else. Eventually, it catches up with them."

She picked up her fork and poked at a mushroom in her salad. "I was lucky 'cause I had Joanna. I never paid much attention to boys. I was so hooked on keeping up my grades and getting into UCLA that no one noticed I didn't date." She sighed. "But Joanna's gone now, and I'm trying to figure out the rest of my life. Before the accident, I felt like an adult sometimes. Nowadays, it's like I've regressed to adolescence."

"What if some guy asked you for a date?"

"I'd tell him the truth."

"You look so regular, Roni." He stared at her.

She laughed. "I look like *you*, wise guy. Everyone says so."

"Do *I* look gay?"

"Oh, honey. Is that what's bothering you?" She noticed how swiftly he ducked his head to study the table top. "Phil, talk to me."

When he looked up, she saw his brown eyes were perplexed. "How do you know if you're gay or not? I like girls, but I've never—"

"If you were gay, Phil, you'd be sexually attracted to boys. Is that what you're feeling?"

He seemed relieved. "Heck, no. I can't even imagine wanting to kiss somebody like Steve Martínez."

She laughed. "I can't either."

"Know what?" Phil smiled. "I understand about lesbians more than I do about gay guys. I mean, lots of women're really awesome—like Siena. Sort of makes sense how you'd be attracted to her. You're not exactly ugly yourself, and you look slick in a bathing suit. Even Steve said that."

"Talk about a back-handed compliment," she teased, nonetheless touched by his assessment. "I don't quite understand about gay men, either. But then I'm biased towards women."

"Me, too." He popped a a cherry tomato into his mouth. "Roni, if I ever have a girlfriend and you think she might be a lesbian, will you tell me?"

"That'd be really awkward, Phil. What if I were wrong?"

"Would you just mention it—if it ever happens?"

"Listen, don't get obsessed with this. I'm not a one-woman patrol for Future Dykes of America."

He hurled a potato skin at her.

To cope with Joyce's luggage, Frank had borrowed his parents' sedan. Veronica parked behind it, rounding the Z to assist Phil with his record store purchases.

"Looks like Joyce's here." The boy winced as he emerged from the sports car.

"Be careful." Knowing his taped ribs were painful, she let him lean on her.

"Roni, how long do I have to be sociable?"

"Give her a chance, okay?"

"Yeah, yeah."

A haphazard pile of luggage lay in the midst of the living room.

"They're probably in bed."

Veronica ignored his sarcastic tone. "Don't play your stereo too loud—not just for their sakes. I'm writing, remember? You'll be on your own tonight, Phil. I'm going out."

Making a face, he headed to his room and closed the door.

Later, Phil entertained René while Veronica changed. As usual, she had failed to notice the time. While she selected casual clothes, she wondered how long the newlyweds would remain secluded. She did not like the idea of leaving Phil alone there. Recognizing her mother's righteous attitude infiltrating her thoughts, she censured herself and strolled out. She found Phil and René watching the original version of *The Fly* and discussing its camera angles.

Talamantes's Texas drawl was evident. "Soon as Phil's cast is off, he's coming with me on a shoot. You never told me how much he knows about film technique."

"Well, he *is* the family photographer."

"Lots of talent in this family," Phil agreed.

"De veras." In a blue chambray jumpsuit, René rose at Veronica's approach. Making eye contact, they both blushed.

Veronica wanted to hold her, but decided to wait; Phil had seen and heard enough for one day. She blew him a kiss while René impatiently tugged her hand. Downing the stairs, Veronica glanced towards Siena's condo and noticed the living room lights were off.

In the van, they kissed eagerly.

"I missed you."

"Aquí estoy," René whispered, caressing Veronica's face. "Sabes qué? I started rewriting this morning. The more I thought about your suggestions, the more I liked them."

"That's a surprise." Veronica rubbed the fine down on Talamantes' upper lip. René's unpredictability intrigued her.

"Hey, I get stubborn sometimes. Besides, I'm the one who asked for advice, so the least I could do is take some." She licked the tips of Veronica's fingers. "You taste good."

"Bet you do, too."

"You won't know till after Santa Barbara."

"That's what we agreed on." Veronica touched the edges of René's black hair. "I rushed with Siena. I don't want to do that again."

"But you're tempted."

"Can I help that with you sitting here giving me the once-over?"

"I like the way you look in yellow—más morena."

Veronica relished the compliment and tugged on the seatbelt. She liked being admired for her dark complexion. Her mother often criticized her for lying by the pool and getting browner. Little did Sara know that being brown had attracted Talamantes in the first place.

"Where are we supposed to meet Michi?"

René seemed amused at the change in subject. "La Strada. Have you met Beth?"

"Not yet. She's supposed to be shy."

"Yeah. Wonder if Michi's scored."

"Talamantes, sometimes you sound so macho."

"*Macha*," René corrected with a short laugh. She gunned the motor. "Hey, I grew up in redneck territory. Sometimes I revert."

"Just don't forget your feminist sensibilities."

"You won't let me, mujer."

"Mom's really glad my job starts Monday." Michi searched for another artichoke heart in her pasta primavera. "In some ways, I am, too. Being on campus might help me decide what to do next."

"Know what you mean." Veronica set down her wine glass. "The campus environment puts you in a particular mindset, but the thought of taking classes and working on academic papers instead of making up stuff freaks me out. It'll take lots of willpower to adapt to footnotes and references again. Hope I haven't forgotten how to do that."

"I'll remind you, mujer." René forked a tidbit of chicken tortellini from Veronica's plate. "And so will Zamora."

While they exchanged smiles, Beth glanced at them. She had a little dot of a mole above her upper lip that complemented an adjacent dimple, and her page-boy hairstyle bounced as she spoke. "Michi says you're both creative types. Planning on being famous?"

"Don't set us up, chica." René grabbed another piece of garlic bread and wrenched it in half. "Being creative and being acknowledged for it are two different things. Just 'cause Veronica's published some stories on campus, and I won an award for one of my films, doesn't mean our futures are sewed up. I see mine—at least—as uphill all the way. How many successful Chicana film makers have you heard of, huh?"

"Substitute 'Asian' for 'Chicana' and you'll understand why our parents encourage us into professions instead of into the arts," Michi interjected with a rueful expression.

A faint crease crossed Beth's forehead. "I've never even questioned that."

Veronica liked the way the young woman's dark eyes glinted when she gazed at Michi, but she did not let that distract her from the conversation. "Well, in my family, Frank's the one who really understands my being creative. According to my parents, I'm weird." Veronica leaned her chin on her hand. "So I agree with René. Being a creative woman of color is a definite challenge. Sooner or later, I'll have to teach 'cause writing alone would never support me."

"Especially on the Westside." One of René's brown arms encircled Veronica's waist and squeezed her.

Michi wriggled her eyebrows. "You two should join forces."

"Believe me, chiquita—I'm working on that."

*

On their way to The Flamingo, a lesbian dance spot, Veronica snuggled closer. Curly head on René's shoulder, she remembered how she and Joanna had rarely attended lesbian events, preferring each other's company. She had behaved likewise with Siena until Michi's persistent encouragement. But, with René, life as an "out" lesbian beckoned. Talamantes had enjoyed the social life of a single lesbian since her arrival in Los Angeles two years before. Veronica knew la Tejana would never be content with a closeted existence.

"En qué estás pensando, mujer?" René kissed the top of her companion's head.

"About how different you are from other women."

"You've only been with two, verdad?"

"You know that, loca." Veronica played with the silver snaps of René's jumpsuit and noticed la Tejana's increased heartbeat; its rapid thumping was visible through the chambrey fabric. Smiling, she kept one hand over René's palpitating heart, feeling the rounded contours of her breast, the aroused nub of her nipple.

"Mira, mujer—if I have an accident, it's your fault."

Abruptly, Veronica lurched away and a solitary tear coursed down her cheek. She imagined Joanna's lifeless face and closed her eyes to blot out that image.

"Corazón, I'm sorry. I didn't think. I just—"

"But you're right, René. I should know better. I'll never do that again while you're driving."

"Hey." Flicking on her right turn signal, René veered the van to the curb. "Is that how it happened?"

Veronica rubbed her eyes. "I don't know. I only see flashes. And then everything fades out."

When René touched her, Veronica crumpled. In her grief, she wondered if the sudden tears were as much for herself as for Joanna. During the months since her lover's death, she had changed; if Joanna were alive, would they still love each other? Veronica could not even bear that thought.

René cradled her. Wordlessly, she kissed Veronica's hair and fondled her arms and shoulders, relying on instinct to calm her.

"I didn't want her to die."

"No one thinks that."

"René, I have to talk with her mother."

"Right now?"

Veronica shook her head. "Before I go to Santa Barbara. Isabel thinks I don't care anymore."

René smoothed Veronica's curls from her forehead. "No, preciosa. She just doesn't like what other people are thinking of her daughter these days."

"I'm here—and Joanna's dead. I have *everything* to do with that." She kept her eyes closed, her head against René's firm breasts. "How can you want to have anything to do with me? I'm an emotional disaster."

A joking element entered Talamantes' voice. "Who ever said I wanted a clean-cut woman? I like mis mujeres to have some character, a tragic or bawdy past. You've had both."

Without lifting her head, Veronica sensed René's smile. "Is that the attraction, then?"

"No. It's *you*—pure and simple." Talamantes' smoky voice trembled. "You've lassoed mi corazón y mi alma. I love you, Verónica. That's all there is to it."

Raising her head, Veronica gazed into those uncommonly serious ebony eyes, drawn to their intensity. She willed away memories of Joanna and concentrated only on the woman beside her. Lightly, she brushed back the thick forelock tumbling over René's brow. She slowly outlined her facial contours, those high cheekbones, her strong jaw and chin, the slight curve in her mestiza nose, the sensual quality of her lips. Leaning closer, Veronica covered that wondrous mouth with her own, unwilling to release her.

"We thought we'd lost you guys." Michi snickered and tossed them a what-have-you-been-doing glance.

Discomfited, Veronica did not answer, but she held René's hand tighter. The bond forming between them was more than sexual; it involved common roots, common perceptions. She did not want to joke about it and hoped Michi sensed that.

Winking at Michi, René guided Veronica to the dancefloor as the familiar strains of Patsy Cline's "Crazy" filled that crowded space.

Forgetting about Michi, Veronica slipped her arms around René. "Remember the last time we danced?"

"I was desperate, mujer. When I saw you with Siena, I figured I didn't stand a chance in hell. If you were into beautiful straight gabachas, I wouldn't even know how to compete."

She rubbed Talamantes's shoulders. "You've found out otherwise."

"De veras." René kept a secure hand on Veronica's waist. "You sure haven't said much about her lately."

At that, she frowned. She knew René did not like Siena, but she would not let that opinion sway her; Veronica was willing to remain friends, for as long as Siena liked. "We've talked things over, and I feel good about that. I like Siena."

Talamantes was unconvinced. "Yeah. Just as long as you don't sleep with her."

Veronica could not resist some sarcasm. "You're

sounding pretty possessive, Ms. Voice of Experience."

René drew her nearer. "Querida, once you've had the Talamantes experience, you won't want anyone else."

Veronica pressed herself even closer, feeling la Tejana's body heat radiating and enveloping her. No matter how much René irked her, Veronica knew she wanted her—soon.

Several women of various ethnicities stopped by their table to greet Talamantes, sharing ribald comments and gossip. When René introduced them to her companions, the women were friendly and playful. Unaccustomed to such attention, Veronica was intrigued by la Tejana's popularity. She wondered which had been lovers, which ones friends.

"The night we met, René, you acted so thrilled to be meeting other dykes." Michi kidded her after the women had moved on.

"I said I was the *token* Chicana dyke in the film school. Never said I didn't know any other lesbians in L.A."

"Seems like you know every woman of color in town." Veronica crossed her legs and tried to look casual.

"Not every one. Just lots." René pointed a finger at her. "And I got to *you* first."

"Is she swellheaded or what?" Veronica offered Michi and Beth a deadpan glance.

"If I knew all those dykes, I'd be swellheaded, too." Michi leaned back and moved her hips suggestively. "Or swollen somewhere else, anyway."

They burst into raucous laughter.

*

Bare feet propped on an opposite chair, Veronica daydreamed of René, recalling her unexpected tenderness, her earthy humor and sexiness. Sighing, she fished a banana slice from the cereal bowl and popped it into her mouth.

"How wonderful! You've already made coffee." Joyce startled her. A statuesque blonde, the new Mrs. Melendez glided in, wearing an aqua romper outfit that accentuated her Caribbean tan.

Scrambling up, Veronica almost knocked over the cereal bowl. "Welcome back," she sputtered.

"Don't I rate a hug?"

Awkwardly, she opened her arms for her beaming sister-in-law.

"Frank was right, Veronica. You look fabulous."

She stepped back. "Well, I've been exercising."

"It shows." Joyce cocked her head with its trendy hairstyle. "I hear you've had your hands full."

Veronica was noncommittal. Moving away, she took two mugs from their hooks and filled them with coffee.

"We don't have to talk about it." Joyce took one of the cups. "Just want you to know I'm in your corner." She removed eggs and a bacon package from the refrigerator.

Veronica was silent for some moments. "It's too bad you had to end your vacation early." She watched Joyce lay bacon slices in the teflon-coated pan; those shocking pink fingernails reminded her of Siena's.

"Frank was restless. Talked about Phil and you all the time."

"Has Phil behaved himself so far?"

Joyce's blue eyes wavered. "Sure. Your mother's the one I really have to charm. Maybe you can give me some tips?"

"Frank's better at that. I'm not too successful with her myself. I bet by the time I get back from Santa Barbara, you'll be getting the knack."

Joyce looked skeptical.

16

"You're really in top condition these days." Siena had come home early and joined Veronica in the pool. "Remember when you could barely swim from one end to the other?"

Veronica treaded water. "I'm stronger now."

Sitting on the rim, Siena towelled her hair and let it cascade; then she began drying it in sections, the auburn waves glinting in the sun. "What are you doing tonight?"

"Having dinner with my parents."

"And after that?" Siena wrapped the towel turban-style around her head.

Veronica met her steady gaze.

"I miss you, Veronica."

Leaning one arm on the pool's edge, Veronica glided her other hand through the warm water, watching the spiraling ripples and wishing another tenant would decide to take a swim. Alone with her, Siena stretched out one foot and let her toes flirt with Veronica's shoulder.

"Why don't you stay with me tonight?"

Sighing, Veronica drifted back, letting Siena's foot slide into the water. She wished she were already in Santa Barbara, away from temptation. "That wouldn't be fair."

"To who?"

"To either of us." Veronica took a breath and added, "Or to René."

Siena toed the water. "You haven't even phoned me."

"You haven't phoned me either. Besides, I figured you were out with—what's his name?"

"Jack." Siena averted her eyes towards the clump of Italian cypresses across the way. "I went to a movie last night—by myself. This weekend I'm going to San Diego to see my father."

Joining her at the pool's rim, Veronica reached for a towel and threw it over her shoulders. "I think you really need to make other friends—besides me."

Siena would not look at her. Although she felt uncomfortable saying these things, Veronica continued. "I'm ready to explore the world I belong in—that means meeting and being with other lesbians. It doesn't mean you and I can't be friends. I just can't be with you exclusively anymore—and not at all—sexually."

"Why does everyone reject me?" Siena's voice quavered, and she turned troubled eyes to Veronica.

"I'm not rejecting *you*, Siena. Look, Tuesday night, you were with a man. If you prefer men, then be with them. But my main focus has to be other lesbians."

"I wish I could be as grounded as you. I just don't know how."

"While I was in the hospital, I had plenty of time to think about how I wanted to live. And I'll do even more thinking in Santa Barbara. Maybe you need to do that, too. You'd be surprised how many answers are actually inside you."

Siena lay a damp hand on Veronica's thigh. "I just don't regret our times together."

"Neither do I." She had hoped Siena would agree on that.

"Frank said you went out with unas amigas anoche." Sara served Veronica a heaping portion of rice to accom-

224

pany the two cheese enchiladas and frijoles refritos already on her plate.

Across the table, Phil wore an amused expression. Veronica tried to ignore him. At mealtimes, either one or the other was likely to be interrogated by Sara Melendez.

"Sure did, Mom."

"Quiénes son?"

"Michi and some other friends. You don't know them."

Sara pursed her lips at that curt reply. "Y adonde fueron?"

"Out to eat."

Joe filled his daughter's glass with iced tea. He never offered her beer or wine when he knew she would drive.

"Que bueno." Sara set down the serving dish and at last took a seat. "Esa Michi never stays put. Ay, but her hair looks so ugly—tán feo, Roni."

Veronica picked up her glass, but made no comment.

"Parece hombrecito," Joe cut in. "She looks like a little man porque la Michi doesn't have much in front, sabes?" He gestured towards his own barrel chest and laughed.

Phil chuckled at his grandfather's clowning, while Sara frowned.

"Don't give este niño more ideas than he already has," She cautioned. "I hear Jimmy and some of los otro chamacos were looking at a dirty magazine at the playground the other day."

Veronica and Phil exchanged quick glances, looking elsewhere when Sara noticed.

"I don't see how kids can avoid any of that stuff nowadays. It's everywhere." Joe sliced an enchilada with the edge of his fork.

"That's no excuse," his wife scoffed. "All those mujeres sin vergüenzas in those magazines—que escándalo!

Gracias a Dios que Frank es nuestro único hijo. I'd hate to have a teenaged boy nowadays."

"Phil isn't so bad." Veronica hoped to change the subject to a safer topic; this one made her queasy.

"As long as he doesn't go jogging at midnight," Joe agreed, nudging his grandson. "Has ese Steve been in touch?"

The boy shook his head and swooshed the refried beans across his plate.

"Ese Steve es el malcriado who had the magazine! Jimmy's mother told me." Sara's voice emanated disgust. "Has he ever shown you any of those libros cochinos, Philly?"

The boy cleared his throat. Holding her breath, Veronica sensed his reluctance to discuss the matter. "A few times, Grandma."

Sara threw up her hands in dismay. "Que caramba! Ay, mijito, you have to stay away from boys like that. He's a devil, that one."

"De veras. I've thought so ever since he broke the bathroom window," Joe agreed. "Have you told Frank?"

Phil nodded and avoided his aunt's gaze. Feeling nauseous, Veronica wondered for a moment if he would be honest with his grandparents this time. She hated mistrusting him, but this was not the setting she would have chosen for coming out. Her head throbbed. Listening to her mother, she felt demoralized by how quickly the gossip had spread.

"I should talk to Rita myself," Sara sputtered. "Mira nomás! Where does Steve get those magazines? I thought chavalos couldn't buy them."

"From his dad, I think." When Phil poured himself another glass of milk, he dribbled some on the lace tablecloth. For once, Sara did not notice. "Grandma,

Dad's already handled it. And I'm not going to be friends with Steve anymore." His voice sounded firmer than Veronica had expected; she felt proud of him, but prayed he would not offer any more details.

"You're a smart kid, mijo. And I knew this wouldn't get by Frank." Joe appeared satisfied that the Melendez men had dealt with the matter. "You mean, Ben Martínez reads that junk?"

The boy looked up warily. "Steve has a whole bunch of magazines in the garage. I'm just guessing they belong to his dad."

"Apenas se puede creer." When Sara shook her head, greying tendrils escaped the tight bun at the nape of her neck. "Gracias a Dios que tenemos tres hijas."

Joe could not let that comment pass. "Sarita, don't blame the men for everything, eh? If the women didn't pose for those pictures, there wouldn't be any of those magazines in the first place." He gestured with his fork. "Verdad, Roni?"

Veronica blushed and decided this was no time for feminist analysis. "Dad, a lot of those women think they'll be discovered in *Playboy* and *Penthouse*. They see the photos as a career move."

"Discovered by who?" Sara demanded, eyeing her daughter skeptically.

Veronica shrugged. "Hollywood. I guess they figure that's one way to get into the movies." She decided not to contribute further to the conversation; it made her very uneasy.

Her mother had more to say. With a dramatic flourish, she threw down her napkin. "Sin vergüenzas—desnudas y todo! I'm not only blaming the men, Joe. Esas mujeres cochinas don't have to pose for the pictures. But who's buying the magazines, eh? Los hombres animales!"

Before his grandfather had a chance, Phil spoke up, an impish expression on his face. "Grandma, haven't you ever heard of *Playgirl*?"

Veronica kicked him under the table, but the boy moved aside before she could repeat her footwork.

"*Playgirl*?" Sara's brow creased.

"It has pictures of naked men, and women buy it," He explained with an innocent smile.

Sara glowered. "How do you know about that?"

He backed off. "Just heard, that's all."

"Madre de Dios, what's this world coming to?" Sara wiped her forehead with the edge of her apron and whispered another prayer in Spanish.

Phil glanced at Veronica, and she had to bite her lip to keep from laughing. Despite her amusement, she felt faint, knowing she had narrowly missed a potential catastrophe. Somehow Phil had deflected the conversation, and his grandfather was too busy eating to notice. For several more minutes, the family ate in uncharacteristic silence.

Sara fanned herself with a napkin. "Did la Joyce make breakfast for everyone this morning?"

"Bacon and eggs." Phil rolled his eyes. "Overdone."

This time his antics did not amuse Veronica. She did not like his participation in trashing his stepmother. "Joyce is a really sweet woman."

Sara dismissed that comment with a flip of her hand. "She was hanging all over Frank's arm last night. I thought she was going to wind up in his lap."

"Or in his plate," Joe added with a wink. "Sarita, they're in love, eh? Frank's a happy man. You can see it in his eyes. He's had enough sadness in his life. You'll change your mind once the babies start coming."

"Babies?" Phil looked astounded at that suggestion.

"Dad, don't worry Philly. He already has enough adjustments to make."

"Do you think esa career woman wants babies?" Sara was unconvinced. "Que crees, Roni?"

"I don't know their plans. All that's been on my mind lately is going to Santa Barbara."

"Thinking about being a nun?" Joe teased.

"No! Just about how peaceful it'll be. No phones, no TVs, no stereos—"

"Yuck." Phil grimaced. "Don't nuns even have electricity?"

"Of course they do." With affection, Sara patted Veronica's hand. "Just be respectful to las monjitas. Be as quiet as you've been tonight."

"You sure have been silencita," Joe interjected. "Todo esta bien, hija?"

"Sure, Dad. Things couldn't be better."

To her surprise, Sara leaned over and kissed her, fondly pushing aside Veronica's curly hair.

For a Friday night, Mi Wey, a Culver City women's bar in a working-class neighborhood, was sparsely inhabited. The few women there hung out at the billiard table in the rear. Sitting with René in a booth, Veronica sipped a Miller Lite.

"Siena wanted me to spend tonight with her."

"Pendeja."

Veronica touched Talamantes' cheek. "Chill out. Things haven't been easy for her."

"I know her type. I saw how uptight she was at the dance. She likes what dykes do, but she doesn't like dykes."

Veronica moved her hand away and picked up the beer again. "A rather succinct appraisal."

"Hey, don't get snotty. I don't think I'm wrong."

Veronica licked the bitter foam from the edge of her mug, and said nothing. Why did she see Siena so differently from René's and Michi's perceptions? Was she more gullible, or simply more generous in her appraisal?

Surveying her, René reached over and fingered her hair. "Did you write a lot today?"

Veronica tried to sound casual, but she was irked by the earlier comments. "A few pages."

"I still think we should collaborate."

"Let me finish this project first."

Talamantes rubbed the tension gathered in Veronica's upper back. "Preciosa, I know I'm blunt—about Siena. Just don't want you going back to her."

"Do you see me with her tonight?"

René smiled sheepishly. She wore a violet western-styled shirt tucked into snug black jeans.

Chin in hand, Veronica watched the laughing women in the rear of the bar. She continued to be alternately pleased and annoyed with Talamantes's candor; at least, René was aware of that. Sometimes she wished René possessed Joanna's tact; but, she reminded herself, Talamantes was not Joanna Nuñez and never would be.

"Almost had to come out to my parents tonight." She offered a capsulized version of the dinner episode. "Mom was in one of her states of moral outrage—lashing out at porn magazines. She didn't say anything in particular about the *Penthouse* pictures. She's really straitlaced about sex. Maybe she couldn't bring herself to be specific about the lesbian stuff." Veronica toyed with her glass. "Of course, maybe she didn't go into detail because Phil was there. Or maybe Mrs. Gómez hasn't told her the whole story."

"Know what I think? Your mother's warning you, in a

230

not-so-subtle way. She's probably wise to you. Mine sure was."

"I've wondered about that, René. My parents are both so indirect—especially where sex is involved. But I still kept expecting Mom to drop the bombshell. She didn't say anything about Steve's mouthing off, or even about Joanna's brothers getting banged up." She took another sip of beer. "Phil surprised me—the way he turned the conversation around. He'd never admit it, but he's protective, in his own way."

"Like you are with him."

Veronica smiled into those ebony eyes. "What haven't you noticed, Talamantes?"

René grinned. "Who am I going to spar with while you're in Santa Barbara?"

"You have lots of friends, loca. You won't be lonesome. Besides, you can revise your screenplay in the meantime."

"And you know exactly how I should do that." René caressed Veronica's shoulder. "Sure wish I could spend tomorrow with you, but I promised to videotape a wedding. Getting paid by the hour and I'll be gone all day. You know how Chicano weddings are."

Veronica smoothed Talamantes's coarse hair. "But you'll still drive me to Santa Barbara—"

"Preciosa, I want to deliver you to the convent myself. Besides, I have to meet this Sister Lucy. I've always had a thing about nuns."

On Veronica's bed, Michi lay on her tummy, supervising the packing. She munched on pretzels and provided a running commentary. "Don't forget those baggy T-shirts."

Veronica peered from behind the closet door. "I usually wear just panties underneath instead of shorts. Can I get away with that in a convent?"

"That's one way of scoping out the lesbo nuns, Roni. They're bound to notice your legs."

"Very funny." Veronica tossed a couple of T-shirts at her. "How's Beth?"

Michi peeled the shirts from her head. "What made you ask? She remind you of a nun?"

"A bit defensive, aren't we?" Veronica squatted beside a dresser drawer, fishing out culottes and shorts, piling them on the carpet. She hoped this relationship would work for Michi; but Beth was shy—maybe too shy.

Glumly, Michi met her gaze. "Beth lives with her parents. Where're we supposed to get together—in the back seat of my car? Not only that, but she's cleaning teeth right this minute. Her cousin's a dentist, and Beth works Saturday mornings in his office. Talk about Asian solidarity."

Veronica reached for the pretzel bag. "When you're my roomie, you can bring Beth over any time."

"Do you plan to be entangled with René in the other bedroom?"

"Sounds rather orgiastic. You're really looking ahead, Mich." Sitting cross-legged, Veronica smirked. "But if ethnic groups can express solidarity, so can dykes. Mi casa es tu casa, amigita."

Michi giggled. "You're acting more like the old Roni. Have you noticed that?"

Veronica responded with a self-conscious shrug, though she welcomed Michi's appraisal; after all, who knew her better? Sorting through the pile of clothes, she wondered if she could *ever* revert to her old self. So much had happened since the accident; so much had changed.

"I want to go to the cemetery tomorrow, Mich."

"Sure." Michi did not seem surprised.

"I want you and René to come with me."

Michi sat on the floor beside her. "Okay."

Veronica pulled a couple of pairs of jeans from another drawer. "When I phoned Isabel this morning—"

"About the letters?"

"Yes. I want them before I go to Santa Barbara." She glanced at Michi. "Anyway, Teddy answered the phone and—he wasn't friendly, Mich. He didn't ask about Phil either. I'm not even sure if he'll tell Isabel I called. What's happening to everybody?"

Michi helped her fold some T-shirts. "Teddy might be a kid, but he's still male—and sexist and homophobic. If Rubén's overreacted, don't be surprised if the boys have, too. Remember, we're talking about their big sister here—your lover. You know how crazy those kids were about Joanna."

Veronica lay the jeans across her lap. "The whole Nunez family probably sees me as an evil influence."

Michi touched her shoulder. "Roni, we both know that isn't true."

She sighed. "I'm strong enough to deal with it, one way or the other. I worry about Phil, though. Those boys are his friends—Larry, Teddy and Jimmy Gómez, too. He's already lost Steve. What if none of the other kids wants to hang out with him anymore?"

Michi took the jeans and lay them in Veronica's suitcase. "Phil can handle a lot, and he has a supportive dad. His relationship with you hasn't changed."

"Sometimes I wonder. It seems like he's projected his resentment to Siena. That bothers me. I really expected him to be cool to Talamantes, but he's jazzed about her being a film student."

"That could be 'cause René's her own person." Michi offered her another pretzel and stretched flat on the bed. "Siena doesn't have that kind of self-assurance. By the way, have you seen her lately?"

"She wanted my company last night."

"Melendez, I don't know what you've got, but you're hot. You have to fight off women, and I'm really jealous." Michi stuck out her tongue.

"Is that a come-hither invitation?"

"Take it any way you want to." Michi giggled and pretended to unzip her denim shorts.

After lunch and an impromptu shopping mall trek with Michi, Veronica relaxed in the pool with her brother's family. Even Phil, cast-bound arm, taped ribs and all, sat on the pool's rim, cooling his legs in the water.

"Roni, be sure to exercise," Frank advised. "It'd be a shame if you started getting stiff again."

"I plan to walk all over the convent grounds. Maybe I'll drag Lucy along with me." She sat beside her nephew and nudged him. "Phil thinks I'm crazy."

"Weird vacation, if you ask me."

"Sounds like it'll be quite an experience," Joyce chimed in.

Veronica noticed how the boy avoided her gaze. Clasping his hand, she squeezed it once. Phil looked at her then and smiled slowly.

At the freshly mown gravesite, Veronica rearranged the resplendent birds-of-paradise and assorted greenery, grateful that René and Michi had allowed her an interval of solitude. They had wandered off to explore the marble and glass mausoleum atop the hill.

"I'll be gone a while, Joanna." She bit her lower lip, anticipating the coming tears. "Why won't people understand that we loved each other? Why does it matter that we're both women?"

She stared at the rose granite stone, embedding its rectangular dimensions and carefully lettered carving in her memory. "I thought your mother understood about us, but—I don't know anymore." She plucked a withering leaf from its thick stalk. "I'm trying to go on without you, Joanna, but I miss you. I wonder if that'll ever stop."

She stood, a slender but resolute figure amid the summery gusts of wind. She glanced about for René and Michi; instead, she saw Joanna's mother advancing.

"Hello, Isabel."

Her unsmiling mouth seemed clamped, the muscles of her face strained. "Why do you keep coming here? Roni, why don't you leave her in peace?"

At that unleashed anger, Veronica flinched, but her voice remained firm. "I come to honor her. And as long as I knew her, Joanna *was* at peace."

Isabel spat out her words. "How can she be, knowing her father broke down and cried when I told him everything? Do you think she's at peace, knowing her brothers have to face insults about her? What do *you* know about peace? All you ever wanted was to touch her—ruin her. She's burning in purgatory now because of you!"

Trembling, Veronica took a deep breath. "No matter what you say, I loved her. Joanna was a woman of integrity. If you believe I could ever force her into anything, you're wrong. We *loved* each other." She caught her breath, barely noticing her friends' return. They halted a few feet away and tried to make themselves inconspicuous.

Veronica repeated her declaration in a stronger voice.

235

"Joanna and I *loved* each other. And I want the letters I wrote her."

"They're gone." Isabel's eyes never left her daughter's grave. "I burned them."

"Oh, Isabel—" Veronica stared at her. "Why?"

"I didn't want Rubén to read them. I couldn't let him see—" Her anger dissipated into shattering sobs. On reflex, Veronica went to her.

"Roni, she was a such a good girl. But why did she keep secrets? Didn't she trust me?"

"We were afraid. We didn't think anyone would understand."

"I still don't."

Veronica's eyes were wet when they met hers. "Do you have to understand in order to accept our love for each other?"

Isabel shook her head perplexedly and attempted to withhold her tears. "I think your mother knows. After Mass this morning, she came up and put her arms around me."

Veronica felt chilled. "Did she say anything?"

"She didn't have to. It was the way she looked at me. She hasn't hugged me like that since Joanna's funeral. She must've heard about—"

Veronica's gaze focused on the birds of paradise; such regal flowers for her beloved. "She hasn't asked me anything."

"You have to talk to her, Roni."

"I don't know how." Stepping back, Veronica looked at the grave again; she would not see it for weeks. "I love you, Joanna," she whispered. Turning, she hurried towards her friends. She wanted to leave right away.

17

Veronica kept her eyes on the coastal route. She watched the Pacific's rolling tides and remembered, in the months following Joanna's death, how tempted she had been to merge with the ocean, to be swallowed by its blue-grey water. Sometimes that image still haunted her. Rubbing her eyes, she did not participate in her friends' banter. Michi and René sounded so frivolous.

The confrontation at the cemetery had unnerved her. If Isabel, who had seemed supportive, could turn on her, how would her own mother react—in righteous anger, with sobbing prayers? Veronica could only guess. She was unaccustomed to being perceived as Joanna's corrupter; she knew the letters, full of intensity and passion, had contributed to that image. No wonder Isabel had destroyed them. But if Isabel had truly known Joanna—she had been a sensual lover, fond of double entendres and bathtub sex. With teasing toes, she would arouse Veronica clitorally; there was no sensation comparable to that sudsy foot rubbing against her underwater. No, Isabel would never know about—or understand—that.

Sighing, Veronica noticed the highway sign announcing Oxnard. That town was an anomaly along the scenic route, dotted with industrial areas and neighboring barrios. She liked its scruffiness, its sprawling car dealerships and Spanish-language movie marquees. It reminded her of similar sections in her hometown.

Wedged between her friends, she appreciated their tolerance of her anti-social mood. René regaled Michi with Tejana tall tales, and Michi bounced back one-liners. Glancing at them, Veronica longed for the awaiting solitude. But Santa Barbara, she realized, would be only a temporary refuge.

In Oxnard, René stopped for gas and jumped out of the van.

"Roni, what's with you—laryngitis? No wonder you wanted me here—to keep René entertained."

Veronica rubbed her stiff leg. She could not bring herself to face Michi. "I'm sorry."

"Isabel came down hard, I guess."

"I've tried to explain why we kept our relationship secret, Mich, but she doesn't want to hear that from *me*. She wants to hear it from Joanna."

Michi pressed Veronica's knee. "Wish I knew what to say."

Veronica shrugged. "Isabel has to work it out herself. At least, *I* know Joanna and I were honest with each other. Isabel doesn't even have that consolation."

Wielding a squeegee, Talamantes cleaned the dusty windshield, mugging outrageously. For the first time that day, Veronica laughed at the clowning and noted the triumphant gleam in René's eyes.

"She's going to miss you, Roni. Suppose I will, too."

Veronica did not trust herself to speak.

Opening the glove compartment, Michi removed a package of Hershey's kisses. She offered Veronica one and took another for herself. "Joanna and I spent lots of time together the summer you were in Mexico."

Veronica unwrapped the candy and popped it into her

mouth. If only she had retrieved the letters from Isabel—like Joanna, they were gone forever.

Michi's voice was quiet. "She was so smart—and classy. I really miss her. René has lots of rough edges."

Veronica reached for another candy. Talamantes was an altogether different type of Chicana, barrio born and bred. "René's older, Mich. She's had to face much more."

Michi did not have a chance to respond because Talamantes hopped inside and slammed the van door. "All set, mujeres. Have you lured her back to terra firma, Michi?"

"I've tried."

Veronica snuggled closer to René. As much as she craved solitude, she did not even want to think about missing her. "I have a tendency to fade out sometimes."

"As if I haven't noticed. I'm waitin' for the day I'll fade out with you."

They rattled into the seaside city in time to visit the natural history museum located near Santa Barbara Mission. When Veronica introduced Talamantes to the Chumash displays and showed her the local seismograph, René admitted being ignorant of those indigenous Californians, but she had already experienced an earthquake or two. When they left the museum, the trio headed towards State Street where they explored art galleries and browsed in bookstores. Finally, they stopped to eat at Stearns Wharf.

Over seafood, Veronica listened to their witticisms and smiled at their competitive humor. She sensed her growing detachment, observing her friends with a combination of longing and distance. She let her mind drift, wondering how Siena fared during her San Diego

239

weekend. She thought about Phil, battered from the accident, faced with adjusting to his new stepmother. She thought about her parents, clinging to traditions while coping with disparate children. And, as always, she recalled with a bittersweet twinge, her love for Joanna. How long ago that other life seemed.

Rosy twilight enhanced the rustic setting of the Convent of St. Teresa. Situated near the edge of Los Padres National Forest, the Carmelite convent and neighboring retreat house resembled a Spanish colonial compound, while its outlying bungalows and dormitories reflected a similar tradition. A decade earlier, a wealthy Santa Barbara family had donated their estate to the Roman Catholic Archdiocese with the intent of keeping the grounds intact. The Church hierarchy had opted to conduct spiritual retreats and related activities in that secluded setting.

"Reminds me of San Simeon, Catholic-style." Michi leaned out and inhaled the fresh air while Talamantes guided the van along the narrow road guarded by shadowing pines.

René nudged Veronica. "Maybe Lucy could put up all of us."

"*You're* out of luck. There are definitely some advantages to having a nun in the family."

"De veras." As soon as René parked across from the main house, the three scrambled out.

With an agility that surprised her, Veronica toted her suitcase and bounded up the convent steps. She had not been to St. Teresa's since the previous summer, when the whole Melendez clan had come for Lucy's birthday. Her sister had last visited Santa Monica in May, and Veronica was eager to see her again. She fumbled with the intercom button on the oaken door. René and Michi tagged along with the portable typewriter.

Within moments, Lucy welcomed them, her decorous face wreathed in smiles. She hugged her younger sister to her brown, floor-length habit; away from the convent, Lucy wore more modern apparel. Her habit's coarse fabric made Veronica's arms itch, but she did not care. She hung onto Lucy with all her might and almost toppled her. They both laughed.

Shorter than Veronica, Lucy resembled their mother more than any of the other Melendez siblings. However, at age twenty-seven, accustomed to spartan meals, the nun did not share their mother's round figure.

"Bienvenida, hermanita. You're finally here!"

In the convent's terra-cotta floored entry, a tile mosaic of Our Lady of Guadalupe dominated the wall behind the nun. On viewing that familiar Mexican icon, Veronica felt at home.

"Lucy, you can talk me into anything." Holding her sister at arms' length, she inspected the youthful face framed by the heavy veil. Lucy had Sara's large brown eyes, ready to either laugh or cry. Her eyebrows were full like Veronica's, but other than their skin tones, that seemed their only similarity.

Veronica wondered how Lucy could stand wearing that heavy habit in warm weather. She recalled their girlhood days of roller-skating and bike-riding, both of them sun-bronzed in T-shirts, cotton shorts and sneakers, their flying hair braided and beribboned. Of her two sisters, Lucy was her favorite, yet Veronica remained mystified by her religious vocation.

She gestured towards her friends. "Lucy, this is René Talamantes. And I'm sure you haven't forgotten Michi."

"How could I?" Lucy smiled and slipped a thin arm

around Michi. She looked a bit chagrined by the crewcut, but did not comment.

Michi grinned from ear to ear, for once without a ready quip. Sometimes a nun's presence could make any parochial school graduate revert to adolescent shyness.

Lucy turned her attention to Talamantes. Studying her rangy figure, she took her coppery hands. "Hello, René. Where did you meet my sister?"

With uncharacteristic embarrassment, Talamantes grinned. "She came to see my film on campus."

"You're an actress?"

At that, Veronica and Michi exchanged glances and snickered, enjoying the mild-mannered interrogation and René's unaccustomed restraint.

"No way." Talamantes threw back her shoulders in a semi-swagger. "I'm a grad student in Film."

"Ah. Creative like Roni." The nun's eyes narrowed. "How old are you?"

"Twenty-six—your contemporary." René seemed to regain her usual aplomb. "Any other Chicanas stationed in this joint?"

"Two more." Lucy raised her brows. "Why do you ask?"

"I think she's plotting cinematic possibilities," Veronica remarked, noting the film student's sardonic expression. She wanted to deflect any outlandish Talamantes remarks.

"Just like you dream up literary ones, mujer." René winked and turned again to Lucy. "I've always been curious about monjitas, sabes? Here you are, a woman of color living in a community of predominantly white women, subject to a patriarchal hierarchy, and—"

"Sounds like another feminist analysis in the works," Michi interjected.

Veronica was relieved by that interruption. While the nun maintained a placid smile, her sister recognized the Melendez stoicism at once. It was obvious Lucy was not eager to engage in a controversial topic. René shrugged good-naturedly.

"Well, Roni, you need to get settled. Vespers will begin soon. I want to show you the bungalow before then."

"Bungalow? I never expected that."

"Mother Superior insisted. She's so pleased you've decided to spend time with us. She and the other sisters have prayed constantly for your recovery. They'll be delighted to talk with you in the morning." She paused, allowing her sister to see her friends off.

Taking the hint, Veronica smiled at them. She would miss Michi's wisecracks and everything about René, but she did not want to linger on that. "See you guys in a few weeks. Thanks for driving me here." She hugged Michi first, one cheek against her moussed crest.

"Work hard, Roni. But play some, too."

"I will."

Letting her go, Veronica embraced René. When she felt those firm breasts against hers, those wide hips pressing against her own, Veronica almost changed her mind about staying.

"No me olvides, preciosa." Talamantes' deep-set eyes caressed her. "Hasta la victoria siempre."

She nodded and tried to smile. "Ten cuidado, loca."

Talamantes grinned and touched her cheek. "Finish your stuff so we can collaborate."

"It's a deal." Veronica knew she referred to more than a screenplay. With reluctance, she let her go.

Amidst waves and smiles, the two departed, shutting the oaken door with more finality than anticipated. Bereft, Veronica stood, blinking away tears.

"Let me help you, Roni." Lucy reached for the suitcase. "Did I tell you how wonderful you look? I'm so happy to see you walking without the cane. You're a miracle, honey."

Veronica squeezed her near again. "I've had lots of people rooting for me." She wiped her eyes with the back of her arm.

"René's a character."

"Tell me about it."

Smith-Corona in hand, she trailed the brown-garbed nun down the tiled corridor.

She sat on the narrow bed, absorbing the bungalow's austerity. Veronica sensed she would be able to work there, undistracted, undisturbed. There would be no phone calls from her mother, no gossipmongers, no tempting ex-lovers, but also no joking Phil, no reliable Frank, no cajoling Camille, no teasing Michi, no unpredictable René. Yet she needed time for herself, no matter how much she already missed everyone. She had to finish at least a first draft of the promised stories. And she had to decide when and how to come out to her parents.

After moments of contemplation, she emptied the suitcase's contents into the plainly designed bureau's drawers. Placing her underwear and toiletries in another drawer, she closed the suitcase and set it in the adjacent closet. She wanted to be settled in tonight.

To her delight, an old-fashioned desk, the functional wooden type she remembered from her parochial school principal's office, occupied the wall beneath the casement windows. Rubbing its polished surface, she opened the burlap curtains and discovered a twilight view of the fruit orchard and its surrounding garden. The trees provided a natural barrier between her window and the next bungalow.

Wasting no time, Veronica adjusted the gooseneck desk lamp, removed her typewriter from its case and inserted a sheet of paper, prepared to work.

When Lucy paid a visit later, Veronica marvelled at her demure manner. She recalled her sister's tomboyhood—climbing trees, pitching softball, beating up the neighborhood bully. The quiet nun in the straight-backed chair, hands folded in her lap, hardly seemed the same person. Veronica began to feel uneasy when Lucy spoke.

"Mama phoned. She wanted to know if you'd arrived. I got the impression she didn't think you were really coming."

"You know Mom. Always suspicious."

"Does she have a reason to be, Roni?"

"She said something about me?" Veronica leaned against the desk.

Lucy's face altered slightly. "She's worried."

"What else is new?"

"You're her baby, Roni. You came very close to death last year—she's still affected by that."

"You think *I'm* not? It's on *my* mind every minute of the day." Hands in jeans pockets, Veronica faced her, sandaled feet restless on the hardwood floor. She did not like this cat and mouse game. This was not what she had anticipated; her bravado began to dissipate. Too nervous to tough it out, she slumped into the desk chair. "Will you just tell me what she said?"

"There's been talk—about you and Joanna."

Veronica exhaled, feeling all energy seep away. "It's true." She picked up a pencil and tapped it against the typewriter. "And I'm writing about her—or trying to."

The nun leaned forward. "Roni, I know about particular friendships."

"Were you involved with someone?"

"It was never sexual, if that's what you mean." Lucy looked out the window at the darkened orchard. "During our novitiate, we were very close. The novice mistress advised us to make other friends. When the other girl didn't make the effort, she was asked to leave. I don't know whatever became of her."

"Jesus, Lucy!" Veronica banged the pencil against the desk. "That's incredibly oppressive. Hasn't there been *any* contact between you?"

"Of course not." Her sister's eyes flashed at that outburst. "My life is dedicated to Christ, to the Carmelite community. No one forced me to live this way. I chose the communal life, not one in which individual relationships prevail." Lucy spoke earnestly, but her sister rejected her words.

"I don't believe Jesus would expect you to cut yourself off from a friend. He cherished his." Veronica used the pencil point for emphasis. So much for Santa Barbara's tranquility.

Lucy's tone became calmer. Like Frank, she had often been the family conciliator. "I realize I'm speaking as a woman who's been a member of a relìgous order for almost ten years. I live by the rules of my superiors. It's a different world outside our gates."

Veronica left the chair and began to pace, too agitated to keep still. "*Totally* different, Lucy. Sometimes—" She gestured with the pencil, "—especially when I was in the hospital—I used to envy you. I'd think about you here, sheltered from stress and emotional pain, dedicated to your religious ideals, and I used to long for that kind of peace. But your life *isn't* for me, any more than mine is for you." She tapped the pencil against her thigh. "I'm just beginning to find *my* community, to meet other women like me. I know where I belong, Lucy, just as you do. I suppose Mama expects you to deprogram me."

The nun reached for Veronica's hand. "I'm here to listen, if that's what you want. After all, the order sent me to college for my counselling degree. You may as well take advantage of that," she added with a tiny smile.

"I don't need a shrink." Veronica pulled away and began to pace again. "I saw one in the hospital, remember? I can take care of myself, Lucy. Sure, I'll talk to you, but only as my sister. Don't start feeding me any religious or psychological gobbledygook. That's not what I'm here for."

Lucy wore that infuriatingly placid smile again. "Not everyone comes here for religious or psychological reasons. We've often had writers in residence, although we don't advertise that. Many people come to recharge their batteries before plunging back into the world. They want peace and solitude, time to reflect, to make decisions."

Veronica halted. "Exactly what I came for. To do some writing. To escape the gossip. To allow Frank and his family to get acquainted." She rubbed her eyes. "Phil's friend Steve is the one who started the talk. This hasn't been easy for Phil either."

The nun looked concerned. "Have you talked with him about—?"

"And with Frank—and Isabel."

"But not with Mama and Dad?"

Veronica threw up her hands. "Jeez! Of course not."

"Oh, Roni." Lucy pursed her lips like their mother did. "You're as indirect as they are."

"Where do you think I learned that?" She was exasperated; Lucy had been away from home too long. "Come on—we're talking about Sara and Joe, our parents. The ones who never breathed a word about menstruation, much less about sex. If it hadn't been for you, I'd still think my period was a hemorrhage. How can I possibly tell them I'm a lesbian?"

The nun's eyes widened at that admission. "Es la cultura, Roni. Besides, you're the baby of the family. I think Mama wanted to keep you inocente as long as she could. By the time you were ten years old, I decided to tell you about the changes that would happen with your body. Mama was furious when she found out."

"I never knew that." Veronica sat on the edge of the desk, inches from her sister. She had often wondered how she would have survived her preteen years without Lucy. Because of their early confidences, she did not hesitate to be blunt. "Well, no one stays innocent for long. Joanna and I started playing around when we were in grammar school. I still can't believe no one caught on."

Lucy's face colored, but she behaved as if she had not heard her sister's remark. "Since I've been doing counseling for the Archdiocese, I see more and more cases of Mexicanos not being open about intimate matters."

"Have you counseled any lesbians?"

"A few—mostly teenagers." Lucy hesitated. "I've also spoken with Mother Superior about such matters."

Veronica touched her shoulder. "Are you shocked about me, Lucy?"

The nun sighed. "You loved Joanna from the day you met her in kindergarten. Everyone knew that. We just never looked beyond the friendship." She gazed into Veronica's eyes. "Now that she's gone, I only hope you weigh the consequences."

"Of being a lesbian?"

"The Church views homosexual acts as sinful."

Veronica grimaced. "What do you expect from a patriarchal and heterosexist institution? The Church has no right to judge me for loving the only way I know how." She put down the pencil and ran both hands through her tousled hair. "The irony is, if I were to marry a man—which would be not only hypocritical, but also psychologically harmful for myself and the poor sucker—I could be back in the Church's good graces because heterosexual marriage is sanctioned. Lucy, I won't accept that hypocrisy. Jesus said, 'Love your neighbor as yourself.' He never specified heterosexuals only."

"Roni, the modern Church is far more complex than when Our Lord founded it."

Veronica spread her hands. "My point exactly. Jesus' intent was to move away from the Hebraic tradition of endless precepts and proscriptions, not create more. Oh, Lucy, I'm so frustrated about the Church's attitude! That's why I quit going to Mass. I feel so out of place among that patriarchal hogwash." Moving back further on the desk, letting her legs dangle, she used the pencil as a pointer. "But Catholicism is part of our cultural heritage—Our Lady of Guadalupe, Las Posadas, the blessing of the animals at Easter. Rejecting the Church entirely is like rejecting Chicanismo, like denying a whole part of myself. How can I justify doing that? Instead, I pick and choose what I want from the Church and from la cultura."

"And you're not the only one doing it, by any means." Lucy seemed unwilling to confront that issue as well. She glanced at her watch, and Veronica realized her sister had to be in bed by a certain time. That annoyed her, but she decided to keep that opinion to herself.

The nun lay her hand on Veronica's knee. "When Mama told me about these rumors, I said your personal behavior—from the family's standpoint, anyway—has always been impeccable. Yes, you're sarcastic, sometimes even a little pompous—"

Veronica arched a protesting brow at that.

"—but we've always been able to count on you. You're a Melendez through and through—stubborn, proud, sometimes unreasonable—but extremely loyal. You're also a college graduate, capable of deciding how to live your life. We don't have to agree with you, but we do need to respect you. You owe the same to the rest of us." She went on with a slight smile. "I remember when I decided to enter the novitiate. You were only thirteen, but you stood by me, Roni. Of course, Mama was in favor of it. But Dad balked; even Frank and Angela did—probably because they felt I was too young to make the decision." Lucy took a breath. "I'm not equating your position with mine, though. Mine was definitely a choice."

Veronica was about to cut in. When the nun held up her hand, her sister backed down.

"I chose to dedicate my life to God and made my final vows. If I hadn't chosen that, I probably would've married and had children. However," Lucy said, meeting Veronica's eyes, "from what I've studied, homosexuality is not a matter of choice. Perhaps it's genetic—the evidence is not in yet. If you have the predisposition to be sexually attracted—"

Veronica could not keep quiet any longer. "It's *more* than sexual, Lucy. It involves an emotional, intellectual and spiritual attraction as well. You can't expect me to be celibate for the rest of my life because the Church doesn't recognize same-sex relationships." She leaned towards her sister in her fervor to explain. "I loved Joanna with my whole being. How can that be a sin? Her death left me desolate, so full of grief I wanted to die, too. And despite what Isabel says, I absolutely cannot believe Joanna is burning in purgatory because of me."

Lucy's eyes welled and she reached over to clasp her sister's hand. "Dios mio. When did Isabel say *that*?"

"This morning—at the cemetery."

"She's displacing, Roni. Her real fury is towards Joanna."

"I know, but the words still hurt." She grasped Lucy's hand. She wanted so much for her to understand. "I love Joanna, and I miss her every day. As much as she loved me, too, I know she wouldn't expect me to spend the rest of my life alone. She'd want me to find another woman to love."

Her sister's voice was steady. "Have you?"

Veronica felt shy for the first time that evening. "I was involved with someone, but that's over now." She sighed and went on. "Lucy, I've begun to care very much for René—and she feels the same about me."

Rising, her heavy brown skirt whooshing against the hardwood floor, the nun kissed Veronica's forehead. "You've always been such a complicated kid."

"Do you have to leave?" Veronica leaned against her, wanting to stay up all night with her.

"Yes. We can talk more tomorrow." Lucy moved towards the door. "Sleep well, Roni. Breakfast is at 8:00 in the main dining hall. I have Mother Superior's permission to eat with you."

"See you then. Buenas noches."

"Y que Dios te bendiga, hermanita."

In the uncommon silence, punctuated only by the staccato chirping of crickets, Veronica undressed for bed, attuned to each movement of her body in that barren room.

Removing her shirt, she felt her shoulder blades crack, protesting the sudden movement after immobile hours at the typewriter. She sat on the edge of the bed and rotated her neck, barely loosening the tension congealed there.

The cool evening air drifting through the window caused her to shiver. She pulled on a cotton nightshirt and tugged off her jeans. Nestling within the frigid sheets and woolen blankets, she sought warmth. Her conversation with Lucy, as frustrating as it had been at times, had rekindled memories. She remembered how she and Joanna had snuggled together that last Thanksgiving weekend in Idyllwild, their combined body heat and physical passion obliterating the mountain chill. Cuddling Joanna's tawny body, Veronica had never felt so wanted, so loved.

Alone in the darkness, she tried not to remember those loving nights, those glorious mornings with Joanna. Lulled by the encompassing silence, exhausted by her verbal exchanges with her sister, she closed her teary eyes and slept.

18

THE MORNING DAWNED in grey mist, swirling patches of fog among the pines. In the dampness, Veronica awakened, at first disoriented. Realizing she was not in the Idyllwild of her dreams, but alone in Santa Barbara, she shook the sleep from her eyes. She showered, donned jeans, a white pullover and Nikes, and ambled outdoors.

Pausing at the bungalow door, she inhaled the piney scent and noted the blanket of drying needles beneath her feet. Briskly, she strode towards the fruit orchard, swinging her arms in unison with her strides. She walked the perimeter, intent on her surroundings. Sunlight filtered through the drifting fog.

Shifting reality to the background, she pondered the work ahead, deliberating unwritten dialog, unspoken action. Preoccupied, she did not notice she had reached the refectory until she smelled freshly brewed coffee. Hands in jeans' pockets, she pushed open the dining hall's heavy door with her elbow and stepped inside.

Clumps of early risers milled about, breakfast trays in hands, forming a haphazard line. She noticed the only other brown-skinned people were the kitchen help; that did not surprise her. She dallied by the doorway, uncertain as to where to find her sister. Then she felt Lucy's hand cup her elbow.

The nun guided her into a private dining area and Veronica picked a corner table overlooking the woods.

Lucy had no trace of sleepiness in her voice.

"I went by your bungalow and couldn't believe you'd already left."

"The coffee lured me."

"It couldn't be the people," her sister remarked wryly. "Be right back with your breakfast—and don't argue. It's taken me forever to get you here. Let me at least wait on you."

"Who's arguing? Just hurry. I'm starved."

Veronica and Lucy shared family gossip and avoided the previous evening's topics. The nun was concerned about Phil's stepmother dilemma, and she and Veronica discussed this at length. Before Veronica returned to the bungalow, Lucy persuaded her to meet with Mother Superior and the others. Veronica was touched by the nuns' solicitude; they were sincere, caring women, and she felt cynical in comparison.

In the late afternoon, she wandered into the orchard, through clusters of peach and fig trees, and followed a trickling stream leading further into the woods. Striding parallel to its rippling waters, she relished the verdant solitude of the pines and the clean mountain scent. Like the air, her mind seemed clear, focused on writing rather than worries.

For nearly an hour she traversed the narrow path, plotting her next day's work and daydreaming about Talamantes. She missed the verbal give-and-take of their creative sessions. In fact, Veronica found she missed Talamantes more than she had expected, emotionally—and sexually. She hardly thought about Siena; René stayed on her mind.

And her days fell into a predictable pattern: early

morning walk, breakfast with Lucy, working on the stories, no lunch, an afternoon hike, dinner with Lucy—their conversation often continuing in Veronica's bungalow—and nights of uninterrupted sleep. She had no nightmares, few flashbacks about Joanna's death. Once in a while, she envied the nun's structured life; yet Veronica realized her own self-discipline, attuned to fiction writing rather than to religious ideals, served her equally well. Not only had both sisters found their places, but also they respected each other. Veronica promised herself this time at St. Teresa's would not be her last.

While Lucy conversed with an elderly couple, Veronica left the main dining hall and dashed into a tiny alcove housing the public telephone. She inserted coins and deftly punched in the area code and seven memorized numbers.

"Bueno," A contralto voice announced. For a moment, Veronica was taken aback before remembering René's mother did not speak English.

"Buenas noches," she stuttered in California-accented Spanish. "Está René en la casa?"

"Pues, si. Quien habla, por favor?"

"Veronica Melendez."

"Ah, la escritora." Senora Talamantes no doubt had heard about her. "Un momento, querida."

Before she could contemplate how much René had confided, Veronica heard that longed-for voice zing through the phone cord.

"Hey, mujer. I was about to send up a smoke signal for you. Did you jump over the wall?"

"Not quite." Veronica tried to sound nonchalant, despite her hammering heart. "Just thought I'd call."

"Miss me?"

"Now and then."

René laughed at that. "Too busy to think about me all the time, huh? How's the writing?"

"Frustrating at times, but I'm determined to meet Zamora's deadline. I have no excuse now, René." Veronica leaned against the stucco wall and wished Talamantes were not so far away.

"Que suave."

"Well, there's nothing here to distract me."

"No black-haired Tejanas with flashing eyes?"

"I wouldn't mind one of those."

"Soon, preciosa," Talamantes drawled. "Saw Camille yesterday. Says she got a postcard from you. Seems glad you're hard at work."

"I thought I'd let her know I'm here. Otherwise, she might think I skipped town for good."

"She knows I wouldn't let that happen."

Veronica frowned into the receiver. "What've you told her about me?"

"Nada—other than we've started checking out each other's work. Camille's cool. She knows I'm a dyke, pero she's too discreet to get personal."

"I should be so lucky. *I* get the third degree from her."

"'Cause she cares. By the way, cómo está tu hermana?"

Veronica ran a finger along the rough plaster. "Lucy's a good listener. Sometimes she's amazed at how vocal I am about being a lesbian. We've had some interesting conversations."

"I miss you, Verónica."

"I'll be home soon." René's fervor excited her, but she kept a steady tone. "Have you seen Michi?"

"She's fine—likes the job. I've had lunch with her a

few times. Mainly, I've been rewriting 'Adobe.'"

"I'd like to see it."

"You will. When should I drive up, mujer?"

"I'll let you know. René—"

"Dígame."

"Come alone."

"Si quieres." Talamantes laughed. "I'm beginning to get the picture—it was a little hazy at first. You're serious?"

"Very. I'll phone again next week. Ten cuidado," she whispered and hung up.

Veronica wished she had a radio. Feeling giddy after talking with René, she wanted to boogie to golden oldies, sing aloud with the Supremes or Aretha, do something outrageous. For the first time since her arrival, she left her day's work untouched. She went into the bungalow's small bathroom and peeled off her clothes. In the shower, she belted "Baby Love," "Come See About Me" and "Back in My Arms Again," shimmying out in her sleek brown nudity. She grabbed a a towel and even did a few bumps and grinds while drying herself. Amused by her undulations, she giggled at her reflection in the misty mirror. After towel drying her hair, she bounced into bed and made herself comfortable before pleasuring herself. She dreamed of René's loving fingers arousing her.

One afternoon not long afterwards, Lucy poked her head through the casement window, her veil almost catching on the latch.

Veronica paused at the typewriter. "Hey, flying nun—what's up?"

"For you." Lucy smiled and handed her a rectangular brown-wrapped parcel. "I have a counselling hour, Roni.

See you at dinner."

When Lucy departed along the gravelled path, Veronica stared at the taped parcel, noting its Santa Monica return address. Slowly, she began to undo the wrapping. Within layers of pale pink tissue paper, she found a beautifully designed purple silk caftan. As she removed the robe from its box, a small envelope slid out.

Dear Veronica,

I've decided to spend the rest of the summer in Sonoma with my mother and grandmother. After you left, it finally dawned on me how lonely I've been. I've seen how you've gathered strength from Frank and Phil, and I need my family, too. I know it won't be easy, but I'm going to tell them about the abortion.

I'm not exaggerating when I say you're the best friend I've ever had. You've convinced me to believe in myself, no matter what anyone else thinks. You've always been upfront with me, more than I was with you, and I'm sorry.

Sometimes I wonder if you'll be the only woman in my life. Before you, I never would've considered loving a woman, but now—I don't know.

I'm not sure if I'll be back in L.A. for the design class in January. Right now, I'm just not sure of anything. Whether I come back or not, I want us to be friends. You mean very much to me, Veronica.

Good luck with your stories. I want to read them someday.

Your friend, Siena

She let the letter slide through her fingers to the neat folds of tissue paper. Siena had left no forwarding address.

With a sigh, Veronica rose and lifted the silk caftan from its box. When she tried it on, the rich fabric fell over her gracefully, concealing her slender form. Unlike Lucy's coarse woolen habit, the caftan seemed elegant, luxurious. Veronica remembered the Latinas in Talamantes's film, clad in transparent robes, and she whirled and twirled in awkward imitation. Feeling dizzy, she sank to the narrow bed. She touched the caftan's silken texture, and cried.

"I never expected her to pack up and head for Sonoma, but once Siena makes up her mind, that's it." Veronica swirled the mashed potatoes, topping them with an array of peas and carrots.

"You said she'd gone to confession after—the abortion?"

Veronica nodded.

"As long as you're staying here, I wish you'd talk with Father Riley—"

"Lucy, you're the only one I'll talk to about personal stuff. Don't need any judgmental priest telling me I'm hell-bound."

Her sister took on a placating tone. "Roni, the Church does not consider the state of being homosexual as sinful. It—"

"—considers the *practice* of homosexuality to be. In other words, I shouldn't look forward to a future with René." Veronica cocked a dark brow. "I'm to be commended for saying 'bye-bye' to Siena and freeing her for some unsuspecting male, but *I'd* just better not make plans for the next woman." She pointed her fork at Lucy. "Listen, all my life I've heard 'God is love.' If that's true, why should the love I feel towards a woman be sinful? Love is love. Why should it matter whom I direct it to? It's a human emotion—a human response. Am I supposed to deny my humanity just because some celibate geezer in the Vatican says so?" She flicked the air with her hand, a gesture reminiscent of her mother. "Give me a break, Lucy. I'm an intelligent woman. I'm not falling for that."

The nun kept her voice modulated. "I would never try to make you change your life. You've told me you loved Joanna, and I believe you. But can't you see? Not every woman you meet is Joanna. I think Mama and Dad would've accepted your love for her, and tried to understand it. But I doubt if they'll be receptive towards any other—"

Veronica leaned forward. "Joanna has been dead almost a year. I miss her terribly, but as each day passes, I've become stronger, less dependent on memories. Right after the accident, I didn't want to go on without her. I've found out since that I can, and that I'm lovable—not only as I was to her—but to other women as well. There's absolutely no way on earth I'll deny myself the right to love and be loved. If Mom and Dad don't like it, that's too bad." She paused, running a hand through her hair. "They didn't like Joyce either, and Frank didn't let that stop him—he married her anyway."

Lucy folded her napkin and set it on the table. "More than anything else, Mama and Dad are going to have trouble with the religious aspect—or I should say, with the lack of religion in your life."

"Am I immoral?" Veronica sighed. "Why should I pledge allegiance to a Church that denigrates me? I live by the Golden Rule. What more do Mom and Dad want?"

"They want you to accept their values, not reject them."

Veronica felt her exasperation rise. What had happened to the adventurous Lucy, the one who had lobbed baseballs on the garage roof just for the chance to climb up to retrieve them? This brown-garbed nun, with her conservative talk and knit brows, hardly seemed the same person. But then, Veronica mused, she had changed, too.

"Mom loves having a daughter who's a nun. That's fine—but I'm not you, Lucy. Anyway, Mom and Dad are from a different generation, a different sexual orientation. How can they—or anyone else in our family—possibly understand me? *You* don't even understand my need to write, much less my being a lesbian."

Lucy sipped her tea and seemed determined to ignore this latest outburst. "Your supper's getting cold," she advised, taking no notice of her sister's glare. "I only want you to be prepared for the worst, Roni. Sometimes I wish you didn't have to tell Mama and Dad anything."

"Would you rather have me stay in the closet and lead a double life? I've done that already, and I don't want to keep doing it. Besides, according to Isabel, Mom already knows. I'm surprised she hasn't driven up here, just to pin me down."

Lucy sighed. "I think Mama would like to erase it as much as possible. Actually, Frank has the best idea. Don't say anything unless you get involved with another woman."

Veronica met her gaze. "I'm on the brink, in case you haven't noticed. René's going to drive me home."

The nun refilled their teacups. "I don't think you should implicate her in all this."

"She wants to meet them. And, believe me, René can handle anything."

Veronica sat motionless for several moments, unrolling the last page from the platen. Setting it beside the others, she rested her dark head on the silent typewriter. Ahead lay the editing of these latest three stories for Camille Zamora. That process would be time-consuming, challenging, but the groundwork had been laid; the foundation was in place.

Throwing on a sweatshirt, she jogged to the refectory and darted into the alcove. A grey-haired man in a business suit, briefcase by his side, clutched the phone possessively and ignored her restless pacing. Irked, she headed into the orchard. Kicking several stones from the path, she wondered why she felt more depressed than euphoric.

"Se acabó," She whispered to René a few minutes later.

"Ay, mujer. Estoy encantada! Let's go out and celebrate."

Veronica smiled into the phone at hearing the joy in Talamantes' voice. She wished she could feel as ecstatic. "Hey, loca—this is just the beginning. I still have to clean up my drafts before showing them to Zamora. There're tough times ahead."

"I know, but loosen up a little. Editing can be a bitch, sure. I just about pulled out my grenas when I was working on 'Tortilleras,' and I still think it could use some changes here and there. Pero, don't forget—you've got three stories plotted out, ready for fine tuning, plus the three Zamora's seen already. A few months ago, you were flat on your back in the hospital. You've done a lot since then, mujer."

Veronica sighed. "I've lost a lot, too."

"Es la verdad, preciosa," René said softly. "It must be real hard to write about Joanna. You've said yourself that one way of cherishing her memory is to write about her—"

"When I put her in a story, René, I can bring her back—even it's for a little while."

"Si. And she'll always be in your corazón. When your stories are finished, she'll come alive for others, too."

"That isn't the same as having her here." Veronica closed her eyes and leaned against the stucco wall. "We grew up together and shared *everything*. A part of me wants to share this with her, too."

"That makes sense."

"Be honest. Does that bother you?"

"Un poco, but I can handle it. Can you?"

"René, if I couldn't, I wouldn't be asking you to come for me tomorrow." She hesitated for a moment. "Sorry I've sounded so low tonight. Comes with the territory, I guess."

"I've been there myself, preciosa. And I'll be there for you."

"We *will* celebrate, René, just the two of us. I miss you so much."

Talamantes took on a teasing tone. "I could drive up right now."

"No. Be here early instead. We'll find a place to stay and spend the whole day together."

"I love you, Verónica."

"Hasta mañana."

She padded barefoot from the bathroom with a bag of toiletries. "Don't know exactly when I'll be home, Lucy, but I don't want the family worrying about me. I'd appreciate your not mentioning when I leave."

"I don't like being a party to this."

Veronica slipped an arm around Lucy's thin waist.

"Relax, sis. Don't be such a prude. I remember when you used to neck with Johnny Hernández in the balcony of the Criterion."

"I was a silly teenager then." The nun's face reddened. "And how did you ever know about that?"

Veronica grinned and squeezed her closer. "Joanna and I used to spy on you. Afterwards, we'd go to her house and practice kissing."

"Too precocious for your own good." Flustered, Lucy moved across the room, picked up her sister's dictionary and thesaurus and set them in the suitcase. "You're more opinionated than ever, but I must admit I've enjoyed your visit."

"Me, too." Veronica approached and gently encircled Lucy's waist again. "I love you, sis."

Lucy pursed her lips. "I love you, too, Aztec-nose. And no matter what, you know you can count on me." She nudged her sister's chin. "I have a feeling I'll hear the fireworks all the way up the coast, but I really hope everything goes fine when you talk with Mom and Dad. I'm proud of you, Roni, for sticking to your principles, even if I don't agree with them. You don't let anyone push you around."

Veronica hoped not to cry, but already she felt the sting of tears. "All of a sudden, Lucy, I wish I could stay. I needed quiet time, away from everyone, and you made that possible. How can I ever thank you?"

The nun gazed at her fondly. "By coming back. Don't wait for a crisis next time, Roni."

"Just try keeping me away. Can I bring René with me?"

"Ay, muchacha—what am I going to do with you?" Lucy looked more amused than exasperated.

*

Veronica piled her belongings near the desk, left a note tacked on the door, and went off for a final hike. At sunrise, the country air was invigorating; her breath vaporized as she tramped through the forest. She touched the gnarled tree trunks, bade good-bye to those steadfast friends and saved their verdant leaves for remembrances. She straddled a fallen log, plucked dandelions and whirled their fluffy tendrils into the wind. She surveyed the stream with its smooth colored stones and listened to its ageless secrets; its whispery tones seemed to mimic her thoughts.

"René's coming. She'll be here soon. Why am I so nervous?"

Grabbing a handful of rocks, she tossed them into the stream, watching the heavier ones settle at the bottom. Then, restless, she followed the path further, sunlight beaming at her through the forest shadows. Soon she realized she had hiked further than planned and reversed direction.

Rounding a hairpin curve, she glimpsed Talamantes striding towards her. Veronica stopped and stared at that tall, full-breasted Chicana.

Talamantes' voice was smoky. "De donde vienes, mujer?"

"De mi corazón a ti."

Then she could not wait to be with her. Running, she laughed aloud in her exhilaration. René stood grinning, arms outstretched.

When her sneakered feet fell on mud-caked leaves, Veronica slipped. Reaching to catch her, René also lost her footing. They tumbled in a heap, wrapped in each other's arms. Their dark eyes mirrored mutual delight. With no hesitation, their yearning lips met and held. On the leaf-covered forest floor, they continued kissing and holding each other.

"You really came for me." Veronica smoothed Talamantes's thick forelock from her brow.

"You knew I would."

"Will you always be here?"

"Para siempre, preciosa." She held up a motel key attached to a plastic rectangle. "And this is for today, for us."

And they kissed again and again.

19

Touching her, Veronica's fingertips tingled. René's coppery skin was faintly brushed with down, from her firm arms to her long legs, a fine down attesting to a long-ago conquistador. It swirled at the nape of her neck, meeting her thick black hair, glossy and straight as that of any Azteca. Another whorl decorated the base of her spine, where her slim buttocks fanned from her hips. Veronica's errant fingers traced that velvety path, and she listened with pleasure to René's sudden intake of breath. But she did not linger.

Lying beside her, she instead guided her wandering hands to those high symmetrical breasts, each tipped with a prominent ever-darkening nipple. Along the encircling areolae grew more sparse hairs, as black as René's mane, trimming her bosom with their primitive design. With her tongue, Veronica teased each nipple, smiling as they grew taut. As her eager lips surrounded one, she heard René gasp again.

Then she felt warm hands encompassing her, one on each buttock, drawing her nearer. While Veronica continued sucking her, René allowed her fingers to begin their own exploratory journey. She touched Veronica's scarred leg, outlining its surgical incision. Lifting her head, Veronica looked at her questioningly.

"Eres tan linda," Talamantes whispered.

Veronica smiled. She knew René wanted her; their

desire was identical. She's like me, she thought—so brown, so Chicana.

René brought her mouth closer and they kissed repeatedly, tongues enraptured. fingers relentless, bodies reeling. Their combined feminine scent defied the motel room's air-conditioned ambience.

Legs askew, Veronica shuddered when that nimble tongue found her aching clitoris. She closed her eyes and moaned, feeling René's loving mouth provoke her. Her pleasure was intense, and she spread her thighs apart. She opened her eyes briefly and became even more excited at seeing that dark head between her legs, that passionate brown woman making love to her. Dizzy with ecstasy, Veronica came over and over, then lay still.

René sprawled beside her. "Como te sientes, hermosa?"

"Maravillosa. Y muy contenta." Breathless, she gazed at Talamantes. "Ahora, mi mujer, que quieres?"

With a sly grin, Talamantes rolled closer, still caressing her. "Te recuerdas que soy tortillera?"

Still aroused, Veronica nodded, watching René mount her outstretched leg. Moving one hand between her slim thigh and that juicy vulva, she slipped two fingers within, her thumb inciting René's clitoris. Yearning mouth at Veronica's breast, René rode her emphatically, groaning at the multiple sensations of her lover's fingers and her own vigorous exertions. She pressed herself against the bony ridge of Veronica's thigh and came convulsively, her long body sinking on her lover's. Entwined and exhausted, they exchanged lazy kisses and slept.

Heavily lashed eyes closed, René seemed vulnerable, her sensual lips parted, her blue-black hair mussed against Veronica's arm. Her coppery complexion accentuated the whiteness of the sheets, and her willowy body remained still, a definite contrast to her customary restlessness.

Veronica caressed her lover's wide shoulder, encouraging her closer. René snuggled, her lips inadvertently brushing Veronica's breast. And in her sleep, René seemed to welcome that fleeting contact. On reflex, her mouth surrounded the already erect nipple. While she suckled, Veronica tenderly embraced her, securing her near.

On many other mornings, long-ago but not forgotten, Joanna had lain with her, offering and sharing these same pleasures. In that silent motel room, Veronica squeezed her eyes tight at the memory of that tawny body beside hers, those memorable lips at her breast. Sometimes Joanna would nip her and laugh, her brown hair cascading. In her mind, Veronica could hear Joanna's bell-like voice, see her glorious eyes. She would never forget her; yet those days were gone forever. Enjoying René's suckling mouth, witnessing her tranquil sleep, Veronica rejoiced in the promising future.

"Estaba tan cansada." On awakening, René grinned at Veronica's skeptical expression. "De veras, mujer. Hardly slept last night, and then drove a couple of hours to get here."

Veronica leaned over and kissed her. "I didn't mind. I love watching you."

René looked embarrassed, but accepted the kiss, her ebony eyes appraising. "You're speaking English."

Veronica laughed. "What?"

"You spoke only Spanish—before. Sin duda, I bring out your Chicana nature." Talamantes fingered her lover's tousled hair. "Quiero vivir contigo."

"René, you're so impulsive. It's much too soon."

"But I love you, mujer."

"I—I love you, too." Veronica felt herself blush.

Laughing, René continued surveying her. "We do have to be realistic, huh? I have to figure out what to do about my mother. And—"

"I have to come out to my parents."

"Yeah." René's eyes met hers. "Ven aquí, preciosa." Flat on her back, she opened her arms. Unhesitantly, Veronica lay over her, her head cushioned on those warm breasts. "I want to be with you when you tell them."

"Oh." Remembering Lucy's admonition, Veronica raised her head. "I don't know about that."

"They'll more likely believe you if I'm there. My mother thought I was jivin' till I introduced her to my first lover. She'd figured it was all talk." Talamantes continued to smooth Veronica's hair. "Besides, I charmed your brother and Phil. Just wait till Sara and Joe meet me."

Veronica was unconvinced, but she did not want to argue, too distracted by those deep-set eyes.

Raising herself on her elbows, she offered her breasts and aimed one towards René's ready mouth. Talamantes bit her nipple, causing Veronica to moan with anticipation. And while she sucked her, René groped between those already parted legs. Veronica touched her, too, one thumb endlessly provoking her while her fingers moved inside. Intent on each other's pleasure, they kissed, tongues teasing.

Pausing, Veronica ducked downwards; she wanted to taste her. She revelled in René's opaque secretions, her womanly fragrance. She liked the purplish tinge of René's velvety labia. Her clitoris stood to meet Veronica's tongue, and she licked it repeatedly before sucking it. René groaned anew at each brush-like stroke. And she came suddenly, strongly.

Moving over her again, Veronica waited for René to acknowledge her. Breathless, she nodded and Veronica straddled her, tensing when René's long fingers reached her cervix. She wanted more and more pleasure. Mesmerized by each other, they made love endlessly.

Ravenous, they found a nearby restaurant and dined on salad, baked potatoes and New York steaks, but their eyes remained solely on one another.

"Tell me about your stories."

Veronica sipped the zinfandel. "Well, the new ones are about adolescence—with some lesbian hints. I wonder what Zamora will think."

René munched some steak. "She probably won't be too surprised since you're hanging out with me. So the new stories are about dykes?"

"One of them involves sexual experimentation between Chicana teenagers—obviously, it's autobiographical. If Zamora wants Chicana stories from me, that's what she's getting. Anyhow, besides Cherríe Moraga and Gloria Anzaldúa, who else writes about Chicana lesbians nowadays?"

"I do." Talamantes grinned at her lover's omission. "But you don't think screenwriting's legit."

"When did I say that?"

René filled her glass from the carafe. "I've read between the lines."

"Talamantes, 'Adobe' is a very compelling piece."

"As long as I make *your* revisions." She gave Veronica a teasing glance. "Actually, I'm glad you gave me those tips. Sometimes being with your own work for too long makes you insular."

"Which means you want to read my stories."

René picked up the glass and saluted her. "Not exactly subtle, am I?"

"No. Look, as soon as I have all six stories xeroxed, you can have copies. Just remember they're not in final form. It'll probably take you all day to read them."

"All day, huh? What about—"

"Talamantes, you have to plan your time." Veronica enjoyed their bantering, but she did not really want to discuss the stories. She wanted to return to the motel for more private moments instead. "Loca, where's your self-discipline?"

"Back in Venice." Talamantes laughed, caressing Veronica's hand. She signalled the waiter for the check.

"Did you think of her while—"

"Not during—afterwards. Joanna still flashes into my mind, but it's different now. I'm learning to let go. It's strange—" Veronica paused, leaning against the pillows.

"Que, preciosa?"

"Even though you and Joanna are completely unalike, being with you seems so familiar. Maybe it's because you're Chicana, too, and there are so many things I don't have to explain. For instance, with Siena, there was a cultural difference—"

"Not to mention she's also straight."

"Well, yes." Veronica shrugged. "I don't know, René. With you, I can really be myself. I feel this tremendous connection between us—maybe 'cause we're both writers."

"This is mainly an intellectual attraction?"

Veronica felt herself blush. "It's much more, loca."

"Is the supposedly articulate Veronica Melendez tongue-tied?"

"Momentarily." Dropping her gaze, Veronica drew a lazy index finger along René's sloping shoulder. "Before I met you, I was so lonely. I missed Joanna. Even with Siena, I had this feeling of isolation—of being with her sexually, but not really otherwise. Of course, that didn't stop me." She glanced at Talamantes before continuing. "When Michi and I saw 'Tortilleras,' I was fascinated, not only by the film, but also by your finesse with the audience. You were so in control, René."

"I was scared shitless."

"You didn't show it. And—this probably sounds odd—I was so proud of you! I didn't even know you, but I felt such admiration. You stood up to that mostly male audience and showed your pluck. I was very attracted to you that night."

"You didn't say that then." René watched her, twirling a strand of Veronica's hair.

"Of course not."

Amused, René lifted Veronica's chin and kissed her full on the lips. "Playing hard to get."

"No. I was involved with Siena. René, I'm not a two-timer. Anyway, I don't rely on sexual attraction only."

"That's right. There has to be some intellectual stimulation, too." Talamantes smirked, one finger poking Veronica's left nipple.

"Stop it." She tried to stay intent on her narrative. "Of course, my opinion changed at the dance. You were horrid then."

"De veras. Consumed with jealousy."

"I hope that isn't typical behavior."

"Hey, I lost my cool that night. Haven't made an ass of myself since."

Veronica pretended to mull this over, laughing outright at her lover's perplexed expression. "No. You've been exceptional."

Talamantes leaned closer. "That's why you love me?"

Veronica slipped her arms around her. "I love you because you're not afraid of being René Talamantes. You're proud of your roots. You're a tantalizing blend of hardheaded Tejana traditions and lesbian creativity. And I want to learn from your fearlessness."

"Veronica, sometimes it's an act."

"Not where I'm concerned, I hope."

"Ni modo, preciosa. Just don't idolize me."

"I won't," She whispered, her lips inches away. "But I will love you."

Before leaving Santa Barbara, they visited the botanical gardens, not far from the Mission. They hiked its winding trails, stealing kisses behind lush vegetation. Pausing, they sat on a large boulder, arms around each other, and observed the panoramic view.

Lips nibbling Veronica's ear, René sighed. "Too bad we have to go home."

"We can't afford to stay another night."

"We could camp on the beach, sleep in my van."

"And eat seaweed for breakfast, I suppose."

"Where's your spirit of adventure, Veronica?"

She leaned against Talamantes. "I don't want to go back either, but postponing it won't solve anything. Anyway, I have to pack my stuff for the move this weekend."

"Michi's looking forward to that. Have you been back to the apartment since—"

Veronica shook her head.

"Are Joanna's things still there?"

"Her parents left only her books and record albums."

René touched her lover's shoulder. "Can I stay with

you the first night?"

Veronica met her gaze again. "We'll see."

Taking the coastal route, they left picturesque Santa Barbara, its pink and white oleander bushes waving in the distance. Veronica's eyes were on the southbound traffic and she kept a reflective silence.

"I don't want to be dependent on you."

"Always thought you were *independent*."

"I did, too—till Joanna died. I relied on her a lot, René. She used to pull me out of my down moods. I tend to be a pessimist—sometimes I'm not too much fun to be around." She faced her with a challenging look. "Anyway, I'm not going to rely on you to snap me out of—"

Talamantes pushed back her unruly hair. "Veronica, if you can put up with me, I'll put up with you."

Veronica laughed then, recognizing the veracity of those words. Unlike Joanna, René could be mercurial, maddening, and even downright obnoxious.

"Maybe *I'm* the one who'll have her hands full."

"You said it, not me." René grinned across the cab. "Mira, mujer—I love you. That's all that really counts, verdad?"

She patted Talamantes's slim thigh. "Verdad."

By twilight, they arrived in Santa Monica, avoiding the beach traffic by heading inland past Oxnard. With no one home at Frank's condo, they headed to Veronica's parents' house.

"You don't have to tell them tonight."

"I want to get it over with."

An ocean breeze rustled the eucalyptus trees on the

corner. Leaving the van, Veronica strode hand in hand with her lover, pausing to survey her childhood home. She admired the neatly mown lawn with its rainbow border of azaleas, sweet peas and pansies.

René seemed to read her thoughts. "How come dykes aren't identified with flowers?"

"Your hair's on end in the morning, just like those birds-of-paradise."

Grinning, René squeezed her hand. She studied her lover's face. "You really want to go through with this?"

Veronica nodded, afraid to lose courage by waiting another day. She felt queasy, but determined.

"Caprichuda. So stubborn."

"Get used to it." Veronica tried to be flippant, knowing René sensed her apprehension.

Together they approached the modest Spanish-styled house. Starting up the brick walkway to the front steps, they were almost overrun by Phil. He darted out the front door with a can of Budweiser in one hand and a Pepsi under his cast-bound arm.

"Hey, Roni." He halted at once. "Everybody's been wondering where you've been. Hi, René," He added, staring at their interlocked fingers.

"Everybody?" Veronica frowned. She noticed the boy seemed lankier; he would probably grow taller than Frank.

"Well, Grandma," He corrected. "Grandpa's in the garage, waiting for his beer." He was about to bound away.

"Wait, Phil." Veronica rubbed his thin shoulder. "How've you been, honey?"

He grinned at her affectionate action. "Okay."

"Getting along with Joyce?"

"Yeah." He did not seem eager to talk about that.

Veronica did not press him. "Is Dad alone?"

He nodded.

"Then we might as well see him first." Veronica slipped her arm around her nephew. René shrugged and followed them towards the garage.

"Look who I found, Grandpa," Phil shouted, leading them inside.

"Dónde estabas, muchacha?" Joe boomed with mock sternness. Wiping his greasy hands on a torn towel, he accepted the beer can while wrapping the other husky arm around his youngest daughter. "Roni, have you seen your mother yet? She's been on and off the phone with Lucy since you left St. Teresa's."

Veronica kissed his unshaven cheek, tickled by its scratchiness. He kissed her, too, resoundingly, but seemed to avoid her eyes. She wondered how much he knew.

"There was no need to worry. We just decided to spend another day in Santa Barbara." She gestured towards the tall Chicana beside her. "Dad, this is René Talamantes."

"Mucho gusto en conocerle, Señor Melendez." René eyed his oil-stained hands and instead clasped his hairy right wrist, giving it a firm squeeze.

At her spontaneous gesture, Joe chuckled and leaned against the Pontiac sedan. He was not much taller than his daughter's lover. "El gusto es mio, René. You're the movie maker, eh?"

Veronica noticed Phil's sheepish smile behind his Pepsi. How much else had he revealed?

"My reputation precedes me." Talamantes laughed, giving Phil a playful nudge. She displayed her usual self-assurance. "What kind of car trouble are you having, Señor?"

277

Joe slapped the Pontiac's hood. "Dead battery. Mi esposa forgot to shut off the lights after the novena last night."

"That isn't like Mom," Veronica murmured.

"Está preocupada por ti, Roni. Go in and talk to her while I put in the new battery."

She preferred to postpone seeing her mother for the time being. Instead, she nestled against her father, feeling his solid strength. His muscled brown arm remained around her.

"Dad—"

He kissed the top of her curly head. "Next time, phone if you decide to stay longer. It's a miracle your mother didn't contact the Highway Patrol. Besides, Frank's ready to move you out this weekend. Your apartment's empty, waiting for you and Michi." At her serious expression, he softened his words. "We missed you, Roni. Todo está bien?"

She nodded. "I feel better than I have in months."

He kissed her forehead. "You look it, too. And Lucy says you behaved yourself."

At that, Verónica smiled. "According to Mother Superior, I'm an ideal guest."

"Otro milagro." He toasted her with the beer can.

"She's in the kitchen." Veronica and René stood in the Melendez living room. "Stay here."

"Veronica—careful what you say."

She nodded and moved away with more determination than she felt. Peering into the kitchen, she saw her mother. Sara hummed to herself, her stout body moving efficiently as she dried the dinner dishes and utensils, storing them in cupboards and drawers.

"I'm back, Mom."

Startled, Sara dropped a handful of silverware with a clatter. Leaving the utensils scattered on the linoleum floor, she whisked her daughter into her plump arms.

"Ay, Roni. Por Dios, dónde estabas?"

"Dad said you were worried." Her mother's arms hardly let her move. "I didn't mean to—"

"I thought you were never coming back." Sara broke into harsh sobs.

"Mama, please don't cry." Veronica felt her own eyes mist. Telling her was not going to be easy. "Why did you think—?"

"Because everybody's talking about—you." Wiping her eyes on her gingham apron, Sara stepped back and clasped her daughter's hands.

"Oh." Veronica made herself look at her. "That's exactly why I had to come back, Mama—to tell you everything."

Sara wept, her round face dissolving into distressed creases.

Veronica caressed her mother's quivering back. "No llores por mi, Mama. Ven conmigo. Mi compañera está en la sala."

Sara gasped. "She's here?"

Veronica gently tugged at her. "Yes. I want you to meet her and know why I love her. Please come with me, Mama."

20

Sara impassively studied René. Knowing her mother's aversion to darker-skinned Chicanas, Veronica was sure Talamantes's coppery complexion, her long-legged height, the mestiza coarseness of her thick hair, and her assertive dyke stance scored negative points. Her mother no doubt remembered Joanna had been the opposite in appearance.

René grinned, ignoring the unspoken animosity. "Siento mucho que llegamos tan tarde, Señora Melendez."

"Roni knows she should have phoned."

Veronica took note of that curt rebuff in English.

Maintaining a stoic demeanor, Sara glanced at her daughter and settled into one of the corduroy easy chairs. "Lucy told me to listen to what you have to say."

Queasily, Veronica sank next to René on the flowered sofa. "Mama, you said everybody's talking—not only about me—about Joanna, too." She hoped to keep the tremor from her voice. "She and I loved each other. We weren't ashamed of it then, and I'm not ashamed of it now. I'm a lesbian, Mama."

She saw her mother recoil, and felt René's hand clasp hers. Not daring to let Sara to speak yet, Veronica continued quickly. "I'm not going to hide anymore. I thought Joanna would always be part of my life. I was very happy with her. But she's dead, Mama, and I'm still here."

Sara stared at the Sacred Heart statue atop the dining

room hutch. Was she even absorbing her daughter's words? Veronica could not tell, but she kept talking.

"It hasn't been easy, but I've learned to live without Joanna. Even so, I don't intend to stay alone. I love René, and she loves me."

"Y tu religión?" At last, Sara turned to look at her. Her voice was tremulous, eyes anguished.

"The Church says we're wrong. I refuse to believe that—and I feel no guilt." Her eyes never left her mother's wounded ones.

"Have you talked with a priest?"

Veronica shook her head. "I know what's right for me, Mama."

Sara glared at that. "*You* know better than the Church? Since when? We sent you to Catholic schools, Roni—for what, eh? Is this why your life was spared, so you could wind up—" She waved her hands disdainfully in René's direction.

Her mother's angry words stung. Veronica did not want this discussion to disintegrate into finger-pointing and blame-finding. She wanted to keep it rational. "Lucy knows I'm sincere. She believes me."

"She doesn't agree with you, and you know it." Sara's hands clenched the border of her apron and she twisted its edges.

Veronica leaned forward, gesturing. She had let go of René's hand. In fact, she had almost forgotten Talamantes was beside her. "Lucy and I talked about this a lot, Mama. I'm *not* going through a phase. This is the way I want to live."

"Quieres vivir en pecado mortal? Your father and me didn't raise you for this, Roni."

"No matter how you raised me—I'm a lesbian. That's a fact." Veronica ran shaky fingers through her hair. "I should've told you this a long time ago. But I was afraid you'd hate me, disown me. Mama, I'm not afraid to be myself anymore."

"No puedo comprender todo esto. Y no quiero oirlo tampoco," Abruptly, Sara went back to the kitchen.

Veronica rubbed her eyes and felt her lover's arms surround her. "This isn't working, René."

"Go to her," Talamantes urged. "Tell her you're still her daughter. Tell her you haven't really changed. She needs to hear that. Verónica, *talk* with her."

"What if she doesn't listen?"

"You have to try, preciosa. Go ahead."

Steeling herself, Veronica began to rise, but René interrupted with a reassuring kiss. "I'll be here."

At the kitchen counter, Sara stood weeping into a dish-towel. She had picked up the fallen silverware and put it away. Quietly, Veronica approached and touched her shoulder. Sara stiffened, but did not otherwise move. "Ay, Roni."

Leaning against the sink, Veronica drew her near. "Mama, when I realized I was in love with Joanna, I didn't understand it either. I was very scared, but I knew she wasn't a bad—"

"That girl was an angel. Mira, hijita—sometimes chamacas get very attached to each other and—"

"No, Mama. I *loved* Joanna—the way you love Dad. That's true, whether you like hearing it or not. I'm only sorry you had to hear rumors before I had the courage to tell you myself."

Sara began to cry again, and her daughter embraced her.

"Maybe I shouldn't have brought René with me tonight. Maybe that was inconsiderate. But I just wanted to convince you that my feelings are genuine. Joanna was my first love. Now I love René."

Her mother sobbed harder.

"You were so upset when Frank started dating Joyce. Mama, I haven't forgotten that. It probably would've been easier for you if I hadn't told you the truth. I could've saved us all this turmoil. I could've denied the rumors. I could've lied to you. But I didn't want to, Mama." Veronica took a deep breath to keep herself from sobbing.

"Can you imagine how broken-hearted I was when Joanna died? Mama, I had no one to talk with about losing her. I couldn't tell you or Dad—I didn't know how you'd react. That's why I'd keep to myself, and not want to discuss the accident. That's why I acted cold sometimes. I didn't mean to pull away like that, but if I didn't, I thought I'd lose my mind. I wanted to die, too. No one understood that I loved Joanna with all my heart. Everyone thought she was only my friend—but, Mama, she was so much more."

"Ay, hijita." Sara raised her head and gazed at her daughter with growing compassion. She opened her arms, and with no hesitation, Veronica moved into them. Months' worth of pent-up tears flowed, and in that instant she realized how much she had longed for her mother's consolation.

Sara crooned to her, wiping her daughter's eyes with the edge of the dishcloth. "You've kept this secret so long. And you've been so brave since the accident. Pobrecita, mi niña. Yo no sabía tus sentimientos. Pensaba que no me querías. No sabía que me tenías miedo. Perdóname, por favor, Roni. Perdóname." Sara struggled with her emotions.

"Mama, there's nothing to forgive. You had no real idea of my feelings. I only wish you'd accept me as I am—because I love you very much."

"I love you, too, Roni. And you're still my baby."

Veronica smiled, lips quivering. "Well, I don't know about that. I'm grown up."

"You'll always be mi morenita," Sara chided. "Y nunca podia rechazarte." They hugged each other again.

"Mama—" She enjoyed snuggling against her mother and decided to take advantage of the situation.

"Si?"

"Do you think you can accept René as the woman I love? She's part of my life now."

Sara reached over and grabbed a paper towel. She blew her nose heartily, then frowned. "Pues, quién es esa mujer?"

Veronica smiled. Her mother was not one to give in easily. "Why don't we talk with her? You can ask her yourself."

Sara looked wary, but she took her daughter's arm, returning to the living room.

"Parece india," Sara muttered as she resettled into the easy chair. Veronica sat on its arm.

From the sofa came a throaty chuckle. "Parezco india porque mi abuelita tenía sangre Tarahumara. Pero no se apure, Señora Melendez. Soy civilizada, más o menos."

In her embarrassment, Sara's tear-swollen face became even redder.

Before her mother had a chance to apologize for the

frank remark, Veronica cut in, amused at Talamantes' audaciousness. "René's mother was born in Chihuahua, Mama. That's where your relatives are from, right?"

"Sí, casi todos." Sara straightened in her chair and crumpled her apron's edges. "I have nothing against los indios. I didn't mean to sound prejudiced, René."

Talamantes was undaunted. "You didn't, Señora. Even if you had, I'd understand, under the circumstances."

Wiping her eyes, Sara seemed baffled by the self-assured Chicana on the sofa, but her tone remained cool. "Is your family in Los Angeles?"

"I live with my mother in Venice. My father's in El Paso. They divorced about fifteen years ago."

"Que pena. Any brothers or sisters?"

"My father has three kids from his second marriage." Talamantes grinned, anticipating more questions.

Veronica looked at her mother, afraid the animosity would resurface. She aimed to keep the conversation light. "Mama, you'll never believe this, but I speak Spanish a lot with René. Remember all the times you've scolded me for not being bilingual? All of a sudden, I'm finding it easier to communicate in Spanish. You can give her credit for that."

Sara did not seem to listen. She allowed her gaze to drift again to that unflappable Chicana. "Do you love my daughter?"

René's answer held no trace of self-consciousness. "Con toda mi alma y corazón."

Leaning back, resignation and apprehension etched on her face, Sara sighed. "No puedo argüir con eso. Pero todavia no lo comprendo."

Veronica's voice was gentle. "Mama, you may never understand it." She hesitated, before adding, "Just please accept us."

With tenderness, Sara touched her daughter's cheek, but she did not look at Talamantes.

"Grandma wouldn't have liked Siena." Phil leaned on the open window when they drove him home.

"I'm not so sure she likes *me*," René admitted.

He smirked. "Jeez, don't complain. You've made out better than Joyce ever did."

"I'm Chicana, that's why."

"And she spoke Spanish most of the time, Phil," Veronica added. "That racked up some points."

"I bet." He laughed, nudging her. His grandparents had often scolded him for being monolingual; his language skills were even more limited than his aunt's. "Can't wait till we tell Dad. Even Grandpa was laid back."

"You never can tell with him. He hates personal conversations. But you'll have to let Frank know yourself. I'm staying at my apartment tonight. I'll be over tomorrow to get my stuff."

Phil gaped and Veronica pressed his knee. "René and I need to be alone."

"Oh." In his corner of the van, the boy was quiet. He did not seem to notice the smiling exchange between the women. "It's sure going to be different when you're back in your own place, Roni."

Talamantes halted the van at the condo's parking stalls.

"I won't be far." Veronica ruffled her nephew's hair. "And I'll always make time for you, Phil."

The boy cleared his throat, reluctant to leave.

With a rush of sentiment, Veronica hugged him, kissing his smooth forehead. "Will you help me with the move?"

"As much as I can with this bum arm."

"You can carry boxes on your head or balance them on this." René reached over to knock on his cast.

Phil smiled at that, but squirmed when Veronica kissed him again.

"Hey, amigo, you're not getting off that easy," Talamantes drawled when he began edging away. She grabbed his thin arm and pulled him across Veronica, towards her.

"Buenas noches, Felipe." René smooched him right on his bashful lips. He reddened considerably before slithering out.

"You guys're too mushy."

Honking the horn, they zoomed off.

On Amherst Avenue in West Los Angeles, 1950-era apartment buildings were sprinkled among single-story houses. Veronica began to open the passenger door even before René had parked. She faced the home she had last seen the previous November. In the summer darkness, she focused on the unlit second-floor balcony window.

"You want to go up first? I can bring your stuff in."

Veronica shook her head. "Come with me." She hurried across the lawn to the stairway.

The apartment building seemed unchanged, though recently painted. Joanna's favorite rosebush bloomed against the front wall. Climbing the stairs, Veronica's legs trembled. She grasped the steel railing and pulled the key from her canvas bag, trying not to recall her excitement that last weekend with Joanna when she had scampered down these same stairs to help her load the Rabbit for their Idyllwild weekend.

When René caught up, Veronica had unlocked the

door, but had not pushed it open. The doorknob looked more tarnished than she remembered.

"Que tienes, preciosa?" Talamantes squeezed her fingers.

"I'm scared."

"Hey—I'll be with you."

Veronica brought René's hand to her dry lips. She rubbed those strong brown fingers against her face and kissed them once more. Then she nudged open the door and found the wall switch. Light flooded the shadowy room, but the Chicanas remained in the threshold, hesitant to enter.

The small living room contained crowded bookcases, a secondhand loveseat covered with bright pillows, and an overstuffed chair. Georgia O'Keeffe prints highlighted the stark white walls. Noting the carpet looked freshly vacuumed, Veronica suspected Frank had been there earlier.

Everything looks the same, she thought—except Joanna is gone. She noticed the books remained in alphabetical order by author, and she ran her fingers along one shelf. It had been dusted; the fragrance of lemon oil still lingered. The living room seemed in a time warp, with no evidence that anyone had lived there since November.

René broke the silence. "Have to tell my mother we're back. Do you think the phone's hooked up?"

"Why don't you try it?" Zombie-like, Veronica moved into the adjacent hallway.

At the bedroom soon to be Michi's, she flicked on the light for an initial glimpse of its white-walled void. Joanna had kept her clothes there, the closet jam-packed. By the window, a twin bed had been dominated by her teddy bear collection. Next to it, a chest of drawers had been topped with musical jewelry boxes and glass atomizers.

But nothing of Joanna remained, only memories.

With a shudder, she went to the other bedroom. Through the open mini-blinds, the street light cast an eerie glow on the queen-sized bed's lacquered headboard. How often they had lain there, awakened by chirping finches or street sounds. Joanna would kiss her into consciousness; sometimes she would even rub a tempting nipple across Veronica's lips. She smiled at that delicious memory. What would it be like to live there without her?

Veronica leaned over and turned on the bedside lamp. The clock radio had been unplugged. She bent over, inserted the electrical prongs into the socket, and set the digital timer, feeling disjointed at being there without Joanna. She was relieved Michi would move in soon. Maybe she needed to share the place with her first before living with a lover again.

Veronica moved around the room, checking the closet, finding her winter clothes neatly hung. But the jeans and turtleneck sweater she had worn the evening of the accident were nowhere in sight. Joanna had given her that royal blue sweater; Veronica never asked what had happened to it.

In the living room, René conversed by phone with Guadalupe Talamantes, but Veronica did not listen to the content of her lover's speech. She heard only its distinctive rhythms—jesting, Tejana-flavored Spanish. She longed for René to hold her, to quell her fears and lull her to sleep. The evening had been exhausting and anxiety-ridden.

She needed to contemplate her revelations to her mother. She did not know how Sara would react in the days to come. Would she make references to religion again? Would she become self-righteous? Veronica suspected so. She knew this truce was temporary; the matter remained unresolved.

Wearily, she noted the bed had been stripped and the mattress pad laundered. Leaving the room, she sorted through folded sheets in the linen closet and found her favorite pair. She smoothed them, outlining their embroidered patterns; they could tell so much.

"Cómo te va, preciosa?"

Viewing the unhidden concern in her lover's eyes, Veronica dropped the sheets and hurried into those ready arms. Her sobs startled her, even though her emotions had been on edge all evening.

René soothed her, massaging the tension gathered in her neck and shoulders. Veronica rested her curly head against her until the sudden tears gradually ceased.

"René, this place seems so empty."

"Ya lo se. I love you, Verónica."

"I love you, too—very much. And I only want to think of *you* now." She gazed into those ebony eyes, wanting René to believe that.

"I know, corazón." She held her a while longer before letting go. Stepping aside, Talamantes seemed eager to avoid a serious conversation. She unbuttoned her striped shirt. "Look what you did, loca—got me all wet! Guess I just have to take this off to let it dry."

Tossing the shirt aside, René again drew her close. Veronica smiled at those surefire tactics. She pressed herself near and relished René's bare-breasted warmth. Sniffling, she wiped her eyes with the back of her hand before her mouth found René's waiting nipple.

"Ay, mujer." Talamantes sighed.

For several moments, Veronica licked and sucked her. Then she stopped. "If you want more, Talamantes, you have to help me make the bed."

*

They leaned on lacy pillows propped against the headboard. René sat with her legs wide, Veronica nestled in front, within their possessive borders. Kissing her lover's supple neck, René moved lean hands across Veronica's breasts, teasing her nipples. Her fingers made sweeping circles and inched lower towards Veronica's abdomen, eventually to the moistness below.

Head resting against René, Veronica moaned at those arousing actions. Her slender thighs parted further with each consecutive movement of René's hands. They had never made love like this, and she relished the novelty of Talamantes' controlling position.

"I love what you're doing. Please don't stop."

"Nunca, mi amor. Nunca."

René's lips and tongue were at Veronica's neck and shoulders, one hand continuously caressing her breasts. While her strong thighs surrounded Veronica's, René moved her other hand within her lover and her thumb towards her clitoris. Veronica could only lean back and enjoy the adulation, feel those firm breasts against her back. Her lover's breath warmed her shoulders, and those indefatigable hands remained on and inside her.

When Veronica was on the verge of orgasm, René tilted her body to allow their lips to meet. And while they kissed, she came spasmodically, clinging to her. Continuing to cradle Veronica, Talamantes rocked her, tenderly easing her into an encompassing sleep.

"Listen, you dyke lovebirds, I've been ready to move for the past two days!" Michi chattered over breakfast at Bagel Nosh. "It's about time you're back. Wondered whether you'd driven off into the sunset."

Veronica yawned and spread a hefty portion of cream

cheese on a cinnamon raisin bagel. "That's what Mom thought. Why was it such a shock that we decided to spend extra time in Santa Barbara?"

"Sure, Roni." Michi's black eyes danced. "I can imagine the type of sightseeing you did—cruising through René's erogenous zones."

Guffawing, Talamantes nudged her blushing lover. As their laughter subsided, René stole some hash browns from Michi's plate. "How's the Beth game going?"

"René—" Veronica frowned over her coffee cup.

"Well, that's about what it is," Michi confessed. "I'm hoping Beth'll want to stay overnight after the move. That okay with you, Roni?"

"Fine. We're going to my folks' for a barbeque that night, anyhow." Michi looked astonished as Veronica continued. "It's Dad's idea, Mich. He doesn't say much, but he seems to like Talamantes. Can you believe her mother's invited, too?"

"Sounds like one big happy family, huh?" René grinned. "Guadalupe's all excited about meeting the Melendez clan."

"Your mother's named Guadalupe?" Michi looked up from her scrambled eggs. "How perfectly Catholic."

"Yeah, I wanted her to change it to Tonantzin—the name of the Aztec goddess who preceded Guadalupe—but she wouldn't buy it. Catch this: Maria Guadalupe Carrizosa de Talamantes. A real low-down Mexicana name, huh?"

"And how. What's your father's name?"

"Everyone calls him 'Hank.' Actually, it's Enrique de Jesus Talamantes y Ayala."

Michi clicked her coffee cup to René's. "With those credentials, you must've made a hit with Roni's mom."

Talamantes rolled her eyes. "Oh, yeah? She thinks I'm

too india-looking."

"She said that?" Michi clapped her hands and giggled, familiar with Sara Melendez's outspokenness.

Veronica reached for more cream cheese. "Mom's so color conscious. She classifies Latinos according to the Spanish caste system, with darker-skinned people at the bottom of the scale. Remember how she scolds me for getting browner?"

"*I* love mujeres morenas, especially you." René hugged her. "Listen, Sara'll come around—in time."

Veronica gave her a skeptical look. "The fact that I'm living outside the Church will be a continuing problem. I can guarantee that."

"The prodigal's returned." Frank found his sister and René surrounded by large boxes and mounds of possessions.

Leaping up, Veronica threw her arms around him. "How's mi hermano?"

"Great." He returned her kiss and kept his arms around her. "Joyce'll be home soon. She dropped me off and went to the market." He looked over Veronica's head. "Hi, René."

"Orale." She got to her feet and let him hug her, too. "Must be late, huh?"

"Almost 6:00."

"Éjole!" René threw up her hands. "Promised Mama I'd have dinner with her. Better get going." She grabbed her hemp bag from the bed. "We can take these boxes over later."

"Okay, chula." Veronica accompanied her to the living room while Frank tagged behind. "What time will you be back?"

293

"In a couple of hours, preciosa."

They kissed before Talamantes took her leave. Closing the door, Veronica turned to meet her brother's smiling face. "What's so funny?"

He rubbed his chin. "Looks like the assertive dyke won. Bring me up to date, hermanita."

Later, René lounged on the apartment sofa, dark head in her lover's lap, while Veronica conversed by phone with Lucy. Though relieved at their parents' reaction, the nun agreed with Veronica's assessment that the matter remained unresolved. Lucy still had doubts about her younger sister's way of life; however, the Melendez sisters did not argue about it and promised to talk again soon.

On Saturday, the Melendez and Yamada families assisted with the move. After Frank, Joyce, Phil and both sets of parents left, René and Veronica finished helping Michi.

"What time's the barbeque?" Michi stuffed a mass of underwear into a dresser drawer.

"Around 5:00." Veronica watched her friend's slovenly methods with amusement. "Are you nervous about Beth?"

"You better believe it. Whatever made you ask? And, so help me, René, no wisecracks. I'm terrified. I've never seduced anyone."

"Chiquita, you won't have to *seduce* her." René hung a batch of shirts in the closet. "She's attracted, right—and you've already played touchie-feelie games."

"Yeah, but—"

"But what?"

Veronica stacked nightgowns into one of the drawers. "René, let her talk."

Shrugging, Talamantes kept quiet. Veronica slipped a supportive arm around her friend. "What is it, Mich?"

She welcomed the gesture and nestled nearer. "What if Beth doesn't want to make love?"

"Then you don't have to. You can cuddle instead."

"Sure. But soon enough one thing'll lead to another," René concluded with a smug grin.

"Beth's shy," Michi mumbled, not looking at either of them. "She thinks *I'm* not. But you know I really am."

"Tell her that. Let her know you're edgy."

"I'm not crazy about that strategy," René grumbled, hanging more clothes in the closet. "*I* like to exude confidence."

They burst into laughter at her swaggering attitude. Still giggling, Michi sank to the floor and pulled over another box.

Talamantes glared. "Veronica, you know damn well my methods work. You dykes were both salivating at my film screening." Striding over, she grabbed Veronica in a spontaneous abrazo.

Her lover tingled, but pretended to be unaffected.

"Preciosa, since when're you immune to my charms?"

"Whatever you say, loca, I still like to see a woman's vulnerable side."

"She likes absolutely all sides of a woman, Michi." René winked. "I can verify that."

"Talamantes, you're hopeless." Veronica released herself and snatched her wallet off the dresser. Michi needed concrete advice, not teasing. Maybe if she left them alone, René would quit showing off and listen instead.

Talamantes stared. "You're going somewhere?"

"To the drugstore to buy lightbulbs."

"Don't be mad, preciosa." René gently kissed the tip of Veronica's nose.

"Just need some exercise. Be back in a snap."

It had been a long time since Veronica had stretched her legs along Amherst Avenue. She had even forgotten the bus stop located a corner over. Come fall, she would have to get used to taking public transportation to the campus, unless she left early enough to drive in with Michi, or René came by to give her a lift. But she did not want to be dependent on either of them; the more independent she remained, the better. Faced with Talamantes's strong personality, she was determined to maintain her sense of self.

Sometimes she worried about the dynamics of their relationship. She and Joanna had been so compatible. In contrast, René relished a difference of opinion, a chance to verbally spar. Veronica liked that, too—aside from lovemaking, their creative wrangles were among the most fascinating aspects of their relationship. She only hoped they would not burn themselves out. Yet as much as René exasperated her, Veronica could not imagine a life without her.

In the cashier line, she was impatient until she noticed Steve Martinez browsing at the magazine rack. On impulse, she decided to deal with some unfinished business. When she tapped his beefy shoulder with the lightbulb carton, he whirled and gawked.

"Checking out the latest *Penthouse* issue?"

The boy seemed at a loss for words. For all his bluster, he was, after all, an adolescent with a misguided outlook.

"Been a long time since I've seen you, Steve. Guess

you're running with another bunch of kids these days."

"Leave me alone, bulldyke," He muttered, relocating some bravado.

"My pleasure." Veronica's lips eased into a smile. "After all, dykes like me prefer powerful Amazons to boring little boys like you." She tossed him a carefree wave and strolled away.

21

"Que feisty eres, mujer. Bet that little bastard never expected you to meet him head-on." Talamantes guided the rattling VW van along Lincoln Boulevard.

Veronica laughed. "Halfway home, I got scared when I remembered he'd beaten up Joanna's brothers."

René made a sharp right off Lincoln Boulevard. "That damn kid won't dare come near you anymore. He knows he can't intimidate you." She glanced over and grinned. "Looks like you're finally all the way out."

"Still have to meet your mother. She'll think I'm an ignorant pocha—my Spanish isn't exactly fluent."

"No te apures, preciosa. She already likes the sound of your voice. Dijo que eres muy simpática."

Unconvinced, Veronica shrugged. She noticed the neighborhood had become increasingly seedy. These dilapidated wood-framed homes and narrow car-lined streets were a far cry from her parents' tree-shaded home and her own Westside apartment. Here scruffy Chicanitos played baseball in the street, ignoring occasional beach-bound traffic. René slowed the van several times and even cheered when one kid hit a soaring flyball. Being in the Venice barrio increased Veronica's edginess. She wondered if René ever felt safe here.

She rubbed clammy hands along her arms. "So you think she'll like me?"

"We're about to find out." Talamantes stopped the

van before a small green house. "Home sweet home."

Veronica stared at the rickety fence surrounding the scraggly lawn; it looked ready to topple. The house did not look too sturdy either. A strong earthquake would no doubt knock it off its foundation. Her hands shook when she unbuckled her seatbelt. Talamantes locked the van and pushed open the creaky gate, beckoning her to follow.

Standing on the cracked cement steps, Veronica envied René's equanimity. She would be too embarrassed to bring a lover to this run-down house. René did not seem to mind as she ushered Veronica inside. The interior reminded Veronica of her deceased grandmother's home. It had been almost identical—cluttered and inelegant. She knew Sara would be critical of these furnishings; the phrase "que rancherita!" echoed through Veronica's mind.

A black and purple serape draped the sagging sofa. *La Opinion*, the Spanish-language newspaper, lay unfurled on the scarred coffee table next to a flyer announcing "un gran baile" at St. Mark's Church. A makeshift altar adorned with lace dresser scarves dominated one corner of the room; votive candles flickered in homage to El Santo Niño de Atocha and La Virgen de Guadalupe. Atop the television set, among clay pots filled with feather blossoms, were numerous photographs of René, no doubt the apple of her mother's eye; more photos covered the drab walls.

Veronica studied one, viewing a gangly brown child with heavy black braids, rumpled jeans, T-shirt, sneakers, and an exaggerated tomboy stance. Sara had a similar one of her youngest daughter at about the same age.

"Wasn't I a tough little baby dyke?" Talamantes joked, nudging her. Then she called to her mother. "Dónde estás, mi Lupita? Vámonos, mujer. Se va hacer tarde si no te apuras."

A contralto voice answered from the direction of the hallway. "Un momentito, querida. Ayúdame con este zipper, por favor."

Tossing Veronica an exasperated look, René ambled into the hallway. Seconds later, she proudly emerged with a handsome woman. Guadalupe Talamantes did not have her daughter's height, but she possessed the same coppery skin and compelling eyes. She had fashioned her abundant black hair, accentuated by greying strands, into a sleek chignon, and wore a smart two-piece red and white ensemble, revealing shapely legs in red high heels.

What a beautiful Mexicana, Veronica thought. She glanced at her own clothes and wished she had chosen a spiffier outfit, instead of white jeans and a pale yellow camp shirt. But she was charmed by Guadalupe's smiling approach.

"Que gusto me da en conocerte, Verónica! Hace mucho tiempo que le dije a esta renegada que te debía invitar a cenar con nosotros. No sé que tiene esta muchacha caprichuda!"

Veronica could not resist a smile. "René hace sus mismas reglas, Señora Talamantes." She liked the easy way Guadalupe treated her as a co-conspirator.

René came to her own defense. "Pues, como no?"

"Váyate, hija." Guadalupe shooed her daughter. "No puedes ir asi. Cambiate a tu jumpsuit blanco—el nuevo. Adelante!"

"Okay, okay." Backing off, René left to change her clothes.

Guadalupe smoothed her skirt and gestured for Veronica to be seated. "Mira, querida. Puedo conseguir trajes muy guapos porque trabajo en el garment district, verdad? Díme si quieres algo, hermosa. Tienes un cuerpito tan chulo. Que size eres, eh?"

"Siete, más o menos." Self-consciously, Veronica took a seat and hoped René would not take too long. Was Guadalupe referring to her casual taste in fashion, or was she merely being friendly? Veronica tried not to stare, but could not avoid it. The Talamantes women had a definite presence.

Guadalupe continued smiling. She seemed to expect Veronica's admiration, and her warmth was captivating. "Como te fué en Santa Barbara? René me dijo que estabas visitando tu hermana monjita."

In her limited Spanish, Veronica chatted about her weeks at the convent. She wondered about Sara's reaction to this woman. There was at least a fifteen-year age difference between the mothers. She hoped they would get along, but one never could tell.

While she explained that being alone in Santa Barbara had allowed plenty of writing time, Guadalupe listened intently. Veronica suspected she sought clues about her own daughter's creativity. Eventually, Guadalupe glanced towards the hallway. "René, ándele!"

"No puedo hallar mis aretes," Talamantes shouted. They heard much drawer slamming while she searched for the errant earrings. Trying not to laugh, Veronica and Guadalupe exchanged knowing glances. She lay an affectionate hand on the younger woman's shoulder. "Me dijo que quiere vivir contigo."

Veronica blushed. She had not expected Guadalupe to know René hoped to leave Venice in the future to live with Veronica. She aimed for tactfulness in her response; she understood René had qualms about leaving her mother alone. "Si es posible, Señora. Pero ella no la quiere dejar a usted sola."

"Algunas veces René cree que *ella* es la mamá. Muchacha loca! Tengo dos amigas que quieren vivir cerca de la playa. Puede ser que—"

Before Guadalupe could detail her own plans, René burst into the room in a white open-necked jumpsuit which emphasized her brown skin. She wore dangling silver and turquoise earrings, and grinned with some of her usual self-assurance. Veronica decided the wait had been worth it; her lover looked dazzling.

"Ahora, guapa, nos vamos, eh?" Guadalupe strolled across the room and blew out the votive candles. She adjusted René's collar and fanned her coarse hair over it. "Tienes bastante gas en el van?"

"Si, si, si." Talamantes slipped an arm around each woman and hustled them outside.

Halfway to Santa Monica, René pulled into a liquor store parking lot. "Botella de vino," She called over her shoulder, hurrying out.

"Pobrecita. Está tan nerviosa." Guadalupe spoke with fondness. "Pero yo estoy contenta, Verónica. Eres simpática, inteligente y de buena familia. No me gustaba cuando tenía compañeras que no hablaban español."

Veronica dared herself to be direct. "Es verdad que ha tenido muchas compañeras?"

"Algunas." Guadalupe's answer was evasive. She no doubt decided to let Veronica find out for herself about René's previous lovers. "Las muchachas se vuelven locas por ella. No lo entiendo, pero dice que asi es." She patted her upswept hair. "Ella no es tu primera novia, verdad?"

"No." Veronica was equally unwilling to offer more.

René clammered back inside. "White zinfandel for us and Dos Equis for the men. Is that okay?"

"Fine. René, I've never seen you so jittery. Don't worry. We'll get through this together."

"This is big time, Verónica. Never been to this type of

family shindig with a lover. Look at Lupita—she's all jazzed."

Pursing her lips, René's mother pointed to the car keys. "Ándele, muchacha. Se va hacer tarde."

"A sus órdenes, mi jefita." René saluted, starting the ignition.

Midway through the evening, Veronica wandered indoors and found her mother warming more chili beans.

"Roni, ayúdame con esos platos, por favor."

Veronica placed the stack of dishes next to the stove. "I can handle this, Mom. Go outside and relax."

Sara ignored the offer. "I don't know what to do with myself, hija. Your father's over there, joking around con la Senora, like he's dealing with your boyfriend's mother. But esa india flaca *isn't* your boyfriend—she's your *girl* friend." She sighed, fanning herself with her apron. "I phoned Lucy this afternoon. Ay, Roni. She's probably tired of hearing from me."

No wonder her mother had come inside; at least she had not made a scene. So far Sara had treated the Talamantes women cordially; Veronica was grateful for that.

"Mom, I wish there were an easier way to cope with all this, but I don't know what it is." With a fingernail, Veronica rubbed a speck of chili sauce from the edge of the stove. "Before tonight, I used to feel dishonest at family gatherings because I wasn't open about myself. I don't want to feel that way anymore." She touched her mother's arm. "What bothers *you* most?"

Sara's dark eyes glistened as she stirred the beans on the stovetop. "Pues, todo! I used to think—even if you

303

have a smart mouth—that you really were inexperienced about life. Sin duda, the accident changed you. But you were already different before Joanna died, and I didn't even know it! Me da pena, Roni."

"Mama, I'm sorry." She leaned against the counter and rubbed her eyes. "Don't you think I wanted to tell you? I just didn't know how—or when."

Sara appeared not to notice her daughter's remarks. She seemed to be thinking aloud, unburdening herself. "I wanted all mis niños to get married and have their own familias. Instead—look what's happened! Frank's Connie died, leaving him with baby Phil to raise. It took Frank a long, long time to get over Connie. And who did he finally marry? Una gabacha que no quiere tener hijos!"

In a way, Veronica felt relieved that she was no longer the topic, but she grew impatient with her mother's continuing put-downs of Joyce.

"She hasn't said she doesn't want kids. You're making that up."

Sara shook the serving ladle at her. "Esa gringa's a career woman. She's out there talking about architectural design con tu—amiga. I heard her, Roni. She's not planning babies."

"Mom—"

But Sara was intent on her own woes. "And then your sister Angela married un buen hombre, but they moved to Arizona, of all places! I hardly see mis nietas except at Christmas or when we visit each other. My sweet Lucy's a nun—I shouldn't complain about that—but she would've made a wonderful mother. And then—there's you."

"Yeah—the black sheep." In exasperation, Veronica threw up her hands. "I didn't plan this, by any means—"

"Ay, mija, pero esos chismes! Todo el pueblo's gossiping. I can't face Isabel and Rubén. Everyone thinks you were the one who—"

"Who what?" Veronica's temper flared. "Seduced Joanna? That's an absolute lie—our relationship was based on mutuality. Joanna and I were sexually involved even before we were teenagers—"

Sara gasped at that admission.

"—and we *both* wanted it. We loved each other, Mama!" She wanted to shake the truth into her. "But now I have to live the rest of my life without her. That wasn't an appealing prospect—until I met René. Would you rather have me shrivel up and turn my back on love?"

"Cálmate, Roni." Sara glanced worriedly at the kitchen's screen door.

"How can I calm down when you're accusing me of seducing Joanna?"

"Shhh!" Sara whisked a dish towel at her. "I'm not accusing you of—anything. I don't even understand todo esto. Pero no me gusta éste escándalo. And I just wish you would've waited for the rumors to pass before—"

Veronica took a deep breath, hoping to subdue her anger. She did not want to argue with her mother, yet Sara could be so frustrating. "Mama, the timing suits René and me fine. I'm not going to allow you or anyone—"

Guadalupe peered through the screen door. "Sara, puedo ayudarle con algo?"

"No es necesario." Sara tried to mask her agitation.

Guadalupe entered anyway, sizing up the situation. "Verónica, René quiere hablar contigo. Vete con ella." Like her daughter's, her ebony eyes would not be challenged.

Sensing her intent, Veronica nodded and left.

*

305

She found René downing a Dos Equis at the far corner of the picnic table. Phil had spread several rows of photos on its surface for inspection.

"Las madres are in a huddle."

"If we see Lupita hurled through the window, we'll know Sara had the upper hand," René drawled, provoking a snicker from Phil.

"There's nothing funny about this, René. Mom was ranting about the rumors right before your mother went in. I really didn't want to leave them alone, but—"

"Lupita's slick. She can handle herself fine." René put down her beer. She seemed in no mood to speculate on their mothers' conversational topics. "Phil, these shots are great. You have a fabulous eye, kid."

The teenager beamed. Disgruntled with Talamantes's casual attitude, Veronica wandered off to chat with the others.

Leading a raucous discussion about Santa Monica politics, Joe Melendez held court in a patio chair beneath the avocado tree. Egging him on about the recent city council election, Frank served himself another helping of barbecued beef. He grinned when his sister joined Joyce on a redwood bench. Veronica sat quietly; her head had begun to ache.

"Veronica—" René called from the back door.

"What is it?" Trying to avoid thinking about Sara, Veronica had been listening to her father's lively description of working with an integrated crew on a street construction project.

Talamantes ran a hand through her unruly hair. "They're getting bombed in the living room."

"Oh, no. Did you hear, Dad?"

Joe whisked the air with his outstretched palms. "Pues, no le hace, Roni. Your mother'll just fall asleep. She can't hold her liquor."

"Never seen Grandma plastered," Phil said, awe-struck. He was about to enter the house when René barred his path.

"Hey, buster," Frank cautioned. "I think it's time for us to leave. Or would you rather have us stay, Dad?"

"I can handle this, hijo." Joe Melendez got up and brushed past René. "You girls are taking Guadalupe home, eh?"

They nodded in unison.

With an amused expression, Frank gathered his family. "If you need any help, holler. Ma'll be in bad shape tomorrow."

Bidding them goodnight, Veronica and René followed Joe inside.

The mothers sang an off-key rendition of "De Colores" and toasted each other with dinner glasses filled with Gallo Tyrolia. Sara's face was flushed, her apron dis-arrayed. Veronica wondered if she had been crying. On noting their audience, Guadalupe tried to regain her poise, minus one earring. Her elegant coiffure was slightly as-kew. Unable to restrain himself, Joe chuckled and wiped his eyes.

"Lupita, que voy hacer contigo?" René scolded as she approached. "Vámonos, mamacita. Tienes que dormir ahorita."

"No me molestes, René." Guadalupe edged away from her daughter's ministrations, but Talamantes was in-sistent and helped her up anyway.

"Let me—" Veronica offered.

"No. Just open the door."

To Veronica's surprise, René smoothly swung Guadalupe's pliable body into her arms. Even Joe gasped at that abrupt action. Rather than protest, Guadalupe leaned her dark head against her daughter's shoulder and smiled.

"Buenas noches, Sarita. Y gracias por todo."

"Buenas noches, Lupe." Sara seemed unperturbed at the sudden departure, but she had trouble rising to see her off. She pushed aside her husband's assisting hands. "No estoy boracha, hombre. Nomás estábamos platicando de nuestras hijas."

"I'll be back later, Verónica," René yelled from the van.

She nodded and waited until they had driven away. Closing the door, Veronica felt her headache intensify; she was not eager to face her mother again.

Sara seemed unaware of her. Stubbornly, she refused any assistance and tottered to her bedroom. Joking about her condition, Joe accompanied her. After thirty-six years of marriage, he knew how to deal with his often volatile wife. Usually, he wound up making her laugh.

Veronica picked up the empty wine bottle and glasses and went into the kitchen. Trying to keep her mind blank, she found that menial chores suited her fine for the time being. She reached into the cupboard for an aspirin and downed it quickly. Filling the sink with suds, she began to wash the pots and pans. Eventually, her father joined her.

"Women," He grumbled. He opened the refrigerator and pulled out another Budweiser.

Scrubbing a pot, Veronica surveyed him. "Is Mom all right?"

He popped open the can. "Claims she is, but she's no drinker, and wine hangovers are no picnic."

"Dad, I've never seen her like this."

"She's a proud woman. She takes things hard." He stood beside his daughter and rocked on his heels. "Tell me, hija. Is René moving in with you?"

Veronica grabbed the remaining pot and dunked it underwater. "We've talked about that. We just don't know when." She turned towards him. "Is that a problem for you, Dad?"

She noticed how tightly he held the Bud and remembered how, in her childhood, he had crumpled beer cans to demonstrate his might. She had been awed until she had tried it herself and discovered the flimsiness of aluminum. Since then, her father had not again attempted to impress her; maybe he knew that was unnecessary.

"I'm not sure, Roni." He shrugged and continued to sip the beer. "Would she help pay the rent?"

"Of course." Although he did not state it, Veronica realized his concern centered on more than financial details. She was used to his indirect communication. "René has a graduate fellowship, and makes extra money videotaping weddings and parties. Right now, she doesn't want to leave Guadalupe alone in Venice. It may take a while to find someone to share the house."

Joe scratched his greying head. "She's a good daughter. You can tell by the way she deals with Guadalupe. Sure must be hard for that woman, having only one kid, and having her be a—"

"Lesbian." For the first time, Veronica said that word in his presence.

He did not answer, but frowned and looked away.

Veronica wiped her hands on a dishtowel and met his gaze. "Guadalupe's known about René for about ten years. She's had lots of time to absorb it, Dad. And I think René's very lucky to have her for a mother."

For several minutes, neither of them spoke. Occupied with her tidying tasks, she moved about the kitchen. Her headache lingered, but was not as intense. Joe seemed reflective, and she knew him well enough to avoid intruding into his thoughts.

"Roni—"

She glanced up while sealing the lid of a Tupperware bowl.

"Is there something I did that made you—you know." At a loss, he spread his hands.

"That made me turn to women?" Her eyes welled at the self-doubt in his voice; what it must have taken him to ask that question. "No, Dad. It has nothing to do with how you and Mama raised me. I saw nothing but love in this house—I still see it all the time. You two really love each other and I find that very beautiful—very comforting." She paused. "If there's a reason for my being different, I think it's biological. So far, that's only a theory—it hasn't been proved."

Concentrating on her words, he frowned. "Have you talked with anyone about it—you know, a priest, a doctor?"

"Only Lucy—mainly to explain who I am, not to ask advice. Lesbianism isn't a sin, Dad—or a disease either. It's only another way to be."

Joe looked skeptical. He seemed about to respond, but the door chimes interrupted.

Veronica watched him head for the living room, and knew, for the time being, the moment had been lost.

22

"Preciosa, want to just snuggle tonight? I'm beat."

Veronica nodded and tossed her canvas bag on the easy chair. On the coffee table were two half-empty glasses next to a copy of Adrienne Rich's *The Dream of a Common Language*. Veronica picked up the poetry collection.

"The bookmark's set at the twenty-one love poems. And Michi's door's shut. Very positive signs."

"Guess we'll find out in the morning." René grinned and followed her into the bedroom. "Know what I'd like? A warm bath with you."

"We'll probably fall asleep in the tub." Liking that idea, Veronica poked through her toiletries for a fragrant packet of bubble bath.

"Anywhere with you is fine, corazón."

Though she had not expected to, Veronica slept soundly. In the morning, she lay quietly and wondered if her parents had. She thought about them for several minutes before her thoughts drifted to Michi and Beth; she heard no sounds from the other bedroom. She hoped René would not be too curious about them; they needed their privacy. Her lover's dozing head lay inches away, one brown arm flung across Veronica's breasts. She smiled and whispered, "René Talamantes, I love you."

René stirred, a tiny smile forming on her sensual lips.

She opened her drowsy eyes and moved nearer. "Nothing like palabras de amor first thing in the a.m."

"Well, why not, chula? Before I fell asleep, I kept thinking—what if I hadn't gone with Michi to see 'Tortilleras.' I never would've met you."

"Hey, I would've found you, preciosa. I mean, how many Chicana lesbians are there on the Westside?"

Veronica shrugged. "You're the only one who matters." She outlined Talamantes' lips with her fingertips.

Those ebony eyes glimmered. René leaned forward and kissed her. "You know, mujer, I've been meaning to tell you this—"

"Hmmm?" Veronica fondled her lover's back and shoulders, enjoying her warm body.

"While you were in Santa Barbara, I went to Sisterhood Bookstore looking for a biography of Dorothy Arzner. Then I got to talking with one of the owners. Next thing I knew, I'd signed us up for a joint presentation."

"René!" Glaring, Veronica pushed her aside and pulled herself into a sitting position; so much for pillow talk. "How could you do such a thing without telling me first?"

For her own safety, Talamantes sat up, too. "I meant to, preciosa. It must've slipped my mind." She took on a humble tone. "Look, corazón, it'll be great exposure. By that time, most of your stories will be polished. You can read them, and I'll show 'Tortilleras.' Tell you what, for an added bonus, I'll even videotape your reading. Wouldn't that make you happy?"

In spite of her annoyance, Veronica had to laugh at René's contrite demeanor. "All right, Ms. Wise Guy. But don't get into the habit of making commitments without telling me. Sometimes you're such a smartass." Sighing, she studied her for several seconds. René's ebony eyes met hers unwaveringly, and Veronica knew she could not remain irked for long. She leaned over and found her ready mouth.

Talamantes kissed her longingly.

"You maniac. When's the presentation scheduled?"

"Not till October."

"So we do have plenty of time, loca."

"For what?"

"Making love, of course," She whispered, pulling René down again.

"How long'll you be on campus? Want a lift home?" Michi lay on the rolling lawn of the UCLA Sculpture Garden, her fuzzy head near Veronica's sandaled feet.

"Maybe. After I meet with Zamora, I'll swing by Melnitz to see how René's doing. She's critiquing Jorge's latest edit."

"Okay. I'll leave at 5:00 sharp." Michi glanced at her watch and grimaced. "My lunch hour's up. Better get going. Do you miss having the Z to drive around?"

Veronica stretched her full length on the grassy carpet, her strong arms and brown muscled calves offering the garden's female nude sculptures some healthy competition. "Actually, I like riding the bus so I can people watch and eavesdrop. And I'm going to like being back here on a regular basis." Slowly, she pulled herself up and brushed off her turquoise shorts. "I'll walk with you to Campbell."

The friends strolled past Bunche Hall towards the building housing the ethnic studies programs.

"Roni, I think I'm in love."

Veronica grinned. "I was wondering when you'd tell me." She slipped an affectionate arm around Michi. "I'm so glad. Even if you're a lovebug, will you still be my roomie?"

"Honey, you bet. I'm as ready to live with Beth as you are to settle down with René." She wriggled her eyebrows at Veronica.

"You've got that right. Let's stand on our own two feet first."

Outside Campbell Hall, the friends came to a halt. They hugged each other long and hard before Veronica headed towards Rolfe Hall.

She peeked around the corner, spotting Professor Zamora busy at her IBM PC, typing bibliographic entries from the stack of books beside the computer.

"Camille, I'm early—for once."

Zamora glanced at her over wire-rimmed glasses. "Que tal, Veronica. Cómo te fué en Santa Bárbara?"

"You be the judge of that." She set a hefty file folder atop the professor's crowded desk. "Three more stories."

Zamora swiveled her chair away from the computer. "Being away was good for you, then."

"Yes." Veronica took the hard-backed chair Camille offered. "What are you working on?"

"A reading list for my new upper-division class—Contemporary Womanist Fiction. I'm including Audre Lorde, Sandra Cisneros, Mitsuye Yamada—Native American, Jewish and lesbian writers, too. Interested in being my T.A.?"

Veronica crossed her left leg over her right, her fingers instinctively outlining the scar. "Sounds challenging. Why didn't you offer this course when I was an undergrad?"

"What a difference tenure makes, verdad?" Camille laughed. "For one thing, we have a new department chair this year—he claims he's all for innovation and diversity."

"I'll believe it when I see it."

"A skeptic como yo." She touched her student's hand. "I've missed you—and I hear René did, too."

Veronica felt herself blush, but she made herself keep her eyes on Camille's. "We're thinking about collaborating."

"Focus on your own work first. I'd like to see your stories published."

"You say that without even looking at the latest ones. Camille, I've ventured a bit into René's territory." Veronica uncrossed her legs and stretched them out, wriggling her toes in their leather sandals. Since being released from structured physical therapy treatment, she had become more conscientious about unkinking any accumulated tension.

"You're taking risks."

"Yes, and that's scary. The stories aren't totally autobiographical, but they come close." Veronica rubbed the edge of the thick file folder with her index finger. "Camille, thanks for encouraging me to—"

"Couldn't allow you to stagnate for eight months, no?" Zamora offered a slight smile. "The incoming editor of *The Jacaranda Review* keeps asking for contemporary fiction from student writers. Why don't you submit at least one of the first three stories?"

Veronica's gaze was direct. "I'd rather wait till you read the next three. Maybe one of them would be better."

"Bueno." Zamora took the thick folder and put it beside her briefcase. "Pues, what about the TA-ship? Do you want it?"

"Of course." Veronica pulled her chair closer. "Let me help you with that reading list."

*

"So how come you don't want to hang around and wait for me? We can have dinner with Mamá later." René turned away from her consultation with Jorge to meet Veronica's gaze.

"I want to see Frank and Phil—and use the pool while I'm at it. Chula, we don't have to see each other *every* night."

"Why not?"

Jorge excused himself to go out for a cigarette.

Veronica gave René an exasperated look. "'Cause sometimes we both have other things to do."

René looked skeptical. "Did Camille give you some pointers about me?"

"You're paranoid, Talamantes."

"Not me." She grinned. "Okay. Go do your thing. When I finish here, I have some phone calls to make anyhow. Some Latinas run a literacy program out my way. They want me to tape some sessions so they can use the video for funding purposes."

"Sounds great." Veronica started to move towards the door and René followed her.

"No besitos ahorita?"

Veronica planted a little kiss on René's chin. "I'll phone you later, loca."

She decided to take the bus instead of waiting for Michi. Veronica disembarked on Ocean Park Boulevard near her brother's condo and walked half a block towards it. Since no one was home, she changed into the swimsuit she kept there and went to the pool. She was taking a breather on the chaise longue when Frank arrived. He came over when she waved.

"Hey, little sis. Que pasa?"

"I turned in my stories today."

"Terrific! That must be a relief."

"Kind of nervewracking, actually."

He grinned and squeezed her shoulder. "Want to split a salad with me?" He gestured with a plastic container.

"Sure. Where's Phil—and Joyce?"

"He's at the beach with Jimmy and she's at the manicurist."

Veronica tugged on her robe and followed him inside.

"Good to see you by yourself once in a while," Frank drawled as he divided the Caesar salad betweem them.

"Feels good, too," she admitted. She handed him a fork and took one herself.

"Getting pressured?"

"Now and then. Nothing I can't handle. Has Mom said anything about me lately?"

He shook his head. "I wasn't referring to Mom. I was wondering if René's been pressuring you to live with her."

"Oh, yeah." She looked at him and smiled. "But you know how stubborn I am. I'm not ready for that—not yet, anyway."

"She could sure give you a run for your money."

"Definitely." Veronica munched a sourdough crouton. "I still have lots of adjustments to make, Frank. I feel very safe with Michi for the time being—and vice versa. Michi and I are usually on the same wavelength; she's so easy to be with. Some nights we just sit around and talk about Joanna. I suppose that's therapeutic."

"It is, honey," he said gently. "Can't be too easy for René to compete with that."

"She understands—or tries to. I try not to make comparisons between Joanna and her, but sometimes I can't help it."

"Well, you'll work things out. Why rush? Listen, have you ever heard from Siena?"

"Just that one letter." She forked through the salad and searched for more croutons. "How're things around here?"

"Oh, Phil gets moody just about every other day—but that's adolescence, right? I tell Joyce not to take it personally. He's going through a phase, so he's bound to be cranky. I'm glad he's so interested in photography. He really wants to go on a shoot with René sometime."

"She's been trying to convince me to go along, too." Veronica poured herself a soda. "As for Phil, he has lots of time on his hands, all these changes in his life. Once he's back in school—"

"Sure hope that's true."

"For him and for me."

Sorting through their just-washed laundry, Veronica and Michi sat on their living room carpet one evening in late summer.

"Hey, Roni. Remember when we were little kids and we used to pretend we were invaders from outer space?" Michi grabbed a pair of pink cotton bikinis and stuck them over her head, haphazard tufts of her moussed hair poking through. She crossed her eyes and made a playful lunge at her friend.

Veronica giggled and toppled over on a pile of folded towels. "Mom used to get furious whenever we did that. She thought it was nasty. I suppose it embarrassed her. She's such a prude."

"Mine, too. It's like—how were we ever conceived in the first place? The folks don't like to deal with anything even slightly related to sex." Michi pulled the panties from her head and continued searching for more of her T-shirts.

Veronica lay back for a moment, watching the whimsical expression fade from her friend's face. "What's happened?"

Michi glanced at her. "Nothing. That's the point." She sighed. "Yesterday after work, I went to the flower shop 'cause Beth likes bonsai rose bushes and I wanted to surprise her with one. So I'm there looking at what Mom has in stock. When she asks how come I'm all of a sudden interested in flowers, I say I want to buy something for Beth. Mom gives me this look. 'You see her a lot. Where did you say you met her?' 'At a woman's dance.' I'd never said that before."

Veronica leaned closer. "Then what?"

"She went back to the stockroom and phoned a client about details for a wedding bouquet. She was on the phone forever, Roni. I got tired of waiting, so I left her a check for the bonsai bush and left."

"That's it?"

"Yeah. I mean, I gave her a wide opening and she just ignored it." Michi sat cross-legged, elbows on her knees. "She's impossible."

"She's pulling the oblivious act, Mich—evasive tactics. What's Beth say about this?"

Michi's mouth turned downwards. "It doesn't bother her 'cause she *doesn't* want to come out. She thinks her family would disown her."

"Sounds familiar. After all, once you say those words, you can't take them back. If it hadn't been for the letters and the Siena episode, I could've stayed in a while longer."

"You think so?"

"Yeah. I don't regret being out, but I would've preferred doing it in a thoughtful way. Sometimes the unspoken tension gets to me. I came out with a bang, Mich—but my own procrastination had lots to do with that."

"Finding the right time isn't easy. Roni, sometimes I get so pissed about the whole thing."

"Me, too. I don't like conflicts any more than you do. I'm surprised your parents haven't heard about *me* by now."

"Maybe they have."

Veronica placed a gentle hand on Michi's knee. "Well, whatever happens with them, remember I'm your amiga."

"All the way," Michi agreed with a little smile. "The thing is, how long can this last? You and me, I mean. One of these days, René'll want to move in with you."

Veronica sat up and moved nearer. "That won't happen soon, Mich. I won't let it."

Her friend looked at her questioningly.

"I love René, but I like the status quo. She can be overpowering sometimes—and I need to get stronger. The other thing is—" Veronica hesitated momentarily. "You know Talamantes. She's more adaptable, more flexible than I am. Mich, her neighborhood freaks me out. There's gang activity there, dope pushers down the street. I'm not used to that—it's scary. I'd rather have her come here, but she doesn't like leaving Guadalupe alone so much. She's much closer to her mother than I am to mine. Anyway, whenever I go to Venice, I start feeling edgy—and I guess it shows."

"I can relate. In a way, it's like Beth and me. Her family's in professional fields—her father's an orthodontist, her cousin's a dentist. Heck, my family owns a flower shop. We're comfortable, but we're a step lower on the economic scale. The same goes for you and René."

"That sure can be a sensitive issue. Sometimes she calls me a snob. Guadalupe seems to understand my attitude more than René does."

"Yeah, 'cause she and René are on different levels, too. She works in the garment district and her daughter's a film student. What a difference, huh? And, man, whoever thought we'd have to deal with class issues besides everything else?"

"Not me."

"Me neither, Roni."

23

"Hey—that's Grandma's car." Phil leaned out the window of René's van and pointed to the Pontiac sedan.

"I wonder what she's doing here." Veronica followed her nephew out to the sidewalk before the Talamantes home.

"What're you so surprised about, corazón? I told you Lupita and Sara'd stay in touch." Talamantes grinned and handed Phil the video camera and a roll of coiled cable. "Let's take this stuff inside, carnalito."

Hoisting the equipment, he opened the gate and started up the walk. Veronica grabbed the audio monitor and tagged behind him.

On the sofa, the mothers shared coffee and Mexican sweet rolls. They looked up when the three young people entered.

Guadalupe accepted her daughter's kiss and glanced at the others. "Quieren pan dulce?"

Phil did not need a second invitation. He quickly buzzed his grandmother's cheek and plopped himself beside her, grabbing a sugar-coated roll in the process.

Sara nudged him reprovingly, and he got the message. "Thanks, Mrs. Talamantes."

"Cómo no, mijo. René, trae más tazas, por favor."

When René went into the kitchen to bring more cups, Sara turned her attention to Veronica. "What have you been up to, hijita?"

322

"I was about to ask you the same thing."

Sara pursed her lips at her daughter's impertinence.

Veronica smiled and continued. "We were at the community center most of the day, helping René with her latest project. She's making a video about the Latina literacy program."

"Saw some really awesome girls there, Grandma."

"I hope you kept your eyes in your head, Philly."

"Just looked, that's all. René kept me too busy to do much else." He winked at his grandmother. "It was pretty interesting, you know? But I sure don't know what I'd do if *I* couldn't read."

"Pues, when people come over the border, most of the time they don't know English." Sara cut a sweet roll and offered Veronica half.

"Thanks, Mom. The thing is, the women there *aren't* immigrants. They were born *here*, just like us."

"They're from poor families, broken homes, eh?"

"Some. Actually, Senora Melendez, most are high school dropouts—either 'cause of being pregnant or being into drugs. They're women who need a second chance," René explained while she set the cups on the table.

"Why would you girls want to get involved with esas cholas?" Sara gave her daughter's knee a reprimanding pat.

Veronica was about to answer, but deferred to Guadalupe.

"Ay, Sarita. Nomás quieren ayudarlas." Guadalupe gazed at the older woman fondly.

"Well, not exactly, mujeres. I was there just to videotape, but now I'm thinking it wouldn't be a bad idea to volunteer for the project now and then."

"I'm starting to feel that way, too," Veronica agreed. "All my life, I've had much more opportunities than those women. When I was a teenager, I liked being in school, learning new things—and I sure wasn't distracted by boys."

Phil smirked at that, but Sara ignored it.

Veronica continued. "So why not give some of my knowledge and skills back to the community?"

Sara seemed unconvinced. "Ay, Roni. Those cholitas are probably lost causes. They'll wind up pregnant again or back on drugs. Even if they learn how to read and write English properly, who says they'll be able to hold jobs? Besides, when will you two find the time? In a few weeks, you'll be back in school yourselves."

"Mom, *you* always find time to volunteer at the parish. René and I could make time, too."

"In fact, I think Lupita could benefit from that type of program herself," René remarked.

"Que dices?" Guadalupe turned her dark eyes to her daughter's.

"Sabes que tienes aprender a hablar ingles y leerlo tambien, Lupita."

"We've already talked about that," Sara said, wiping crumbs from her lap. "Lupe y yo are going to get together in the evenings and I'm going to teach her English myself."

Guadalupe smiled and poured herself another cup of coffee.

"Mom, that's fabulous. But how are you—" Veronica thought better of it and asked another question instead. "When did you decide to—"

"Pues, I was down at the Santa Monica Farmer's Market the other morning and saw Lupe trying to tell un chinito that she wanted half a dozen oranges. I helped her out, but that got my mind going. It's not easy to go back to school when you're older. And since I'm bilingual and always have been—why not help her, eh?"

"Que buena idea, verdad?" Guadalupe reached over to caress her daughter's shoulder.

René brought her mother's hand to her lips. "Maravillosa, Lupita." She grinned at Sara. "Señora, you're going to do something I've been bugging her about for a very long time. This means a lot to her—and to me."

Sara seemed embarrassed by the sincerity in René's voice. "Pues, I think Lupe would do the same for me."

"Cómo no, Sarita," Guadalupe agreed.

Despite their age difference, the mothers gradually became friends, drawn together by religion, culture and common experiences. Through their twice-weekly English lessons, they became even closer. Both devout Catholics, Sara and Guadalupe attended religious services together and even registered for a bilingual women's retreat at the Convent of St. Teresa in the fall. Veronica was relieved her mother had found a local confidante, especially another mother of a lesbian daughter. Since Guadalupe had accepted René's lesbianism throughout the past decade, she was more than willing to counter Sara's—and even Joe's—misconceptions and prejudices.

When summer faded into autumn, Veronica returned to graduate studies, dividing her time among course work, reediting her short stories, and volunteering for the literacy project. Professor Zamora was a demanding mentor, prodding her into rethinking themes and character motivations; although they argued occasionally, Veronica relished the older Chicana's diligence and perseverance. Often René would find her lover in the University Research Library, nestled into a carrel, surrounded by textbooks and dog-eared manuscripts, hard at work.

At the beginning of fall quarter, one of Veronica's stories appeared in *Ten Percent*, the gay and lesbian students' newsmagazine. Another was accepted by *The Jacaranda Review*. By early October, she found herself anticipating the reading at Sisterhood Bookstore. And in her happiness with herself and with René, she brooded less and less about the past.

"How do I look, Mich?" In a lavender shirt and ivory cords, Veronica handed her an Afro pick. "Will I attract groupies?"

In the rear of the bookstore, Michi fluffed Veronica's hair, rounding it into flattering tendrils. "I really wish you'd use mousse—it'd give you a different look. But no matter what—once you start reading, you'll knock everyone's bra off."

"Yeah, if anyone here's wearing one," Talamantes drawled. She wore a form-fitting black jumpsuit with strategic zippers. Against the west wall, she set up a portable screen.

"Listen, Mich, during the reading why don't you do a nipples check? If everyone's perked, give me the high sign. That's a sure way to gauge audience response." Veronica smiled and rearranged the tall stool by the microphone.

Michi giggled. "Goddess knows you've been around Talamantes too long. You never used to say things like that."

"Not out loud, anyway." Veronica flipped through the manuscript to check that the pages were in order. "So glad I'm first—if I had to sit through 'Tortilleras' again, I'd collapse. I'm really uptight about Zamora. Maybe she'll change her mind. She's not here yet."

"Dreamer." Michi offered her a consoling pat.

"We could always have a quickie in the back of my van, preciosa," René suggested with a wink. "That'd relax you."

Blushing, Veronica turned away to huddle with one of the store's owners, reconfirming the time allotted.

When women began drifting in, Talamantes found a ready audience for her outrageous comments and soon caused a noticeable stir. Despite her nervousness, Veronica was amused by her lover's knack for attracting attention and grateful René had ushered Professor Zamora to an ideal spot. Soon one of the bookstore owners began the introductions for the afternoon event.

"We're proud to present a program featuring Chicana creativity. Today we have with us two UCLA graduate students—Veronica Melendez, a short-story writer, and René Talamantes, a screenwriter and film maker—"

Hearing their names linked, Veronica felt queasy. Sometimes she felt a competitive edge towards René's work; both Chicanas used different media, yet similar themes. She saw Camille Zamora's nod of approval, but when Veronica noticed Talamantes's eyes, she blushed. Had René sensed her rivalrous thoughts?

Veronica took several deep breaths and tried to relax. Although she had rehearsed for weeks, she felt her confidence fleeing. Striving to calm herself, she remembered the many readings she and Joanna had attended in this room, the lesbian authors they had admired, the autographed books they had collected. Her gaze wandered to that enviable south wall and she recalled the summer afternoon she had confided to Siena her wish to be there, too. Those times seemed so long ago.

Veronica closed her eyes, pushing the memories aside.

She breathed again, and focused on the owner's conclusion. "—and now Veronica Melendez will read 'Recuerdos.'"

When the applause ebbed, Veronica adjusted the microphone, tilting it towards her mouth. For one absurd moment, she imagined herself grabbing the mike and bursting into song. That whimsical thought caused her to smile and slacken her tense posture. Holding the manuscript, she glanced at the audience before beginning. As she started to read, she reminded herself to speak slowly, distinctly.

René had cautioned her to look up often, not only to connect with the audience, but also for the success of the videotaping. Keeping that in mind, Veronica paused at the end of the first page and again scanned the women. Their presence filled her with a deeply rooted sense of accomplishment. Seated in a semi-circle before her, they allowed her dream to come alive.

Her eyes lingered on them, and Veronica wanted to memorize each of their faces: the butch-femme couple holding hands, nestled in a corner; the chubby dyke, arms crossed, slouched in a folding chair; the thin black woman with the majestic profile; the blue-jeaned, long-haired Latina tapping her sandaled foot. She smiled again, seeing some of her tutorees from the literacy program; this was their first time inside a bookstore—and with her encouragement, Veronica knew it would not be their last. All these were the women she longed to touch with her stories, to reach with her words. And she wanted to know them all.

Michi offered a thumbs-up signal. Veronica was proud that her friend shared this day, that she would hear for the first time in public the fictional recreation of Joanna. Veronica was ready to move beyond societal and cultural boundaries, beyond her stories' well-defined margins. She was determined to say aloud, to Camille Zamora and all the women present, that being a Chicana lesbian encompassed not only her writing, but also her personal reality. She felt empowered by the collective women's energy electrifying that narrow room. And finding René's steadying presence behind the video camera, she gazed at her and smiled. Talamantes winked and gestured for her to continue.

Facing her audience, Veronica spoke, her voice strong and clear. She read with conviction, with passion—and the women listened.

About the Author

Terri da la Peña is the Chicana daughter of a Mexican immigrant mother and a Mexican-American father. She is a native of Santa Monica, California, where her father's family has lived for six generations. She has been awarded the Chicano Literary Prize from the University of California, Irvine, and has taught in the Writers' Program at the University of California Extension, Los Angeles. Her fiction has appeared in numerous anthologies.

Selected Titles from Seal Press

VOYAGES OUT 2 by Julie Blackwomon and Nona Caspers. $8.95,
0-931188-90-3   In this second volume of our series designed to
showcase talented short fiction writers, two fresh voices report on
lesbian life in distinctive ways.

THE FORBIDDEN POEMS by Becky Birtha. $10.95, 1-878067-01-X This
powerful first collection of poems by the noted African-American
lesbian writer explores recovering from the loss of a longtime lover.

CEREMONIES OF THE HEART: *Celebrating Lesbian Unions* edited by
Becky Butler. $14.95, 0-931188-92-X   A celebration of love and
lesbian pride, *Ceremonies of the Heart* takes us into the lives of twenty-
seven couples who have affirmed their relationships with rituals—
weddings, handfastings, holy unions and ceremonies of commitment.

LESBIAN COUPLES by Merilee Clunis and G. Dorsey Green. $12.95,
0-931188-59-8   The first definitive guide for lesbians that describes the
pleasures and challenges of being part of a couple. Audio version also
available. $9.95, 0-931188-84-9.

DISAPPEARING MOON CAFE by SKY Lee. $18.95, 1-878067-11-7
A spellbinding first novel that portrays four generations of the Wong
family in Vancouver's Chinatown.

ANOTHER AMERICA by Barbara Kingsolver. $10.95, 1-878067-15-X
(paper), $14.95, 0-878067-14-1 (cloth) A beautiful collection of poetry
exploring themes of courage and resistance by the author of *The Bean
Trees* and *Animal Dreams*.

GAUDÍ AFTERNOON by Barbara Wilson $8.95, 1-878067-89-X
This high-spirited comic thriller introduces Cassandra Reilly as
she chases people of all genders and motives through the streets of
Barcelona.

SEAL PRESS, founded in 1976 to provide a forum for women writers
and feminist issues, has many other books in stock: fiction, self-help
books, anthologies and international literature. You may order directly
from us at 3131 Western Avenue, Suite 410, Seattle, WA 98121 (add
15% of total book order for shipping and handling). Write to us for a
free catalog or if you would like to be on our mailing list.